THE SWINDLER

Michelle Kaye Malsbury

"The Swindler" - an incredibly fast-paced roller-coaster ride through the world of illegal commodities trading with enough sun and sin to heat up every reader's day (and night.) Michelle Malsbury at her finest! A definite must read!'
-**Marilou Trask-Curtin**, Author of "In My Grandfather's House: A Catskill Journal"

Boy, can Michelle Malsbury write a tight 'suck-you-in' novel! Intriguing from first page to last. Loved the ride. Great characters and a heap of twist and unforeseen turns. This is a great holiday read if ever there was one.
- **Shane Briant**, best-selling author, actor, and screenwriter. His latest work is titled "Worst Nightmare."

During a long and successful career in the trucking business, I always carried a stack of books to entertain myself and hopefully learn a little something also. One of my favorites was Steven Frey because he always had some insights into the dark side of finance along with great characters. Move over Frey and make room for Michelle Malsbury!

The Swindler has great characters, some lovable, and some not, but all believable. Indeed, I felt like I already knew many and was acquainted with several others. There were the obvious evil ones but the mindset of good ones being led along and seduced by money and the good life was particularly poignant.

...I began to study finance moved to being a Senior Financial Consultant. In the process of interviews and study I felt like I met many of her characters, things just didn't feel right, but oh so seductive!

All this set in quirky and sultry southern Florida, I could feel the humidity, see the pastels, and revel in the ambience. What more could anyone want in book?
- Bill O'Toole, Senior Financial Consultant, Southern Commercial Group

THE SWINDLER

Copyright © 2010 by Michelle Kaye Malsbury

ISBN: 978-0-9844219-4-7

Library of Congress Control Number: 2010904953

Edited by: Marvin D. Wilson

Cover design by All Things That Matter Press

Published in 2010 by All Things That Matter Press

Acknowledgments

I would like to thank my friend, Thomas Keyes, for acting as my second set of eyes in the initial readings of this manuscript where we tried to ferret out any grammatical or spelling errors and correct them before eliciting the services of a professional editor. Thomas also posed many questions about situations that arose in this book and invited me to write some scenes with more clarity. Thank you, Thomas!

Huge thanks go to my official editor, Marvin Wilson, who initially read this manuscript three or more times before sending it back to me for revisions and polishing. Without his criticism, tweaking, and sage suggestions this book would be nothing like it is today. The final version is a compilation of our work. Thank you Marvin, you really are the best and I honestly could not have done this, at least not nearly as well, without you!

I would like to thank Phil and Deb Harris from All Things That Matter Press for pushing me to be my personal best and believing that I could always do better. Thank you both! Without your support and open door I may not have aspired to become better than I was. And most of all thank you for leading me to Marvin!

AUTHOR'S NOTE

The Swindler is based on a real story. The names of the characters and the circumstances have been changed entirely and fictionalized. Any reference which bears likeness to actual persons or events is purely coincidental and should not be relied upon as fact. The cities and places written about herein are real places that many of you may want to visit and enjoy. Any inconsistencies are the fault of the author alone.

CHAPTER ONE

Ft. Lauderdale, Florida

Charles (Skip) Horowitz was just finishing one of his marathon Friday afternoon meetings in front of his team of account opening experts. Seventy brokers – including six people from trading, A.J. from compliance, and Matt from lead generation, sat half sleeping as Skip droned on. They wanted to get to the bank, deposit their checks, and have a nice weekend, but that would have to wait for Skip to get off his soap box.

"You know each and every one of you has the potential to earn hundreds of thousands, even millions of dollars from this enterprise. I've provided you with the tools, skills, and training. That is enough to surpass even your wildest dreams. I came from nothing – even less than nothing. And look where I am now. I've businesses across the USA, the Bahamas, Costa Rica, and my newest jewel is going to be an office in Key West."

Skip was wearing one of his handmade silk and linen blend suits with a cotton linen blend shirt, silk tie, eighteen carat gold Rolex, Presidential version with a diamond bezel, solid gold pinky ring with three carat VVS diamond, and Bally slip-ons. He hiked his sleeve up to show off his watch. "I've got many of these and you can have them, too. I've got a Rolls Royce Corniche, a Bentley Turbo sedan, a Contender yacht, and more. You may ask what you need to do to get where I am? Let me tell you this – all it takes is hard work and dedication."

Some of the brokers stifled yawns while others stole glances at their watches or the clocks on the walls wondering how much longer Skip was going to go on about himself. Those long in his employ knew he loved to hear himself talk and brag. The newcomers would catch on soon enough.

"A.J. and I put this business together over fifteen years ago and did it on a shoe-string budget." Skip looked in A.J.'s direction and smiled. "Today money is no object, but as we know – it takes money to make money and I've invested a bundle in lead generation. Some of you have not fulfilled your obligation toward turning those leads into investors. You are on thin ice. Unless you begin to produce you will be unemployed. I do not mean to sound crass, but this is the harsh reality."

Skip leaned forward and held up a forefinger, shaking it for emphasis. "We are only as good as our last deal. Those of you who are relatively new to our family, know this. We set our expectations high." Skip pointed at the ceiling. "If you do not have goals you stand little chance of being successful. On average, eighty percent of our investors will lose all of their investment within a twenty four to forty eight hour period of time. Those are just raw statistics. Those that do not lose will recoup some of their investment by being paid thirteen percent on their capital over the twelve month period following their first year of investing with us. Afterward, consider them wiped clean."

Skip had been on a roll for two hours. He was a handsome, successful, and vain man. Most of his audience had long since tuned him out, but he didn't care. He loved that he could make them do anything he commanded. He relished the money he made off the losses of his duped investors. He savored the power he had over his employees and the women he had on the side. Skip was beginning to feel invincible.

***

Key West, Florida

Monday, eight a.m., Catherine's' cell phone rang and vibrated steadily on her bedside table. The ringing and vibrating were magnified by the incessant pounding inside her head. Sunday night had been dark, dreary, and rainy. So much so that Catherine opted to stick close to home instead of going out. Her mistake, and sole reason for suffering this morning, had been being fool enough to play a drinking game with her best friend, Connie Portner. Catherine had no idea what time she'd gotten home or how. She tried to focus her bleary and bloodshot eyes. She realized she was in her own bed, alone. That was, and was not, a relief. She preferred to share her bed with a man and there were times when any man would do. Her clothing was strewn halfway across her room. She did not remember taking them off. She figured she must have teetered in her drunken stupor toward her bed, tossing off her clothing, and passed out.

Catherine had a headache pounding loud enough to rival the University of Miami's marching band drum section. Her mouth was as dry as a bag of cotton balls and her tongue felt stuck to the roof of her mouth. Just prior to the messages being transferred over to voicemail she rolled over and palmed her phone open. Her voice came out as a dry croak, "Hello." She looked down and noticed she was still wearing her bra and panties. Ugh.

"You don't sound very good," Connie said, "Are we feeling our age today?"

"How can you be so cheery?" Catherine vaguely recalled sharing a bottle of red wine followed by a half bottle of port and then topping that off with some tequila shooters. She grabbed her head. No wonder I feel so horrid. Stupid. Plain stupid.

Connie's tone was caustic. "Oh, do I sound cheery? Sorry. Let me begin again."

"Seriously," Catherine said, rubbing her throbbing temples. She envied Connie for not feeling as bad as she did. Girlfriend could drink vast amounts of alcohol with no ill effects the next day. Catherine wondered if that was a curse or a blessing. She would gladly take the blessing now.

Connie and Catherine were unlikely friends. Connie owned an ice cream shop and Catherine worked in real estate. Connie had moved to Key West in 1979 from Erie, Pennsylvania, and Catherine was a Keys native, born and raised. They had met a decade or so ago, became and remained best friends ever since. They were opposites in many ways, but they shared a passion for men and casual unprotected sex – a topic they most often discussed. Men gave them the desire to dress and face each day. Connie had been married twice before and Catherine was still, ostensibly, waiting for Mr. Right. It dawned on Catherine, Men … that's the reason we had the drinking contest.

"Rise and shine." It was a command.

"I am." Damnit. " I am."

"Meet me at Scotty's in forty five?"

Scotty's was not just a breakfast joint. It was an institution, at least to the regulars, nestled away in downtown Key West. Scotty's was a diner with diner appeal and little more to offer than that. It was clean, bright, and served good food for a fair price. The owner, Scotty, had been an occasional lover to Connie over the years, a number of one night stands, and she still enjoyed his companionship from time to time. He was getting older, not as sexy as back in 1980, but he was a kind and gentle man.

"Connie, please." Catherine placed her head back on her pillow. "Give me one hour." She rubbed her aching temples again, to no avail. Resigned to having breakfast with Connie and overcoming this horrible hangover, she tossed back the sheet to get some fresh air on her legs.

"Okay, see you then," Connie rung off.

Connie had been sitting atop her outdoor deck in a sling style lounge chair, wearing only her bra and panties and sipping a steaming cup of cappuccino, watching the morning unfold when she decided to call Catherine to rouse her. She was generally known by her friends as being a wonderful cook and she loved to host lavish dinner parties to show off her culinary skills. She always used the best and freshest items she could afford. For her, coffee first thing in the morning was no less exotic than any of her fine meals. She steamed whole milk and doused the cup with raw sugar cubes. Her favorite choice was freshly ground Starbucks morning blend, which cost twice as much as regular morning blend, but its great taste was well worth it. She enjoyed the morning hours before the work day began at her ice cream shop almost as much as she liked sex. Connie desired and got sex as frequently as some people took a bath. She could never get enough. Some people believed she was a nymphomaniac, but she always said, *if it's good for a man why not a woman?*

She placed her cordless phone on a side table and took a few final sips of the splendid java. Her mind clung to a recent sexual encounter with her new friend, Ray. Ray had been a very adept and thoughtful lover and had pleased her in many ways. She knew they would be at it again in the days to come and she was looking forward to it like a cat would a cup of warm milk.

Catherine reached over and hit the snooze button on her alarm clock, setting it to go off again in five minutes. She rolled over on her stomach and grabbed the pillow beside her to shutter the light streaming in through the window from her red eyes. Her bra felt like an anchor. She unlatched the hook in the middle of her chest and let her petite but perky breasts hang free. Did that ever feel good! She shrugged out of it and tossed off to her side.

A loud clamor shook Connie from her relaxation and recollection of sex with Ray. She sprang from her chase and rushed to the railing, nearly toppling her coffee cup, forgetting she was wearing nothing but panties. A Waste Management truck was lumbering down the tiny and narrow street. It squeaked. It groaned. It moaned as if alive and unhappy to be so. The rear door was ajar and it emitted an odor that reeked like skunk or worse. Large blackish-blue flies hovered around the foul trash heap. Connie held her nose, sucked in her breath, and thought, you'd think at this hour they would try to be a little quieter, but no. Assholes. She had not bothered to comb her hair before going outside and it was standing straight on end. Blond spikes protruded outward in every direction.

One of the garbage collectors looked up and saw Connie, her small breasts resting over the edge of the porch railing, cup in hand. He couldn't tell if she was scowling or smiling because of the blinding early morning sun. He was filthy from head to foot, with soot and trash all over his ruddy, moon-shaped face. His eyes were dark and beady like a rat and he had a unibrow. His protruding stomach was barely covered by his grimy t-shirt and his pants gaped where his back met his bum leaving a clean view of his crack. Covering his eyes against the sunlight, he called out, "Hey baby – want some of this?" With a lascivious smile he grabbed himself.

Connie flipped him the bird and walked inside. She left the door from her balcony open to keep a breeze flowing. The hardwood floors felt cool under her bare, manicured feet. A bird chirped outside and settled into song. Connie tried to rid her mind of that rank and smelly garbage collector before hopping into her shower.

In the shower, Connie's thoughts went back to when and how she had managed to buy this house. She recalled the conversation she'd had with her ex-lover, Carl.

"Carl, I'm pregnant," Connie blurted out, and waited for some reasonable response from Carl.

"And?"

"And nothing. It's yours and I expect you to do right by me."

"Right meaning married?" Carl was indignant and put off by the idea.

"Exactly."

"There's no way that's going to happen." He stopped and thought before continuing on. "How about we make a deal?"

"A deal? What kind of deal?" Connie walked to the refrigerator and took out a cold beer. She opened it and chugged the entire can while Carl was considering his next move. She licked her lips and looked hard at him.

"What if I give, well not exactly give, but sell you this house?"

Connie wrinkled her nose. "That all depends."

"Depends on what?" Carl's eyebrows knitted.

"What do you want in return?"

"Oh for Christ's sake, Connie," Carl said with his eyes rolling up in his head, "why do you have to be so difficult?"

"I'm not the difficult one. You are!" She stomped her foot.

Carl rose and regarded her for a second. His tone was final as he said, "Look, here's the deal. You are going to have an abortion and I'll make you a very good deal on this house." He looked around and said, "I'll even finance it for you at first and then we can roll it into a regular loan. That way you can get some good exposure for credit too." He winked and smiled. "Deal?"

Connie pondered this a moment and then said, "Deal."

Carl had sold her the house, which had been sectioned into three units, for a meager $138,000 and financed it for three years so she could effectively have 20% as a down payment before going to the bank. Connie had gotten an abortion and only sometimes looked back with regret. When all her tenants paid on time she was able to meet her monthly obligation to Carl. When they didn't, she would pay late or sometimes would pay him in trade. The barter was sometimes sex, but more often it was a finely prepared meal.

Connie still had it bad for Carl, even though the relationship had ended in all sincerity long ago. He was one of three men who had managed to break into her psyche and dwell in her conscience in a way similar to people who could stay married for fifty years or more.

Connie was a fanatic about having things orderly and clean. She kept her home pristine and impeccable. On a personal note she was less tidy. She oftentimes went out after sex without taking a shower or even brushing her teeth. She got a rush out of kissing one guy with the fresh sex of another still lingering on her lips. She almost never allowed men to stay overnight, but kicked them out of bed soon after orgasm. Carl, Christian, and Bennet had been the exceptions to that rule. Now, of course, Ray Georgeakopoulos was warming her bed and turning her thoughts toward domesticity.

Connie had met Ray at a CIA/FBI reunion that also allowed members of the SEC, Securities and Exchange Commission, NFA, National Futures Association, and CFTC, Commodities and Futures Trading Commission to attend. In the early 1970s she had done some contract work for the CIA and still kept contact with people who worked there. She was always invited to their non-critical, but informative, inter-governmental get-togethers. The meeting at which they had met was one such picnic/information exchange forum, targeted at getting the intelligence organizations to work better together instead of parallel to each other. Ray had been presenting information about suspected Ponzi schemers and Connie had sat in on the lecture because Ray had been tall and handsome – *and* Greek. She had not had a Greek man before and she had an often stated goal of wanting to have sex with at least one man from every country in the world. After the lecture she had approached him to pick his brain on those suspected of these Ponzi schemes.

Connie had worn a short skirt that showed off her sinewy legs to that reunion. Ray had noticed her, too. Sitting in the front row, she had crossed and uncrossed her legs several times, wide enough to reveal her naked pussy. He had had to regroup a couple of times to continue his presentation.

Connie had approached him after his talk was over and said, "You certainly are well versed on Ponzi schemes."

"That is more or less my specialty of law."

"Mmm," she'd said with a coo, "So you're a lawyer too?"

"Yes."

She had given him a demure look and said, "Would you like to get a drink and talk about this more?"

His eyebrows had lifted. "Yes, that would be nice. And – what is your name?"

"Connie Portner." She'd reached out her slender hand to Ray.

After shaking hands they had walked off for a few drinks and conversation. Their personalities had meshed; both on an intellectual and personal level. Before she could bat her eyelash extensions she'd had him in her lair. She'd learned that Ray was involved in some high profile investigations. That, as well as his sexual prowess in the bedroom, had fascinated her. She'd figured she could do Greek for a while and had even boned up on Greek cuisine to help keep him.

***

The alarm chirped once and then again. Catherine had just fallen back into a rapid and deep sleep. She rolled over and hit the off button. She was still discombobulated, fuzzy and groggy, but managed to get out of bed and into the bathroom. She looked at her reflection in the mirror and groaned, then reached into the medicine chest and downed two tabs of Advil before hopping into the shower. The running water was as soothing as it was cleansing. She let it run down her back for a full five minutes before doing anything else. The pulsating action of the shower head massaged her muscles, still aching from having slept splayed in many disjointed directions. She tipped her head back and let the water run through her thick red tresses then reached for the Breck shampoo. She closed her eyes and let her mind wander as she rubbed her aching head. She thought of Max, her office cleaner. He was very married and had two children, but she thought he was always coming on to her. He was from Brazil and spoke passable English with a cute accent. Max was short, but well built and sexy in a macho Latino sort of way. He had told Catherine that he was an attorney back in Brazil, but could not take the bar in Florida because of his poor English. There was also the illegal citizenship issue to deal with. So he and his wife had to work as maids.

Catherine wondered what Max was like unclothed. She wondered if he was good in bed. Thinking about Max did nothing to dull her headache. Her hands were too shaky to risk shaving so she put that off until later. The cool shower had renewed and refreshed her more than she thought possible if even for a short while. She stepped out, turned off the water, and blotted herself dry before walking to her closet to see what to wear. She dropped her towel as she exited the bathroom, leaving it in a damp heap on the tile floor – typical for her, she was fastidious about her personal hygiene and appearance, but a bit of a slob about cleaning and keeping up the house. With regard to that shortcoming she often wished she were more like Connie. Her wet tendrils were still dripping down her back. The cool drops of water kept her cool on this humid morning.

Connie had showered and made it to Scotty's in record time.

She had her hair closely cropped, almost a military buzz cut, and bleached nearly white.

7

The busy waiter looked up as Connie came in. He couldn't help think how she looked like a walking garage sale. And how super thin she was – legs like a scarecrow. Maybe a drug addict, he concluded.

Connie sat at the bar on a red vinyl stool reading a copy of the latest Key West Citizen Newspaper, sipping a café Americano, waiting for Catherine to join her. The story that captured her eye and sense of humor was in the crime section. It was about a 911 call to one of the gay women's-only guesthouses over on Caroline Street. Allegedly two women were fighting over a double ended dildo because one had caught the other with another girl. Connie laughed so hard tears ran down her cheeks. She couldn't wait to relate this one to Catherine.

Several minutes later Catherine straggled in. She spotted Connie and waved. She carefully made her way through the crowd toward the left end of the bar. She had not blown her hair dry: it was still damp and fragrant, leaving wet rings on the shoulders of her green silk blouse.

"Hello," she said in a flat voice.

"I assume you look better than you feel?" Connie said, wiping the fresh tears from her cheeks with a stiff paper napkin.

"Why do you say that?" Catherine looked down the length of herself to be sure she was not wearing two mismatched shoes or something equally ludicrous. "And why are you crying?"

"You said you had a big head for one thing, but you don't look too worse for the wear." Connie took another sip of her café, neatly folded the newspaper and placed it off to her side. "You've got to read the crime section of the paper today. It is a real doozy. If only I were a writer. I would never lack for tales to tell."

Catherine took the seat to the right of Connie and perused the menu. "What are you having?"

Connie glanced across the bar at a swarthy young man, easily a decade her junior, licked her thin lips and said, "I think I'll have him." She smiled at him as he caught her eye.

"Don't you ever stop?"

"There will be plenty of time to stop when I am dead."

Lori Katz, Connie's accountant and dear friend, walked in the door. Connie, oblivious to the other patrons, waved and called out, "Lori, you've got to read the crime section." She held the newspaper over her head and waved it back and forth.

Lori meandered through the crowded restaurant toward Connie and Catherine. Catherine turned to Connie and said, "Do you think she owns anything besides spandex?"

"Look – most overweight women wear spandex for some reason, but let's not dwell on her weight. Look at her face instead."

8

"Well, it looks to me like she's got a new crop of zits working or something."

Connie swatted her with the newspaper. "Be nice. Of the three of us she is the only one with a college education and a regular paying job."

"I know, I know." Catherine paused and then said, "Don't you think she looks a little bit like Petunia Pig?"

Lori knew most of the people in the restaurant and she worked the crowd like a politician at a fundraising event as she maneuvered her bulk toward the counter.

She lumbered over to Connie and Catherine, arriving in a sweat, huffing and puffing. With her long fake nails she clipped the newspaper from Connie's hand and spread it across the counter to search for the crime section. After a short quiet read she burst into laughter so loud her triple chin quivered.

Lori howled as she read the last line and said, "Oye----how I wish that was me!" Wiping away tears, she parked her behind onto the stool next to Connie, smothering it by several inches. "What I would do with that double ender." She continued to pat tears of laughter as the story faded from her mind.

"You're no dike. You can get the real thing."

"With the men around here …" She glanced across the noisy and brightly lit restaurant. "… you might as well double your chances of having sex by taking all you can." She snorted and grunted, turned to Connie and said, "Like you've never tried it?"

"You know I have," Connie said blandly and without animosity.

"Then?"

"Then nothing." She lowered her head. "Do you see that hottie across the bar from us?"

Lori looked up from the menu to check him out.

Before Lori could utter a word Connie said, "I saw him first."

"Nothing like a little age before beauty. You can break him in for me." Lori clucked.

A prissy waiter stopped in front of the three women and said, "Are you ready to order?"

Connie ordered boiled eggs with rye toast and butter and another café Americano. Catherine ordered a short stack of hotcakes with bacon and coffee. Lori ordered a large stack of hotcakes, sausage, bacon, two scrambled eggs, toast with butter, and a large chilled orange juice. Breakfast conversation hinged on two things: men and sex. Lori shared Connie and Catherine's pension for one night stands and each enjoyed trying to top the other two's stories. Slowly Catherine's massive headache began to abate. She glanced at her Swatch watch and said, "I hate to spoil a good thing, but I better get to the office before Shamus."

"Shamus, Shamus. When you are really done with him, send him my way," Lori said with another grunt. "I'll teach him to ride the wave." She slapped her wide thigh and laughed at herself.

Catherine sighed, dropped a ten-dollar bill on the counter and said, "Yeah, Shamus, Shamus … what a tired old story that one is, him and me, huh? But look, I gotta go. Sorry to eat and run. See you ladies later."

CHAPTER TWO

On the drive to her office, Catherine thought back on how her family had come to America and especially how they came to reside in the Keys. Catherine's parents' family migrated to America via New York City during the potato famine in the 1850's. During the coming decades the O'Reilley's and some special friends nudged their way southward out of New York City. The trip down was a rugged trek at best, but they persevered. The children were always restless, hungry and tired. Key West to them was as heavenly as they had been told to expect. More than a place in the sun, it had been a welcoming seaside community that embraced those Irish emigrants as if it was truly home. There the O'Reilley clan found peace and eventually prosperity.

Key West was rather bohemian and unpolished at that time. Jobs were plentiful. Pay was low, but consistent for those who were willing. If a person was so inclined he or she could work all year round – unlike some occupations that were of a seasonal nature in the north. Those who were not so inclined could sleep under the palms and not be castigated for doing so.

Thirty some years and many calluses later, Catherine's father had taken over the sponging business from his aging boss who had fallen ill and had no children who wished to pursue that type of rough manual employment. Oliver Stern and Danny O'Reilley had come to an amicable arrangement.

Catherine paused in her reflections as she turned a street corner. She lowered the sun blinder to take a glance at her reflection in the mirror. What? Am I seeing more wrinkles around the eyes? She sighed, and thought back to days gone by.

As a younger woman Catherine O'Reilley had had her share of men ogling her large full breasts, shapely legs and round, robust hips. She matured early and her brother's young friends were always trying to sneak a glimpse of her as she changed clothes. The more adventurous young men went so far as to erect ladders to peer into her bedroom window. She knew they were watching. Sometimes she even made a show of it for them with a seductive strip tease.

She smiled to herself as she drove, remembering those delicious moments of her youthful dazzling dalliances. Ah, but that was then, she thought, and sighed again. Now I'm a full figured woman in my mid thirty's, beginning the battle against aging. Weight gained is becoming difficult to lose and wrinkles appear where none were before. At least I'm not fat, not compared to Lori, anyway. All the diets I've tried and no use. There are some things in life one cannot change. Like family genes.

Catherine still lived at home and had never ventured off the Florida Keys. Her family was a tight-knit group and, as long as there was room under their roof, her parents wanted her in their house. Catherine had enough freedom that the arrangement never infringed on her overzealous sexual lifestyle. There was a wide world out there ripe for exploration and sometimes she had a desire to get out and experience it. At other times she was fearful of the unknown, reluctant to leave the safety and security of her small, hometown, island community.

Catherine looked at the dashboard clock. Still enough time to get to the office before Shamus. She knew she had Shamus, if and when she wanted him, but she was not really certain that he was the *one*. She had known him her entire life. Their families had always assumed they would marry. Shamus had had the hots for her forever. The way she toyed with him was shameless, leading him on when her intentions were unsure. Lately she had let that relationship cool in pursuit of other more interesting and lesser known men. She thought she wanted change. Shamus was not change. Shamus was safe. Maybe it was her age. Maybe it was the ticking clock that all women in their twenties and thirties talk about. She could not place her finger on it, but she was not content to be where she was now, doing what she was now doing.

She contemplated her life situation as she drove, half-paying attention to traffic, half lost in her somewhat melancholy muse. Many would have thought Catherine lucky to have been born, raised, and still living in Key West. It's considered a paradise. She did not entirely disagree, but *was this* all there was? Occasionally she watched the nationwide news channels, home decorating, or the travel channels when she, Lori, and Connie were not out and about chasing and sleeping with men. Catherine was filled with wonderment and curiosity about the differing cultures in far off places.

Will I ever go to places like that? Somehow I doubt it.

Catherine blinked her eyes, realizing she was at the office. She parked her jalopy under the fir tree near the edge of the street and walked toward the front door wondering what this day would present. Her father had always said, *life is largely what you make it*. Words of wisdom, she had always thought, and tried to live by them.

Once inside, Catherine stood brooding over her jammed Xerox copy machine, deep in thought and annoyed. She pursed her full and pouty lips. Her worn out patience was giving way to an electric frustration. She silently cursed the day she rented it. Damn thing never seems to work when I need it to most. Not one day has gone by without some problem with this high-tech machine. She cursed it again and kicked at its wheels. Worthless piece of shit!

Catherine thought back to the time when she and Shamus, her partner of nearly seventeen years, had rented this space. She was full of energy and pride back then. They had spent six months seeking a place that was affordable and in a good location to open their real estate empire. Previously the place had been a hair salon and then a bathing suit shop. It was the sixteen inch variegated gray marble tiled floors, tall ceilings, and big French doors that had first lured them in. They had worked hard to create an atmosphere that was professional, a place where other agents would want to work. Most of the money had been from Shamus, but the elbow grease was mostly Catherine's. Both considered that an honorable trade off.

Shamus, she thought in a moment of pause, dear Shamus. Catherine was well aware of Shamus' burning passion for her. He had made no secret of it over the years. She had mixed feelings about setting up a home and family with him. He was too familiar. He was almost like a brother to her. She and Shamus had had a fling in high school. He had taken her to the junior and senior proms. They had had sex, quite a few times, but she considered that as juvenile lust and inexperienced hormones.

She thought about his family, the Nelsons. They have money, lots of it. That's how he can afford the way he's recently become such a playboy. Flinging money around at hot babes rather than concentrating on the sale of real estate. He's working hard to make me jealous .But I'm playing it cool. I don't want him to know how much I care about him. I can't be controlled by him, or anyone. Still, lately I have been rather cold, even nasty toward him. I should stop. By now he's probably thinking the best he can hope for between us is a truce. And he's probably right. My idea of a relationship – a real relationship, is to him just some sort of fantasy. The stuff one reads about in childhood picture books.

The antique brass sleigh bells on the front door handle softly rang, reminding Catherine she was at work and not alone in her thoughts. Work, she thought. Someone has to do it; especially if all Shamus is doing is playing with his favorite flavor of the day.

Catherine looked up from the dreadful malfunctioning copy machine to see who had entered her not-so-hallowed space. Who could be intruding on her not-so-precious thoughts? While she had been fussing with the machine some of her staff had collected at their appointed desks, including Shamus. They now sat in idle conversation about their weekends, paying no attention to the man at the door.

Annoyed, Catherine surveyed her staff, which was made up of two middle-aged drunks, and one young, but naïve, girl named Alexis. Nobody budged. She silently wondered, how long will it take for anyone to address this handsome, well dressed, stranger standing on the doorstep? Nobody moved an inch. She smoldered with anger and her eyes flashed from grey green to nearly black. In a huff she said, "Is there anyone else working here today, or am I it?"

When nobody responded, she stormed toward the front door fuming out loud, tugging at her too short and tight skirt that had ridden well up her thighs, trying to make herself presentable. The man on the doorstep took in every action. The look on his face was one of mild, placid amusement. As Catherine approached the stoop she officiously addressed the attractive stranger with a fake Irish lilt she took on whenever nerves got the best of her. "Oh, hello there. Is there something I might help you with?"

He wore crisp white linen slacks and a light blue silk designer shirt, open enough to see a dusting of dark chocolate colored hair on his tanned and muscled chest. Catherine bit her lip. He tipped his Maui Jim sunglasses back. Good god, Catherine thought. Gorgeous black hair, matching long lashes, and striking deep blue eyes. Hang on to your panties, girlfriend.

He offered Catherine his hand and said with more than a trace of egotism. "Hello, my name is Skip. Skip Horowitz." He smiled, revealing sensuous dimples. Catherine felt a tingling in her lower belly. "I am interested in previewing some commercial properties." He looked around her office again, then directly at Catherine's breasts. He smiled wide before moving up toward her eyes without the least bit of embarrassment.

Strangely, Catherine was entranced with this man, but unsure why. He makes no apology for gawking at my boobs, and offers his hand with the arrogance of a king or some shit. Am I ready for this? Numbly she shook his hand. She noted his skin – soft and smooth, not at all like her brothers who had spent their lives doing manual, outdoor work along with her dad. As she disengaged his handshake she said, "Commercial, eh? Would that be for rent or for sale?"

Skip's eyes drew her in like a hypnotist placing her into a trance. They were alluring and unsettling at the same time. Like he's staring into my soul. The hackles on her neck rose and her skin became goose-flesh as if he had some evil edge lurking just beyond those sexy eyes. Pull yourself together, Catherine. She regained her composure and said, "Would you be interested in Key West or up the Keys somewhere?" She had people come in wanting to look as far up as Key Largo. Sometimes she serviced them, other times she referred them to a friend more familiar with the market there. With sex on the brain she decided, not you, Mister. You're all mine.

Skip paused a moment to consider her question, then said, "Key West is where my interests lie." He took a step toward Catherine. "At least at this particular time." Skip held Catherine's gaze until his azure eyes, flashing and growing in intensity, forced her to look away.

God, he's captivating. Flirty, vivacious, and fresh. Reminds me of the wolf from *Little Red Riding Hood*. Will I get eaten? Would I even care?

Skip broke her thoughts off. "What a wonderful accent you have … Irish, or Scottish?"

Catherine stammered and stuttered, managed to get out, "Thank you. It's Irish. My family is Irish-American." Her heart was racing. She felt her face flush as she got a whiff of his exotic after shave. Still flustered, she stepped over to the reception desk, picked up a note pad and pen. As she bent forward Skip got a good glimpse of her open bum in lacey thong. Catherine could feel his eyes following her every move and curve. It excited and thrilled her. She jotted down some notes and began factoring in the available commercial possibilities before glancing up to ask, "How much space might you require for your business."

Before Skip could reply Shamus barged into the front office with a clang and a bang. He'd seen enough, he wanted to check out this guy. He gave Skip a sideways glance and sneer that could have killed a dozen seagulls. It froze Catherine in mid sentence. Shamus took a distinct dislike to men he considered pretty boys, even though by most standards he himself was good looking. Under his breath he said, "Freaking faggot," wandered back toward his desk, then thought better of it and tromped back to stand close to Catherine and Skip.

Catherine winced at Shamus' rowdy entrance, childish utterance and untimely re-entrance. She hoped he would leave, but knew better. She proceeded with as much professionalism as possible.

Skip, unfazed by Shamus, took a glance around and said, "I'm not really sure. But something, oh, I'd say three or four times the size of this office might be adequate. It might also be a good thing to have some room to expand if business necessitated that."

Catherine had another vision of the wolf licking his chops, readying to devour the chickens in the hen house. She let it pass. I'm the chicken and you're the wolf. Honey, you can eat me any time.

Shamus stomped between them to the back of the office, muttering something in Gaelic under his breath. Alexis looked up from her mess of a desk just in time to catch the cord from her phone before a grumbling, marauding Shamus snagged it and hurled it onto the marble tiles. She, like the rest of the office, was no stranger to Shamus' angry tirades and usually used them as an excuse for a fast exit. She gathered her things into a backpack and slithered toward the door. Nobody took notice, nothing was said.

As Alexis exited, Catherine noticed outside, on the front stoop, stood three charming and well-dressed children. Two sweet looking brunette girls with topaz-hazel eyes and a young boy with blondish hair, ruddy skin and green-blue eyes. All three were dressed as if going to church. With a crook of her neck in their direction she asked Skip, "What adorable children. Are they with you?" Is he married? How do these kids fit into this picture?

Skip's million-dollar smile broadened into multi-millions. "Yes, the two girls are mine and the young man is my sister's son. Before coming in I had asked them to please wait there for just a moment." He pointed to one of the girls. "Evelyn wants ice cream and I can never say no to my kids. Promised her and all of them a cone once I got through with our meeting."

Catherine wondered where the wife was and why Skip had been so friendly and flirtatious with her if he was already attached. She did not take kindly to married people catting around. She forced her inquisitive mind back to the business at hand and said, "I'll put together a few things. Perhaps we can hook up later in the day and do some drive bys to see if any of them are of interest to you."

Skip's face took on a puzzled look. "Drive bys?"

Shamus laughed out loud at this ridiculous question by the pretty man. Catherine shot him a withering glance. Shamus moved a little closer to not miss her reply.

Catherine smiled despite Shamus's toxic behavior. Why can't he grow up and act like an adult? "Ah – sorry, that's realtor talk." She began to speak with her hands. She always did so when she was nervous or under pressure. Flustered now. "I meant that we can preview some properties from the outside." Her gestures became more animated with each sentence. "So we can determine if you are interested in one or more of them. If so, we can make an appointment to go inside."

"How long do you need to get something together?" Skip said with genuine interest. He found Catherine attractive and knew he would easily bed her in the not too distant future. She was older and wider than his typical interests, but she looked to him like an eager lover.

Under his breath Shamus said, "About five minutes with me ought to do it you bloke. Toss pot."

Catherine shot Shamus another annoyed glance, grateful it appeared Skip had not heard the exact content of his crass remark, and thought for a minute. She looked down at her watch and said, "Is five o'clock okay for you?" Catherine knew Shamus had a softball game at that time and would be unable to track her whereabouts. She thought, I'll fix him.

Satisfied, Skip said, "I'll see you then. I'm staying at the Pier House Resort." Skip took two steps toward the door. Just prior to stepping outside he turned around on his heel. With his hand perched on the door handle he smiled the widest, sexiest smile that Catherine had seen since Calvin Klein underwear ads. She melted. Without a word he exited.

Shamus smoldered. Catherine grinned to herself. She thought she could see steam rising from his ruffled, shaggy head.

Skip gathered up the three children and walked across the street toward Connie's ice cream parlor.

"Did you cum yet?" Shamus blurted out as Catherine followed Skip with her eyes. He lowered his voice, knowing he was being too loud, but damn it. "You act like he's some god, but I guarantee you ... deep down he's just a married scumbag looking for something on the side."

"Why do you have to be such a dick, Shamus? Grow up," Catherine spat. She wondered what Connie would have to say about Skip and made a mental note to give her a call after they had left her shop. To nobody in particular she said, "That guy has class."

"No, he has money. Money and class are not the same."

Catherine's eyes followed Skip and the children until they were out of sight and inside the ice cream parlor. It was fifteen or so minutes before they all emerged with double dipped cones in hand. As soon as they were out the door she rang Connie and said, "Boy, he is a hottie."

Shamus moaned. *She really is impossible.*

Connie said, "Is he ever. Tell you what ... I'm going to walk over to your place where we can talk this over in person." She hung up and jogged across the street. She did not bother to lock the door because she could see her entrance from the front of Catherine's office.

Shamus hated Connie. He made no secret of that. He felt she was a bad influence on Catherine and bad for their business. She was never dressed appropriately when she came in. Shamus exhaled loudly and said, "Slut."

Connie heard that, was not bothered by it, and said, "Takes one to know one." She took the seat across from Catherine at the reception area with a smile that looked like she was the cat who just ate the canary.

Catherine rolled her eyes in Shamus' direction. "Why do you even bother to indulge him?"

"He makes the sadist in me glow red hot." Connie turned to smile at Shamus like the devil about to snatch out his soul.

Shamus thought she looked like some weird jack-o-lantern in a nightmare or horror show.

"So what is he looking for besides a date?" Connie toyed with the tiny toothpick dangling from her necklace chain.

"Commercial property. So he says."

"What does he do?"

"Beats the hell outta me."

"I do hope you will find out," Connie said with a raised eyebrow.

Shamus mimicked her from his desk and the other two male brokers, John and Dan, cracked up laughing.

"Don't they sound like cackling hens?" Connie said with a hitch of her neck.

"Don't dignify them with any comment, please. They are worse than children."

"Anyway, he's a hunk with a capital H." She stopped to pluck a crumb from her teeth and let it fall to the floor.

Shamus grimaced. *Wanker.*

"Yes, indeed."

Two tourists stopped their brightly colored mopeds at the curb and began to walk into the ice cream parlor. Connie stood and said, "Duty calls."

"Thank God," Shamus said to himself. "Good riddance"

John added, "Do you think someone should find an exorcist?"

More laughter came from the back office.

Catherine called over her shoulder, "Children." She hit the enter button to awaken her sleeping computer and began surfing for properties that might fit the short description Skip had given her. Six were close enough that she thought they might work. She hit the print button and walked to the rear of the office to retrieve her documents. All the guys followed her every move. She said, "Don't any of you have something better to do? Oh, I almost forgot. That would require working ... something that none of you have the vaguest idea about." She gathered her documents and rummaged for a fresh manila folder to drop them into.

"For your information I have a showing tomorrow," John said.

Catherine ignored him.

CHAPTER THREE

Two federal agents from the SEC sat in a plain blue Ford Taurus watching Catherine as she drove in to pick up Skip. Ray Georgeakopoulos was the senior of the two. Their radio was tuned to NPR and the speaker was lamenting the presidential election of 2000 and comparing it to that of 2004. He remarked, in conclusion, that in Ohio a nervous, feverish recount was in progress.

Ray said to his junior partner, "This is the second presidential election that's been skewed. I don't remember anything like this since Nixon. Or was that Mondale?"

"I don't know. This must make us look weird to the rest of the world. Like we can't even elect a president without controversy. And then there's Iraq."

"And Afghanistan."

"Both black holes."

"Don't get me started." Ray held up his hand.

"So what do we know about this Skip guy?"

"For one, his wife, the fair Frederika, is speaking to Marek and offering tidbits of information that have been helpful in piecing together Skip's past business dealings and seeing where all of this may be going," Ray said as he turned the radio off.

"Whew," his partner said, looking around the car. "Get serious – his wife?"

"Yea. Marek thinks she is going to be of benefit to our case on the witness stand if she will agree to testify against her husband."

"Man, that is no kind of marriage. Wicked wrong. The wife talking shit about her husband and going to the Fed's."

"Apparently she's had enough of his affairs with young titty dancers and the likes."

"Stakeouts are boring," junior said with a yawn. "I could go for a titty dancer about now."

"In your dreams, junior. In your dreams." Ray laughed.

"So, again … what do we know about this guy, really?"

Ray took a sip of his now cold coffee and said, "What do you want – his life history?"

"Something like that. Just tell me what's in his dossier."

"You've not seen it?" Ray was incredulous.

"No, man. I don't rank that high yet. You know the *eyes only* stuff."

"Okay. It goes something like this. Skip is the bastard son of a maid from New Jersey." Ray waited for a reaction. When nothing was offered he continued, "That is when she worked. Apparently she liked to drink, have sex, and do drugs more than anything else. She got pregnant at the tender age of sixteen. Not being into motherhood she left Skip to fend for himself."

"So his mom's a zero. Not surprising, all things considered. What else?"

"He was in and out of juvie. Began when he was ten or something like that. He did manage to graduate from high school, but nothing else especially outstanding for a number of years. He opened his first brokerage about twenty odd years ago. Over the past few years he seems to have branched out and made quite a bit of money. He was not a favorite of the older sage Wall Streeters because he was the new kid on the block, but he did manage to piss off some of his investors from time to time. That's when he popped back up on our radar because there were a lot of complaints from his investors. He'd promised some pretty high rates of return – and as you know, nothing in the market is an absolute."

"How many's a lot?"

"Over the years I'd say thirty or more."

Junior nodded and stroked his chin. "That is a lot."

"Yes and no. There are some people who just like to complain, but say we cut those out there are still about half which might be of substance. Somehow those complaints were never fully investigated or didn't net anything we could use against him. My quick take on this guy is, he's just a scammer and a hustler."

"But a crafty bum, or we wouldn't be staking him out, right?"

"Seriously. The guys got a rap sheet a mile long." Ray sighed, had a sip of cold coffee and belched.

"Duh, tell me more." Junior rolled his eyes.

"Mostly petty theft things in his youth," Ray said and yawned. "But then he graduated to bigger stuff. They all do."

"Guess the lack of parental oversight is a common thread in many juvenile crimes. We can't fault him for that."

"Don't go gettin' all psycho sympathetic on me. We..." He pointed back and forth between them for effect. "...are here to do a job. The job is catching him in the act and that's just what we're going to do. Got it?"

"Yea, I got it." The rookie lit a cigarette, took a drag and let the smoke out slow. "Where ya think he learned this Ponzi scheme stuff?"

"If I had to guess, and this is an educated guess, he met some wall street white collar criminal types or their bosses when he spent his last stint, or one of his many previous stints, in the pen. And with the time they had on their hands, day after dreary day, they taught him the basics. Gave him some clues specifically in the areas of high-end extortion or investment crimes."

"This Ponzi scheme stuff is actually a clever kind of scam. It's equally as amazing that someone could learn this shit while in the big house. I'd guess perfecting this type of scam could take years."

"Getting the ball rolling does take years. This guy is just one of those lucky fuckers that got a head start." Ray paused. "But you know what they say?" He kept his eyes on the entrance to Catherine's office. "All good things come to an end and his time is about to come to an abrupt halt."

"Don't we have anything concrete on this guy?"

"We've had complaints for years, but nobody took the time to follow up until now. Except me. I've done some digging and research on him. Seems Skip was a quick study in his early years. He was fascinated by the stories he heard in jail. Reports I've read say he vowed when he got out he would create the largest and most profitable Ponzi scheme ever."

"I didn't know those things had been around that long."

"There's a lot you don't know, junior."

Junior frowned.

"And there's this A.J. guy. A friend he made. He helped prime him for this adventure. Perfect fit, the two of them. Skip now looks like some model Wall Streeter to everyone. He's learned how to dress for success by wearing expensively tailored hand-made suits and shirts, name brand watches, and hand crafted Italian leather shoes. Drives expensive cars and hangs with fast women." Ray stopped to have another sip, groaned at the taste, and farted.

Waving the air out of the window, junior spotted something, pointed and said with urgency, "Ray – there she goes."

"I wonder what's going on with those two. She doesn't fit his typical profile for love interests."

"Maybe it's nothing to do with love."

"Maybe."

Catherine stopped in front of the Pier House Resort promptly at five, as she and Skip had agreed earlier. Her blue Mercury was eight years old, dented in places and the paint was faded. Patrick, her brother who owned and operated a car detailing business a block from her office, had helped her wash it an hour before, but washing never made it look new. At least it's almost paid for, she thought as consolation. Patrick's such a sweetie. A true O'Reilly, never too busy to help out family. So proud of him too, the way his business has grown. Good service and great prices always spells success.

Skip had stepped off the curb in front of the main entrance as soon as Catherine wheeled into the parking lot. The Fed's took a few snapshots and cued up their microphones. Skip was dressed casually with navy pleated slacks and a white polo shirt. In his hand he carried a brown leather folder with a shiny golden pen.

Catherine drew down the window and said, "Good afternoon, Sir. Please get in."

The Fed's snapped another picture.

Skip opened the door and slid carefully in beside Catherine, trying not to wrinkle his nose. He said, "Thank you for taking the time out of your day to help me with this." Skip was being polite, but he meant it. He liked Catherine and hoped to know her better.

"Where are those darling children I saw you with this afternoon," Catherine asked as she pulled out of the driveway and turned left onto Duval Street, unaware of the Fed's following at a discreet distance.

"I've left them with their nanny. They'll stay with her in our rooms while we take care of business," Skip said with an easy smile. His expensive after shave wafted around inside her car thanks to the fan from the over-burdened air conditioning. Skip could tell Catherine felt comfortable beside him. She's helpful without being too presumptuous, he thought. I like her style.

Catherine drove Skip all over town to acquaint him with the business district and the buildings or spaces that were available for rent. Showing off Key West was easy because the island ran in one big circle from the business side of the island, where the shopping centers and hotels were, to the airport and beaches.

Daylight was closing into dusk. The sky went from blue to pink to violet to orange and gray. Streaks of muted light cast a soft haze over the hot pavement and bathed the buildings in hues of gray. A soft breeze came out of nowhere and swirled the fallen leaves and debris around the gutters. A flock of wild parrots squawked overhead.

The Fed's followed and videoed as they drove. The microphone caught their suspect's amicable chatter, but nothing incriminating.

Catherine said, "Key West is small, but it's a lively and interesting place if you've not been here before. The small narrow streets crisscross the main segments of the town and oftentimes ended up as dead ends. Drivers have to know their way around to navigate the one ways and dead ends." Catherine brought the car to a stop at a red light. "I've been doing this since the age of twelve under the direction of my elder brothers and sisters."

Skip looked deeply into her eyes.

Catherine added, "Driving that is." She smiled.

Skip felt certain that Catherine was an ace. His ace. He smiled and said, "I guess I'm glad I found you then."

"Let's just say we're both lucky," Catherine said with a wide grin.

"I'm very impressed with your knowledge of commercial properties and your professional mannerisms. I also like that you follow through with what you say you are going to do. On previous trips I've invited a couple of other realtors to show me around and none could find the time or the right space. Maybe you are my good luck charm."

The Fed's laughed at that line. The agent manning the recorder waved his hand for them to shut up.

"Fine. I'll consider their loss my gain. Thank you for the opportunity, but I don't think I would get very far in business in Key West if I didn't go the extra distance. On this small two by five mile island there happens to be more than 400 realtors."

"That's quite a lot. Is there enough business for everyone?" Skip said with sincerity.

"About like everything else. Twenty percent of the people have eighty percent of the business. I just want to be in that twenty percent." She paused. "What sort of business would you be opening here?" Catherine thought she detected reticence on Skip's part at that question. Evasive.

He said, "I'll tell you what. If we find the right location, I'll let you know what my intentions are. Deal?" He flashed his most winning smile.

"Fair enough," Catherine said with a wink. Yeah, he's a bit evasive all right, but somehow he comes off without seeming rude or standoffish. Guy's got game.

Inside the Fed car someone said, "We already know what he does. What we don't know is what he is doing with her. If we can figure that out maybe we can catch him."

Catherine was thinking about the nanny and Skip. She decided to broach that topic with him now and get it over with. "You said the children are with the nanny?"

"Yes, that's right. Why?"

"Well, I was just wondering if she might be more than just the nanny?"

"No she is just the nanny. She's quite a nice girl and the kids love her."

"What about your wife?"

"What is this – twenty questions?" Skip smiled, despite being grilled.

"No, sorry," She stammered, "I just wondered why your wife is not with you – now?"

Skip looked away out the window. "My wife and I are separated."

"Sorry, I didn't mean to …"

He waived her off with a hand and said, "Don't be. She is a great lady, but we've got some things we just don't see eye to eye on." Skip paused and then said, "Would you allow me the pleasure of your company for dinner this evening? I'm sure you know of a local place where we can dine in privacy and continue our discussion about my property search." He fluttered his eye lashes and smiled. Catherine was thinking. He waited for an answer, patient.

"Thank you for the invitation, but I've got to decline. How about a rain check? You see, I've already made some plans to meet up with my favorite artist friend and his wife, Greg and Wanda Sobran. They are a delightful couple. If I had known you would be here at this time I would've invited you, but … as I mentioned I already have plans. Sorry." Painfully sorry. How can I find an excuse to meet him later, perhaps just for a drink?

"Oh? Well, maybe we could meet later. That is, if later is not too late, whenever the social engagement you have is over with. I'm sorry, what was your artist friend's name again?"

"Greg Sobran. Greg is just the best watercolorist. Wanda, his wife, handles his sales and marketing. They really are a great couple, great people. I've made a deal for them to exchange art for accommodations and tonight they are having an informal showing to see how much public interest there is for them." I'd invite you to come in a heartbeat, she thought, except Shamus is going to be there. How uncomfortable would *that* be. Plenty. "I guess I could ring you when it breaks up if … that is, if it's not too late, I'm guessing ten-ish?"

Skip smiled. "That would be fine. Actually better than fine."

Catherine dropped him back at the Ocean Key House, thanked him for the generous dinner offer, and they cemented plans to meet later.

The Fed's watched and listened.

***

The party for Greg and Wanda had gone off without a hitch for the most part. Shamus had the audacity to bring one of his new conquests along. Catherine wished she'd gone ahead and invited Skip.

Shamus called out to Catherine, "Come here, Cat – I want you to meet someone."

Catherine did not want to meet her, but walked over anyway. "Hello, Shamus," She said with a tight lipped smile.

"Catherine, this is my new friend, Roberta. "

Roberta's smile was a little too sweet for Catherine as she said, "So nice to meet you. I've heard so much about you and the office."

Tussy, Catherine thought.

"Roberta is studying to be a dental assistant," Shamus said, "She's working for Dr. Eaton and Smith over on Fogerty Street."

Catherine took an instant dislike to her. She was too perky and smart. She really wanted to get even with Shamus for playing around with this girl. As the party wound down, which *was* around ten that evening, Catherine rang Skip. She did it intentionally within earshot of Shamus, and with smug pleasure arranged to meet him down in the lobby at the Charthouse Bar for a drink.

Catherine arrived at the bar a few minutes later. Skip was seated in a booth near the back. He waved her over. She took a seat opposite him.

The Chartroom had been the only bar at the Pier House before they redesigned the entire property in the mid 1990s. It was small and cozy with enough seating space for about twenty people. Tonight there were fewer than six. The lights were dim and the room smelled of fresh popped popcorn.

The bartender asked, "What may I get for you this evening."

Catherine looked at Skip's glass. He said, "It's just a coke. I don't drink, but go ahead and order anything you like." He smiled.

Catherine said, "I'll have a brandy, please."

"Why don't you drink?" Catherine said as the bartender left to get her brandy.

"I'm AA. I used to drink too much and things got out of control. I found Father Zeke and he helped me stop drinking and get my life back on track." He reached across the table and touched her hand.

"I guess just about everyone in Key West could use a little dose of AA from time to time." She smiled and enjoyed his hand lingering on hers. She'd have left it there longer but the bartender arrived so she pulled her hand away to receive her drink.

"Why don't you tell me a little about you," Skip said.

"Oh," Catherine said with a toss of her hair, "there's nothing to tell, really. I was born and raised in Key West. I've hardly been off the Island. It's really all I know."

"Small towns can be charming."

She sighed, "Well sure, charming – but also boring a lot of times." She gulped her brandy and Skip motioned to the barkeep for another round.

Skip said with a pat on the seat next to him, "Why don't you come sit over here? We can talk more intimately if you are next to me."

She did. She liked him. He was more intriguing than men she knew in Key West. And after two more rounds of brandy he was becoming more appealing all the time – even if it was the enhanced effects of inebriation. Skip's eyes were mesmerizing. Her heart jumped when he pulled her close and kissed her – lightly at first, and he pulled back to see her reaction. Her expression was one of 'give me more,' so he kissed her passionately. She did not resist. She became jello in his hands, melting with his touch, wet from his long, deep kisses. She thought she should put a stop to it, maybe she should go slower with this man, but she was powerless under his spell.

The bartender called out, "Last call. Does anyone want another drink before we close?"

Catherine looked around. She and Skip were the only ones left in the dark bar.

"Do you want another?" Skip said.

"Oh, no. I better not have another or I may not be able to make it back home."

"Would that be so bad?"

Catherine resisted the temptation to say no. "I've really got some urgent things waiting at the office for me in the morning. But I've so enjoyed this night." She blushed at the thought of how easily he had put his moves on her and said, "And thank you."

Skip paid the tab and walked Catherine out to her car. He kissed again, with such intense passion she nearly swooned. His hand caressed her breasts. She felt the electricity flow between them like strikes of lightening across a summer sky. She opened her car door and slipped inside. Skip closed it behind her and watched her drive away. As she drove she was second guessing why she hadn't chosen to bed him on the spot.

CHAPTER FOUR

Catherine arrived at her office just before ten the following morning. She had spent the better part of her night thinking about Skip. He was a complex and interesting man. She wanted to know more. At this hour the streets were mostly vacant and the tourists were only out in small numbers. One or two cruise ships were scheduled to park at the docks on Mallory pier. Soon the Conch Tour train would be trailing them all around town.

The first few minutes to a half hour of the day always began peacefully because Catherine was alone in the office. She jiggled her key in the lock, and swung the door open. She felt the left side of the wall next to the door and flicked on the overhead lights. She then moved toward the reception desk and dropped her personal items off.

The peace and tranquility was disturbed by the *swoosh swoosh* of the noisy Conch Tour Train as it lumbered down South Street and came to a jerking halt at the corner of South and Simonton Streets before continuing on its island tour. The driver honked the horn at random to businesses or people along the route and made a show of waving for the tourists. This morning as the horn was honking, tourists were gawking, and the striped awning covering them from the bright sun was flapping in the warm, humid breeze. In the wake of the train came the unmistakable waft of burning propane and suntan lotion. It drifted and lingered along the street long after the train had passed by.

Most people who resided in Key West agreed the train had turned a quaint little Island into a virtual fishbowl, or something like a reality television show, in the matter of a few fleeting years. Ed Swift, the proprietor, had made it impossible for any street or alleyway to escape the leer or shutter of a camera from a tourist riding his trains and trolleys. Catherine hated the intrusion. Perhaps she differed in opinion from most residents because she recalled how private the island was as she was growing up. Travel and tourism had changed all of that long ago, but her childhood memories were still fond, vivid and clear.

Catherine had to turn on the copier, reboot the desktop computers so they could be updated on real estate transactions from the previous day, and check the voice mail for messages on a variety of things ranging from plugged toilets in rental properties to people looking for places to rent or own. Usually this was not a big deal, but today she felt the weight of the business more than the day before. Today she wanted to see Skip. She wanted to bed Skip.

Catherine touched the button to replay messages from voice mail. One of the first ones had come from Skip. His message said, "Hello, this message is for Catherine. Could you please call me when you get this message? There are some things I would like to discuss with you regarding the spaces we previewed yesterday. You can reach me on my cell phone at 954-527-5406."

Catherine smiled to herself and allowed her mind to drift as she listened to Skip's message a second and third time. She already loved the sound of his voice. It was symphonic to her ears. He was so professional and handsome. She jotted down the number on a notepad and stored it in her purse. Skip's message was only one of lots more. Someone had not forwarded the phones the previous night and the messages were stacked up like a large, overdue order of cold hotcakes. In the office Catherine was helpful and solicitous. She wrote detailed messages in hopes the rest of the office might follow her lead. She filed the messages into the slots labeled with the names of each agent for them to pick up from her desk when they arrived. Her own messages were neatly stacked to the right and placed in order of priority. One by one she began to ring them back.

Shamus arrived next at 11:15, walking in with a cup of hot coffee from up the street. The minute he shut the door a blend of sweet musky cologne and aromatic, Columbian-blended coffee permeated Catherine's nose. She liked it. She wanted to see what he was wearing, but didn't want him to know she was checking him out. His iPod was hooked into his ear, preventing him from conversing with Catherine, so he just nodded. She understood that to be his 'good morning.' He ambled toward his desk at the rear of the office.

Shamus parked his coffee onto his desk and began to sit. His cell phone vibrated in his pocket and he twisted it out of his pants. He opened it without looking to see who it was. It was Roberta. Sweet, he thought, and said, "Hello, lady. Did you have a nice time last evening?"

"Indeed I did, Shamus. As a matter of fact, that's why I'm calling you now."

"Really? What's cooking?"

"You were last night, baby. I wondered if you were free tonight?"

Shamus blushed. "I've got a softball game at six. It should be over around nine. Usually the guys go out for a few beers before heading home. Do you want to meet us at say, 9:15 at Finnegan's Rainbow?"

"Actually I had something more intimate in mind," she whispered.

"Really?" That sexy little New England accent drives me wild, he thought. What a bombshell. Thank god she doesn't like snow and moved here from Rhode Island. Get a grip, Shamus; let's not go sounding too eager. He said, "Is ten too late?"

"Ten will be just fine. See you then."

Catherine had overheard Shamus' side of the conversation and fought off pangs of jealousy. She looked him over. How handsome he looked! He was dressed better than she could remember him being. His olive linen trousers were expertly pressed. His starched, white Guyaberra shirt was a nice compliment and contrast to his dark linen slacks. She decided to call Skip. Humph. I'll one up him. And that Roberta floozy.

A couple of the other guys straggled into the office, creating noise as Catherine was about to dial Skip. They were exchanging hangover stories from their previous night's endeavors on their way to their respective desks. They smelled like day-old beer left in the sun and stale cigarette smoke. Their clothing was wrinkled and hair all askew. Catherine greeted them with as cheery a voice as she could muster. "Good morning."

They nodded, solemn and engrossed in sordid tales, and muttered back, "Yea, you too." They shuffled toward the back where they took up more interesting conversation with Shamus. Catherine was aware that the guys loved Shamus and only worked there because of him. She was high maintenance according to their low standards. She was not the kind of woman they could be bothered with. They had told Shamus many times he should let her go.

"Man, that was some game last night, Shamus," John said as he plopped in his chair, pulling open a drawer to prop his feet up on.

"It sure was, my man," Shamus said with pride. "We kicked some major booty didn't we?"

Dan said, as he fell into his seat, plopped his coffee on the desk top, and kicked his feet up on the edge of his desk, "What about that gal from Boca? Was she hot or what?" He grinned.

John replied first, "Hot like titty bar hot if you ask me."

"I tend to agree," Shamus said and then added, "That does not diminish her innate abilities."

"She was playing with that bat like a real pro," Dan said with a sly wink.

"Ten cents says she's usually on the other end of a bat or should I say pole," Shamus said.

Raucous laughter filled the back office.

"I'd like to have her on the other end of my pole," John said with a lascivious grin.

"Ditto," Shamus said as he took a sip of his coffee.

John raised his eyebrows. "How was that art show?"

"Better than I expected. I took Roberta. And let me tell ya…" Shamus winked, "…she is quite a gal."

"Now that's what I'm talkin' about. Did you do the nasty?" John said with a cockeyed grin.

Catherine called out to the back of the office. "Hey – some of us, me anyway … I may be the only one, but I am trying to get some work done.

Can you guys keep that cheap talk to a dull roar?" She meant to sound playful, but it came off as annoyed.

Don, unfazed, called back to Catherine. "Hey lassie, you should have seen our man Shamus last night. He hit a triple in the final inning and then who knows what with that Boca Grandie." He turned to Shamus and high fived him across their desks. They exchanged wide boyish grins.

"Yea, right. Whatever," Catherine called back, somewhat distracted at the last comment. She was already angry and jealous about the fair Roberta. *Who pray tell is the Boca Grandie? I can just imagine her. Some city slicker comes to the island to romp and play. Shamus the willing accomplice.*

Catherine was getting ruffled. She knew she smelled alcohol on them from their previous night's adventures. She decided to call them out. "I guess nobody better light a match near you guys or the entire office will be up in flames."

"And who are you? The fire marshal?"

"Seriously, guys." She waved her hand as if to clear the air. "You stink."

Don flipped her the bird. John said under his breath, "Up yours."

"I heard you."

They got a chuckle out of that and continued their semi-sober banter. They could've given a flying fish what Catherine thought she smelled, or anything else for that matter. Each, simultaneously, took a sip of their stale coffees.

John leaned back in his chair and sucked in air. Too much too fast. He let out a terrible sounding smoker's cough that nearly toppled his coffee off his desk. He was bent in half over his desk coughing and wrenching. His eyes looked like a flag in a gale force wind. Attempted words came out as, *choke, hack, hack, choke.* Just when Don thought something was seriously wrong, John stopped … and grinned. He wheezed once, twice, and then took a delicate sip of his hot and not too tasty coffee. "You can never take these things too seriously. Really" And he seemed to believe that, too.

Shamus flicked his chin toward the pack of Camels that sat at the far edge of John's desk next to his bic lighter. "Ever thought of giving that up?"

John said with a smile, "Only for a joint." He gave a hearty laugh. "I tried it for a lady once and look where that got me … the big D. And I do not mean dick ring!" He smiled through yellowed teeth. "I've got some hefty alimony to pay now and nobody to share my bed."

"I would never give anything up for a woman," Don said.

"No woman in her right mind would have you. You sorry fuck."

"Well, what does that say about your deranged woman?"

"More than I care to admit." Another cough, less violent, came and went. "On that note, I better have another smoke."

Don and John had come to Catherine's office as a pair. Previously they worked for the Real Estate Company of the Keys, but when that was sold to two of the top producers, who also happened to be gay, they'd said, *sianarah!* Don was once married and was sworn off that forever. His life now was sports, drinking in excess, and smoking a fattie. John had been married three times and always dug himself a deeper hole financially with each relationship. The ill effects on him had taken their toll. He oftentimes said he'd rather be bitten by a rattlesnake than married again.

Don formed a conspiratorial grin, looked into his shirt pocket and said, "Man. I got a fattie. Wanna step outside?" His eyes were still red from the joint he smoked on the way to the office. A perma-grin was pasted across feeling-no-pain face.

Amy came in silently and took her seat. Head bowed, eyes averted. She did not want to converse with these guys. She thought them gross and vulgar. She never stayed in the office too long, only as long as it took her to return her messages and catch up on any paperwork. Had it not been for her cards on her desk there may have been no evidence of Amy.

Shamus said, "The only fattie you got is that unused thing in your drawers, dude. And it's probably so shriveled you can't find it with a magnifying glass."

Amy's face burned red. She was mortified by such speech. She was the daughter of a local Baptist minister, still a virgin at twenty two, and believed such language was a fast track to hell. She desperately wanted to go to heaven and tried to live righteously in order to get there. Feeling the heat on her face, she looked down at her desk again and hurried to get her list of chores completed.

The men erupted in laughter.

Shamus noticed Amy's red face and said, "Hey Amy, want to join in our reindeer games?"

She pretended not to hear. *Just keep your head down. Do not engage them whatever you do.*

The men laughed louder.

Catherine was really annoyed now. *Jeez.* Maintaining control was going to take every ounce of her remaining self respect. She wouldn't normally be so critical of them, but she felt compelled by forces beyond her control today. I wonder why? She thought. Can't pinpoint it, really. In a way I feel left out. But their childish antics aren't anything I want to get involved in. They're so petty and juvenile. Just big kids. Are they ever going to grow up?

She called out again, "Hey. I've got to leave a few messages – can you pipe down or take that conversation outside?" She realized that sounded like a pious nun in primary school and grimaced. She softened her tone and said, "Please?"

The guys made stupid faces and ugly gestures behind Catherine's back. Amy felt bad for her and was appalled at their lack of professionalism. She came to this office because of Catherine and remained because of her generosity and help in the past couple of years as she was struggling to get a handle on the real estate market in Key West.

"We can take this outside," Shamus said. Collectively the men stood, filed out the back door and onto the small patio where they proceeded to deride Catherine for being so pushy. They understood Amy – she was just a young and innocent prude. The back door had not closed entirely and Catherine overheard one of the guys ask Shamus if that pole dancer he banged the other night was a good piece of ass. That ticked her off again. What a jerk, she thought of Shamus. Thinks he's all that, having sex with multiple partners. Trying to be like me, she realized – and was not happy about it.

Catherine left messages for two of her callers before settling in to ring Skip at the Ocean Key house. She dialed while the guys stood outside exchanging stories about the Boca Grandie. She spoke softly. She especially didn't want Shamus to overhear her conversation. The line rang once, then twice. She got the automated front desk answering machine, was disappointed, and didn't know his room number so she had to wait for the operator. She stomped her foot on the tiles as she waited for a real voice to talk to, hoping Shamus would not come back in too soon.

After what seemed like ten full minutes of boring elevator muzak, the operator came on and said in a cheerful voice, "Good Morning, Ocean Key House. How may I direct your call?"

Catherine took a deep breath and said, "Mr. Horowitz, please."

She connected Catherine to Skip's room. The phone rang once. Twice. Three times. Finally on the fourth ring someone answered. It was the voice of a young girl, sweet and proper.

"Hello."

"Well, good morning," Catherine said as cheerfully as she could manage. She figured correctly the voice belonged to one of the two young girls she'd met with Skip the previous day. "This is Catherine O'Reilley. Is your daddy there?"

The little sweet voice said, "Just one minute please."

Catherine waited while at Skip's suite the young girl looked around the sitting room and realized her dad was in his bedroom. She called over her shoulder without cupping the receiver, "Daddy, it's for you." Then she added, "It's a woman." She placed the receiver on the edge of the sofa and went back into the children's bedroom.

"Be right out," Skip said, getting up from a cushy sitting chair next to the king sized bed.

Skip's dish of the month, Evie, was dressed in a skimpy see-through nightie. She was disturbed by him taking the call. She had other things on her mind. She followed him as far as the doorway, leaned against the frame and struck a seductive pose.

Evie whistled to catch his attention, winked and motioned for Skip to come back to her. When Skip failed to succumb to her thinly veiled seductions she licked her lips and raised the edge of her nightie to expose her perfectly shaved pudenda.

Skip held his hand up to signal five minutes and mouthed, *please*. He was already dressed for business. Despite his usual cool demeanor, he felt himself harden. *Focus, Skip. This is probably Catherine.* He lifted the receiver and said, "Hello, Skip here."

The children ran through the room chasing one another. Evie maneuvered them into their bedroom and said, "Your daddy is on the phone. Please stay in here until he is finished with his call."

The children giggled, but did as Evie had told them.

Evie was not easily deterred. Now with the necessary privacy, she strode provocatively over to where Skip sat on the sofa. Skip fidgeted as she approached. He was trying to maintain his cool, but Evie was not giving in. She pushed him back into the fluffy cushions and straddled him as he talked with Catherine.

Skip covered the phone, took on a stern look and said, "Evie, please. Just give me few minutes. This is really a business call."

Evie shook her head no. She stroked his firm manhood. He squirmed. She nibbled on his neck. He tried his best to keep an even voice with Catherine. As Evie continued her sexual mission, Skip became more and more aroused, thinking, God Almighty!

Evie was pleased. Skip was unable to resist her and hard as a rock. She tapped on his bulge and whispered in his ear, "I guess we know who's boss now."

Skip, squirming to adjust his privates, managed to regain his composure. He said with sincerity into the phone, "Thank you so much for yesterday. I gained a lot of perspective on the available real estate in this area." He dared not divulge his late night meeting with Catherine to Evie, but before thinking it through he said, "I am sorry you were unable to accompany me to dinner. I truly would have enjoyed your company." His memory flashed to their steamy petting session. That thought aroused him even more.

Evie had had enough of Skip's divided attention. "Can't you conduct business later?" She said with an impatient pout. "That was a woman you met last evening wasn't it?"

Skip shook his head in the negative.

"If I ever catch you with another woman I promise I will tell Frederika all about us. Got that?"

"Evie, please," Skip said with his free hand over the receiver.

Evie was getting more impatient with each passing second. She bent down and nipped Skip through his pants on his erect penis.

"Ouch," he called out.

"What's that," Catherine asked.

"Nothing. Just one of my children playing a naughty game." Skip tried to be cool, but anger flashed in his dark blue eyes as he glared at Evie.

"Do you need to go and tend to them?"

"No, they can wait."

Evie's eyes flashed back. "You should know better than to make Evie mad." She stomped her foot and was incredulous.

Catherine overheard enough to wonder what was going on. She said, "I'm sorry, what?"

Skip was now beyond irritated with Evie and her antics. He shoved her off, pushed her aside, motioned for her to sit still and made a zipper motion across his mouth. He stared her down, then went back to Catherine. "Oh sorry, that was just the kids again. You know they get antsy when they have to sit still for too long."

Catherine shrugged in her chair and said, "Okay, whatever." She thought she'd like to be a fly on the wall in Skip's suite to see what was distracting him. "Were any of those properties we previewed yesterday of interest to you? Or would you like to see some more today?"

"As a matter of fact there were two, possibly more, that could be of interest to me."

Evie was back on the prowl, nibbling at his ear and working her hand over his thigh toward her precious. He paused to shake his head free of Evie, brush her hand back, and give another sharp look before continuing. "Could we take another look at Truman Annex ... and the one on the corner of Front and Whitehead?"

"Sure, what time is good for you?"

"Give me an hour and I'll meet you downstairs."

"Fine, see you then." Catherine rang off the line.

Evie, hot and out of control, blurted out, "Hey, what about me? What about me? You treat me like one of your children. I've got feelings too."

Skip hung up and patted the sofa beside him. "Please come over and sit for a few minutes while I recover from that bite you gave me." He smiled. "Whatever possessed you to do that? Show me you can be a good girl." God – she's so full of stubborn youthful exuberance, Skip thought.

Evie hesitated, arms folded and fuming. She regarded him, thinking. She sighed, acquiesced and stepped between the sofa and the coffee table. She lifted her hem on her flimsy nightie and danced a little jig.

"Evie, I should call you Dr. Evil," Skip said with a giggle as he pulled her near. "You are wicked beyond belief. Incorrigible in fact." He kissed her passionately. "I can't wait to get inside you."

Skip and Evie made quick love. They lay beside each other on the sofa, panting and sated.

"I wish you didn't always have to leave me." Evie pouted.

"Evie, you know I care about you deeply." Skip looked into her eyes as he smoothed her kinky hair away from her moist face.

She kissed him on the tip of his nose. "I know. I just wish things were different."

"Maybe someday Evie, but this is all I can give you right now."

"And it's good. Honestly."

"What about school?"

"School isn't for me. I could've gone to school back in Trinidad. My parents wanted me to. I want to work like you." She put on her best pampered princess expression and said in a pouty whine, "I want to be rich and powerful and tell people what to do."

Skip chuckled, sat up and said, "We can talk more about that later. Right now I've got an appointment to keep."

"When will you be back?"

"In about an hour. Can you get the children dressed, packed, and ready to go while I am working?" Skip said as he walked into the bathroom to straighten up.

Evie frowned and said, "Sure, babe."

Skip looked at his watch. Time to get moving. He said, "I'll be back in time for lunch and then I think we're headed back to Ft. Lauderdale."

Evie began to pout again. She said, "What could be more important than me?"

Such a naïve little girl, so unwise in the ways of the world, Skip thought. He felt he needed to protect her until his next fling came along. He said, "It's business. I want to open an office here and I've got to look into some possible rental properties."

"Does that mean you would move here with me?" She brightened.

"No, probably not. But I would spend more time here and that means more time with you." He smiled again. "I've got to run. I'll be back as soon as I can. Please stay here with the children." He walked out the door.

Evie followed him and stood beside the door naked. Skip looked at her longingly. She was a beauty and she pleased him in bed. She saw the wolfish look on his face and said, "How about one more time?"

Skip put on his husky macho voice. "Babe, no. I've no time for round two." He smiled and winked. He took the stairs instead of the elevator and picked up a copy of the local newspaper in the lobby before standing out front, waiting for Catherine to arrive.

Exactly as scheduled, Catherine drove up in her clunker. She waved at Skip and smiled. He walked over to the car, opened the passenger door and slipped inside. She said, "Ready?"

"Ready as I'll ever be."

Catherine slipped the shift into drive. "I thought we'd go to Truman Annex first and then to the one on Front and Whitehead."

"You're the tour guide. I'm just along for the ride."

Catherine looked at him and grinned. "I enjoyed last night."

"Me too. I'm really glad you could stop by. And getting to know you, ah …" he winked, "… a little *better* was fun."

Catherine fought back a blush and said, "I thought so, too. Too bad this trip is so short."

"There will be other opportunities, count on it."

The only gate driving into Truman Annex was on Simonton Street. She drove there and pulled up to the guardhouse. The attendant waved her inside.

"Good memory," Skip said, with a nod toward the guard.

"Actually, I called ahead and told him we would be coming back to look some more at the Administration Building. So technically he was prepared for us." She smiled.

She turned right and drove toward the Admin Building. There were only six parking slots behind the building and Catherine was lucky to find one that was vacant. She parked and she and Skip hopped out.

"This is the only completed commercial portion of Truman Annex at this time, Catherine said, pointing. "This structure was the old Naval Administration Building. There are two floors of offices, many of which adjoin and can be expanded if need be."

The property was spectacular. Skip, taking it all in, said, "The landscaping is fabulous. Attention has been paid to every last detail."

There was no trash on the grounds or the sidewalk. The streets were cobblestone and reminiscent of times gone by. The air was fragrant with jasmine and honeysuckle. Skip liked what he saw and hoped the interior was as remarkable as the exterior.

"The sales offices for this property were housed here prior to Leah and Bud Brewer purchasing it," Catherine said. "Do you know that in one weekend alone the original developer sold 85% of this property on reservation?" She glanced Skip's way and then continued. "There was nothing like it here or anywhere else in the Keys for that matter. People flocked here in droves as soon as they heard about it. The frenzy was short lived, though."

"Oh? What happened next?"

"As time went on, fifty percent of that eighty five percent dropped out because the property took so long to develop. It really was a shame."

Skip had seen that scenario replayed time and again, he nodded his head. "Happens all the time up in Ft. Lauderdale. Seems like one developer's fallen dream is always scooped up by the next money man." He snapped his fingers for emphasis. "Dream realized."

"I guess so. We've never had much exposure to that kind of rampant development here in Key West. Many of us natives were against this project from the beginning, but it sure is nice now."

Skip touched her hand and she felt an electric pulse course through her. *God he is sexy.*

Catherine showed Skip a few office suites. They then got back in the car and she took him to the office on Front and Whitehead. Their day's mission accomplished, she took him back and was close to dropping him off at the Pier House when Skip said, "Do you have time for a coffee or tea?"

Catherine bunched her lips and bobbed her head. "Sure. Do you? Wait – let me guess. Bet you do." She grinned at him.

"I've always got a few minutes when I want them. Where would you like to go?"

"How about the Pier House Bistro? It's right on the way."

He made a two handed 'please show me the way' gesture. "I'll follow your lead."

Catherine was pleased he was not rushing off. They went to the bistro where Skip ordered a Café con Leche and Catherine had a Perrier with lime. Inside was noisy with the mid-morning breakfast traffic. Catherine apologized for the din, explaining that the place was a tourist Mecca. Plates and silverware clanked as table were prepared for the next seating. Ceiling fans with large frond-like blades stirred the aromatic air. People were lined up at the counter to pay. Catherine ushered Skip outside. They took a table on the porch where they could have some privacy and enjoy the day.

"I really liked the spot at Truman Annex. What I'm unsure about is the size."

"All of that can be changed as necessary."

He reached across the table and placed his hand on hers. He looked straight into her eyes and said, "Thank you."

"It's been my pleasure."

Like bugs drawn to a flame they met halfway across the table and kissed. Soft, yet with passion. Once, then again. Catherine was breathless. She wanted so much more.

Skip said, "We're going back to Ft. Lauderdale today, but I'll be in touch."

Catherine's disappointment was visible. She said, "Oh, so suddenly?"

"Yes," he said with a hand waving as if all is hopelessly out of control, "it's always business." He smiled. She melted.

"So tell me," she said, leaning in, "Just what is your business?"

Skip had that far away look. Evasive again, Catherine thought. Skip tugged at his cheek and said, "Investments."

Catherine prodded a little. "I've always had an interest in investments. What sorts of investments do you do?"

"We sell an assortment of things." Skip took a sip of his java. "We actually sell commodities more than anything."

"You mean like the movie *Trading Places?*" She was curious to hear more.

Skip laughed and said, "Yes. Like in Trading Places."

"Sounds fascinating,"

"Next time, okay?"

She held a palm in the air. "Providing there is a next time." Not so certain now if there will be a next time, she thought. Hope so.

"Do you believe in fate?" Skip leaned back.

She considered this for a moment and said, "I guess so, why?"

"Because I think it was fate that I met you." He bent forward and kissed her again, this time on the forehead. "Sorry, but I've got a flight to catch."

"Can I give you a lift?"

"Well, I hadn't thought about inconveniencing you that way, but if you have the time that would be nice." He stopped to look her straight in the eye and said, "Are you sure?"

Catherine winked. "Sure I'm sure. Now go round up those children before I change my mind."

"Thank you. We will see you by the check-in desk, okay?"

"Fine."

Skip walked back through the bistro and Catherine went around the side to retrieve her car. Skip rounded up the children and their luggage and sent them down the stairs toward the front desk. He turned to Evie and said, "Good bye, love."

She pulled him to her and kissed him, long, hot and wet.

He broke the embrace and handed her an envelope. She opened it and counted out the crisp one hundred dollar bills. She broke into a wide grin. "Three thousand dollars! Oh, thank you, baby. Kiss me again."

Skip kissed her, enjoying a fondle of her tight, plump derriere, and said, "I told you I would take good care of you, didn't I?"

"Yes, you sure did. I love you so much, Skip." Tears formed in the corners of her eyes.

Skip chuckled and wiped the moisture from her eyes. "Take a cab home and I'll call you when we land."

They kissed once more and Skip went down to join the youngsters at the front desk. Catherine was already there, shepherding the kids and putting luggage into the car trunk. Skip tossed his valise into the trunk and closed the lid. When they were all inside the car Skip said, "Do you all have your seatbelts on?"

"Daddy only one of them works."

He looked back and smiled. "Okay"

Catherine said, "Sorry. It's not very often I have passengers in the back seat."

"I guess it will be okay just this once. It's a short drive."

The children smiled. Catherine drove out of the parking lot and turned left onto Duval Street. She said, "Did you know this is the only street in the USA that goes from the Gulf of Mexico to the Atlantic Ocean?"

The little ones chimed in, "Really?"

Skip was impressed too, but said nothing.

Catherine turned left onto South Street and said, "Do you mind if I stop for just one minute at my office?"

"That's fine. Our flight doesn't leave until twelve forty five and it's barely noon now."

Catherine stopped on the opposite side of the street and left Skip and the kids in the car while she scampered over and into her office. She breezed through the door and said, "I'll be right back. I just wanted to check in." She stopped to see if she had any messages and then turned to leave.

As soon as the door had closed, John spoke. "How much says she's going to meet that bloke from yesterday?" He smacked a well worn dollar bill down on his desk.

Don dropped another dollar on top. "Two dollars says she's going to meet him." He smirked. "I think we all know exactly where she is going." He made a loop with one hand and poked an index finger in and out several times.

John chuckled. "You are such a juvenile."

"But the sad thing is, he's not wrong." Shamus stood and walked to the front door where he had a clear view of Catherine's car and Skip and the children. *Where are they going now?* He trotted back to the money stacked on John's desk and reached into his front pants pocket. Out came a shiny silver money clip with his initials engraved on it. He turned it over and over in his hand as if seeing it for the first time. He detached his money from the clip and unfurled a one dollar bill which he added to the short stack. "Why is it that women have to be so damn difficult to figure out?" Shamus sighed. "Why can't they be more like us?"

"Hey – there are some things about women that I want to *keep* different, dude. I'm no fag."

Shamus regarded John and his silly outburst. "He's a homophobe. That's the one thing he can't deal with, homosexuality."

John huffed and said, "You know the old saying?" He paused to be certain he got it right. "Can't live with 'em, but don't want to do without."

"You dope. That's not how it goes," Shamus said with another sigh. He was brooding.

Catherine pulled away from the curb and continued down South Street, making her way to the Roosevelt Boulevard.

The Fed's were watching and listening, too. By now they knew Skip was interested in expanding his scam into the Keys. They planned to have surveillance in place throughout the entire process. As Ray drove along the perimeter road surrounding Key West, following Catherine and Skip toward the airport, his mind went back to Connie. He was beginning to like her quite a bit, more than he had ever liked anyone. It scared him to think about a future with just one woman and all that that entailed.

The rookie tossed a cigarette butt out the window.

Ray clucked his tongue. "Anyone ever tell you not to litter?"

"Well, I'll be. You've got a voice after all."

"What are you talking about." Ray's voice was a low growl. "Of course I've got a voice."

"Well, you were so deep in thought." Rookie snickered. "I figured you must have lost your voice."

"I was just concentrating on the tailing."

"And I'm Mr. McGoo." The rookie laughed. "Where are you from originally?"

Ray sighed, put off with all the questions. "Why do you want to know?"

"Just making conversation that's all."

"Illinois. Happy?"

"That's a big state. Where in Illinois?"

"Champaign," Ray said, making a turn. "And what the hell is this – an interrogation?"

Rookie frowned. "Jeez, dude. Why you so uptight?"

"I'm an investigator and an attorney. Need I say more?" Ray looked at the clueless kid cop and huffed. Why can't I get a veteran partner? He shook his head and, realizing he had been a bit smug and short with the new guy, he smiled and lightened his tone. "Look – investigators are always suspicious, looking for clues to solve their cases and attorneys are by nature uptight." He shrugged. "It's the nature of the way things work, okay?"

"What about your family?"

Jesus Christ. Does he ever stop or shut up? "What exactly do you want to know? And what about your family?" Oh shit – big mistake, now he'll talk my frickin' ear off.

"My family is in Texas. We're all immigrants from Mexico." He scratched his dark thin hair as he contemplated his next question. "You got any sisters?"

Mexico, Ray thought as he made another turn. That figures. And Texas. Jeez. "Yes, and they wouldn't give you the time of day." Ray thought about his sister, Zelda. She was a doctor now and he was so proud of her. Both he and his sister had managed to break the family mold and not spend their entire lives working in the family restaurant, Diana's. Not that there was anything wrong with carrying on the family tradition, but both siblings shared a desire for getting more out of and doing more with their lives than their parents had.

***

Catherine dropped Skip and his charges off in front of American Airlines outside the terminal building. When they went inside she started to drive off, ready to return to her office, contemplating how meeting Skip fit into the larger puzzle of life.

As she was pulling away from the curb her eyes were struck by a slick, black-haired he/she in a short yellow dress. Adeptly it crossed the crosswalk in stiletto heels. A baggage claim man was caught off guard by the sight. He stood stone still, mouth agape, watching this strange creature come his way. He looked paralyzed – afraid to move. Catherine laughed at his dismay over a relatively common sight in the Keys. He must be new to the area, she thought, he'll get used to it.

CHAPTER FIVE

In the days following Skip's departure from Key West, Catherine's life had gone back to its normal boring status. The only interesting part was the fresh details Connie shared with her about her new love interest, Ray. Connie was now seated across from Catherine in Gerome's, a small restaurant across the street from Catherine's office and next door to Connie's ice cream parlor. They were having their second cup of coffee and sharing a little gossip from the previous day's activities.

"So tell me more about your new lover, the Greek God, Ray."

"Well, he is amazingly adept at loving and he's Greek---but you knew that already. I've not had a Greek man before." Connie was practically salivating. "What *great* hands. And he's not just a great lay, he's smart. He is ruggedly handsome. Kind of like a younger version of DeNiro." Connie sighed. "What else do you want to know? How many times we do it?" She laughed and took another drag of her cigarette.

"Well, yes." Catherine laughed with her. "But no, really. Tell me more. How did you meet him?"

"At a government picnic. He was giving a lecture. And as for the sex---whenever he's around we spend most of the day in bed." Connie did not want to betray the confidence that Ray had asked her to keep regarding his employment and on-going investigation of Skip. She had to keep the conversation light.

Catherine purred and said, "So when am I going to meet this mystery man?"

"When am I going to meet this Skip fellow?" Connie was curious about Skip. The picture she got of him from Catherine differed dramatically from what she'd heard from Ray.

"Well, I don't know when he's coming back to town, and ..." Catherine's voice took on a tone of depression, "... I don't really know if he is interested in me—the person----or if this is just business."

***

Buckhead, Georgia

Six months before looking into Key West, Skip had opened an office in Buckhead, a suburb of Atlanta. He had sent two of his best brokers, Gary and DeRon Frost, to head it up. Gary was the elder, thirty years old, and DeRon was twenty seven. Both were educated and well-traveled young black men looking for a better station in life.

Gary was dressing for another day in the swanky Buckhead office. He was wearing a Brooks Brothers double-breasted, light blue with gray pin-striping suit and a crisply pressed white shirt. He called out to DeRon, "Hey bro are we living the high life or what?"

"You know, Atlanta is a black man's paradise. I love everything about this town."

"It was a big trust for Skip to give us this operation. And man, oh man, are we raking in some serious dough, especially from the Falcon's. Do those guys know how to party or what?" Gary smiled at his reflection in the mirror.

DeRon's voice was exuberant. "They are party *animals*. And today I'm going to reload Jameson for five hundred large."

Gary walked past and gave DeRon a knuckle bump. "Way to go bro."

The Frost brothers had fallen into Skip's enterprise three years before. Previously they had worked for one of Skip's competitors who had been shut down for his unholy investment scam. They were well versed in how Ponzi schemes unfolded. They began as lowly brokers and had worked themselves up to loaders. Loaders took the new accounts and churned them a time or two for good measure before burning them out for good.

"You know Skip's mantra?"

"Churn and burn, baby. Reminds me of that movie, *Talagia Nights* – where those two racers used to knuckle bump and say, *shake and bake!*"

"That's us bro, the shake and bake specialists." They knuckle bumped again.

Churning was illegal according to regulations set forth by the SEC, NFA, and CFTC, but Skip had no reason to believe he or his brokers could be caught or held accountable for such wrong doings. And churning was the least of his transgressions.

Each state had slightly differing rules and regulations associated with licensure. Georgia did not require people opening accounts or doing any trading to be licensed, so Skip hired non-licensed brokers to act as his account openers in that locale. Most investors were not shrewd enough to ask about licensure or much of anything.

Gary and DeRon's office was nestled between an up-scale women's shop and a men's haberdashery on one of the most prominent corners of town. Skip had had it furnished with faux Louis XIV furniture, plush carpets, and soft lighting. Thirty two account openers worked under the supervision of Gary and DeRon.

Since Buckhead was an up-scale suburb, Skip was able to attract some of the best and brightest scammers to this new enterprise. From this office he had great plans to garner the huge funds from sports stars and the like who would never notice a few hundred thousand missing between all of the millions they made each year.

Gary and DeRon were adept at helping his new brokers to loosen large amounts of capital from hundreds, nearly a thousand, of unsuspecting investors in a short period of time with the promise of huge returns. Many were players for the Falcons or the Braves. Most were as green as lush Georgia grass where investments were concerned. Easy prey.

Gary and DeRon had just walked into their plush office when DeRon noticed a copy of their new prospectus on the secretary's desk. He picked it up.

"Yo, bro look at this."

"Nine percent returns is sweet."

"And those are paid out monthly. The new dudes are going to *love* this."

"I'm going to make some calls to the Braves' management today and try to get them in on this."

"Let me know if you need any help," DeRon said with a cocky attitude and walked off toward his private office.

"I think before we get going I'm going next door to speak to Skip's new dish, Allison. She's hot. Girl's got bang *and* pow." Gary made hand gestures to indicate big boobs and booty.

"Too hot for you, bro – and if Skip gets wind of you sniffing up his dip's dress you're toast, homes."

"I'm not giving anything away. Trust me …" Gary did a little moonwalk and finished with a suave bow, "… I am *smooooooth*."

DeRon snorted. "Yea. And I'm Cinderella."

Gary cocked his head to the side and brought a finger to his lips with a frown. "Hmm – I can't quite picture you in a dress." They both laughed as Gary walked out the front door and headed next door.

Skip paid returns only on the first three to six months that any account was open, after that all were losses. Gary and DeRon's office, unlike Skip's other offices, allowed people to walk in from the street and open accounts. Most of his other offices were cloistered away from where prying minds might seek retribution from losses accrued over time. The Buckhead office had made Skip a multi-multi-millionaire. He was extremely pleased with the outcome there. The Buckhead office's profitability had allowed Gary and De Ron to purchase brand new BMW's and live in the prominent and swanky Anstey Park area of Atlanta where they leased brand new top of the line condos to the tune of $25k per month.

Allison was one of the elder women Skip dated, at a ripe age of twenty-eight going on twenty-nine. She owned the women's boutique next door to his office and was supposed to be a second cousin to the famous women's wear designer, Vera Wang. She was petite with long black hair that looked like liquid silk hanging to her tiny waist with a face made of porcelain, fitted with fine features. She kept herself impeccably manicured at all times because her exclusive clientele expected that. She owned her own ten thousand square foot home in one of the affluent neighborhoods nearby. Allison had been married once, but was now divorced. Work was her only passion … until Skip came along.

When Gary reached the door to Allison's shop he found a sign on the door telling him she was out on a shopping spree and would be back later in the week. Gary was depressed only a moment and walked back to the office to get down to some serious business. *Girls and shopping. I'm going to make some money.*

When Gary got back to the office, Althea, the secretary, said, "Boss – a rich looking, well dressed man just came in and inquired about opening an account with us. Do you wanna take him or should I give him to DeRon?"

"We'll both speak to him and welcome him to our operation. Where is he?"

"In the waiting area. I told him someone would be with him promptly."

"Well let's not keep him waiting. Send him into my office and then call DeRon to meet us there." Gary walked along the plush carpet toward his office.

"Gotcha." Althea got up from her desk and walked to the waiting area where she said, "Mr. Laroc, please follow me. Mr. Frost will see you now."

The man followed her, appearing to admire and appreciate the swanky office. In his briefcase camera was recording this well planned meeting. Nick Laroc was posing as an investor. He was a federal investigator from the NFA and CFTC. Nick and Ray had met in law school where they had been classmates and best pals. Both had felt the calling from the investment world ahead of private practice and landed in the investigations department of the SEC, heading up special investigations for the NFA and the CFTC. Nick's cover was as an agent for affluent athletes in the greater Atlanta area.

Gary and DeRon greeted Nick Laroc, and when they were all seated Gary said, "Althea, please bring us an urn of coffee and some croissants."

A few moments later Althea returned with a silver plate tray holding a large coffee urn, creamer, three silver spoons, and three Royal Doulton bone china cups and saucers. She placed them on the marble coffee table across from the sofa and chairs and exited as silently as she had entered.

"Thank you," DeRon said, and he thought, she is efficient even if she can be a pain in the ass. He looked between Gary and Mr. Laroc. "Now we can get down to business. Any quick questions?"

Nick asked, "Yes. Do you have a minimum account opening balance?"

Gary whipped out the new glossy prospectus and opened it to page three, account opening information. He pointed to the small print and said, "As you can see here, Mr. Laroc, we do not open accounts for less than one hundred thousand dollars." Gary let that sink in before moving on. "Is that approximately what you had in mind?"

"Why yes, that is what I would expect from such a classy operation. I've got a certified check right here." He patted his breast pocket. "How do we proceed?"

DeRon said, "We'll get to that right away. But first, just curious, what is it that you do, Mr. Laroc?"

Nick eased back in his seat, calm, enjoying the sport of reeling them in. "I'm a sports agent. I work with the NFL, NBA, and MLB. If this works out maybe I can push some of my sports representatives your way."

Gary and DeRon directed Nick through the numerous account opening pages requiring a signature while glossing over the risk disclosures. Nick signed them, handed over the check and waited for his copies.

"What do you think we'll invest in first?" Nick said with a raised eyebrow.

"Well," Deron said, fingering his chin, "We'll take a look at what the markets are doing and then see where we see some resistance or support and determine what's the best move for you from there."

Nick knew this was double talk. He understood the language of investments. But let them lead him down their Ponzi path. Give them enough rope, eventually they'll hang themselves.

Gary walked over to his desk and keyed up the real time trading page for commodities from the CBOT on his screen. His tone was calm and professional. "The markets have just opened. Maybe we should dive into soybeans. That market is *hot*. If that pans out we may divert into oil as that is the next item poised to make some major moves."

"That all sounds good to me. I don't really understand all of that. So I'll leave the details up to you worthy fellows. Thank you both," Nick said, and he stood to leave.

"Welcome to Newland Investments. We'll be in touch," DeRon said, and walked Nick to the door.

Outside their office door Althea met Nick, walked him out to the front office and out the front door.

Over the next several months Nick tracked the trades DeRon and Gary had placed him in. His numbers never quite jived with those of Newland Investments. It was slightly after their six month anniversary when Nick began to see staggering losses and the 9% promised return was drying up. When Nick inquired as to why this was occurring, Gary and DeRon told him that if he invested more money he could probably recoup those losses. Nick was passing all this information up the chain of command for further analysis and investigation.

CHAPTER SIX

Las Vegas, Nevada

A couple weeks had gone by since Skip had been down in Key West. He had spent the time visiting Buckhead and his next office which was slated to open at the end of the month in Las Vegas. Skip's rapid expansion and early success had him feeling powerful and growing in influence.

Now in his Las Vegas office, Skip was talking on the phone with his interior designer. This office was going to be garish, to blend in well with all the Vegas businesses. He said, "I want bright neon lights, lots of chrome, and cheap Formica furniture."

"Are you sure you don't want to go with something more sophisticated?"

"No. Listen to me. I am absolutely positive about what I want. How soon can you have it done?"

"How soon do you *want* it done?"

Skip hated it when his questions were answered with questions. He said with hint of impatient sarcasm, "How about yesterday … does that suffice?"

The designer's voice took on a concerned edge. "No reason to get testy."

"Look," Skip said, "you'll have a check for the first half down this afternoon. And I want you to get it done aysap. You'll be paid in full as soon as you finish, same day. Got it? Good. Then get on it." and he hung up.

Skip settled on Vinney Garcia and Eddie Nunzio, friends of his good pal A.J., as his managers for this venture. Vegas had no regulations for what was acceptable or not with regard to commodities trading. Capitalism at its best, Skip thought with a sardonic smile, Vegas doesn't give a good god damn about regulating hardly anything. Makes it a cakewalk around here for a guy like me.

Skip called Vinney and Eddie on his three way calling system. When both were on the line he said, "Vinney, Eddie, I want you two to be the managers of our Vegas operation. I need you to hire seventy account openers."

"Seventy? That's a lot boss." Vinney knew to sound polite. He was well aware how Skip got his dander ruffled in a hurry over too many questions. Still, he had to ask, "Are you sure about that. Seventy."

"Yes, Seventy. Which leads me to one more thing."

"What, Skip – you name it."

"I want this office to be open twenty four seven. Got that? Work them in shifts."

"That *is* something boss. Twenty four seven just like the casinos."

"That's right. I want this office to outshine all of the rest." Skip looked at his Presidential 18 carat gold Rolex and said, "I'll check in with you this afternoon." He hung up and dialed Lola.

In Vegas, Skip currently kept company with Lola. Lola was different from his previous Vegas playthings, in that she did not have a powerful position that could help Skip further his business. He didn't even know her last name. She was a showgirl at the MGM Grand. Skip had been there gambling with A.J., Vinney, and Eddie one evening when they met. She was tall and lanky and lovely, but dumb.

Skip attributed her brainlessness to being raised in the corn country of Nebraska. He considered Midwesterners boring and conservative. So did Lola, which is why she, two years ago at age eighteen, left for Vegas and lied about her age to get hired. She craved excitement. Skip looked past her dim wits. *Can't screw that organ, anyway.* Lola was sexy, well endowed physically, always pleasant, and eager to please him. Skip paid her well for that.

Vinney had a friend, Grant Long, who ran one of the charter flight services out of the Las Vegas FBO. He had introduced Grant to Skip just prior to Skip securing the office space two blocks off the strip. Skip liked Grant and had engaged him in his flights back and forth between Buckhead and Las Vegas.

Grant had dropped Skip off in Vegas earlier today. As they landed and Skip was deplaning he had said, "I've got some clients I can steer your way."

Skip had pondered it for a minute and then said, rather dubious, "Do they have money?"

"Money? Hell, yes. These people are richer than the Shah of Iran."

"Really?" Skip's money wheel had started turning. "We'd appreciate that, Grant. Thank you. You can work the details out with Vinney and Eddie."

Grant had spoken to Vinney and Eddie as soon as Skip was off the tarmac. Vinney and Eddie had said they would pay him one percent of every account he helped them open and trade.

The Las Vegas office, 'The Hildebrandt' as Skip had named it, like the Buckhead operation, had a prospectus touting its high rate of return, as well as a minimum amount required to open an account.

The office was furnished in short order. Vinney and Eddie knew the scam and worked it well. Before long Skip had over a thousand rich investors investing in the Hildebrandt. Vinney and Eddie handled the account summaries and the payment of the accrued interest at 10% for the first four to seven months.

One day Vinney said to Eddie, "How long you think we can keep the worm turning?"

"I've not heard anything about the Fed's sniffing around here. Have you?"

Vinney shook his head. "No, not a peep."

"You still have those numbered accounts in the Cayman's for us working?" Eddie loosened his neck tie.

"Sure do. That's our retirement fund." Vinney smiled a toothy grin.

Eddie thought he looked like Bugs Bunny, his big teeth and all, but he kept quiet about that.   "Skip says no trading at all from this office."

"That's right. And nobody loses until about the sixth month into it." Vinney knocked knuckles with Eddie.

"I'll be reloading them by that time and convince them that in order to win back what we've lost they've got to toss the dice again."

"You? What about me. I'm ten times the loader you are."

"In your dreams, buddy. In. Your. Dreams."

***

Key West, Florida

Catherine had not heard from Skip in the past two weeks. She still had a fading, but lingering memory of the sexy man he was, even though her faith in his opening an office in the Keys was rapidly diminishing. Connie had come over and asked her about him a time or two. Catherine always tried to be upbeat, but as time dragged on that was getting more difficult.

Ray called in to headquarters. Marek answered on the third ring.

"Ray, what news do you have from Key West?"

"Skip hasn't been down here since the last time. We've still got shadows on Catherine's phone in case he happens to call in."

Marek groaned. "I hope this cat has not given us the slip … again."

"I do too. I've got information from my source that he was expected here. Anything from Nick?"

"Nick said he had seen Skip in Buckhead, but that was a week or so ago."

Ray's voice rose with a quick thought. "Hey – did he open the account as we planned?"

"Yes, it went off without a hitch." Marek took on a syrupy tone. "He said Skip's boys there were quite nice."

Ray snorted. "Slime is always nice in the beginning when it wants your money. Give them a little time and I'm sure they'll show us what's really going on in that glitzy joint."

"Hope so. So far we've got some complaints, very little follow-up, and that amounts to about zip." Marek paused to sneeze. "Sorry. Bit of a head cold. Look – if we don't get something concrete soon I'm afraid higher up is going to pull the plug."

Ray sighed in exasperation. "We can't let that happen."

"Then I suggest you get busy and get us some information we can use." Marek's other line buzzed. "Got to run." He hung up and pressed the button for line two. It was Armando.

"Armando, how are you?"

"We've found the missing link. He's in Vegas. Looks like he's setting up another shop." Armando Leon lit a Camel and puffed on it as he spoke and listened.

"Can you get inside?

"Negative at this time boss," Armando said with a smoky exhalation. "We can, however, tap the lines and tape the conversations. See what's going on."

"Do it."

"We've also got a possible CI."

Marek liked that, and his voice sounded it. "Really? How? Who?"

Armando let out another puff and said, "His pilot. A man named Grant. We're still dancing with him, but I think he's going to turn."

"Good work. Keep working it and let me know what he reveals."

"Will do. All right, I'm out." Armando clicked off.

Marek reached inside his desk drawer and drew out a package of Tic-Tac's. He had recently quit smoking and his new crutch was sweets. This could be as lethal as smoking, he knew, only in a different way. He sighed as he popped two in his mouth. Well, hell – at least I'm working out four to five days a week.

CHAPTER SEVEN

Clark, Shamus' younger brother, was like a smaller version of Shamus in most ways. He had long shaggy hair, but instead of reddish brown it was golden auburn. He was upbeat, sincere, and inquisitive by nature. Having begun to work out, he was developing the build of a man. After breakfast one bright and sunny morning on their back porch, he asked, "Shamus, how are things going with Catherine. Any chance we might see the two of you getting hitched in the near future?" The entire Nelson family believed that Shamus and Catherine would end up married and happy. Shamus wasn't so sure. He stared off in thought, contemplating a reasonable reply. Clark rapped Shamus on the shoulder.

"Hey. Shamus." Clark waved a hand in front of Shamus' face. "Hello? Anybody home?"

Shamus snapped out of his trance. "You know, Clark, women are strange animals. I'm not sure that men were ever intended to understand them. Catherine and I have known each other all of our lives. We've dated. We've partnered up in business. I wish I could say after all this time that I could read her like an open book, but that wouldn't be true. Matter of fact, she seems to be harder to read with each passing year."

"Is that a no or a maybe?" Clark smiled.

"Let's leave it at a maybe, but even that ..." Shamus looked down and away, "... may be optimistic."

Shamus' father, Byron Nelson, walked out and joined in. He patted Shamus on the shoulder and said, "Hey, I was just on my way to the bar but couldn't help overhearing. Look, son. Women can be hard to read. Don't I know?" He grinned wide. "But I would've thought the two of you had already sewn enough wild oats and were looking at settling down."

Clark said, "Isn't her biological clock ticking?"

Shamus' father's eyes twinkled. He said, "Clark, what would you know about a woman's biological clock?"

Clark squirmed.

"What could be better than the sound of little feet pattering around our home?" Mr. Nelson said with a nod and a wink.

Shamus plucked a dying rose from the nearby rosebush. "Well, to be quite honest, Clark, one would hope so, but she flies off the hook at the slightest little things these days. It's almost like I don't know her anymore." He started picking petals off the rose one by one. "I've tried just about everything I know. I've been nice to her. Mean to her. I've even paraded other women, and I do mean hot ones, too – right under her nose. Sure, she seems steamed once in a while, but nothing I can hang my pecker on." He sighed. "At times she doesn't even seem to notice me. I just don't know what's inside her. She's not the same girl we both knew growing up."

William, the third from the eldest Nelson son, came out and joined them. He said, "Well, Shamus, my brother and good friend. Maybe it's time you ... you know the old saying about knowing when to fold up? The country song about the card game?" He looked Shamus directly in the eye. "Perhaps it is ... time to fold. Cast Catherine to the wind. Quit pining for her. Move on and be happy."

Shamus winced with the discomfort of his entire family swooping in and pressuring him with advice. He plucked the last petal, tossed the flower's core at the trash can, missed, sighed and said, "Can we please talk about something else?"

"Sorry man," William said. "Seriously. I didn't mean to get a rise out of you."

"No worries, bro. Maybe I over reacted." He clapped them on the shoulder and said, "Brothers through and through." He turned to leave. "I gotta go. I've got some things to do back at the office."

Clark stood, frowning, mulling over what he could do to help Shamus. William seemed to understand, too. They both felt bad for him, but at the same admired him. Shamus had helped them both out of some tight places. They both wished to return the favor one day, if and when the time was right.

Mr. Nelson said, "William, Clark, come along. We've got three beer deliveries due this morning and I'm going to need both of your help."

Back at the office Catherine sat at the reception desk licking stamps for some mailings that needed to go out. The postman always came early in the morning and he was due to arrive any minute.

Shamus arrived, appearing solemn and reflective when he walked inside. "Good morning," he said, and headed toward his desk alone in his thoughts as he prepared for the day.

Catherine considered him. For the past few weeks Shamus has been impeccably dressed and perfectly groomed. I wonder if it's because he has a new love interest. She got a small pang in her heart thinking she could be so easily replaced. The phone rang before she could say good morning back to him. She picked up and said, "Good Morning. South Beach Real Estate. How can I help you today?"

Renee, one of Skip's secretaries from the Ft. Lauderdale office, was on the other end. She said, overly officious and somewhat cool, "I've got a call for Catherine O'Reilley from Skip Horowitz. Can you please get her on the line?"

The listening Fed's sat up straight.

Ray and the newbie were stationed down the block from Catherine's office, within eyeshot and with their recorders poised. Ray turned to the rookie and said, "Let's roll."

"I'm on it."

"Turn up the volume."

He did. "Should we patch a call into Marek?"

"Yes, good idea. Tell him to key up his mike and listen in with us." Ray turned his attention back to the conversation.

Renee spoke in a monotone like a recording. Catherine was somewhat annoyed, tried not to be flippant.

"This is Catherine," She said through clenched teeth. "You can put him through."

There was a series of clicks and Skip came on the line. He was all business, but pleasant. "Oh hello, Catherine. So nice to speak to you again." He paused to look down at his agenda. "I plan on returning to Key West to make a decision on what I want to lease." He did not wait for her to speak, but continued. "I would like to make arrangements to look again at the two spaces we saw before, if that's okay with you?"

Catherine was idly fidgeting with the pens and pencils on her desk. Hearing Skip's voice was putting her in a pleasant mood. It reflected in her voice. "Great. Just let me know ahead of time and I'll have it all arranged."

From the back of the office Shamus could hear the cheery tone of Catherine's voice. He felt jealous and annoyed. He thought about what Skip had that he did not. And had not a clue.

John jabbed Shamus in the chest with his open fist. "Hey man, looks like you've got some serious competition there." He pointed toward the front of the office where Catherine sat conversing with Skip. "What are *you* gonna do about it?" He paused to spit a small piece of meat left over from his lunch onto his desk top.

Shamus and Don made a face.

"Clean his clock." A newly cleaned and wide toothy grin crossed John's rugged face. He seemed pleased to have the meat free from his teeth.

"He's not competition in the true sense of the word. I tell you, *that man has no honor.* He's just a pretty boy. He's not as clean as Catherine believes. I know there's some dirt there. Sure – Catherine thinks he's the Holy Grail. She's probably not the only one, bet on it. But I betcha he's not half the man I am."

"Well that says it all. The whore-mongering Shamus has spoken. Does anyone care to listen? Please raise your hand if you are listening?" John said louder than he wanted to. He laughed in spite of himself and moved on.

Don said, "What do you think he is----E.F. Hutton or something?"

Skip told Catherine the dates and times and then said, "My entourage will be staying at the Ocean Key House this time. I've heard the accommodations there surpass those of the Pier House. The arrangements are already made. And by the way, would it be too much to ask you to pick us up at the airport, or is that over the top?"

"Sure. Of course I will."

"We will be on American again. The flight is scheduled to land at ten forty five in the morning."

Jotting the information down, she said, "See you then."

Skip hung up. Catherine fidgeted with the papers and the phone. She wondered who else Skip might be bringing with him this time. It certainly didn't sound like he was bringing the children.

Ray said to his partner, "Did you write down those dates and times?"

"What do I look like – your stenographer?"

"Smart ass," Ray said with a playful smack to the back of his head, "Just do it."

Rook pointed to the recorder. "We've got it all on tape. What's the big deal?"

"There is no deal. Do it because I said so."

Youngblood jotted down exactly what they had overheard. His handwriting was pathetic. Ray would end up listening to the tape again to be sure of the exact dates and times. "I guess we'll be ready for him when he comes back?"

"That's right, Dick Tracey."

Catherine turned her attention back to the office and the boisterous conversation coming from the back between Shamus and the guys. She said, "Do you think when someone is on the phone----talking business, the rest of you could have the good sense to either shut up or talk quietly?" She paused before adding, "You sound like a bunch of school children."

Nobody replied, but they gathered near the back door and made their typical lewd gestures and punk faces toward Catherine.

After a few moments John spoke. "Hey Shamus – want to go grab a bite?" It was a bit early for lunch and late for breakfast. 'Getting a bite' was code for *let's get out of the line of fire to have a couple of cold brews and calm down.*

Don said, "Count me in." He began to close his desk drawers and pack some notes away.

John tapped away at a crumpled pack of Camels on his desktop as he waited for Don and Shamus to tidy up.

Catherine said, "Yes. That's a fine idea. Why don't you *all* just leave? That would – that would ... *make my day.*"

Shamus slammed a couple of desk drawers shut to let off steam and then stood. "John, Don … let's go."

They flew off like bees after honey.

Connie walked up the front steps just as they were leaving. She stopped to tip her oversized oriental hat at them and said with a polite and demure smile, "See ya, gents."

"Where'd you get that awful hat?" John said with a laugh and a snort. "Off some dead Oriental?" He used his best raunchy voice. "What was that poor fucker … your last supper?" He laughed louder than the noisy, honking traffic as they continued across the street to their favored watering hole, Gabriel's.

"You know what?" Connie hollered over her shoulder, "You're all a bunch of assholes. Fuck you!" She reached for the doorknob and stepped inside, seething as she heard John yell from across the street, "Anytime, baby – got ten long, fat inches for ya if ya think you can handle it!"

Catherine was brimming with excitement. She could barely contain her bubbly excitement Connie came inside, doing her best to shrug off the insipid remarks from Catherine's buffoons. Grinning like a school girl on her first date, Catherine said, "Hi. Guess what?"

Connie was unfazed. "You got me." She paused to listen. "So – what?" She continued to walk toward the nearest chair, and … "Damn!" She ducked in time to avoid the ceiling fan snagging and messing up her lovely new hat. She pulled up the chair and sat squarely in front of Catherine's desk, paying full attention. "Well. I'm ready now. What gives?" She opened a pack of Carletons and fiddled with them.

Catherine was beaming. She said, "I heard from Skip again."

"Really?" She feigned surprise. "Never would have guessed."

"And he's coming back to town to see some more properties. Isn't that exciting?"

"Well, now, isn't that special." Connie said with all of the charm of a rattlesnake. She softened her tone. "Really. I'm happy for you. He is an extremely, emphasis on *extremely*, handsome man." Connie licked her lips and smiled. "Just a word of caution about starting something up with a new man. New? … as in not you and Shamus' usual sparring? This guy is different." She leaned forward with a straight face. "Be. Careful."

"Honestly, Connie. First of all, there is no Shamus and me in the romantic sense of the word or otherwise. And second of all, Skip's interest in me is purely business." What am I doing. Trying to convince Connie, or myself, she wondered. "You should have heard his call today. He was all business, really and truly." Myself. Definitely trying to convince myself. "And I don't see what one thing has to do with the other." She couldn't help frowning as she looked down. I do have to concede one point; I wish his intentions were anything *but* business.

"Yeah, right. Do you forget how long I've been around and how many men I've slept with? I know a wolf in sheep's clothing when I see one." Connie toyed with her cigarette. She winked at Catherine. "Wolf or sheep – I wouldn't mind taking him for a spin."

"Thought you gave them up," Catherine said, looking at the smokes.

Turning the cigarette around and around between her lithe fingers, Connie said, "I did, but does that mean I can't play with them?"

"Whatever. I really don't know what's going to happen. I mean with Skip … business or pleasure," Catherine said as she marveled at Connie's dexterity with the twisting cigarette. "I promise to tell you everything. That is if, and that may be a big or wishful if, there is anything to tell."

Connie leaned forward and dropped a brown paper bag on the desktop. "I almost forgot. I made a tuna nicoisse and I want you to tell me honestly how it tastes. Willing?"

"Of course I'm willing – as great a cook as you are. And what's the big worry? It's only me." Catherine opened the bag and took out the sandwich sized zip-lock bag with care. She did not want tuna to fall off the bread and stick to the bag. She glanced around her messy desk for a fresh napkin.

"It's in the bag," Connie said.

Catherine chuckled. "What are we now, a mind reader? How did you know what I was looking for?"

"The same way I know everything. Observation. Witchcraft. Telepathy." Connie mocked the divine with hand gestures in the air.

Catherine huffed and pulled out the napkin as she thought, she does possess remarkable skills of intuition. She's on top of her game in areas of the supernatural, boggles everybody. She looked up at Connie with a mock expression of worship and said, "I am duly humbled." She set the napkin on the desk and placed the sandwich on it. "It's pretty." She gave it one last look before lifting it up and taking her first bite, a huge one. With food still stuffed in her mouth she bobbed her head up and down and said, "This is good, really good." She swallowed, picked up the napkin and wiped the mayonnaise off her mouth. "Seriously delicious."

She had another few bites before saying, "Have you ever considered opening a restaurant of your own?" She knew in fact Connie had. "And don't be trite. I am totally serious. And you know you have. What are you waiting for? You love this way more than ice cream."

"Yes, you're right. You know I have, but the ice cream shop is all I can manage right now." She paused and then said, "I am not Houdini and I don't happen to have an endless flow of cash at my disposal."

"You could start out small---maybe just making sandwiches for lunch. Add that to your ice cream menu and before you know it …"

Catherine raised her voice and both hands in the air, "… *you are a restaurateur.*"

"If it were all as easy as that don't you think I may have done it already?"

Outside the wind blew and rain crashed across the windows. Ominous gray clouds swept across what had been a pure blue sky as if pushed by a broom. *Plop, splotch, plop.* Tourists ran for shelter as large drops of rain splattering into the street gained momentum.

"Who'd have thunk?" Catherine said, her eyes pointing at the weather outside.

"I didn't see any rain in the news this morning. Did you?"

Catherine shrugged no.

Once the rain lightened in intensity to light spatters Connie made her exodus back to her ice cream shop. Catherine was again left alone in her thoughts. They drifted onto Skip and his intentions. Not just his business, but with her as well. She hoped that when he was back in Key West she would get to the bottom of this question and have a sunny report for Connie.

The mailman entered. He was dripping wet from head to toe, but he was his pleasant self as always. "Good afternoon, Catherine." He reached into his deep, wet mailbag perched on his shoulders, dug out a stack of envelopes of various sizes, and deposited them on the desk in front of Catherine.

"Thank you." Catherine avoided looking straight at him. I know he's sweet on me, and he is such a nice guy, but good lord this man is uglier than an apple pie ran over by a scooter and left too long in the sun.

"You're welcome." He stood there waiting for her to look up like a puppy dog desperate for some love and attention. His crush on her was obvious to the point of uncomfortable to Catherine.

Catherine peered at him, noting his tiny apple shaped frame, thin narrow shoulders, pin shaped head, long rubbery looking neck, bulbous nose and beady eyes that pried. She shuddered as a rogue thought of having sex with him raked through her brain. *Ugh – rather have oral sex with a six-foot cockroach.*

He turned and left, leaving a pool of water where he had stood. Catherine grabbed the leftover napkins and mopped the tiles. When she was done she leafed through the mail. One envelope was thicker than the rest and came from an attorney's office over in Sarasota, Florida. Catherine opened it and read the contents. It was about past due child support. John's past due child support. Funny, she thought. I didn't even know John had children. It required her to garnish two thirds of his wages, up to but not exceeding, the amount of $725.00 per month. John is not going to like this is, she thought, as she refolded the contents and placed it in the top drawer of her desk for safe keeping.

CHAPTER EIGHT

The next day John, Don, and Shamus arrived at the office well after noon. They were filled with jolly spirits that could be attributed to the pitcher of beer they drank instead of having lunch. Catherine could tell it wasn't the best time to talk with Shamus regarding John and the child support. She decided to handle it herself. The men ambled back to their respective desks. John was about to sit in his chair when Catherine called out to him. Due to the delicate nature of the issue she thought it best to speak to him in private. She said as nicely as she could, "John would you please come here for a minute?"

Don and John passed each other in opposite directions while going to their seats. Don stuck his tongue out at John.

John said, "Moron," and silently marched toward the front to meet Catherine. As he walked he glanced at Shamus.

Shamus put his hands in the air and shrugged. "Me no sabe, Keemo Sabe."

Don bent over his desk and whispered to Shamus, "What's up with this? What did he do now? She never talks to us for any reason unless she absolutely can't avoid it."

"You're right. I wonder what it's about."

"Should we go up there and try to overhear their conversation?"

They both sat still and pondered that last thought. Shamus said, "No, that would just piss her off."

"I guess you're right. We'll just have to wait for John's return."

John was in no hurry. He could not imagine what she wanted to say to him that the rest of the guys couldn't hear. When he arrived, Catherine held the door open and they stepped outside.

She got right to the point and said, "I got this letter today." She passed it to John. As he read she said, "I thought you should see it before I do anything about it."

John read the letter in stunned silence. His skin took on a white pallor. He looked like he might faint. His face and voice were ragged as he said, "Please don't do this." Sweat began forming on his brow. "I'll handle this. Really. This has nothing to do with you."

Catherine was concerned for John, but not 100% trusting of him. She remained calm and said, "John you can either handle it – and I do mean *now*, or according to how this reads – it leaves me no alternative except to comply with their request. This is not personal. I hope you understand that and make no further problems for me or South Beach. I won't break the law to save your ass."

Shamus and Don had moved up near the big front window where they thought they might be able to overhear the conversation. They stood in silence as Catherine delivered the crushing news to John and watched him turn a sick ivory color.

"Wow, that looks like bad news to me. Did you hear any of it?" Don whispered to Shamus.

"Not really – couldn't make out anything definite. I know one thing, John sure doesn't look happy."

"Do you think she fired him or something?" Don was incredulous.

"No, she wouldn't do that without talking to me, and I would never allow that to happen."

Don brightened, but still wondered. "What else could it be?"

"Don't know, dunno. I sure wish I could read lips."

John stood facing the door and caught a glimpse of them trying to listen in. He tried waving them off without letting Catherine know. They didn't budge. John rolled his eyes at them and pleaded his case to Catherine. He said, "Look, Cat, I really need all of my commissions just to get by, bare bones." He was sweating profusely. She was not buying his line. He put his hands together in a praying gesture and said, "And my wife … she gets wind of this? She'll leave me."

Nice try, Catherine thought, but not impressed. She crossed her arms and said, "Look, John … none of that is of any interest to me. That's your business." She held out the document of doom. "I have to follow the law."

"Can't you give me a little time? Please"

Catherine almost felt sorry for him, but not quite. "How much time?"

"A month or so?"

"Not gonna happen, John. You read this. It's effective as of your next paycheck. Unless you can contact them and somehow satisfy the debt immediately, my hands are tied. They could fine me and cause all kinds of trouble for this business. Sorry. It's time, sir. This is it."

Shamus and Don gave up on hearing clearly what the problem was and slunk of to avoid being discovered and reprimanded by Catherine.

Shamus said, "Man, did you see him sweat. Did you catch what I did – something about being in trouble with his wife? He looked scared as hell."

Don snorted and said, "I don't know what he sees in his old lady anyway. She's as ugly as an old dried up crow. And all she does is bitch."

"One thing for sure, he's scared shitless of what she might do. Apparently she can be rather unpredictable."

Don snorted again. "That may be the understatement of the year. She's a whack job. Plain and simple." He thought for a moment before continuing with sincerity. "You know she could be the next Loraine

Bobbitt." He laughed at the thought. "Picture that if you will. If John comes in tomorrow with his voice a few octaves higher, we'll know why." They both broke out laughing.

Outside John and Catherine continued. "I should think your new wife would be the last of your worries with this," Catherine said, sounding more like a boss than she wanted.

"You obviously don't know my wife. I hate to admit it, but she does wear the pants in our house."

"I'm genuinely sorry, John, but I've got to comply. I don't want any legal problems. I'm not going to be called on the carpet for something that I can't control."

John clasped his hands together in pleading fashion again. "I'm not asking you to not comply. I just need to buy some time."

"You know what I think? I think ..."

John cut her off. "Let me tell you what *I* think. I think you just enjoy seeing me squirm. It's no secret you don't really like me, or Don, or even Shamus for that matter." He threw both hands in the air. "This whole thing stinks!" He stomped a foot and spat. "Well, you'll be the sorry one if you really go through with this. I promise you that." With a spin of the heel he turned and stormed back into the office.

Catherine, exasperated, called out to the back of his fuming head, "John, for god's sake be reasonable."

For a few minutes Catherine stood outside, lost in her thoughts. A gaggle of rain-soaked spring breakers on scooters came cruising by. They were weaving across the street, honking their horns for attention. Catherine gave them an annoyed look and walked back toward the front door of her office, muttering, "Damned spring breakers have no consideration for anybody except themselves ... just like John."

Back inside, Catherine took a seat at the reception desk, pulled out her mirror to check her hair and make-up, and corrected what was needed after the wind and rain. She could overhear John's explaining his side of the story to Don and Shamus in the back, in spite of his hushed tone.

"The way I see it---she can give me a little time to sort things out." John stopped in mid step and pled his final thought. "As a matter of fact ..." He turned to look directly at Shamus, "... you own half of this business. Shamus, don't you have any control over her these days? Maybe she would be nicer if you gave the gal a bone?" John grabbed his crotch and did a Michael Jackson hump.

Don burst into laughter.

Before Shamus could reply, Catherine surprised the men and said in a cold voice, "Not gonna happen. Sorry." Speaking straight to John she said, "Like I said before – this is business, not personal."

John was livid, seething, and shouted, "Then I'll tell you what. My wife and I are going on vacation beginning right now. How do ya like that?" His parting words as he marched out of the office were, "You can go fuck yourself!"

"Way to go, Cat," Don said without emotion. He was drained from John's show and now needed a cold beer or a joint, perhaps both.

Shamus shot Don a withering glance. They both slunk down in their seats, giving Catherine time to cool off.

Fine, John. Just fucking fine, Catherine thought before speaking. As evenly as she could, given the circumstances, and to nobody in particular, she said, "Okay, have it your way." John's slamming of the front door behind him was a final punctuation. He was gone. She was pissed. She got up and strolled back toward Shamus and Don. "How long did he think he could continue to play these games? How long do you all think *you* can keep playing games?" They tried to not snicker, but couldn't help it.

Catherine was seething and spat out her words. "This is serious. Very serious, despite what the three of you might think. You're nothing but a bunch of aging children!"

Shamus and Don glanced sideways at each other as John stormed back into the office. He got up in Catherine's face and said, "You know, you would think as long as we've known each other you might muster a little compassion, but no. You're just a dried up old witch." He spit out his words. "I'll be gone couple of weeks. That should be adequate, give or take. I just want to put some distance between my current wife, my ex, and my ex's attorney." He closed his eyes, took a long, deep breath, sighed, and calmed down some. "That's all."

Catherine knew he was lying. He figures he'll put some distance between me and the attorney who has his nuts in a vice. This mess he's gotten himself in has caught up with him and it's more than he can fathom, let alone handle. Her thoughts must have shown on her expression because John's face was again turning white with anger.

He looked nervous, pulled out his pack of Camels, withdrew a cigarette and wagged it at her. "You know what I think?" He tapped his cigarette case on the desk top as he waited. "I think this is a woman's conspiracy to keep men down. Between the miseries that my ex put me through when we were married, and then as we were getting divorced … and now this shyster attorney woman gets into the mix. Life is more than a bitch. I hope the whole lot of you rots in hell!"

Shamus whistled. "Whew. John, you really had us going there for a moment. And then, nothing. I thought you really had something important to say. Don't you know they *are* all going to hell?"

John shot Shamus the bird, stalked back to his desk and meekly sat.

Catherine couldn't let it go. "John, please. That is just plain cowardice. Madness. Sheer foolishness. I think you should offer this woman some sort of payment plan. Let her know that you are sincere. Make it something that can work for both of you. Hiding or running is no way to solve this situation."

John had both hands over his ears. Catherine smacked her palm on his desk. "Listen to me!"

John was beyond angry, nearly gone mad. He shook his index finger at her, his face boiling crimson with forehead veins threatening to burst and said, "You – you … you don't know what you're talking about, Missy. I've been around a lot longer than you and I know how these things work. Color me gone! Just paint me out of this office picture."

Catherine folded her arms. "John, if you don't want to consider your ex-wife then consider your children. Do they deserve this? They didn't ask to come into this world. You and your wife had a choice in choosing to be parents. You both have a responsibility to take care of them."

John hurled his Bic lighter squarely at Catherine. She ducked just before impact. Shamus and Don doubled over laughing. That enraged her even more.

John could've spit nails and sounded like it. "I don't have to take this shit from you." He stood and was gone in a huff.

Catherine shook her head. "I can't understand such irresponsible behavior, but if he refuses to work or take some responsibility for this, then I'm not about to force him." She trudged over to her desk, slipped on a wet spot, and fell into her chair. She landed awkwardly because the wheels were already moving as she tried to sit. The phone rang. Frazzled and still heated with anger, she gathered herself and answered on the fourth ring. "Hello, South Beach Real Estate. How can I help you today?"

The caller was an advertiser asking if Catherine wanted to take out an ad in the *Key Wester*. She respectfully declined, but promised to look into the periodical before the season went into full swing.

Still pissed, Catherine walked to the back of the office, hips swaying, chest heaving, and shoved the letter in Shamus' face. "Well, what would you have done differently?"

Shamus shrugged and said, "I guess you did what you thought was right, but I would've liked the opportunity to talk about this before blindsiding John with it. This business is supposed to be a partnership and you act like a dictator. You left him no alternative. You cornered him."

Catherine glared at Don. "If that was cornering I never saw the ambush. Someone had to deal with it. Today that someone was me. The way I see it … the sooner the better. Good riddance."

Shamus said, "Personally, I think John is a stand up sort of guy. I say give him some time." He avoided looking her in the eye.

"You … you're such a pig!" Catherine said. "You would say or do anything just to be contrary to me. I did what I had to do and you damn well know it. Maybe you should think more about what's good for this business rather than just blindly siding with your little silly boy chums all the time." She spun around and clomped toward the front.

Shamus hunched his shoulders and grunted, but stopped short of continuing the verbal confrontation. Don waited until Cat was far enough away and went into a spell of hearty laughter. Shamus couldn't look at him without laughing too.

CHAPTER NINE

Catherine met Skip and three of his cohorts later the same day at the airport. She was still in a foul mood from her nasty confrontation with John. She hoped her miserable disposition wouldn't show.

Skip and A.J. were reminiscing while waiting for Catherine to arrive. Skip said, "My very first operation was in Lauderhill and you were there with me."

"Yes. And we did pretty well there, too. Now we've got the Bahamas, Vegas, Cypress Creek, Costa Rica, Buckhead, and the Keys coming on line. That takes us from small time trading firm to the major leagues." A.J. winked and snapped his fingers.

"Yeah. And finding that loophole in the CFTC/NFA law where we can opt to be licensed and do some trading or remain unlicensed and do no trades ... what a major boon that was. If anyone ever got wind of the Ponzi scheme we have going we'd have to run for our lives."

"Never happen," A.J. said with confidence, "We're too slick. Isn't that such a gas? The very people who make the laws left us with a golden egg." A.J's eyes lit up. "Hey – did Gary or DeRon tell you they lured Michael Vick into their firm?"

"No shit? That's great news. When does he start trading?"

"Maybe already has. Want me to check on that later today?"

Skip nodded, pursing his lips. "Yes, that and the rest of our offices. Best to stay on top of everything ourselves, if you know what I mean." He winked and then said, "Speaking of which, have you spoken to Tony or Tommy?"

"Not yet today. Is there something specific you want me to talk to them about?" A.J. sounded concerned.

"Not right now. I just wondered how much money we've taken in and if they have transferred it to the Caymans or are keeping it locally in Nassau."

"Their play is still the currencies, right?"

"Yea, but I don't want those accounts traded at all. That's exactly why we opened that office in the first place. It's a super haven for keeping potential prying eyes out of our double dipping."

A.J. brought a finger to his chin, rubbing it as he said, "We've all been together for quite some time. I've come to think of our tight knit group of guys as ..." he smiled at Skip, "... as family."

"Me too. I've been with you and Tommy since the bad days in Jersey. Man ... how things have changed, eh?" Skip looked down at his golden and diamond encrusted presidential Rolex and noted the time.

"And Tony had a very swanky job with the mob before coming over to work with us," A.J. said.

"If you call killing 'swanky' that's true. And the mob is not like some country club you can just up and quit. Took balls. I don't think a day goes by that Tommy doesn't look over his shoulder and wonder if the mob is going to hit him."

"Yea. That can wear the hell out of you, but … that's why we sent him to the Bahamas, right?"

"Absolutely why." Skip saw Catherine's clunker drive toward them. He waved and stared in her direction.

"Still got the Contender over in Nassau?"

A.J.'s question gave Skip a slight pause, brought his mind back from focusing on Catherine. "Uh, yea … Tommy is more or less taking care of it."

"What did she set you back?"

"About two hundred fifty large." Skip grinned, the proud owner of such a magnificent vessel.

A.J. whistled through his teeth.

"You guys ready?" Catherine said, having rolled her window down after stopping.

"Is this our chariot?" A.J. said with an askance expression.

"One and the same. Hop in."

A.J., comfortable in most every situation, chatted amiably with Catherine as she drove. "I've not been to Key West in quite some time, but Skip tells me this is where he wants to open his next office. Actually I'm excited to see what types of office accommodations this small place has to offer. When he told me about this I was a little uncertain, but I'm behind him now."

Five people with luggage were a tight squeeze in Catherine's mid-sized car. "Sorry about the stifling heat. I've had my air conditioning looked at and it'll work for a while and then not work again."

"This would be one of the times when it definitely is not working." A.J. said as he fanned himself with a flyer.

"I honestly think it has a mind of its own," Catherine said.

"Lucky for us this Island is small. Everything is a short drive to get to," Skip said.

"Well, there were two places that Skip expressed interest in the last time he was here, but that was quite some time ago. I checked yesterday to be sure they hadn't been taken and am happy to report they haven't." Catherine smiled into the rear view mirror.

Skip was riding shotgun. He shifted in his seat and said, "I've been giving this some thought and the place at Truman Annex is probably the best fit for us."

Matt concurred. "Yes, that does sound like a perfect fit. At least in the beginning."

Ralph, always the pragmatist, said, "Well, I won't vote on this until we have actually seen the place. From what Skip tells me, the space will be tight."

"Ralph, don't worry about the intermediate phase. Focus on now – startup needs. This way we can start out small, get things together, and grow," Skip said.

Ralph's expression was doubtful, but he said, "You----are the boss." And he meant it.

The drive back from the airport was uneventful. Businesses were open and ready for business.

Catherine pointed to the sale racks staged on the sidewalks. "All of this is out there to entice potential buyers. When the cruise ships are docked at Mallory Pier they are all vying for the maximum business they can."

"How many restaurants does this town have," A.J. asked. "Seems like there's at least three on every block."

"Wow, look at those bicycle cabs," Matt said.

"Those are called pedi-cabs," Catherine said, chuckling.

"Cool. Different."

Catherine turned left off of Duval into the parking lot and dropped them at the portico for the Ocean Key House. One of the Conch Tour Trains was parked across the street boarding new passengers and off loading passengers from their last tour. Indian summer-gone-into-winter heat mingled with the pungent odor of trash and puke from local bars. The smell was sickening. "I'll wait here while you check in." She wrinkled her nose and looked at her lipstick in the rearview mirror.

Skip walked ahead of the gang, his posture upright – borderline regal. He spoke to the attendant behind the front desk, "Hello."

The stout woman did not move, but peered over her reddish-rimmed glasses at Skip. "May I help you?" she said with a tone devoid of sincerity.

"Do you have reservations for Skip Horowitz?" Skip smiled, ever the polite gentleman.

She was incredulous. "Well, let me see here." Slowly she pecked at the keyboard in front of her. "Horowitz did you say?" Her glasses slipped down her greasy wide nose and came to rest near the tip.

"Yes, Ma'am." Skip almost laughed, but held it, considering her attitude.

"Mr. Horowitz ..." She rummaged in the cubbies on the back wall and came out with a handful of keys, which she dropped on the counter in front of her, "... here are your room keys." She glanced down over her reading glasses to double check. Certain they were the right keys, she pushed them with her chubby hand over toward Skip. She shoved up her glasses and looked squarely into Skip's eyes. She did not smile.

When Skip had collected all the keys he went outside to have a few words with Catherine.

Federal agent Ray and the new recruit, Eddie, listened in. Eddie was bored. He said, "Hey Ray, have you noticed any discomfort in the ranks due to the recent across the board budget cuts?"

Ray scoffed at him. "No, no way. Everybody on the force is happy." He punched Eddie in a playful way. "What do you think, dummy – of course there is ... *discomfort*. Our budget is always the first to be cut. We always get the shaft and feel the pinch."

"You know with two wars in the middle-east and maybe more flaring up," Eddie said, "we're lucky just to have a job. At least that's what my girlfriend Dorothea says. You know, come to think of it, she follows that stuff pretty closely."

"Shhh."

"Don't shush me. These two----what ever they are – aren't saying anything the least bit interesting to me."

"Oh good, perfect, junior," Ray said, "and when the next set of budget cuts come round maybe we can cut you."

"Don't be a wise ass, Ray. I was just saying ..."

Ray held his hand up to stop. "Give me a minute here, please." He listened, then said, "We've already arranged to have the rooms bugged, but we've got to get some good stuff----some solid stuff on this Skip guy soon or we may all be out of work."

"Drama queen," Eddie said in a mumble.

"Shut up." Ray looked more annoyed than before. "God you're like a child. How many times do I have to tell you to shut the pie hole?"

"Cool off, man. I got the message."

"Yeah, whatever. Just keep it shut. They're talking. And some of us take our jobs seriously."

Skip touched Catherine's arm and said, "It's important to me that you get along with my crew. Ralph White, A.J. Longo, and Matthew Riser are my three right hand men. I trust them explicitly. Their judgment is of great importance to me."

"Skip, I totally understand and will more than include them in all that we talk about and do."

"Well, maybe not everything," Skip said with a wink and that sexy sly smile he had in his arsenal.

Catherine blushed.

A couple of bikini-clad girls walked out of the front doors of the Ocean Key House, turned the corner and sashayed toward the ice cream parlor next door. Skip turned to watch.

Catherine observed him watching and was mildly amused. "See something you like?"

"Actually I do, but they are a little young even for me." His smile widened.

"College girls," Catherine said. "Around here we call them 'spring breakers.' And where the girls are …" She nodded toward several young men staring at the plump tight rumps of the bikini twins from behind "… the guys are sure to follow." She and Skip both laughed.

Matt came out the door and immediately spotted the girls as well. "Whoa – nice asses. I think this is going to be a fun trip after all." Matt was not tall, Catherine noted, but had an incredible build going for him.

Ralph came out next, laughing and sniffing the air. "Whew! Did you guys get a whiff of that?" Medium height, thick dark hair, muscular and dressed to the nines, his cheesy smile didn't detract from his handsomeness.

"You bet we did," A.J. said. "Did anyone think ahead to bring the kitty litter? I smell fresh pussy." He arched his neck, raised a hand in a 'stop' gesture and said, "Wait – I think I hear the kitties calling."

Ralph made a show of looking at his two-tone Rolex Submariner. "Hey boss – we got enough time to play a little cat and mouse?" He and A.J. laughed and high-fived.

Skip ignored them. He had kept an eye on Catherine during the lewd remarks, hoping she wasn't offended. When she didn't appear perturbed by his guys, he said, "They can be an incorrigible bunch, but for the most part they're harmless."

A.J. said, "Speak for yourself, boss. I am *highly* dangerous." He laughed.

Catherine giggled at that and did a quick mental assessment of A.J. Balding a little, but bald can be sexy. Ooh, and those intelligent looking dark eyes that sparkle when he smiles. Nice. Very nice.

Catherine also checked out Ralph. Nice tan and the bright white of his smile against his dark skin is totally alluring. I can't wait to tell Connie about these guys. They're all gorgeous and sexy. Nines and tens on the hunkometer.

Catherine looked at Skip. "So tell me." She nodded toward the fellas. "What's the story with these guys?"

"What makes you think there is a story?" Skip smiled.

"Always is. Do tell." She leaned in.

"A.J. here was a cop. We met a long time ago and our friendship runs deep. He's like a brother to me. He's been through some ups and downs in life, had it all, lost it all, and now he's got it all back. Isn't that right, A.J.?"

"A.J. fist pumped his heart and pointed at Skip. Yep – thanks to you, my friend. But hey – you didn't quite tell all."

"What's more to tell?"

"You left out the part about my owning a restaurant."

"Oh, yes. A.J. fancies himself a chef and, as such, good food is what wins over his heart."

"I'll keep that in mind," Catherine said with a lighthearted chuckle.

"Not just good." A.J. struck a pose. "Exceptional. Does Key West have any restaurants that are known for first class gourmet food? Or exotic and exquisite cuisine?"

Catherine said, "Many, A.J., you'll see." She pointed at Matt. "Okay Skip, now tell me a little bit about this one."

Matt stepped right over to Catherine, wedging between her and Skip. He winked at Skip and said, "I've got this boss," then stood at attention and saluted with such comic aplomb the whole group burst into laughter.

"Let me guess – standup?" Catherine said between chuckles. "Skip found you in a nightclub and you were on stage, too funny to let go?"

Matt shook his head and wagged a finger. "Nah, nothing so glamorous or regular." He spoke with sincere emotion, "I came from a prominent Wall Street trading and investment firm. I, unlike the rest of these slobs, actually have a pedigree. This stuff is a perfect fit for me with my Ivy League college education, 4.0 GPA, and all."

"Ivy League? You?" A.J. squelched a laugh. "You can't be serious."

"Did any of *you* attend NYU and get a four point average in economics or finance? Well I did."

Nobody said a thing. Matt continued. "I did the high profile brokering thing for six years. Made a boatload of cash." He paused for a moment to reflect. "Spent a lot of it too – too much. Before long I ran into a little … problem and had to move on. Fortunately I ran into Skip here and haven't looked back since. So you see …" Matt patted his boss on the back, "… he really is a pretty amazing guy."

"Problem?" Catherine looked between him and Skip. "Care to elaborate?"

Skip waved her off. "Ah, it's nothing. Really. I'll fill you in sometime. It's not relevant for what we're doing down here." He didn't want Catherine to know Matt had been caught for insider trading and his license was suspended indefinitely. Or the fact that he did no jail time because he squealed on those higher up. With no other firm that would have him, a friend who knew about Skip hooked them up. Skip said, "Matt has a lot of upsides for this business. He runs the training program and hands out leads for our operation in Lauderdale. He's indispensable, a good man, and loyal." *Loyal because I pay him over $320,000 a year plus performance bonuses,* he thought. *That and the fact he has no license to worry about losing makes him perfect as a profit churner.*

Skip nodded toward Ralph. "Now Ralph here, he's not a trader. He acts as an intermediary and oftentimes doubles as my bodyguard." *Guy is smooth and tough---so play up the good and down the bad.* "He was raised in Texas and still carries that no-nonsense cowboy attitude. He can control a group of arguing brokers like nobody else and even reduce them to sheep that solemnly follow his lead. He's also a quick thinker and tends to act rather than react, both admirable qualities in our line of business."

By now all the men were a shirt and hat size larger and several inches taller from Skip's generous helping of compliments.

"Why don't you park your car and come along with us?" A.J. said, thinking that her car was not much, especially if you compared it to the vehicles that he and the guys drove back in Lauderdale.

Catherine looked at Skip. Skip said, "That's a good idea. Please join us?"

"Since you said it like that----who could resist. Meet you inside. I'll park my car in a guest slot in the parking garage."

Skip, Ralph, Matt, and A.J. walked inside and waited. Skip said, "Now we want her to feel welcome. I do want her to join our little club, so please be persuasive."

Matt said, "Are we looking for a shill? Need to add that Yiddish element for luck and all."

Nobody said anything, but all knew that was how things would unfold. She may give a legitimate and unassuming air to the business in the Keys. And she knew nothing about what they really did.

A.J. said, "Maybe I ought to be the one to broach that subject – her joining us – unless you'd rather Matt or Ralph?" He looked directly at Skip and waited.

"No, you A.J … you've always steered us right and kept our operations out of the prying eyes of the NFA and CFTC." He looked at the other two. "No hard feelings, boys."

Catherine came breezing into the lobby. "Oh, isn't it nice and cool in here?" she said, "And don't you just love the understated elegance of this Tommy Bahamas décor."

All four men bobbed their heads in agreement. Skip said, pointing down at the floor, "Oriental. Nice touch." He glanced at the lamps. "Subtle mood lighting, too. I've seen those before. They give off a suffused lighting day or night."

"Do we want to have a drink and talk before we go to Truman Annex?" Skip said.

"Yes, a capital idea," Matt said.

They went into the hotel café and looked at the drink menu, a wide variety of soft drinks and fizzy waters, also one drink with an alcoholic content.

"Quaint little joint," A.J. said, surveying the small shop's floor plan with its iron tables and chairs scattered here and there.

"Mmm, look at this display. A wonderful assortment of sweets and pastries," Catherine said, bending over the attractive glass counter display.

A very fat woman in white popped up from behind the counter and said, "What can I get for you?" Her chubby gloved hand was poised in the air.

The drink orders were placed and served rather quickly – considering her excessive girth. She tallied up the prices and presented the bill. "That'll be thirteen sixty five. Would you like to pay with cash, credit, or charge it to your room?"

Skip placed a crisp twenty on the counter and said, "Keep the change." He moved off toward a large table with six chairs and took the first seat as the rest of the group followed.

The server stood at the counter in a cloud of utter disbelief. She had never received a tip greater than a dollar no matter what the tab came out to. As if struck by the thought that he might change his mind, she snapped out of her stare, waddled over to the tip jar and stuffed the twenty inside.

Once the group was all seated, A.J. said, "Catherine, Skip has told us all a lot about you. As you know, we do want to open a commodities trading office in the Truman Annex property. But there's more that you don't know. And I'm going to come right to the point." He leaned forward for emphasis. "We would like *you* to be part of that operation."

Catherine jolted up straight. It took her a few seconds to process and think of what to say. With both palms up she said, "What can I do for you – past securing the property?" She looked around the table, stopping her gaze on Skip. Skip directed her eyes back to A.J. with a nod and with two fingers wagged for him to go ahead and continue.

A.J. cleared his throat, clasped his hands together with a clap, then raised two forefingers in a steeple and pointed at her. "We want you to come to work for us."

She swallowed hard and said, "Really?" This is unbelievable.

Skip said, "Yes. I think you would be especially good at this line of work. We all do. With your experience in real estate you have no qualms asking for large amounts of money. We open our accounts with a minimum of one hundred thousand dollars." He let that sink in.

"I've never earned a hundred thousand."

A.J. said, "That and much more is possible if you come to work for us. "We ..." He pointed around the people, "... will help you study and sit for the licensure exams." He smiled. "And another thing, *you* can be instrumental in helping us hire local talent here in Key West."

"I'm overwhelmed. I know nothing about this type of business. I don't see how that can help you." Catherine scratched her forehead, dumbfounded.

Skip grinned and leaned back, hooking his right arm over the back of his chair. He flipped his right palm up. "Let us worry about that for the time being." He looked directly at Catherine. "Okay?" She squirmed. He continued, "Let's do something you are good at. Let's go look at the new office space."

CHAPTER TEN

There was lots of scenery to take in along the way to the Truman Annex. Two cruise ships were parked at Mallory Pier. As the group walked by, Catherine called the guys' attention to them.

"See those cruise ships over there?" She pointed in the general direction of Mallory Pier where only the very top of the stacks from the cruise ships were visible. "Key West made a recent deal to allow cruise ships in during the daytime hours. They'll be parked there for the rest of the afternoon. According to the agreement they'll pull out before sundown, though."

"Why so short?" Matt said.

Sunset is a big deal here in Key West. That's Mallory Pier and every night it's filled with buckers and other street performers, trinket dealers, psychics, hawkers for the local restaurants and bars, and just about anything else that might be loosely construed as a freak show."

As they walked along a man waved and called out, "Hello, Cat."

She waved.

Matt looked dubious, but said, "Friend of yours?"

Catherine looked at Matt. *Ooh, he's so delicious looking.* She said, "Yes. He's the cat man. Real name is Dominique, but he's known as cat man. He'll have his regular station set up for the evening ceremony. Always does."

"The cat man, eh? What exactly does the cat man do?" *Only in Key West,* he thought.

"Well, he's taught his six cats to do a lion's act. You know like in a circus. They walk a tight rope above the ground. They jump through hoops of fire. Actually, they're pretty darn amazing."

"Well thank you for that stunning review. I guess that's something I should add to my list of must sees for Key West. You know, Catherine, you are one fine lady." Matt stopped his gait long enough to perform a small bow along with a gracious smile.

Catherine blushed and smiled. *Add well mannered and full of compliments to this guy's resume. What more could a girl want?*

"Skip tells us that you are very capable – perhaps even better than the cat man." Matt gave a sly wink. "Seriously, I hope we are able to do business together. Skip really knows how to pick 'em."

Keep it coming, sir, Catherine thought as she regarded him. *He's got some game, that's for sure. Love how playful he is. If I didn't have the hots for Skip I'd take a great big bite out of that man. Wait'll Connie gets a load of him. She's a sucker for blue eyed players in white linen slacks. And the blue silk shirt just sets his blue eyes off perfectly. God, he's* edibly cute. Focus, Cat. Focus. Skip. It's Skip that's the boss and the one with the money.

Skip let the guys walk ahead as he fell back alongside with Catherine. He spoke to her as if nobody else was there. He had observed her reaction to Matt, believed there was an attraction there, and he said in a low voice, "You'll need to have a good working relationship with Matthew." He paused for emphasis. "All of them really, but he's my trainer and the best in the business. He's an expert at what he does. Also a brilliant trader. So I'll expect you two to get to know each other extremely well and stand behind each other in all decisions dealing with the office."

I haven't yet agreed to come on board, Catherine thought. This is all so confusing, Try to keep pace with the conversation as it changes and evolves. And for god's sake don't look as confused as you feel.

Dressed like a tourist, federal agent Ray was on a scooter following a safe distance behind Skip and Catherine. He had a high-tech super small microphone attached to the front of the scooter that allowed him to hear even muddled conversation from over 100 feet away.

"These iron gates mark the end of Key West proper and denote the beginning of tranquil Truman Annex," Catherine said.

From the moment they entered they were mesmerized by the differences, the silence, and the grandeur of perfectly planned flora and fauna. Cobblestone walkways led up to the old pump house-turned-post office and the Administration Building that Skip was interested in. A brick fountain was filled with cool, colored water.

"Anyone wanna make a wish?" Catherine said.

They stopped briefly to cast out a few coins and make a silent wish.

A.J. said, "Wow this is spectacular. I don't know what I was expecting, but this was soooo not it."

"I've been to Key West lots of times before and never even knew about this place," Matt said in awe.

"I thought you'd find it nice. I did too, the first time Catherine brought me here." Skip said.

"If the inside is as nice as the outside, I'm sold," Ralph said as he continued to take it all in.

"Shall we?" Catherine gestured with her hand. She guided them into the Admin Building. "The foyer is a combination lobby and information stop."

Expensive Clarence House fabrics had been used on the sofa, chairs, and wallpaper. Mahogany tables with marble tops and gilding graced the lovely and ornately decorated Oriental wool rug that was the room's centerpiece. It was obvious this area had been planned by someone with taste and money … no expense had been spared.

"The elevators are over here." Catherine stepped toward the hall in the center of the lobby.

Beside the elevators was a signboard that announced who was in what space. Catherine depressed the up button and the elevator lights overhead blinked from floor two to floor one. In a soft glide the bronze doors parted and they all stepped inside. She hit floor two and they waited in silence as the elevator rose to its destination where again the doors slid apart like silent partners ending a dance.

A decorative multi-colored flat piled carpet lined the halls at this level. The walls were painted soft eggshell beige and were trimmed in a chair rail of white wainscoting. Lighting came from frosted glass sconces at regular intervals along the smooth walls. Catherine turned left and walked five steps down the hall before turning left again into office 201. The label on the door said, *Brewer Companies, Inc.* Catherine popped her head inside and said, "Hi, Kay. I just wanted to let you know that I have Mr. Horowitz and his crew with me. They want to see units 208 and 209."

"You have the key." Kay coughed twice. "Let me know if there's anything else you require of me." She snubbed her cigarette butt into the ashtray and went on typing.

"Thank you, Kay. Please tell Bud and Leah I said, 'hi'."

"Will do," Kay said, not looking up.

Catherine motioned and said, "Follow me."

Single file, they fell into line behind Catherine. At the door marked 208 she stopped, pulled a key from her pocket and unlocked the door. "This is it." She pushed the door inward and stepped back so Skip could enter first. The rest filed in behind Skip. Then she unlocked room 209 and did the same.

"Well?" Catherine said, looking around the rental space and watching them for first impressions.

A.J. shook his head and said, "Actually, far nicer than I had envisioned."

"Sounds to me like your envisioning could use an update," Matt said with a hint of sarcasm. "Nice, very nice."

"It is small …," Ralph said, thinking out loud, "… but if we took both spaces we could have a little separation between the brokers and the secretary. Perhaps place management and/or trading over with the secretary."

"I was hoping you would find it as appealing as I did. Does that mean you all concur?" Skip looked from man to man.

"That's a yes," said Matt.

"Affirmative," said A.J.

"Most definitely," Ralph said.

"Congratulations, Catherine. You have your first round of applause for finding us this wonderful space." Skip moved over to where she stood and gave her a friendly peck on the cheek.

"Does that mean we sign the lease?"

"Yes, probably. Do you have a copy we can look over? Just a formality, of course."

Catherine nodded and said, "Yes. Of course." She paused and then said, "I'm pretty sure Kay has one handy in her office. I have to leave the keys off anyway. I'll ask her about the lease then."

"Great," A.J. said, "Let's go have lunch. We can talk it over more as we have some gnosh. I'm *starving*." He patted his taut and firm waist. "Catherine, can you lead us to one of those many fine restaurants Key West is noted for? Hopefully one filled with incredible culinary delights. The thought of fine food has me practically salivating,"

"I believe I can. What are you in the mood for?" Catherine raised an inquisitive eyebrow.

A.J. fingered his chin. "Mmm, why don't you pick. Just make it something exceptionally good and devilishly delicious."

She thought for a moment, then snapped her fingers and said, "Got just the thing. Let's go to the Rooftop Café."

"We'll follow you," Skip said.

"Wait here for just a minute. Let me return these keys to Kay and see if she does have a copy of the lease we can preview over lunch." She left.

"What do you think really," asked Skip.

A.J. said with authority, "It will serve us just fine for the time being. One step at a time. Rent the space. Bring Catherine into the fold. Let her help us build it. And who knows from there."

Ralph said, "Skip, do you have any idea how many account openers you want to staff here?"

"Not account openers Matt. That sounds so lame. Independent brokers or IB's, okay?" Skip said, "Yeah, I've been mulling that over and I believe about a dozen would do quite nicely."

"Skip, can I have this as my baby?" Matt's tone was imploring. "You know I'm ready."

Skip shook his head negative. "No, Matt. I need you to be available to *all* of my operations. You're the best trainer I've ever had. And another thing, I was thinking this may be a way to pay back Barbara Stanhoff."

Matt brightened like a flower receiving a welcomed watering. "Why thank you, boss. Appreciate it. And yes, I agree about Barbara."

"What would this office have to do with her?" Ralph said, thinking, she doesn't even work for us. Is there something here he is not telling me?

"Well for one thing she was very instrumental in my first office in Lauderhill. Two, she has a son who she wants to groom to take over her business. He is a little green now. But what better place to break him in than with us?"

Oh, Jeez. "You mean that little dandy boy ..." Matt clicked his fingers, "... what's his name? That guy's a real wanker – to use a Chris term. Seriously, Boss, we can do so much better than that."

Skip cooked up a half smile. "Maybe, maybe not. Anyway, that would be the one and the same."

"Kevin or Cam or something like that, if memory serves me," A.J. said, deep in thought.

Catherine came back and said, "Ready?"

They filed out of the offices and she closed and locked both doors. A few minutes later they were back in front of the elevator. "Everyone in who needs to be in?" A.J. said.

The short ride was in silence. Skip was thinking about how fast he could get this office up and operational. A.J. was still trying to remember the name of Barbara's son. Matt was thinking about bikini clad spring breaker babes. Ralph, as always, stayed alert and present. His job. Ever on guard against any untoward situation that may be developing.

Outside again, A.J. said in a reminiscent tone of voice, "One thing you can say about Key West that beats the shit out of most small towns."

"What?" Matt said, still thinking.

"You got to love a place that has more tittie bars in one block and fewer churches in the whole town than any place outside of Vegas." A.J. was beaming.

"Okay, so you know my weakness," Skip said, resolute.

A.J. put on a mock expression of sincerity. "Which – the tittie bars or the churches?" That cracked everybody up. Ralph and Matt doubled over, holding their sides in pain.

"Speaking of which, Matt said, gasping for air and looking at Skip, "do you think – we may ... get some time off for good behavior?"

"Yes, later you can have some private time. You can do whatever you want, but don't make any plans for dinner. I want us all together again for dinner." He turned to Catherine and said, "That includes you too."

Catherine wondered, Do any of these handsome men have a life of their own – or is it always all about Skip.

Skip and A.J. walked off together. A.J. said, "Skip, I've got to hand it to you."

"Why, A.J.?"

"You got some hold over women. You seem to have them all right where you want them from the get go."

"It takes years of practice, A.J." Skip said with an easy smile. Thinking back, he said, "You know where I came from."

A.J. shook his head in the affirmative, but said nothing.

"It's amazing that I got out of all of that alive and in no in worse shape than I am."

"Especially that hairy bit about your mom," A.J. said. He bit his lip in regret as soon as he'd said it. He hadn't meant to bring Skip back to the darkest time in his life.

Skip recalled vividly the day he killed his mother. She had come home … if you could call an abandoned building a home … only to pass out again. That sock in the stairwell was my only salvation. I snuffed out her pathetic life and have never looked back for even a moment. She was just a drug addict whore. Nothing more. Cops even ruled it a suicide. Accidental, of course, but a suicide all the same. Good riddance, bitch.

"I'm sure it was difficult growing up more or less alone, but look at you now." A.J. jutted his chin out in a salute to Skip's accomplished life.

"I've got to admit," Skip said after a sigh, "it is pretty amazing. I never even knew my dad. Hell – my mom probably never even knew my dad. To her he was just another john. Another way to pay for her addiction and keep her highs rolling."

"Just a bad scene all together, Skip. Look forward now."

"Nothing got between her and her drugs. Do you know she never once came to anything regarding my schooling or anything else for that matter? It was like I didn't exist. I was just …" Skip faltered, his voice quaking with the emotion of a lost, starved-for-love child, "… something that happened to her along the way. Nothing more."

A.J. was stunned at Skips' sudden candid display of deep feelings. He needed to change topics. He put a hand on Skip's shoulder and said, "That was a lifetime ago, Skip. You've really done well for yourself. Even your no-good mother would be proud."

Skip put his hand on A.J.'s. "Thanks, man. It's good to know you've always got my back."

"And the women have your front," A.J. said with a grab of his groin and a laugh.

Skip half smiled. He thought back to a comment Evie had made. "You know, A.J., Evie said something that hit me strange the other day. She said that I have no respect for women. Do you think that's true?"

Hell yes, it's true, A.J. thought, but he was not about to say so to Skip. So he said, "Skip you can be hard on your women. You know, demanding and all, but you have a good heart."

"I thought so too, and told Evie as much."

"She digs you, boss."

"I know A.J., but I don't think I could ever see her as my wife."

"Why not?"

"Well, she's a titty dancer and all. She's a long cry from Frederika. Even if Frederika is an ungodly bitch."

"You shouldn't compare the two. There's nothing at all similar in them, Skip." Except both are hot.

"I know, but it's hard not to."

"Remember the Madoff interview?"

Skip thought back. "Yes, I sure do. That was a long time ago now, but *what a man* he is."

"Why didn't you get that job?"

"Not blue enough for his blood. You know those Jews stick together."

"He's all the rage now. Imagine being where he is?"

"We are going to get there A.J. I promise you that. I will have everything that Madoff has and more." Skip raised a forefinger in prophetic determination.

Ray radioed back to Neal in the van. He said, "Did you catch all of that?"

"Yes, we sure did." He looked down at his notes to be sure he relayed the next duties correctly and said, "Can you see if we can get the bugs into the new office suites? Just fill in Bud Brewer. I'm sure he'll be game."

"That old bird is a hard one to read, but I'll see what he has to say and get back to you. Can you take it from here?"

"Will do. Any problems, get back to me aysap."

"Roger that." Ray sped off back to Truman Annex.

Neal manned the van listening devices, which could detect voices and other sounds from distances as far away as three hundred feet. The van was set up to look like a telephone repair truck working on lines near the sewers, conveniently across the street from the Rooftop Café. Neal worked surveillance equipment while Arlen and Trent acted as telephone crew. They gave a believable performance.

***

At the steps for the Rooftop there was a huge signboard displaying the menu for the day. Catherine stopped long enough to point that out to A.J. and anyone else who cared to have a look before heading up the winding staircase. "Here's a sampling of what the Rooftop is known for. I hope there's something there all of you will enjoy. She turned to A.J. "Especially you, A.J"

A.J. read the menu slowly and carefully, noting every ingredient and the preparation of each dish as if it were the financial section of the New York Times. "Impressive," he said, "of course I intend to test at least a couple before rendering my judgment. I tell you what. If they make these dishes as well as they write them up on this menu …" he stuck a thumb up, "… this place gets five stars from me."

At the top of the stairs they were greeted by a sweet young guy who was clearly gay. He swished over and flashed a wide smile at all of the handsome men. He wiped his damp hands on his clean white apron and said, "Hello. Welcome to the Rooftop. Is this your first time visiting with us?"

Catherine took the lead and said, "I'm a local, but it's their first time. Can you find us a table that'll allow us some privacy for discussing business?" Why does he look nervous? Gawd, this guy is a flaming faggot – I can tell by his body language he's uncomfortable talking with or even being near a woman.

The waiter pursed his lips, fidgeting with his puca shell necklace, and shifted his weight from one foot to the other. He turned to A.J. and said, "Why yes. Please follow me." He picked up several menus from the hostess stand and led the group with swiveling hips toward a large table underneath a Banyan Tree, well removed from the nearest other table. The view below was fabulous. When they had arrived he put one hand on his hip and pointed out the panorama with a wave of his other hand. He said, "Hence the name, 'The Rooftop Café.'" He spread the menus out in front of each seat and with a wink and a smile and said, "I'll be right back with some water, fellas." He pivoted and sallied off.

Matt leaned forward with a chuckle and said, "Hey do you think per chance he's gay?"

Catherine fluttered her eyelashes, brought her hand to her breasts and feigned surprise. "No. Ya think?"

A.J. looked at Matt with a raised eyebrow. "Do you have a problem with your manhood or are you just trying to tell us something?"

Ralph said, "No. He's just a homophobe."

Skip waved a hand in the air and said, "Okay, enough. Can we get off that and move on to more pressing things?"

Everyone spent a considerable time reading the lengthy menu before ordering a round of drinks. Catherine and her new male associates ordered alcoholic beverages. Skip ordered a Sprite.

"How long has it been since you've had a drink, Skip?" Catherine said.

Skip thought back to when he had stopped drinking. It was the day he killed his mother. He no longer needed drinking to numb his emotions to her cold and indifferent behavior due to her repulsive addictions. He shook his head to clear the thoughts, heaved a sigh and said, "A lifetime ago." Something dark from deep inside flashed its way onto his sunny facade. He quickly covered it and moved on.

A.J. said, "I met Skip just after his mother died and it was at that moment he gave up drinking for good." He glanced at Skip to ensure he had not given away too much.

Skip smiled and said, "I used to do a lot of things. I drank. I sold and used drugs. I did whatever I could to survive." Plenty else I could tell, he thought, but no – not now, not here. "And then I met Father Zeke and he introduced me to God."

"Yea, Zeke is a good man," A.J. said, thinking, if she only knew, but I'll never tell.

"So your faith helped to get you through a tough patch?" Catherine said.

"Absolutely," Skip said with conviction. "Are you a believer, Catherine?"

Catherine was fascinated by his candor. Strange business question, but what the hey. "Why, yes I am. My entire family is devout Roman Catholic."

"Father Zeke is going to like you," Skip said without hesitation. He held a straight face, not caring to reveal his thoughts. Best not to tell her that Father Zeke was defrocked from his priesthood because he had numerous affairs with his flock. Or his less than moral dealings helping me with my scams. "His brand of Christianity is unconventional, to say the least." Skip did not elaborate. Also no need to mention I met Father Zeke while in prison. Some things need be kept quiet. At least for now.

"Is it ever. Skip bought Father Zeke his own church," A.J. said in a tone meant to impress.

Catherine's eyes lit up. "Really?" She looked at Skip for confirmation.

"Well, yes I did. He hadn't had a church of his own for quite some time. He was helping those less fortunate instead of heading up his own congregation, but I knew he was itching to have his own church again, so I found this sweet little place and bought it – just for him."

"That's wonderful, "Catherine said, gushing. She noticed that faraway look in Skip's eyes again. What's he really thinking?

My way of paying penance for killing my mother, Skip mused in a momentary state of melancholy. But Father Zeke knows that. And the added bonus is the religious cover … it has been instrumental in bringing new clients. Win, win, win. A smile returned to Skip's face.

Matt said, "You know, Father Zeke always blesses our businesses. Sort of gives us an edge with God---you know what I mean?" He smiled at Catherine, then looked at Skip. "Skip, do you have any plans for him to come down to Key West and do it this time?"

"Of course – you know that. Before we actually move in I want Father Zeke to bless the operation and the building. His blessings have never failed me. He's always helped us to be profitable, humble, and plentiful."

Catherine thought, whatever. And the humble part? Please.

The swishy waiter returned with a tray full of appetizers and placed them in the center of the table. He said, "Will there be anything else I can get you?" Nobody replied so he said, "Your lunches should be ready soon," pivoted and disappeared.

A.J. said to Matt with a playful punch to the ribs, "I think he likes you. See the way he winked at you?"

Matt reddened. "Like hell he did. I am one hundred percent man. I only copulate with women."

"Copulate, eh? That's mighty big word for you, son," A.J. said with a smile.

Skip cleared his throat and tapped his glass with his fork, "Gentlemen, can we please get back to business?"

Everyone sat quiet as meditating monks.

"I'd like to explain how I see this new operation starting up. We know we want Catherine to come on board. That means she'll need to study for and pass the series three exam. Matt, that's your job----you help her study." He winked at Matt. "Make sure she passes on the first time. A.J., I need you and Matt to collaborate on ads. Newspapers, radio, online, everything. I want to line up at least three days of interviews and hire a dozen qualified people if we can find them here. Any questions?"

Matt, between forks full of food, asked, "How soon do you want to begin."

"I want this to begin aysap."

"Like in what timetable?" Matt said.

"I want Catherine to review the lease and then she and I will look at it together. We have a general idea from what we've seen of it today, but it's thirty pages long and I don't want anything to come up that we aren't prepared to deal with – if you follow my logic here." He took a sip of his Sprite and dabbed a pot sticker into the sweet and sour sauce. "If we can conclude this while we're here this weekend all the better. If not, then as soon as we can."

Catherine thought things were moving faster than she was prepared for, but kept it to herself. The lease was no problem, but until today she had never thought about changing her occupation and working for Skip. She was not a girl in her twenties ready and willing to try new things. At thirty seven she was fairly settled into her lifestyle. Making such a bold change filled her with apprehension. She squirmed a bit internally, but listened as Skip went on.

"Matt, I know you don't have the documents to move forward with the tutoring at this time, so however things conclude this weekend, you will return to Ft. Lauderdale with me and then come back here – I'm thinking mid-week. Be prepared to stay until she's ready for the test."

Matt gave a quick nod. "Roger that."

"A.J., I want you to be here with Matt and Catherine. You can relieve Matt when he needs a break. Ralph, I want you to begin preparation on the new office. I mean arranging for the t-100 lines, the FOREX/GLOBEX satellite information and links, the furniture that we will take from the warehouse in Sunrise and have delivered here, etc." A.J. and Ralph both nodded acceptance and approval of the plan.

Lunch arrived and another round of drinks was ordered. A.J. had the house specialty, hand rubbed tenderloin of pork with mango pepper sauce, mashed potatoes with garlic, and green beans almandine. Skip had a cob salad with balsamic vinaigrette and foccacia bread. Catherine had the curried chicken salad on a twisted buttered egg roll. Ralph had the asparagus soup served chilled, shrimp cocktail, and thinly sliced beef on rye with creamy horseradish sauce. Matt had a burger with onion rings.

Catherine took her time, eating like a lady, observing the men who ate and sounded like, well … men. Grunts, burps, and smacking sounds replaced conversation for several minutes.

A.J., finishing his last bite of tenderloin, wiped his mouth with his linen napkin and said, "That was *exquisite*. Thanks for suggesting this place, Catherine."

Catherine giggled at his silly and charming mannerisms. "I'm glad you liked it. It's a regular haunt of mine."

The waiter came back, appearing flustered. A busboy had run into him with a tray of dirty dishes and some sauces soiled his pristine white apron. Skip and his crew had heard the crash, but made nothing of it. The waiter was beside himself, chagrined and red faced.

"How was everything," He asked, struggling for control.

A.J. kissed his fingertips and popped his hand wide open with a flourish. "Magnifico."

"Will there be anything else?" There was nothing gay about the poor fellow right now.

A.J. looked around at everyone. "Desert? Shall we indulge?" All indicated yes, so he turned to the distraught young man and said, "Matter of fact, yes – we would like one of each of your deserts and five new forks."

The waiter wrung his damp hands in silence on the only clean spot left on his dirty apron, and went about his duty.

"After lunch I'm giving you guys some free time. I'd like some one on one time with Catherine before we reconvene for dinner."

Catherine had not planned on her whole day encompassing only Skip. She had things that still needed tending to at the office. She stirred in her seat as she thought what to say, if anything. Speak up, Catherine, you know you have to say something. She touched Skip's arm and said,

"I have some things that need my attention at my office. How long do you think this will take?" She caught a certain look as it flashed across his face. Perturbed. He *so* does not like not having his way.

He said, "An hour at most and then you can be on your way. Do join us for dinner though, okay?" He looked into her eyes.

Catherine flinched. God, it's as if he can see into my soul. She said, "Yea, sure."

Desert came, delivered by another flaming waiter in a fresh white apron. When they had consumed the delectable delights, Skip paid the tab in cash and left the waiter a hefty tip. Outside, Matt said with a devilish smile, "I know where I'm going. Anyone game to join me?"

A.J. said, "I was thinking nap after all that good food, but mm – maybe a little action would be good for the digestion. I'm in."

Ralph had his hand in the air. "Always in. Where to?"

Matt said, "That topless joint we saw – ahm, the 'Upstairs Bar' I think it was called? Am I right, Catherine? Back over there in the three hundred block of Duval?"

Catherine looked impressed. "My, my … such observation and memory." She winked at him. "And yes, that's the name and yes on Duval."

Matt chuckled and pointed at his head. "Don't miss a thing, darling – especially not hot, classy looking tittie bars." He turned to the guys and motioned away with both arms. "Okay, shall we?"

Skip linked arms with Catherine and said, "We could talk more privately in my room."

Oh my god, his room and I've no mints. Why didn't I think ahead? "Okay."

They meandered toward the Ocean Key House. They passed sun burnt tourists of every ethnic origin possible all dressed in shabby tourist attire. Skip said, "I hope you know there is nothing you can't tell me."

"I feel like I already know you so well," Catherine said, even though she knew instinctively there was much to know about this man that she had no clue about. But courtesy and appearances are everything. "All of your guys are so nice."

"Yes, they are a dedicated bunch."

"Here we are." At the lobby, Skip held the large and ornate wooden door open for Catherine. He followed her in, walked to the front desk and said, "Any messages for Mr. Horowitz?"

The haggard older woman behind the desk turned around in her rolling chair to check the cubbies for messages and said, "Yes, sir. Just this one." She handed it to Skip.

Skip read it and winced. It's from Evie. I didn't tell her I was coming to town. Intuition – she just knows. I even told the guys not to go to the

Pirate's Den on the off chance they might run into her and complicate things. Great. Just great. He stuffed it into his pants pocket, turned to Catherine and said, "I'm on the second floor."

They went to the elevator and Skip depressed the up button. Silently they both walked in when doors slid open. Inside, Skip reached for Catherine's hand and held it as they rode up one floor. She liked the smooth feel of his soft touch. She thought perhaps she had been too restrictive in her reservations about him. The elevator stopped and Skip acted the perfect gentleman as he led her to his room. "Twenty two oh one," he said, stopping in front of the door. "Here we are." He slipped his card key into the lock and waited for the green light to blink. Opening the door, he stepped aside and motioned her in. "After you."

Catherine entered the living room area, furnished with a sofa, loveseat, and overstuffed chair. Two wooden side tables and a marble topped coffee table completed the ensemble. The carpet is so soft, she thought in appreciation. Soft diffused light filtered into the room through sheer curtains flanking sliding doors that led to a balcony overlooking the bay.

Skip walked to the mini refrigerator and opened it. He took out two Perrier's, filled two tumblers and offered one to Catherine. She said, "Thank you."

Skip took a sip and said, "You're most welcome." He made a sweeping gesture toward the furniture. "Please ... have a seat."

Catherine surveyed the room and chose to sit on the loveseat. Skip came over and sat beside her. He took both of their glasses and placed them on the coffee table, then turned back to kiss her fully on the lips. Her heart felt like it was jumping out of her chest, but his kiss was gentle and so sweet. Skip let his left hand wander toward Catherine's open necked blouse where he toyed with her breasts with his finger tips. Her breath caught in her throat and she knew she wanted him. They were soon naked, consuming each in the throes of wild sexual passion. Forty-five minutes of ecstasy they shared, during which Skip's expert manipulation of her body brought her two colossal climaxes.

When they had both been adequately satisfied, Skip went into the living room and returned with the Perrier. They sat up in his bed and finished them, all smiles and freshly sexed. Catherine felt like rivers of pent up frustration had given way to an orgasmic flood. Her hair was damp and her skin was flushed. Skip looked at her, brushed back a lock of her hair, leaned over and placed a light kiss on her forehead. With that smile that could melt the North Pole he said, "Guess we both wanted this, huh?"

She lowered her eyes, then raised her gaze back to his face. "I can't say I didn't want it ... I mean you, of course. In a sexual way, that is.

Even from the first time we met and made out. And I know that was a long time ago." She let out a long sigh and relaxed back against her pillow. "This was just great, Skip. I feel invigorated and refreshed." She was already dreaming of their next sexual encounter. I know I've got him now, long term. The way we made love – he was so sensitive and sincere, there's definitely a bond now between us.

"Me too," Skip said, looking away. His eyes would have betrayed his real thoughts. No way I'm interested in any lengthy relationship with Catherine. She's too old by at least ten years, and I don't go for redheads. But I made her squeal. Twice. Now I got her right where I want her. A sudden thought made him say, "You do use birth control right?"

"Of course, silly." She stretched and yawned, then noticed the time on the wall clock. "Oop – I better get going. Got things to do before dinner, remember?" She smiled to herself. Wait until I tell Connie what just happened.

"Do you want to take a shower?"

She thought about that, but decided she for once was going to pull a Connie---not clean off the fresh love scent. She said, "I'll do that later, but thank you." She got up and began gathering her clothing. A line was etched on the carpet of strewn garments stretching from the living area to the bedroom. After dressing she walked back to the bed and kissed Skip long and deep on the lips. "What time is dinner," she asked.

"Is six okay for you?" Skip said without looking at her. He was more focused on tuning the TV to the sports network. Got to find out who won the playoff game between the Nicks and the Celtics. Then it's take a shower and plenty of time for a quickie with Evie. One thing at a time. Ah, life is good.

Catherine gathered up her handbag and said, "See you then."

CHAPTER ELEVEN

Catherine went to the ice cream shop. She had to park half a block down and walk, but she was floating in the clouds all the way. She pushed the glass door open and peered inside. Nobody was at the counter and all of the small booths were empty. She called out, "Yoo-hoo, Connie, are you here?"

Connie popped out like a jack-in-the-box. She said, "Oh, it's you."

"Well don't sound so excited." Catherine rolled her eyes, then said in a gossipy tone, "I've got some great news for you."

"Let me make us both a single dip of my newest flavor first. Rum Raisin. It's the best. Take a seat. I'll be right over." Connie went about locating two spiral cones and dished out two heaping scoops. She walked over, handed one to Catherine and began to lick the other herself.

"I've just come from Skip's," Catherine said. She had a quick lick. "Um, this is good."

Connie zeroed in on Catherine's eyes. "What's that dreamy look, Catherine. Did you just have sex?"

"Yes, and it was heavenly."

"How big was he?"

"Connie, honestly." She took another lick. ""He was a respectable size."

Connie held her hands several inches apart.

"More."

"Really? Totally yummy. How about – you know, the girth?"

"About like this cone," Catherine said as she took another lick. Licking the cone reminded her of licking Skip. She smiled with a smug, private satisfaction.

"Wow, cool." Connie's eyes glazed over as she imagined the ride for herself. She leaned forward and raised her eyebrows. "What about foreplay?"

"Just enough to get my pussy purring."

"Is he a good kisser?"

Catherine huffed. "Okay so what is this – I'm a suspect in the interrogation room?"

Connie snickered as her cell phone rang. She answered it and said, "Ray, what a surprise." She listened for a bit and then said to Catherine, "Ray's got tickets to see the Heat. I've got a half hour to close up and get ready for him to pick me up. Do you mind?"

"No, go have fun. I've got things to do anyway."

Catherine left and Connie went about closing up.

Skip took the time between his sexual encounter with Catherine and the six o'clock dinner appointment to take a hot shower and then speak candidly to his troops. He used the house phones and called each one with the instructions. "Meet me in my suite in fifteen."

He went to his closet where the housekeeping staff had unpacked his belongings and selected an outfit to wear to dinner: a pair of navy slacks, a white linen shirt, and his tassel loafers with matching belt. His next call was to maid service. "Could you please send someone to change my sheets after six p.m.?"

"Why of course, Mr. Horowitz. Will there by anything else?"

"Not at this time. Thank you."

Catherine walked across the street and was surprised to see Shamus and Don were actually in the office. She had been expecting to be alone. She opened the door and the sleigh bells rang. She said, "Wow. I was soooo not expecting you two to be here."

Shamus had the PGA tournament at Pebble Beach tuned on his extra large desktop computer screen. Both Shamus and Don were dressed in casual attire and enthralled in the match. Neither said anything to Catherine's comment until she was nearly even with the desk. Don sniffed the air like a dog after a snack and said, "Do I smell sex?"

"I think you do," Shamus said, "And I smell it too."

"Catherine what have you been doing at this hour of the day?" Don said as a mother might to a child.

Catherine was sweating in spite of the air conditioning. Her face flushed. "I don't think that's any of your business, misters." She proceeded on to the restroom and stepped inside. It was not cool in there so she left the door slightly ajar. She was surprised at how red her face was when she caught a glimpse of herself in the mirror. She slipped out of her top and stood in her bra, bathing with a washcloth in the sink. She always kept fresh clothes in the office in the event she did not have the time to go home and change. She undressed, washed up, put on fresh deodorant and perfume, and redressed. She picked her auburn tresses up and twisted them into a bun, clipping it down with a sparkling clasp. Then she went about redoing her make-up.

Don and Shamus continued to watch the PGA match, talking golf and sports, only occasionally looking back to see what Catherine was doing.

Shamus said, "I can't believe this guy. He's an incredible talent."

"And he even took time off for his wedding. Boy wouldn't I like to have his twins waiting for me after each match."

"They are hot." Just then Tiger made a fifty foot putt for a birdie. "Look at that, would you."

"Typical Tiger. Lies back until the final day and then pours on the steam, rolling right over anyone and everyone in his way."

Shamus nodded and shrugged. "Well Don, when you're the number one golfer in the world and you want to maintain that status, making the tens of millions he does each and every year, you have to make every shot count. 'Specially right now." He took a sip of Watney's. "He's only one stroke ahead of Mickelson going down the stretch."

Catherine emerged from the bathroom looking, smelling, and feeling better.

Don couldn't help saying, "Well, was it?"

"What are you talking about, Don?" Catherine said, somewhat surly.

"That smell ... was it sex?"

Catherine put her hands on her hips. "What does it matter to you?"

"Just curious, that's all."

Shamus smirked.

"Can't you be curious someplace else?" She glowered at both Don and Shamus, her green eyes flashing red. "End of subject."

"Don't let a quick fling with a sleezeball cloud your judgment," Shamus said, deadpan.

"Nothing is clouding my judgment. And Skip is not a sleezeball. As a matter of fact, my judgment has never been clearer."

Shamus flipped a hand sideways. "Whatever."

Catherine stormed past them and out of the office. She needed to go to CVS and pick up her next month's supply of birth control pills before the dinner engagement. CVS never filled any order in a timely fashion so she was prepared to wait the half hour it would probably take. By then it would be five forty-five. Good timing.

When the three lieutenants had arrived, Skip said, "I want you all to know I have sealed the deal with Catherine." His eyes sparkled like diamonds on a gaudy bracelet.

"I assume that means you bedded her," A.J. said without emotion, knowing full well the answer.

"Yes, and for an elderly woman she was not half bad." Skip walked over to the mini-bar, took out a Perrier and twisted off the lid. He took a long pull before saying, "Feel free, any of you, to tap that next." He took another swig. "As a matter of fact, the more the merrier."

"You know what they say – keep 'em dazed and confused." Matt smiled.

Ralph was not smiling. "I hate to be the bearer of bad news, but I've got it on pretty good word that the Fed's are taking another look into our operations."

Nobody was surprised to hear that, but it was an annoyance all the same.

Skip hunched a shoulder. "No big deal. We'll deal with it. We've had them hot and heavy on our tails before and always come up clean. But it does mean we shred anything and everything that could even remotely be incriminating. Pass that on. Why don't you all take a seat? Get comfortable. We've got a good half hour before Catherine arrives and a lot of ground to cover."

Skip settled into the chair and propped his feet up on the ottoman. A.J. and Ralph sat on the sofa and Matt sat on the loveseat. When everyone was settled Skip began again. "I was hoping that an office in Key West would not show up on the Fed's radar. Especially not this soon. It's unfortunate they have no better way to spend their time than dogging and pursuing me."

"For the most part this office is going to be legit, right Skip?"

"Well, depends."

"Skip," Matt's said. His voice was even and forceful, calculating, "Will we----or will we not be trading?"

"From time to time. Same as we do in the other offices."

"Then why bother with licensure?" Ralph said, even though he knew the answer.

"If I were to open another operation in this state and not license the brokers, the Fed's would smell something fishy a mile away. They'd be onto us faster than a bloodhound. So. Even if we don't trade I want this entire staff licensed. Understood?"

None of the men dissented.

"Do you think the timetable is optimistic?" Skip said.

A.J. said, "Yea, why the rush?"

"No it's not optimistic. It is realistic, and because I said so – that's why." He thought, and I do so love always having the last say and upper hand. "Do each of you know what is expected of you?"

They all shook their heads 'yes'.

"I plan to pay each of you huge bonuses for pulling this together in record time." He put on a genuine smile for the first time since they had started their meeting. "Matt, I'll give you ten extra thousand for every person who you train and who passes the series three. I'll give you twenty five k for Catherine alone." He let that sink in and then proceeded. "A.J., I need you to assist Matt any way he can use you. The same bonuses he gets you'll get, too. Ralph ..." Skip paused and then said, "... I need you to keep your eyes open and your ears to the pavement. I want to know if you get even a whiff that the Fed's are close to zeroing in on any kind of hard evidence. Can I count on you?"

Ralph was stone faced. "Yes, sir." His eyes met Skip's and held for several intense seconds.

Skip eyed his Rolex. "Time's up. Let's meet Catherine downstairs."

They followed Skip out of his suite and used the stairs instead of the elevator. Skip's orders – he expected his team to stay in shape and not be lazy. At four minutes before six they sat in the lobby waiting for Catherine. At two minutes to, she entered.

CHAPTER TWELVE

"What are you up for tonight?" Catherine said to nobody in particular as she approached the men.

Skip said, "I will defer to A.J. in all things food."

A.J. brightened and sat up straight. "Well, in that case, I would like to have some gourmet Italian. Is there such an animal in Key West?"

"Per chance there is. Let's go to La Trattoria De Venetia. It's real authentic Italian and the owner doubles as the head chef. His name is Carmelo."

"How best to get there?" Ralph said.

"I'd say a cab at this hour. Even though it's winter it has been a warm one compared to some. The night air is sticky. LaTrat, as we locals call it, is down in the eight hundred block of Duval and that's a fair hike from here."

"As you wish," Matt said with a smile.

Skip walked over to the concierge desk. A fiftyish man was seated at the wooden and rattan desk, shifting through a series of papers. Skip said, "Hello, would you mind ordering us a cab?"

The man smiled politely and said, "With pleasure, sir. What is your destination?"

Skip looked back at Catherine and asked, "Was that place called La Trattoria or something like that?"

She put a thumb up. "You got it."

The concierge placed the call and then said, "Yellow will be here in about five minutes."

The cab arrived there in less than ten, which surprised Catherine, considering it was a Saturday evening. "You headed to La Trot?" The cabbie said, idled beside them.

"Yes, we are," Skip said.

Everyone piled in. The driver was a man who said he worked as a librarian by day and cab driver by night. That mixture seemed strange, but nobody commented.

A.J. said, "Skip, what was the name of that girl you dated from Smith Barney?" He was looking for a reaction from Catherine.

"I've not thought about that for quite some time, A.J. Why do you ask now?"

"I was just trying to recall which Ivy League school she went to and why the two of you split?"

"Family," Skip said in a soft reflective voice, and then added, "I think Lori went to Yale."

"Yea, Lori. That's her name."

Catherine felt a slight twinge of jealousy.

Skip thought, if it weren't for her old man I might have been Madoff now. Damn shame that was.

The driver drove them up Duval and dropped them at the restaurant's front entrance. The fare was eight dollars and twenty cents. Skip gave the man a twenty, told him to keep the change, and they all exited onto the sidewalk.

"The smell is heavenly," said A.J. with a smile and a waft of his hand.

"I didn't make a reservation so we may have to wait," Catherine said, a bit pensive. They walked inside.

A raven-haired exotic Italian woman with almond shaped eyes, dressed in a lacy gown that accentuated her svelte figure and ample bosom, greeted them. She opened her enticing, pouty, red colored lips and said, "Welcome to La Trattoria De Venetia. How many in your party?"

Enthralled, and thinking she could double for Sophia Loren, Skip said, "Five."

The woman noticed Catherine. Her brown eyes lit up and her smile widened. "Catherine? So good to see you again."

"Can't keep me away for long. My friends here wanted to go to a first class Italian restaurant and you know I just had to suggest this place." She turned to the guys. "Fellas, this is Antoinette. Remember I told you Camelo owns this restaurant and is also the head chef? Well this is his lovely wife."

"Lucky Camelo," said Matt with a full up and down eying of Antoinette. The guys all laughed. Antoinette blushed, but took it in stride. Comes with the territory when you're gorgeous, she knew.

Antoinette looked at the seating chart and said, "I can seat you in just a few minutes." She motioned toward the bar. "If you would like to have a drink while you wait, the bar is just over there."

Skip was enchanted with Antoinette. Catherine noticed. She could feel him mentally undressing her and imagining her naked in his bed. She felt her second twinge of jealousy this evening over him. I can't compete with a woman of Antoinette's style and passion. Antoinette could melt the Arctic Circle with her lyrical voice, sultry eyes, and winning personality. Bitch. Catherine suddenly felt frumpish and uninteresting.

The enchanting Antoinette came back and took them to a commodious five-seat table nestled away in a nook by the front windows. Starched white linen covered the table and matching napkins dotted where each person should light. She said, "I hope this is all right." Then she gave a smile that could have brought peace to the Middle East.

A.J. decided to test his limited Italian and said, "Gratzi, bella signora."

He grinned as apparently he'd got it right, because Antoinette raised her eyebrows in appreciation, graced him with another smile, curtseyed and said, "Sei il benvenuto, e come un uomo gentile." To everyone she said, "Your waiter will be with you shortly." She turned and walked away. The view of her from behind was every healthy man's dream. Skip leaned over and whispered something into A.J.'s ear. They both chuckled. Catherine fumed. But then she checked herself. Just being men, don't get all bent out of shape, Catherine. She sat up straight, smiled, and did her best to feel pretty.

Dinner was wonderful and everyone enjoyed it immensely, especially A.J., who now patted his full tummy with a proud satisfaction. "That was some meal. Spectacular." He wiped the edges of his mouth with his napkin. "Thank you, Catherine."

"You're welcome, A.J. ... I'm pleased that you liked it." She drank the last sip of her wine and said, "They have a fine reputation and now you can see why."

Skip wanted to get back to business and then catch up with Evie who was sure to be furious that he had not seen her up until now. "I hope you understand more now, Catherine, and I know you'll make a fine broker under the expert tutelage of Matt. He's the best. I'm going to be busy tonight and through half the day tomorrow before catching my flight out. I think it'd be wise if you spent some time with Matt and A.J., learning some of the preliminary terms you'll be expected to master for this business and the exam."

Ralph, Matt, and A.J. knew what Skip was going to be busy with, or better, *whom* he would be busy with, but Catherine was mystified. She said, "When are you leaving?" She hoped her tone of voice did not divulge her feelings.

Skip looked at her with no emotion. "Tomorrow afternoon. We've pretty much ironed out things here, and we can discuss the lease on the telephone. If we need to send funds I can have Rick FedEx them to you directly."

Catherine was struggling to contain herself. A one-night stand. That's all our lovemaking was to him. That's all I mean to him. God what an idiot, what a fool I am. Sure he never said or promised anything more, but I felt for certain ...

She rose from the table and said, "Gentlemen, please excuse me? I need to go to the Ladies." She spun round and walked off in a hurry before her feelings of betrayal got the best of her.

Skip paid the tab and said to his team, "Okay, I'm catching a cab down to the Pirate's Den to hook up with Evie." He started to leave.

A.J. said, "Hang on, Skip. How about we share a cab, drop me off at the hotel. I'm going back to my room and read until I get sleepy, which won't be long after that delicious dinner." Skip agreed and they walked out together.

Matt said to Ralph, "Hey how about we invite Catherine out for another drink. Wasn't hard to tell how she took Skip's obvious jilting of her. A few stiff ones and she'll feel better."

Ralph got a sly grin and wagged his finger at Matt. "You. I know which stiff one you're thinking will make her feel better." He grabbed his crotch. "It's a capital idea, buddy, but one hundred samolas says I get her between the sheets before you do."

"Bet," Matt said, and they both laughed. Matt spied Catherine returning and said, "Shh – here she comes. Let the competition begin."

Catherine put up some resistance to their invitation, but they were so charming in their pleading, and, she eventually decided maybe going out for some fun would take her mind off Skip. They ended up at Margaritaville, Jimmy Buffett's place. Three spots opened up at the bar just as they arrived. They hurried over and sat on the stools before anybody else could.

It was only nine thirty and the late night band was setting up on the forward stage. The signboard said they were 'The Tumblers' and that they played rock-a-billy.

Matt read the sign and said, "So, Catherine – what the heck is rock-a-billy?"

She smiled and said, "Bluegrass. You know bluegrass?"

"Ah – yeah, okay."

"Yup, same thing, basically." She looked around. "Looks like most of the diners have given way to the drinking crowd."

"Speaking of which," Matt said, turning to the bartender and motioning for service, "Three rounds of your finest tequila, please."

"Tequila?" Catherine screwed up her face.

"Don't tell me you don't drink tequila?"

The bartender placed three tumblers with Souza Anejo premium silver label tequila in front of them along with a saltshaker and three slivers of lime. Matt thanked him and said to Ralph and Catherine, "You guys know the drill, right?"

They each took a squeeze of lime and bit into it, then shook a dash of salt on their hands before saying bottoms up and using their other hands to lift and down the shots in one gulp.

"That was smooth," said Ralph as he licked the last of the salt from the crook of his hand.

Matt caught the attention of the bartender and said with a twirling finger in the air, "Another round, please."

The Tumblers began to plug their guitars into the amplifiers and tune them. A loud screech came over the speakers, causing Catherine and several others to grab their ears and the soundman to scramble at the mixer.

"Check out that beefy bouncer over there at the door checking ID's," Ralph said.

Matt chuckled and said, "Me, I'd rather check out that perky young thing waitress beside him. Shit, she doesn't look old enough to drink, let alone serve."

The next round arrived.

Catherine was already feeling emboldened with the booze as she said with a hearty flourish, "Bottoms up!" She salted her hand and licked it off before shooting the shot. "Bartender can we have another?"

The bartender looked between Catherine and the guys. Nobody voiced opposition. He shrugged, refilled their shots and placed them down in front of them. "Here you go. I hope you've got a DD."

Slurring her words, Catherine said, "No worries I'm a local and locals don't get caught drunk driving."

Matt said, "Maybe you've had enough, Cat?"

"Nonsense. I'm Irish and we Irish can hold our liquor just fine. Another round, please." She nearly fell trying to find her barstool. *Who to bed to night? They all look good now.*

"Cat, maybe we better see you home instead?" Ralph said with a sheepish grin.

Matt shrugged. "No es mi problemo."

"Don't you think she's had enough?" Ralph said.

"I say let her be the judge of that."

The bartender arrived with another round. "Here you go. Enjoy." He walked over to the service end of the bar and asked a petite waitresses, "Do you think I should cut them off?"

The waitress stacked her drink order atop her tray and said, "Who?"

"See that redhead over there with those guys?"

"Yea. Them?"

"Well?"

"Ah – shucks not. That's Catherine O'Reilley. I know her and she really can hold her liquor just fine." She walked off.

Catherine dropped her shot glass on the bar top. It didn't break, but made a lot of noise. "Sorry," She said to nobody in particular. "Can we have another?"

Ralph said, "This is the last one. Okay, Cat?"

"Don't be such a spoil sport, Ralph. Let's get good and pissed."

"Pissed?"

Matt interjected, "That is an old English word for drunk or pottied."

"Thanks for the translation."

"Anytime."

The bartender lined up another row of shots.

Catherine was the first to drink hers down, and she gulped it without salt or lime. She licked her lips. "That's so good. Don't you guys just love Tequila?"

"Can we have the tab," Ralph asked the bartender as he passed by.

"I've got to use the girls' room before we go," Catherine said, and staggered off.

"Do you think she's going to be okay?" Ralph said, concerned.

"She's going to be just fine." Matt smiled like the cat that just ate the goldfish.

Catherine was drunk and loving it. She sat on the commode with a sly look of devil-may-care. Damn I feel amorous. Which one?

***

Skip caught up with Evie just prior to her second set on stage. She was cool when he first approached her, but warmed when he said he had a big surprise for her waiting in his room. He had made plans before he left Ft. Lauderdale, instructing Randall to get her an expensive sapphire and diamond tennis bracelet. He knew that would rack up all the pussy points he needed. He settled into a seat near the edge of the stage and watched her dance. The DJ cued up Mick Jagger's, *I'm too sexy.* Evie spun and gyrated. She rolled and slunk. She lifted her thin leg onto the pole and spun more. Skip was getting turned on. The song lasted no longer than three minutes and she collected no less than fifty dollars during that one routine. She then proceeded to weave her way through the crowd and coffered another hundred. She did two lap dances that netted her another hundred and numerous offers for dates, which she declined.

When the DJ cued up the stereo for the next dancer she came to sit beside Skip and nuzzled up to him. Her boss disliked boyfriends or suitors coming in during their sets so she had to be brief. She whispered in Skip's ear that she would see him in about an hour and a half if things went as planned. When the next dancer took to the stage Skip walked out and went back to the Ocean Key House to wait.

CHAPTER THIRTEEN

It wasn't her first time doing two men at a time, but Catherine was embarrassed in the morning when she awoke wedged between two naked and passed out hunky men. She grimaced and smacked herself on the forehead as she remembered the vivid, graphic details of the multiple positions three-way she'd had last night with Matt and Ralph. How many shots did I do? Lost count. One too many, that's for sure.

She gently untangled herself from them and went to bathroom for a hot shower. She closed the door as quiet as she could and turned on the lights. She turned on the water in the shower, letting it run while she had a quick pee. The hot shower felt good and helped to soothe her frustration at her lack of control in drunken situations. I wonder if they thought I was good. Hope so, something at least partially good should come of this.

She got out and dried off, then padded back into the bedroom to look for her scattered clothing. She collected all the pieces she could find, but was unable to locate her bra. She dressed quickly, trying not to waken her slumbering sex partners, then slipped out the door and walked at a brisk pace down the hall toward the elevator bank.

An oriental family had exited their room directly across the hall from Matt's at about the same time Catherine had. They gave her the eye, making her wish she had sunglasses on. None of their business, but still. She arrived at the elevator first and hit the down button.

Before the elevator arrived a beautiful young woman stepped out of the door that Catherine knew to be Skip's. She joined the group waiting at the elevator bank. She was racially mixed, a striking combination of Caucasian and African American, Catherine guessed, dressed in evening attire and sporting a dazzling diamond and sapphire tennis bracelet set in platinum. The stones set off rainbows of color even in the dimly lit corridor.

Now just who in the hell is this pretty young thing coming out of Skip's room at this hour, Catherine wondered, and what is her connection to him? As if you don't know, dummy. She's Skip's, *some things I have to tend to before leaving town.* Jackass. Catherine started feeling frustrated and depressed. Don't let on your feelings. Humph – little miss fine thing looks all fresh and ready to take on the world. The elevator arrived and all stepped in. They rode down in silence.

Skip rang Ralph's room. No answer. He called Matt. A groggy Matt picked up and said, "Hello."

"It's Skip. I need you guys to meet me downstairs for coffee and to check out in a half hour. I've already spoke to A.J.; obviously he was the good one last evening. Do you know where Ralph is?"

Matt looked across the bed and saw Ralph sprawled out half under and half over the sheets. He said, "Yes, I do."

"Good – please tell him the plan." Skip hung up and went about reading the early morning edition of the New York Times.

Matt tossed a pillow at Ralph who flinched when it hit him squarely in the face. "What the ..."

"Get up. Skip wants us to meet him in a half hour downstairs. And he said to be ready to check out, too."

Ralph took the pillow from his face and let it drop to the floor. He looked at Matt through bleary eyes and said, "Did we really do what I think we did?"

"All that and more, my friend," Matt said with a satisfied smile.

Ralph propped himself up on one elbow and rubbed his forehead, yawning. "Did we have a good time?"

"You said you did the whole time. I know I did. She's a wild mustang. Boy, did she give us a ride." Matt got up off the bed and strode into the bathroom to take a leak. He did not bother closing the door or turning on the lights.

Ralph groped for his clothing and rolled off the bed. He dressed partially and then went out the door. "See you downstairs."

CHAPTER FOURTEEN

Skip had taken a copy of the lease back with him to Ft. Lauderdale. He signed it and instructed A.J. to convey the document back to Key West for signature by the Brewer's. Matt and A.J. were packed and waiting in the exterior waiting area adjacent to Skip's office when he walked out and said, "Do you have all of the items necessary to conduct a thorough training for Catherine?"

Matt said, "I do."

"A.J., do you have the lease?"

"I do."

"This is beginning to sound a little like a wedding. Can we use another phrase instead of *I do?*"

A foul memory zipped through Skip's head of what he considered his biggest mistake in life – his marriage to Frederika. He had needed her family money to open his first office at the time, but he had soon grown weary of her and her antics. Just last night the bitch again threatens me with divorce. Says she's going to expose me for the lying, cheating, playboy that I am. Then has the audacity to rant on about how pathetic in bed I am. Dried up old ass cunt, who wants to ride her for very long, anyway? She'll never go ahead with the divorce, but damn – how much better would my life have been without that ball and chain? She pisses me off so bad sometimes I'd like to just kill her. Squish the life out of her the same way I did my tramp, drug-addict mother. To snuff the life from her, to never have to hear her nagging voice---that would be music to my ears. Hold on, Skip. Get a grip. You don't want to go back there – over the edge. That place in the head where insanity becomes rational, the place that's devoid of right and wrong, that dark abyss where you might just …

Matt whistled. "Boss? You okay?"

Skip snapped his head out of his macabre mental state and said, "Yeah. Sorry. Back to business. About Catherine, I'd like to see her ready for the series three no later than next Friday. Do you think that's doable?"

"Depends."

"On what?"

Matt shrugged. "How much she is able to ingest. Whether or not she is a sponge waiting to be filled with knowledge, or a soaked rag unable to absorb any new knowledge."

"Aren't you quite the simile spinner this morning? Well, do your best."

Matt cocked his head and said, "C'mon boss – don't I always?"

"Of course, I know you do," Skip said. He tugged on his cheek. "But look – I want this office open in record time."

A.J. clucked his tongue and said, "Skip. You told us that before. We fully understand your timetable and will do the best we can."

Skip grimaced. How dare you correct me in any way, he thought. Let it go. This time. "Godspeed," He said, shook both their hands and sent them on their way.

***

Catherine had asked Shamus to come in early this morning because she wanted to break the news of her new adventure with Skip to him before the rest of the office staff arrived. He breezed into the office in such a manner it caught Catherine off guard. *He looks and smells great. What gives?*

"Good morning, Catherine. What is it you wanted to talk to me about?"

"I've got some news I want to share with you." She considered how best to select her next words.

"What kind of news?" His expression indicated suspicion, even though he dared to hope she was coming to her senses. *She's changed since she met that Skip guy. I know in my heart of hearts that prick is a dark and dangerous man whom Catherine should avoid.*

Catherine sucked in a deep breath, held it, then sighed and said, "Matt and A.J. – the two men who work closely with Skip Horowitz – they are on their way here now. Shamus, I … I'm going to go to work with them, for them." She bit her lip, took a step back and braced herself.

"You're what?" Shamus was shocked. "We've spent seventeen long years setting this office up and getting things to work out just so, and now you tell me you're leaving? For a huge unknown? He looked down and shook his head with a huff. "I'm sorry Catherine, but this just doesn't make any sense."

"Shamus, please understand. This move has nothing to do with you. I've got to see what else there is out there – you know … spread my wings." She tried to smile. Didn't work, looked forced.

Shamus groaned. "I've never tried to hem you in. You have all of the freedom and none of the real responsibility right here. What more could you possibly want? Why don't you come out and say what the real issue is." He pointed at himself.

"Shamus, really. Don't make this about you and me."

"Well isn't it?"

He stood. Catherine thought he looked more handsome than ever. *Shamus is an honorable man. A hardworking, albeit somewhat* womanizing, man. But Skip has such a pull on me. I can't shake it – even if he isn't really interested in me for a long term love relationship, if I fail to take this golden opportunity I know I'll blame Shamus for the rest of my life. Why, Catherine, why? Figure that out later. I've got to do this. She looked at Shamus, firm and convinced.

"It's bigger than you and me, Shamus. I have to see what else there is out there."

"What has he promised you?" Shamus was starting to boil. "What hold does he have on you?"

"Shamus, get a hold of yourself. This is not a sporting contest between you and Skip. This may be the opportunity of a lifetime. I've got to walk through that door and see for myself. Please just wish me well."

Shamus remembered advice from his father – which he still believed. If you love something, or someone, you do not cage it in. With a sigh of resignation he said, "Fine. Good luck," and sat, facing away from her and toward his computer monitor.

Catherine went about gathering up her personal things. She cleaned out the front desk that she used most. When she was done she called Connie and relayed her good news to her too.

Connie thought back on all the various topics that she and Ray had discussed. Then she said, "You know, Ray knows all about trading commodities. He operated a commodities trading pool for fifteen of his good friends and from what he tells me they did very well. He also said it was risky, but the more risk the higher the potential return. Maybe you should ask him a few questions before jumping in with both feet?"

"If I get stuck maybe I will, but I've made up my mind to give this thing a try, however it ends up. And Skip is sending Matt and A.J. to help me prep for the exam. As a matter of fact, they are due in today."

"I'm not sure Ray has a license. I don't think we ever broached that subject. I've heard some of those exams last as long as eight hours."

"Argh. Eight hours? That can't be right."

"Ask them about that, but I think I'm right."

"Will do. I better get moving. I've got a lot to do before they arrive."

Connie sneezed. "Whew! Excuse me. Well, good luck and don't forget that if you have questions you can always ask Ray."

"Thanks. I appreciate that. We'll be in touch. And bless you."

"Come again?"

"You sneezed." They both laughed.

CHAPTER FIFTEEN

Vinney, from Vegas, called Skip early on Tuesday. He had heard that Bob Rolly was rolling up his offshore gambling operation in Costa Rica and he wanted Skip to jump on it before anyone else got wind of it and shut them out.

Vinney said, "Hey Skip – have I got a windfall deal for you."

"What would that be, Vin?"

Skip was at home dressing when he had taken Vinney's call on his cell phone. He walked over to the full length mirror now and admired his profile and then his full frontal. He pressed his hand along the seam of his starched and pressed linen trousers.

"Remember Bob Rolly? The guy who had the offshore gambling operation in Costa Rica?"

Skip considered for a moment and then said, "Oh yea. What about him?"

"Grant told me this morning he's looking to move his operations to Panama. He's putting the Costa Rica business up for sale."

"And how would Grant know this," Skip said, admiring his smile in the mirror as Vinney continued.

"Well it just so happens he does some charter work for him too. You know he has a big time gambling operation sanctioned by the mob right here in Vegas."

"No I was not aware. Anyway, that doesn't matter. How can I get in contact with this Bob Rolly guy?"

"Does that mean you are interested?"

"Depends ... on what he wants."

"I've got his number right here."

Skip looked around for a pen and pad. "Hold on a sec – let me get ... okay, shoot."

"800-902-8206."

"Okay that was 800-902-8206, right?"

Vinney looked at the small post-it note and said, "Yes, that's right."

Before Vinney could say more, Skip said, "I'll call him now."

The line went dead. Vinney turned to Grant and said, "Looks like he may do it. Of course he said it depends on the cost, but Skip's a shrewd businessman. If he thinks there's money to be made he'll be all over it."

"There is a lot of money to be made, according to Rolly's top dog, Katarina. She's a Russian national and she heads that operation up. Hot broad, too."

"Does she go along with the deal?" Vinney pulled at an earlobe.

Grant pursed his lips and wagged his head. "No idea, but as you know, everyone has a price."

"Why is Bob moving into Panama anyway? Did he have problems in Costa Rica?"

"No, from what Katarina told me, and this is on the fly – Bob got all entangled with another one of those ex-pat Ruskies and she took him for the ride of his life."

"No shit. Go figure."

"Yea. She was hot and young and he's no spring chick, but he's loaded and *made*. Anyway, he married her and they ended up with her name on many of his accounts. Foolish thing in retrospect … I mean what man would let a woman on his accounts----why not just give her one of her own?"

Vinnie nodded. "I guess that would make more sense. Anyway, what?"

Grant smirked and chuckled. "Keep this between us, okay?"

"Sure, what?"

"This is the snow on the mountain top." He whistled between his teeth. "Get this – she closed out one account that had something like two hundred fifty g's in it and skipped town."

Vinnie let out a whoop, flopped into a chair and slapped his knee. "Man – that takes balls. I'd like to meet that gal. She's roguish, but very cool."

Grant grunted an agreement. "Nobody seems to know where she is, but I'm betting when he finds her she's gonna be shark meat."

"No doubt about that, my friend. No fucking doubt." Vinnie's eyes steeled and his face was grim. "You don't fuck with the mob."

***

The 800 number was a direct line to Costa Rica. Skip said, "May I please speak to Mr. Rolly?"

A stilted Russian-English speaking voice on the other end of the phone replied. "May I let Mr. Rolly know what the nature of your call is?"

She sounds guarded, but some of that is a good thing, he thought, then said, "Yes, Skip Horowitz, please. And tell him I've heard from a mutual friend that he has a business to sell."

"One moment, please." She placed Skip on hold and went to fetch Bob Rolly.

Katarina approached Rolly, who was busy setting the line for the next day's bets. "Bob, there is a Skip Horowitz on the line – he's inquiring about a business you are selling." She tucked a pen behind her ear. "I think he's the guy who has the small time operation across town. Do you wanna speak to him or not?"

Bob leaned back. A flicker of fire could be seen in his dark eyes. He ran a hand through his thinning, but not yet graying brown hair, puffed on his Partegas cigar and said, "Yes, I'll talk to him. I think this is the guy Grant was telling me about." He looked up and to the left, recalling, then said, "Yeah – he also has some sort of commodities business or investment something or other in Vegas. Put him through. I'll ask Sid about him when I get done."

Katarina went back to her desk and said, "Just one moment, Mr. Horowitz." She placed him again on hold and transferred the call.

Bob did not rush to take Skip's call. Instead he said, "Katrina, place a call to Sid about this Skip fellow while I speak to him." He then waited a full two minutes before picking up the line. When he did speak, his voice was warm. "Hello, Mr. Horowitz."

Katarina dialed Sid.

"Mr. Rolly, hello. I'm not sure you remember me, but we met in San Jose last fall."

I thought that name sounded familiar, Bob thought. Now I remember from where. "Yes, I do recall that brief meeting." The meeting was so short I don't recall much about him. Hope Sid can clue me in.

"It appears we share the same pilot for our charter service." He let that simmer and then said, "Grant. Anyway, he told my guy in Vegas that you might be looking to sell your Costa Rica operation. Is that correct?"

It never ceases to amaze me, Bob thought, how fast gossip travels, even across entire countries. "Yes, that is true. Why – are you interested?"

"Depends." Skip took a second for game's sake. "Depends on what you want and what all I get for my money."

I like this guy's style, Bob thought with a wry grin. Direct. "Well, I'm not selling my book and I'm not relinquishing my eight hundred numbers. But the space and the people who are not willing to move can be had for, say ..." He hadn't expected an offer so soon. He let Skip wait while he took a long puff on his cigar and considered something that would be fair. "I think three million is about right."

Skip let the old man guess how well he was taking his offer with a short silence, then said, "Seems fair enough. Let me ask you, though – how many employees and how large is your space?"

"Forty three men are staying. I had seventy six in all. The space is all set up for a book making business and it's about four thousand square feet, including the lobby."

"That's a good size. In fact, considering the space and the people, it's very reasonable. How soon do you want to move?"

111

"Obviously as soon as I can." Bob exhaled a wide swath of smoke.

Skip could've jumped up and down. Stay cool, Skip. Business – all business. This man is a player and on top of his game. He knows there'll be no need for written contracts. In fact he, like me, wants no paper trail left behind this kind of transaction. "Works for me. I'll fly down tomorrow to cement the deal. Where should I wire the funds?"

I like this guy more by the minute, Bob thought, repressing a giggle. He said, "Deutsche Bank. I'll have Katarina give you the wiring instructions."

"Great. I'll see you tomorrow and the funds should show up by noon the same day."

"Skip – can I call you Skip?"

"Certainly."

"Great. Pleasure doing business with you, Skip"

"Likewise. Bob. I can call you Bob?"

"Absolutely. Hold on, I'll transfer you back to Katarina." He clicked Skip over and called out, "Katarina – please give the wiring instructions for Deutsche Bank to Mr. Horowitz. We have a deal." He walked over to the mini-bar and opened a cold beer.

After Skip got the instructions from Katarina and called his bank, he got on the phone with Grant and booked a flight. He thought over the new venture.

I'll merge my small operation with Bob's significant leftovers. Right now I've only got five men working in an office barely larger than a phone booth. With the forty-three left that Bob's giving me, that'll be nearly fifty. Skip fist pumped with a grin and said, "Big time here I come."

CHAPTER SIXTEEN

Matt and A.J. arrived in Key West mid-day on Tuesday. Catherine picked them up and delivered them to the Garden's guesthouse on the corner of Simonton and Angela. They hadn't previously stayed there, but Catherine felt it offered a more tranquil setting than the hustle and bustle at the Ocean Key House, and the cost was comparable. She drove into the cobblestone driveway and parked near the front entrance. Signs directed them toward the pool area, massage area, walking path, or the front office.

Catherine said, "I hope you like it here. I've never known anyone who stayed here, but if it's as good as their well done brochure then you should love it."

A polite teenage boy in walking shorts, pressed fishing shirt and sandals, asked, "Do you have a reservation."

"Yes, I believe the name is Horowitz. There should be two adjoining suites," A.J. said.

The youngster looked down at his clipboard and said, "Yes, I see you here. You have suites three hundred and three oh one. Right through the double doors is check-in. Do you have any baggage you would like me to take to your rooms?"

Catherine opened the trunk of her car. The bellhop took the two travel bags out and placed them on the cobblestone drive while they walked inside.

The Garden's Hotel was a large mansion that had been converted to a bed and breakfast during the real estate boom of the 1990s. The polished hardwood floors gleamed like mirrors, as did the wainscoting on the lower portion of the walls. Fresh scent of jasmine could be smelled throughout. A wide and ornately carved staircase graced the foyer and led to the floors above. To the left was a parlor that had been converted to the front desk and concierge. Two gray haired women dressed in all white smiled when Catherine, Matt, and A.J. approached.

The taller of the two said, "Welcome to the Garden's. I understand you are the Horowitz party. You will be in suites 300 and 301." She handed them two keys on white plastic rings labeled with their suite numbers.

The smaller of the two said, "If you'll follow me I'll show you to your rooms." She did, and then said, "I hope you don't mind the shared seating area." The spaces were lavishly decorated. They were impressed. She walked toward the exit and said, "Is there is anything----anything at all that you need?"

"No, thank you very much," A.J. said for everyone.

"If there is anything you require please just give us a ring." She disappeared down the corridor.

"Nice place," Matt said as he looked around. "Wow – look at that view from the balcony." Love Palm trees. "And what's that wonderful smell?"

Catherine sniffed the air and said, "Glad you like it. Gardenias and jasmine, I believe." She walked over a couple steps and pointed up. "And look at this spectacular chandelier."

"Good call, Cat," Matt said with a wink and a smile. He stretched the way a man does when he gets home after work. "Looks like this is home for the next week and a half or until we have you ready for the exam." He suddenly got serious, remembering Skip's expectations. "Ready to begin?"

Catherine looked flustered. She said, "Like in now?"

"Yes, like in now. What did you think I meant?" Matt smiled.

She drew a deep breath and said, "Okay. I guess so," feeling less than enthused.

"I'm going out by the pool for a while," A.J. said, and walked into his bedroom to change.

***

Skip's bank wired the funds to Deutsche Bank in San Jose as directed by Katarina. The wire person there notified Katarina as soon as it was in. She said, "Rolly, the money's here."

Bob smiled and continued planning his exodus to Panama. "Thank you, Katarina."

That afternoon Skip and Grant flew from Ft. Lauderdale to San Jose. They landed at the charter end of the small international airport and checked in. The woman charged them a landing fee then asked them if they needed fuel. They said yes. She arranged for the fuel truck while they went to their appointment.

They stepped out front of the large tin building that doubled as a hanger and charter terminal and saw a beat up Dodge Rambler station wagon with a taxi sign on top. The driver was reading a periodical. Spanish, Skip noticed. They opened the side doors, got inside and gave the driver their destination. The driver didn't understand their English. Neither Skip nor Grant spoke enough Spanish to communicate.

Skip asked, "What do we do now."

"Hold on," Grant said, and went back into the FBO to see if someone would help them direct the cabbie to Bob's office address. Consuela Maria offered her services. She came out to the curb and told the driver where to take them. Grant thanked her profusely, thinking how friendly and gregarious she was.

"Consuela Maria, is it possible we can have this cabbie wait for us?"

"Ah seguro, sí, sí, señor. Un momento, por favor," Consuela said, and asked the cabbie in Spanish if that was possible. He answered her and she explained to Skip and Grant that the cab driver had another fare to pick up from the Barcelona Hotel to take out to Café Brit, the coffee plantation, but then he would be free.

Grant looked at Skip. Skip said, "I guess that would work. About how long does all of that take?"

Consuela asked the cabbie. Skip tried his best to remember enough Spanish to understand the cabbie's response, but was soon lost as he said, his arms gesturing as if in justification, "Usted sabe que los caminos no están bien saliendo aquel camino y luego si hay tráfico. Para estar en el lado seguro yo diría una hora."

Consuela nodded with understanding, then turned to Skip and Grant and said, "He says the roads are not good out that way, and there is much traffic. He said a safe estimate would be one hour." She waited for their response.

Skip consulted his watch and said, "Let's do it. If we have to wait a little on our end, that's fine. But be certain he does come back to pick us up. Okay?"

"No es un problema, señor. I make him promise me he comes for you after Café Brit." She crossed her heart.

She then turned to the driver and said something in Spanish with a finger wagging in his face. He shook his head in the affirmative. A huge bead of sweat dripped from his nose onto the steering wheel. Skip cringed, but got in, along with Grant. The driver took off in a herky-jerky fashion, trying his best to dodge the large and perilous potholes. The drive through San Jose was not memorable for Skip.

Third world country, everything is drab and dirty. Only draw this country has for me is the same it had for Bob Rolly----the ability to operate an illegitimate business outside of the prying eyes of the US government and a place to stash earnings without worrying about paying taxes on them.

A few minutes later, the cab driver pulled up to a non-descript tan building with the address Consuela Maria had written for him. Skip consulted his note from Katarina. Satisfied, he jumped out of the tepid taxi and said, "Cuanto?"

There was no odometer in the cabs, cabbies set fares as they saw fit. He pondered for a moment and then said, "Dies dolors."

"Ten?"

"Sí, señor."

115

Skip reached into his wallet, drew out fifteen US dollars, and handed them to the driver.

"Muchas gracias, señor," the driver said, smiling and pleased.

Skip and Grant looked at the building, sighed together and ambled up the broken sidewalk to the front door that had a buzzer and call box. Skip pushed the call button. A few seconds later Katarina's voice came across the line.

"Sports-R-Us."

Grant said, "Catchy name."

Skip said, "Hello, Katarina. It's Mr. Horowitz."

"Oh, hello. Let me buzz you in."

Bzz, bzz, bzz -.the lock clicked and Skip pulled the door open. Skip and Grant walked toward the next double door and stepped inside. Sports-R-Us occupied the entire building. It was not opulent or luxurious. No frills.

A petite woman in a sundress with short blonde hair greeted them. Traces of her Russian accent bled through her speech. She said, "A pleasure so to meet you, Mr. Horowitz."

She turned to Grant and said, "Welcome back, Grant. Long time no see." She winked. "Mr. Rolly is expecting you." Katarina showed them to Bob's office.

Bob Rolly was sitting behind a sixteenth century hand carved desk. He said, "Grant, great to see you again. Can Katarina take you out for some breakfast?"

"Sure."

Katarina and Grant exited.

"Now down to business," Bob said, and reached across his desk to open a Partegas box. "Would you care for a cigar, Skip?"

"No, thank you. I don't smoke."

Bob Rolly grunted and sized him up. "Suit yourself. Anything else before we get down?"

"No, just the books, the deed, and the people who will transfer with this transaction."

It was hard for Bob Rolly to dislike him despite what he had heard to the contrary. "Well, here is the deed. We can have it transferred once everything is signed." Bob passed a two-page document to Skip.

Skip took it and read it. "I thought you owned this building. This says a 100 year lease." Skip looked back at Rolly.

"Merely a matter of how property is transferred here in Costa Rica. Nothing is ever really owned for longer than the 100 year land lease. Is that a problem?"

"Not really, but it wasn't what I'd expected."

"What – you think you'll live forever?"

Skip ignored the dig. "I see there are eighty nine years to go. Is that right?"

"Yes." Bob cut the tip off his cigar and clicked his lighter. He took a few gentle pulls until it was burning good.

Skip watched him and then reached for a pen. He signed the title transfer and said, "What's next?"

"As I mentioned before, I am keeping my books. I plan to resurrect my own business in Panama."

"What will I do for clients?"

"You've got forty plus of my best people who can open new clients for your business. They have a long string of referrals that can help you get up and running in no time."

Skip looked doubtful, but said, "Okay. I'd like to meet them and discuss those options now."

Bob leaned back in his leather chair and punched the buzzer next to his phone. "Marvella, can you come here, please?"

Marvella said, "Yes, Sir Rolly."

Bob opened the second drawer in his desk and took out a ring of keys. "Here are the keys. I'll be out of here by eleven. If you have any more questions just have Marvella bring you back here."

"Which one goes to this office?" Skip held the color-coded key ring up.

Bob looked at the ring and said, "The yellow one is to this office and only you and Marvella have those keys. You can change that, of course, anytime you like." He exhaled a puff of whitish smoke. "The blue one is the front doors. Marvella can help you with the rest."

Marvella materialized.

"Skip, meet Marvella. She is a very big part of this business and will be most instrumental in keeping things on an even keel while you ease into it."

"Hello." Skip found himself face to face with an extremely large boned woman who looked like she could take him down in two minutes flat. He was unsure if he could or should place his trust in her. "I've got five of my own men flying in tomorrow morning. Maybe you, Marvella, can acquaint them with the business and help them find accommodations for the duration."

Rolly watched the exchange with genuine amusement. He knew Marvella came off brash and strong. She had served him well, but did not want to move again. He was curious how Skip would take to her.

Through her thick Russian accent she said, "Very pleased to make your acquaintance." She did not extend her hand. "Yes, I help your men find lodging. Want to see the operation now?"

Bob cut back in saying, "Skip is the man I told you about who is taking over this operation. Since you do not want to come with me to Panama I told him if he wanted or could use you, that you were willing to stay."

Her frosty gaze took in Skip. She said, "That's right."

"So do you want her or not?"

Skip looked her over and figured he would rather have her on his side than against. "Yes, I'll keep her." At least for now.

"You won't be sorry. She's loyal and hardworking. She puts some of the guys to shame." Bob laughed. "I guess Marva can take it from here." He walked over and gave her a hug.

As much as she could show emotion, which was very little, she reciprocated. She said, "Bob we all miss you. You are very good man." A small smile crossed her tight thin lips.

Skip spent the remainder of the hour with Marva talking over the finer details of how he expected this business would unfold and how everyone was to be paid. On the way back to the airport he stopped at the Canadian National Bank and opened an account that Marva could also sign on for payroll and other expenses. Skip knew the Canadian National Bank was known most for paying 30% per annum, which was unheard of in most banking circles. He was parking a million dollars there in order to receive his 2.77 percent paid monthly.

Riding with Bob on the way back to the Airport, Skip said, "I never realized how many Russians there are here."

"Russians, Checzks, Poles, Germans, they're all here."

"I think I'm going to like expanding here. Can you believe the Canadian National Bank pays thirty percent when back in the states the best we can hope for is around seven, maybe eight?"

Bob pulled out a fresh cigar, eyed it with affection and said, "I've had some money with them for years. I have a lot of customers here and one day, who knows – maybe I'll retire here. This place is peaceful and the people are warm and inviting."

"Better learn Spanish first."

They laughed. The cabbie did not. He spoke no English.

CHAPTER SEVENTEEN

A week later Catherine was finally catching on to the new lingo used for brokering commodities. She learned that investors can make money on a rising or falling market, what a call and a put was, what hedging was and who predominantly used hedge funds, how long and short positions can be combined to mitigate losses, and the various sizes of contracts according to industry. Matt drilled her daily with only a break for lunch and dinner. When Matt needed a break, A.J. drilled her. She was exhausted. When she slept she dreamt of commodities.

Tuesday of that week, Skip called Matt. He was brief. "Matt, how is she doing?"

"I think very well. We've been at it solidly for a week now and she has perfected the various contract sizes and prices and terms."

"Good. Do you think she's ready for the exam on Friday?"

"Barring any unforeseen problems I would say yes."

"Has A.J. been helping?"

"Like a champ, boss."

"Great. I'll have Lilly book the flights for Thursday – that way you can all relax before the exam first thing on Friday."

"Where are you putting up Catherine?"

"At the Ho-Jo's in Lauderdale by the Sea."

"Skip, that place is run down. Don't you think that's not going to look good for us?"

"This is not pleasure, Matt. There will lots of time for pleasure when she passes the exam and we have that office up and making money."

"Right. You're always right." Matt could hear Skip smiling at his abeyance.

"See you Thursday." Skip hung up.

One day and a half. That was what Matt and A.J. had left to ensure that Catherine was going to pass the exam, and on the first try at that. Matt, who had already felt pressured, felt even more so now.

***

The Fed's had been able to keep tabs on Skip's Key West crew from listening to the daily telephone conversations between Connie and Catherine. They also knew about Skip's taking over the Bob Rolly book making facility in Costa Rica – thanks to Grant. However, they had no jurisdiction there unless they could effectively tie that operation to one of the ones Skip had in the USA. Marek Kovackovich, the direct supervisor for Ray and Nick, called an informal teleconference meeting.

Marek said, "Nick, we have a new task for you."

"I'm all ears."

"You will pose as a bouncer/bartender who has won a weekend at the Ho-Jo's on Lauderdale by the Sea. You will meet and hook up with Ms. Catherine O'Reilley and I do mean get cozy. We want her to confide in you. To trust you. Got that?"

Nick was known around the NFA and the CFTC as acting akin to *Dirty Roy*. He sometimes overstepped the typically imposed boundaries when he felt they hampered his ability to get a conviction or bring an important case to trial. So effective was he at his job, the vast majority of the time he got off with little more than a slap on the wrist and a few harsh words of admonishment. Nick was dashing, daring, intelligent, and an ardent playboy. He said, "Does that include anything?"

"I can feel you thinking, and the answer is yes. There is considerable leeway, so feel free to use your ... imagination. This is becoming an important case and may help us set a precedent for Madoff. You know he is even more elusive than Horowitz. And Nick? Don't make me sorry I've selected you."

Ray said, "Why does he get to have all the fun?" and laughed.

Marek said, "Like I'm about to take that seriously. This is not time for playing around, Ray. You got to have an extended duty in Key West when he just stayed for a few days. And we happen to know about your new friend Connie Porter, too. Don't let pleasure get in the way of business."

Ray scoffed and said, "I would never let anything get in the way of business. I'm a professional on every level. And really, Marek ... like she poses any threat to our investigation." He shrugged. "She's helped us keep tabs on Skip's crew down here as well as how Catherine fits into the bigger picture. It's entirely possible that without the Connie Catherine connection we wouldn't even know what they were up to past the rental of that unit in the Admin Building."

"Yes, she has been helpful in that respect. That brings me to the next task. Ray, you need to get an interview for Skip's new Keys operation when his men place the ad in the Key West Citizen. Can you do that without your usual bravado?"

"What? You know me better than that. I can play it cool when things need cool. Nick is the wildcard." Ray huffed.

Marek cleared his throat. "We're not talking about Nick now. We are talking about you. We heard how Connie built you up to Catherine." Marek replayed the tape for Ray's edification. "You should be a shoe-in, but you also need to play it slow and cool. Got that?"

"I think I can manage that. Skip may be smooth, but he's never met the likes of me." Ray rolled his eyes, as if everyone on the line could see him.

"Nick, your room at Ho-Jo's is already arranged. Get there and get ready," Marek said, "and Ray, stay where you are. When they, as in Skip's men and Catherine, head to Ft. Lauderdale, ask the Brewer's if we can put some listening devices into Skip's office. High tech – the best stuff we got. Skip will do his regular sweeps – and our latest bugs, I'm told by our tech staff, nobody has the technology to detect them." Marek paused to consult his memo, a shopping list from the higher ups. "That's about it. Any questions?"

Before anyone could reply Marek noticed one other note and said, "Wait – one last thing … I almost forgot. We are setting up a covert shredding crew to help Skip with his latest propensity to shred sensitive documents. We need to make sure they get hired. With our men doing the shredding it should help us get some of the inside dirt we need. The new name, just for the record, is Farnsdale Shredding."

Always the wise guy, Nick said, "Sounds like some farm implement thing out of the Mid West. Are we shredding cow pies or something?" He snickered to himself at their lack of imagination.

Typical bureaurocrats. "Couldn't you come up with a better name than that?"

"Okay, wise ass. Any other *relevant* questions?"

Since there were no replies Marek said, "Good luck, be sharp, and get it done. We need to nail

this bastard." He disconnected the teleconference. The next call was to Arturo.

"Arturo, have you been in contact with Iggy?"

"Yes, we know exactly when Skip comes for his workouts and how long his sessions last. Is there something else you want me to find out?"

"He just bought the Rolly operation in Costa Rica. See if Iggy can get anything out of Skip about that. And the Keys is moving ahead, too. We'd like to have Iggy wear a wire. Do you think he would play along?"

"That one is hard to call, boss. I've not told Iggy that I am a federal agent. He thinks I'm a trainer just like him. Do you think now is the time to come clean? I don't want to jeopardize this case. God knows this Skip guy has been evading us for eons now."

"Let me put that to the powers above us. Until then just keep the channels of communication open and probe as you can."

"Iggy said that Skip is especially generous during the holidays. I could wear a wire and get close enough that maybe we can overhear something that can help?"

"That could be helpful. Do it and let's see what information Iggy will help us uncover."

"Will do."

The line went dead.

CHAPTER EIGHTEEN

Catherine had not been to Ft. Lauderdale before. Without the pressing exam she may have been able to relax and enjoy it more. She had packed casual clothing, sandals, shorts and halter-tops to show off her figure, because Matt and A.J. said she was going to be lodging at the beach.

Catherine, Matt, and A.J. were out at the Key West International airport by nine thirty sharp on Thursday morning. The flight was scheduled to leave for Ft. Lauderdale at ten fifteen and arriving at eleven – providing there were no delays or inclement weather. Catherine had driven and she parked in the short term parking. She fed the meter, and they ambled toward the terminal building with luggage in tow.

The loudspeaker, heard typically all the way down to Smather's Beach on a calm day, called for a lost child's parents, the Albertson's, to please come to the Hertz rental counter to pick up their child. Another message given over the hailer announced the departure of Cape Air to the Bahamas. Catherine, Matt, and A.J. were scheduled to depart on American.

Inside the terminal building, they walked up to where a crowd was gathering in a haphazard line for ticketing and departures under the large American Airlines banner. They chatted idly as they waited in line. About ten minutes later they got tickets and seat assignments. A sweaty, burly guy at the counter told them to proceed through the scanner to the waiting area where the flights would be called for boarding.

"This way," Catherine said to the men, pointing and leading the way. "This airport is so small that all flights arriving or departing use one common area for waiting. See the two counters?" She pointed them out and giggled. "Two different airlines can use each of them at any given time."

When they had cleared security Catherine looked around the busy and nearly full waiting area for three vacant chairs. As she threaded herself through the crowds and baggage left standing on the floor, with Matt and A.J. following close behind, she said, "Excuse me please," several times. They found three chairs together and had been seated only three or four minutes when the call came to board.

A chubby and scruffy, but cheery, gay chap took their tickets and handed them back a laminated seat assignment card. "Pass through gate A."

Outside, the tarmac was alive with activity. Baggage handling trolleys and fuel attendants were jockeying for space against the ticking clock for departures, and the flight crews were doing their pre-flight preparation for takeoff. A small private plane had just dropped onto the far runway and was cruising over toward the FBO. A rickety and rusty stair was rolled over to it.

Catherine stopped at the foot of the stairs and eyed it suspiciously. She said to the male steward, "This looks old and shaky. Is it safe?"

The steward grasped the stairs with both hands, shook it to display its solidity and said, "Yes, Ma'am, I'm quite sure it's safe."

Catherine gave him a dubious look and boarded with Matt and A.J. right behind, followed by the rest of the full capacity boarders – thirty people in all. At the top and upon entering, a petite elderly flight attendant asked for their passes and told everyone where to find their seats. As Catherine passed the open cockpit she glanced inside to see the pilot and co-pilot going through their pre-flight preparations. God I hate flying, she thought, and crossed herself. Lord, please let us all be safe and may these two men have a wealth of experience.

Catherine feared she might become claustrophobic with people seated so tight together. She and Matt sat together on one side in row seven, and at her request, Matt allowed her to have the window seat.

"Thanks, Matt," she said, taking the sweater she was carrying and putting it over the back of the chair.

Matt pointed and said with more than a little sarcasm, "Sweater?"

She giggled and sat as she said, "Well, yes – I wasn't sure if the air conditioning would be too chilly." Matt chuckled along with A.J. who sat across the aisle.

A rotund mid-forty-ish woman stopped in the aisle in front of A.J. and looked at her ticket. She informed him that she had the window seat next to him and asked if he would please allow her to squeeze by. A.J. stood and disappeared behind a mountain of bulbous flesh for several seconds as she huffed, pushed and squashed her way past him and into her seat. Her sickly sweet cheap perfume made him nauseous. Part of her bulk was spilling over into his seat. He managed with difficulty to sit back down with a visible cringe.

Matt motioned for A.J. to lean over so he could whisper to him. "Looks like you got the daily prize." He snickered.

A.J. gave him a withering glance, shook his head with a sigh of resignation to his fate and squirmed to get comfortable ... without success.

Cat glanced around the packed plane. She had only flown twice before, once to Miami, and once with her friend, Freddy Cabanas, who ran the bi-plane concession at the FBO in Key West. Her palms were sweaty, her pupils dilated, her heart felt like it was beating double time.

Matt said, "Are you okay?"

"Yes. I mean no. Okay, yes and no. I've only flown twice before."

"Seriously? Incredible. You're hardly a child; I'd have thought a woman like you would have had lots of air travel experience."

"I don't really like the idea of being up in the sky. People are meant to be on the ground." She pulled a hanky out of her purse and wiped her perspiring brow.

Matt guffawed. "You can't be serious. If we never went into the air we'd never have gone to the moon and beyond. Flying has opened up a whole new world."

Catherine looked sickly and unimpressed. "Sounds like you're a fan."

"Beats the hell out of driving."

"I guess so," she said, but did not sound convinced.

Soon the engines coughed, sputtered, and then roared to life. The pilot and co-pilot revved one and then fired the other. The aircraft shuddered and groaned. Catherine prayed it would be able to take off and stay in the air. A visual survey of the fully packed craft did little to lessen her skepticism. The flight crew closed the boarding door to prepare for taxiing and take-off. The *no smoking and fasten seatbelt* light bonged. A crackling recording played the emergency instructions and Catherine paid full attention.

The captain's voice came over the intercom. "This is Mike Mahaffy and I am your pilot today. Our estimated flight time is forty-five minutes. The weather in Ft. Lauderdale is eighty-two degrees and sunny with winds at three knots from the west-southwest. Enjoy your flight and thank you for flying American."

Catherine fidgeted in her seat and checked her seat belt to ensure it was fastened – twice. The ground crew removed the chocks from underneath the forward wheel of the aircraft. It jerked once to the right and then straightened up to taxi out onto the runway.

Matt nudged his nervous partner and said, "Take it easy will ya? It's a very short flight." He went back to leafing through his magazine, oblivious to Catherine's wooden glare.

The captain came back on the microphone and said, "We are number two for take-off. Please note the no smoking and fasten your seat belt signs, and remain seated during take-off. Once we are at cruising altitude the signs will ring off and signal that it is safe to move about the cabin." Safe my ass, Catherine thought. I'd never feel safe anywhere in this heap of junk except when it's on the ground and parked.

A few minutes later, the plane was rushing down the runway toward the waiting clear sky. It lumbered up and off the runway with creaks and moans and when it was fully in the air a loud scraping sound caused Catherine to jump like a cat. "Omygod – what was that?"

Matt looked up from his rag and chuckled. "Relax, gumdrop – just the landing gear. It's retracted into the cargo hold."

Several minutes into the flight the dollar-store-variety-perfumed plump lady began to badger the man behind her. She said, "Would you turn off that damn iPod? You can't hear a word the pilot has said."

A.J. stared at her.

She turned to him and said, "It's okay, he's my son."

A.J. forced a smile in acknowledgement and thought, lucky him, as she continued her tirade He tried to ignore her, but she was dogged and when her son failed to speak back to her or do as she requested she turned her charms on A.J.

She smiled, creating a hideous sight..

Good god, A.J. thought, she looks like an obese jackal. The extra skin on her face crinkled and her triple chin wiggled like pudding. A.J. nearly barfed.

"Hi. My name is Charlotte. Charlotte Wimple from Oswego, Wisconsin," she said, and extended a size fifteen hand.

A.J. shuddered. I'd rather swim in urine than shake her hand, he thought, but he managed a forced smile of acknowledgement and said with a flat face and voice, "I'm A.J."

"What kind of name is A.J.?" she said, with more facial wiggles. "What mother would name her child A.J.?"

Make like nice, A.J., do not slap her and tell her to shut the fuck up. He fingered his nose and considered how best to deal with this repulsive beast. "Excuse me, but my mother happens to be a wonderful person. And A.J. stands for Antonio Jameson." He pretended to read the back of the emergency landing card. Can't this bitch take a hint?

Across the aisle, Matt watched the struggling A.J. with sincere amusement. He turned to Catherine and said, "How many gallons in a crude oil contract?"

"Forty two thousand."

"Good. How about a one cent move up or down?"

"Four hundred twenty dollars."

"Very good. You're going to do just fine."

A hostess shuffled down the narrow aisle asking if anyone wanted a soft drink or water. She was harried because of the short flight. A man a couple of rows back from A.J. let loose with a loud fart. The person next to him gasped, choked, waved the air away and uttered obscenities.

A teenager a few rows behind them laughed so loud and hard he was brought to tears and gasping for air. His snorting and gasping got so obnoxious his friend jabbed him in the side and said, "Jeez-us."

Fart man slunk down in his chair as the boys howled again. An elderly woman across the aisle shushed them to little avail.

After several minutes of calamity the pilot came over the intercom and in his pleasant tone said, "We are in the holding pattern for landing at the Hollywood-Ft. Lauderdale International Airport. Please bring your seats back to full upright position, fold all trays up, and fasten your seatbelts. Flight crew, prepare for landing."

Matt said, "Does an option cost more or less closer to the money?"

"More." Catherine winked.

"In our operation most options cost about $1,000. You can buy them for more or you can buy them for less. The same for futures. What makes an option different from a future?"

"The option is the right, but not the obligation to buy."

Matt patted her on the arm. "You're doing great, Cat. Skip is going to be oh so pleased."

The lights flashed and bonged for seatbelts to be fastened. The plane dropped a few feet, settled, dropped several feet more, leveled out, banked left, and took a pass at the landing strip a few hundred feet ahead. Catherine's stomach went to her throat each time the plane dropped altitude and her soft hand on Matt's thigh turned into a grip firm enough to cause him to wince.

"Easy, baby, relax." They both laughed, his genuine, hers nervous.

Once safely landed and after the passengers had been told it's safe to unbuckle and unboard, the flight crew bid them a good day as they filed out and the pilot said, "Thank you for flying American."

Skip had arranged for Randall Sims to meet Matt, A.J., and Catherine at the commuter terminal this momentous Thursday. Matt and A.J. knew Randall well. He was another of Skip's official right hand men. He waved at Matt and A.J. and said, "Greetings. Welcome back to civilization."

A.J. introduced Catherine to Randall. "Randall, Catherine, Catherine, Randall."

Catherine noticed his dark, narrow set eyes. Shifty, she thought, doesn't look straight at the person he's talking to.

Randall eyed her sideways with a quick up and down look over, smiled, looked down and away while rubbing his chin and said, "So this is Catherine. Pleasure, Ma'am." He looked back at her for a second. "Skip's told me so much about you I feel like I already know you."

Catherine blushed and said, "I hope it was all good." She had to contain her facial expression and be courteous. My lord – this small man has a face like a pig. Bulbous nose, thick lips. Certainly not the typical hunk most of Skip's cohorts are. And he's fat, too.

Randall chuckled. "All good, all good. Well, are you all set or do any of you need to go to baggage claim?"

"We're good," Matt said.

They followed Randall out to the valet parking on the main level. Randall handed a coded ticket to the uniformed man at the counter who said, "One moment please."

A few minutes later the uniformed man returned with a shiny, navy colored, Jaguar sedan. Randall tipped the man a twenty and said, "Let's stow those bags in the trunk, shall we?" He hit fob on the key ring and the trunk jumped open. Matt and A.J. placed the bags inside. A.J. took the front passenger seat and Matt and Catherine sat in the back. Randall eased the car into gear and off they went.

Matt said, "So you got the maid's car, eh? What's she driving today?"

Catherine stared at him, lost.

A.J. laughed as did Randall. Randall's hoggish nostrils flared and he said, "Yes, she's away visiting her mother and the Bentley's in the shop. You know Skip, he loves to ride in style and class and *he* can afford the best. Dress for success and drive for success, that's our boss."

Catherine had heard of those brands of cars, but had never seen one up close. The Jaguar was two and a half years old and in pristine condition. She was speechless.

Randall said, "Skip told me to drop Catherine at the Ho-Jo's and then take both of you to his office."

"Whatever he says. He's the Man," Matt said. "Any boss who pays as well as Skip does deserve loyalty and abeyance, right guys?"

"Got that right," A.J. said, "and God help anyone who doesn't figure out soon enough what happens to anyone who tries to go against ..." He crossed himself.

A sharp look from Matt shut A.J. up in mid-sentence. The look reminded him that Catherine had no idea yet just what devilry Skip was capable of when his iron fisted authority was dared to be challenged by anyone. People had lost limbs and even life. And this early in the game was not the time for her to find out.

Catherine noticed A.J.'s abrupt shut up and wondered what the eye contact was all about. An awkward silence fell over the group for a moment. She broke it with an attempt at small talk, even though she wasn't much for that sort of thing.

"Have you worked for Skip very long, Randall?"

"About six years, maybe seven come to think of it. He really is a great boss." Randall looked in the rearview mirror to see if he could change lanes.

Catherine said, "There sure is a lot of traffic here."

"I guess so. You get used to it."

Randall angled the Jag over toward the exit for Atlantic Boulevard East. Cars of every make and model roared and flew by. Catherine had never seen traffic like this. She ducked in reflex when Randall cut a black SUV off in order to make his turn onto the exit ramp. At the stop sign he bore right and continued until he came to A1A where he turned left. He continued on for three blocks and came to a stop at the Howard

Johnson's on Lauderdale by the Sea. Catherine felt small and insignificant in an entirely different world.

Randall said, "Well, here we are." He let the car idle with the air conditioning on while he and Catherine went inside to check in. As they approached the counter he said, "I'll be back in just a minute."

She stopped and he left. He added, "I'm going back out to get your luggage."

In stark contrast to the grandeur of everything Skip owned and frequented, this place looked like the ugly stepsister of Cinderella. The paint was faded and pealing in many places. The windows looked like they had never been washed. The sign was half fallen its pole and only the 'Ho' was lit. At street level, you could smell the carbon emissions expelled from all of the passing traffic. It was oppressive.

Randall held Catherine's small overnight bag and opened the door to the lobby with his free hand. He said, "After you."

"Thank you," she said, and stepped inside.

Either the air conditioning was not working or they had none. A wave of warm air met them immediately. The small lobby was dotted with run down furnishings that looked like they came from a yard sale or second hand store. A beat up and deeply marred counter separated the office workers from visitors. A single bell stood on the edge. A mish mash of brochures dotted the other end, sporting everything from two-for-one dinner specials to twenty percent off on Jet Ski rides. A wiry middle aged man bumped around from behind the counter. Randall approached him and said, "Reservation for Horowitz, please."

The man dropped something, bent to pick it up, then said, "Ah – I see it right here. Two nights?"

"Yes, that would be it."

The clerk shoved a small dirty piece of paper toward Randall and said, "Please fill this in."

Randall looked it over and said, "There will be no car here overnight, so I don't believe this is necessary."

The clerk looked dubious, but said, "Fine," then handed them a plastic key ring with the number 302 scratched into it. "Elevator's right over there." He pointed toward the hallway and then disappeared behind a door just beyond the counter.

"Skip would want me to see you to your room."

"That won't be necessary. I think I can find my own way."

"Are you sure?" He was not, and he was never one to disappoint Skip, either.

Catherine nodded. "Yes, I'll be just fine."

"Okay, if you're sure." He shifted his weight from side to side. "What's the plan from here?"

"Well, Skip wants you well rested for the test in the morning. It begins at eight thirty sharp. They allow eight hours to complete it, but most of the people I know took nowhere near that long." He had hoped to sound reassuring. "I'll pick you up no later than eight. The test site is only about fifteen minutes from here."

"Until then?" Catherine appeared confused.

He patted her on the shoulder. "Relax. I'm sure Skip will be in touch."

Whatever, Catherine thought, as Randall turned and exited the premises leaving her by herself in a dank place – somewhere near the beach in some city she had never visited before. She sat on the nearest chair, heaved a sigh, ran her fingers through her hair … and felt alone.

***

Nick had already gotten his room at the Ho-Jo's, and had been waiting. The agents on detail were to give him the cue when Catherine arrived. From there he figured he would arrange what seemed to be a chance meeting, perhaps in the elevator, or near the pool, or even on the beach, and work from there.

Nick had done dozens of these setups and each one titillated him to find newer and more creative ways to worm his way into the suspecting person's trust. He had studied the background information on Catherine O'Reilley. He knew when her parents had come to America and what path they had taken to land in Key West. He knew how many children were in her family and what each of them did. He knew she had not been a particularly good student and had not aspired to go to college. He knew she had a connection to Shamus who was more than smitten with her. He knew her history of having a propensity for one night stands and her thoughts about having a regular relationship with Skip. He figured he would use the sex angle to get inside her. He had smiled to himself more than once over the pun of his plan.

His cell rang. The caller ID read Daryl Handson, one of the Lauderdale-based agents on detail. He popped it open and said, "Daryl – whatcha got."

"I've got Skip's assistant, Randall, and the pick-up in sight. Picked up on them at the airport and followed them out to their transportation. Looks like they're headed north on I-95."

"Roger that," Nick said. "ETA?"

"I'd guess twelve to fourteen minutes unless there's an accident or unusually heavy traffic."

"Thanks. I'll get in place."

CHAPTER NINETEEN

When Catherine arrived at room 203, she slipped the key into the lock, turned the handle and pushed open the door. It swung inward with a bang. The room was dark, damp, and smelled of stale cigarette smoke. She felt the wall to her left and turned on the lights. Ooh. Harsh florescent lighting made the room look all the more depressing. The carpet was worn thread bare and the upholstery was dotted with spots and speckles of whatever its last residents had spilt. The bed was made, but the pillows looked small, worn, and puny on the king sized mattress. She dropped her luggage on the foot of the bed, kicked off her sandals, and went to the window, or what she believed was a window, and drew back the pathetic half hung curtains in hopes of getting some natural light.

It was not a window, but a dilapidated sliding door. The lock was corroded beyond use. It rumbled and bucked in the frame when she slid and pushed at it. The screen was hanging by a spline that was torn and battered beyond functionality. She took it off the frame and stood it off to the side. The adequately sized balcony had two plastic chairs and one small plastic table, both filthy. Over the side of the balcony looking east she had a fairly nice view of the pool area and the beach beyond. She wondered what Skip was paying per night for this hovel.

Whatever it is, it's too much. Oop – phone's ringing. She answered her cell. It was Connie.

"So how's Ft. Liquordale?"

"Funny." She smiled to herself. "I just got to my room and it is … un-be-lievable."

"Nice, eh?"

Catherine snorted. "Hell, no. Quite the opposite."

"Get out of here. With all of Skip's money and he puts you up in some dump? I'm shocked."

"You sound it. The only nice thing in this outhouse is the view of the pool and the beach."

Connie made a humph noise. "When's the test?"

"Tomorrow morning at eight thirty."

"Are you ready?"

Catherine sighed, trying to stay upbeat. "I guess I'm as ready as I'll ever be. The time is up and here I am."

"You'll do just fine."

"Glad you think so."

"What does Skip have planned for tonight?"

Catherine sat on one of the chairs. "No idea. Randall, his assistant, just dropped me off here at Ho-Jo's and said Skip would be in touch."

"Where are your evil twins?" Connie chuckled.

"I suppose you mean Matt and A.J.? They went with Randall to see Skip."

"And why didn't you go too?"

"Randall said Skip wanted me to wait here, to rest and to be fresh for the exam."

Connie clucked her tongue. "That's it?"

"That's all I know so far." Catherine yawned and stretched.

"Well, it's still early, why don't you go out to the beach or the pool and do a little fishing?"

"You never stop. Seriously. But that does sound like a good idea. I could take my cell phone in case Skip tries to reach me."

"There you go. Have some fun."

They hung up and Catherine went over to her overnight bag and fished for a pair of shorts and a tank top. She had not thought ahead to bring a bathing suit along, but thought maybe there was a shop close by where she could find one. She dressed and combed her hair into a ponytail, then put on her flip-flops and headed out the door.

At the front desk Catherine stopped to ask the aged desk clerk where a bathing suit shop might be found.

He said, "Well I am not one hundred percent sure, but there used to be a Swim-n-Sport in the strip mall across the street. You might give that a try." He pointed west toward the opposite direction from the beach.

"Thank you. I'll check it out."

Catherine walked to the crosswalk and depressed the signal for stopping that was supposed to make the lights turn and allow pedestrians to cross. She waited. And waited. The light never changed. Catherine lost her patience and flung her hands in the air. Damn things never work. Nothing but a damn placebo button. What the hell, I'll make a dash for it.

She bolted across and narrowly avoided being pulverized into a pile of plasma by fast traffic in both directions. One driver honked and another cursed at her, but she made it. She heaved a sigh of relief and walked in the direction of the strip mall. The sun was bright overhead so she cupped her hand over her eyes to read the large sign. *Swim-n-Sport.* Good.

Inside the shop, a young and friendly version of Barbie greeted her and asked if there was anything in particular she could help her with.

Catherine said, "No. I just want to look first, but if there's anything I can't find I'll come looking for you." This little Barbie Doll is too cute, too young, and too coquettish for her own good, she thought. She milled around the small and closely packed shop for a suit that would be suitable and sexy for a woman her age. She found three that had some potential and went to try them on. The first was slightly too revealing. The second was a nice look for a nun. The third suited Catherine perfectly. It was a brown and beige animal print with high-topped briefs and a halter style top.

She looked at the price tag. Surely this must be a mistake. One hundred thirty-eight dollars? I've never spent even fifty dollars on a bathing suit before, let alone one hundred thirty-eight. Decision time, do it or don't do it? She looked again in the mirror. Perfect. Go for it. The hell with the cost and what I might think tomorrow. At least I'll look great today. And I deserve a treat after all the work I've done studying for this freaking exam.

She dressed, paid, and went back to the Ho-Jo's to change, feeling a bit better.

Having watched her every move, Nick was about to make his.

CHAPTER TWENTY

Catherine emerged from her room at the same time as Nick was leaving his. Her room had been bugged. Nick's room was at the other end of the hall, but it also had a view of the beach and pool deck. He waited to see if she would take the stairs or the elevator. She chose to take the elevator and Nick followed. They were the only two in the hall at the time so he struck up a conversation with her as they approached and entered.

"Hi. Up or down?"

Catherine smiled and said, "Down. Thank you."

"My name's Nick. What's yours?"

"Catherine. Catherine O'Reilley." Dreamy, she thought, giving Nick the eye over. Surfer shorts hung low with six pack abs and a sculpted chest. Very sexy. A potential playmate? It's been ten days and I'm horny as hell.

Nick had a difficult time moving his eyes from her extra large mammaries stuffed into her halter top. He eventually got unstuck and looked up to her face, but he also noticed his prolonged assessment of her sexual equipment didn't appear to bother her. Probably used to men's staring, he thought. Wow – for a thirty something she's hot.

He tucked his sports mag under his arm, adjusted the beach towel on his shoulder and said, "Beach or pool?"

"Beach. I like to feel the sand underneath my feet."

Nick bunched his lips and nodded. "Me too. Wanna sit together?"

Abrupt, Catherine thought, sort of refreshing. Guy doesn't play cat and mouse games. "Sure."

They rode down in the elevator engaged in small talk. When it stopped and the doors jerked open, Nick stood to the side with a slight bow to allow Catherine to exit first.

"Why thank you, sir."

"My pleasure," he said with a wink.

Outside a cabana boy asked them if they wanted to sit around the pool or on the beach. He was twenty something and spry. Catherine noticed even at this early afternoon hour he sported a five o'clock shadow that lent his youthful face a rugged texture.

"Beach. Two, please," Nick said with a smile.

The lad hefted two aluminum chairs over his thin shoulders and schlepped them onto the beach. "Anywhere in particular?"

Catherine said, "How about near those three palm trees. That way we have the luxury of both the sun and the shade."

The young man trudged across the hot sand over to the trees and put the two chairs side by side. Then he placed two fresh, but worn, beach towels on each one and twisted them down under the slats so the wind, if there was any, would not blow them away. "Anything else?"

"Just one question," Nick said, "do we get the drinks from you or someone else?"

"I'll send out Cassandra." He began to walk away.

Nick whistled at him. "Hey hold on. Wait a minute."

The waiter turned around and Nick slipped him a ten-dollar bill. He looked at it, grinned and said, "Thank you very much."

Catherine sat on the chair closest to the trees and Nick sat by her. She said, "Thank you."

"For what?"

"Tipping that nice young man."

Nick waved a hand. "Oh that's nothing. I know what it's like to live for tips."

"Oh, really. What do you do?"

"I bartend and bounce for the Buccaneers Restaurant and Bar."

Catherine's eyes shot up and to the left. She shook her head and then looked at Nick. "I've never heard of it."

Nick raised one eyebrow in a knowing manner. "Then you're not from around here."

"No. I live in Key West." She adjusted her halter-top.

Nick took the opportunity to follow her hand motion and relish another good look at her boobs. "Really. That's way cool. What da-ya do down there?" Enunciate or she'll think you're a cretin.

"Real estate. Actually I used to do real estate, but I'm in the middle of a career change."

Nick leaned forward, showing interest. "Real estate should be a booming industry down there. Why are you giving that up?"

"Well, it was a very lucrative business, but the bubble has just about gone bust. I have an offer to work as a commodities broker." She stretched a leg and leaned back.

Nick nodded, but had a wrinkled forehead. "That's a huge change in direction. How did you get into that?"

"It's a long story really, but to give you the short version I met a man who was looking for commercial space and he invited me to come to work for him."

"What does that entail?" Nick folded his arms and then brought two fingers to his chin.

Their waitress arrived and said while smacking and chewing on a mouthful of gum, "Hi. I'm Cassandra. I'm your waitress today. Stan told me you wanted some drinks?"

Nick and Catherine both looked at the chubby, pimply faced and sweaty girl. Her dishwater blonde hair was pulled back in a pony tail that hung halfway down her back. Her denim shorts were riding up on her rump, exposing dimpled cheeks. She shifted nervously from one hip to the other as she waited for their reply.

Nick looked at Catherine and asked, "What would you like."

Catherine frowned. "I don't know. What are you having?"

"I'll have a Jagermeister please."

"Mm – that sounds good. I'll have the same."

Catherine considered this Nick guy. I like him more with each passing minute. He's polite and seems interested in me. Plus, he's handsome and built like a Roman statue.

Nick made a silent gesture with both arms mimicking the waitress' girth to Catherine. They both repressed a laugh. He said, "So anyway … you were saying? About this business?"

"Well his business is commodities. Did I already say that?" Focus, Catherine. Get your mind off of sex.

Nick smiled. She's playing right into my plan. "Yes. Do you need any special licenses to do that?" He rubbed some oil into his ripped pecs. Catherine's gaze followed his every movement.

"Yes, I do. I've been studying non-stop for the past ten days for the series three exam."

Nick's eyes widened. "Some of those exams take a long time. How long is this one?"

"Well, the way I understand it we can have up to eight hours, but according to the men who tutored me I should complete it much sooner than that."

"I see. When do you take it? The exam that is." Nick wiped his forehead and then his hands with his beach towel.

Catherine watched his biceps bulge as his arms folded and the oil glistened in the sun. God I'd like to take a bite out of this man. "Tomorrow morning. At eight thirty a.m.," she said, and sighed, "and I am *so* not a morning person."

Nick nodded. "Understand. So, what's the name … of your new company?"

Catherine shifted her weight in her chair and ran her fingers through her hair. "Well, Skip has several companies, but I think the name for us in Key West is going to be Heritage Financial or something like that."

"Sounds interesting. Good luck on the exam." He winked and gave two thumbs up.

She smiled. "Thanks. I'm sure I'm going to need it."

Chunky pimply face materialized with two cold Jagermeisters and placed one on each chair. "Anything else I can getcha?"

Nick looked to Catherine to see if she had need of anything else. Her look told him, no. "Not right now. Thank you."

"Did you want to charge these to your room or pay me now?" She popped a huge bubble and licked it off her sun burnt lips.

Matt said, "I'll pay you now."

"That's six dollars even."

Nick fished out another ten, handed it to her and said, "Keep the change."

She brightened. "Gee – thanks, Mister."

Nick looked at Catherine as the girl walked away, shook his head and said, "You know you're getting old when girls her age start calling you mister." He laughed. "See the look on her face? Like she's never gotten a tip that size before. Probably not." Nick took a good pull off his drink. "Boy that hits the spot."

Catherine's cell rang. "Hello. Oh, hi Skip. No, you are not bothering me. What's up?"

Skip had the ten-day progress report from Matt and A.J. They were confident about Catherine's being able to pass the series three. If they were convinced, Skip was close to it, but he also wanted to check things for himself.

"I was going to take you out to dinner, but something has come up. Can I take a rain check?" Since Catherine had no idea what Skip's plans were, she said, "Sure, fine."

"You should rest, relax, and enjoy yourself, but get to bed at a reasonable hour. The exam comes early and I want you to be sharp."

"Yes sir." She looked over at Nick and smiled. Hmm, she thought, that look on his face … almost as if he knows who I'm talking with. How could that be? Weird.

"Randall is going to pick you up and take you to the exam. When it's over and we know you have passed, I told him I want you to come to our main office over on Cypress Creek Boulevard. I want you to meet my crew there and see how a first rate operation works."

"Okay."

"Is there anything you need from me?"

She thought, yea, but I guess we will not go there right now. "No, I guess everything's okay."

"Are you sure? You sound tentative."

"Yes. No. I mean, I'm fine." She giggled. "Thank you."

"Great. Good luck on the exam. And please don't let me down."

"I won't."

Skip hung up. Catherine closed her cell, put it in her purse and enjoyed a long swallow of her drink.

Nick leaned toward her. "Don't tell me … the new boss, right?"

Catherine half-smiled and said, "Good guess."

"You don't sound very pleased."

"Sorry." She hunched a shoulder. "I don't know exactly what it is about him, but he is just so intense. And I do mean about everything." She took another long pull of her warming Jagermeister.

"In this case is intense a good or bad thing?" He put a palm up.

"It's hard to describe. I think he is obsessed with money and power."

"Ah." He leaned back and clasped his hands behind his head. "Both can be hard to control. I've met many a man who was drunk on both."

"Well said." She paused. "So. Enough about me. What about you?"

"There's really nothing to tell." He reached for his drink.

"Come on, everyone has a story to tell."

Nick whistled, waved at their waitress and said with two fingers in the air, "Two more please."

She waddled off toward the bar.

"I don't do anything very exciting, but I have fun."

I'll just bet you do, Catherine thought. This guy is a clever one, and there's more to him than meets the eye. Even though he's a hell of an eyeful. Pry a little.

"I bet you meet a lot of ladies."

"Are you trying to ask me if I'm single?" His face lit up in devilish smile. Catherine nearly creamed her new bathing suit.

"I guess I am." She giggled. "Sorry, you don't have to answer that if you don't want to."

Nick leaned close, touched her hand and said, "I am completely single."

She eyed him up and down. "What's wrong with this picture?"

His eyebrows went up. "What do you mean?"

"Well, you're attractive. You're nice. You have an okay job. Why single?"

"Oh that." He leaned back. "My choice. I've never met anyone who made me want to stay attached."

Well you might just be flirting with the one who'll land you right now, Mister, Catherine thought as she gave him a sexy eye.

Pimples on legs came back with two cold and frothy drinks and placed one again on the end of each chair. "Will that be all?"

Nick handed her a twenty and said, "Keep the change."

She jumped in glee at his generosity, almost managing to defy gravity and lift off the sand, and trudged off.

Nick and Catherine sat under the three palm trees for the next two hours drinking and talking about life. Twice they took a dip in the cool ocean. They were both beginning to feel the effects of the alcohol. Catherine was horny and amorous. She rubbed her leg on Nick's. The sun was beginning its descent to the west and the shadows cast on the beach from the palm trees were long and thin. A few seagulls skittered at the edge of the beach where it met the sea in search of something to eat.

"Wanna come back to my room and watch the sun set?" Nick said, his hand resting on her leg.

She placed her hand on his and cooed. "That would be nice."

They gathered their belongings and strolled toward HoJo's. The long shadows being cast by the sun made the structure appear sadder than it was. Most of the people around the pool had gone inside for the night. The cabana boy was busy straightening lounge chairs and picking up soggy towels. The oversized gum-smacking girl was counting her tips.

On floor two, Catherine said, "Give me just a minute to freshen up. What room are you in?"

"Two oh eight."

"See you in about five minutes."

"Fine. See you then." Nick wanted a minute to freshen up too, but he also needed to call Marek to tell him how things were progressing. They should know since the rooms were bugged, but protocol was to check in at regular intervals anyway. He went to his room, took a shower and then placed the call.

"Marek. Nick here. Did you catch most everything?"

"We did, well, except for the time just now at the beach. Good call to keep her entertained. She's already telling you a lot of good information, I hope?"

"Yeah. Fair amount so far. No time right now but I'll fill you in aysap. Gotta get ready right now, she'll be here any minute. Now, look ... there may be some things coming along that I don't want you to hear." Nick laughed, but he was serious. He planned to have sex with Catherine and was always apprehensive when his colleagues had to listen in. This was not the first time. Pricks have a good time eavesdropping too, he thought with a shake of his head. Then afterward when I'm with them they'll imitate the woman I've just laid making jokes and laughing about it. Rude and childish.

A chuckle came over the phone. "Now, partner – you know the rules. We've got to listen. Just try to not be too gooey."

"Gooey? Come on, don't you have a better word than that? Okay, just joking."

Nick knew his partners were equipped with state-of-the-art listening devices that could overhear a seagull's fart from two miles away. They had infrared scanners that measured body heat through building walls. He groaned. They'll hear every word and noise we make.

While Catherine had been on the beach with Nick, Skip had sent a bouquet of flowers to her room with a note that said, '*Good luck with the exam! Love, Skip'.* She thought, what a confusing man. The flowers were magnificent and the fragrance masked the stale cigarette smell, making her room more pleasant. She propped the note up beside the vase and stepped into the shower.

Ten minutes later she was ready for her rendezvous with Nick. She put on the sundress she had worn when she flew in earlier that day and fluffed her wet hair with a fresh towel. The shower had felt good and given her some time to clear off the Jagermeister's. She looked a final time in the murky mirror, stepped outside into the hall, walked over to room 208 and knocked.

Nick opened the door and said, "Please come in."

Nick's room was an exact replica of Catherine's. The same threadbare carpet and stale cigarette smoke, identical faded wallpaper, and flat pillows on the bed. Nick had a bottle of Irish Whisky on the television stand and a plastic bucket filled with ice. He said, "Would you care for an Irish whiskey?"

She smiled and said, "Thank you. Don't mind if I do."

Nick took out two short plastic tumblers and filled them to the top with whiskey and ice. He handed one to Catherine, pointed with his eyes to the balcony and said, "The sunset is out there."

Catherine hesitated with a thought. "If you live here and work here why are you staying in this hotel?"

Nick had anticipated that question. "We have a drawing at the bar once per month. All of the staff participates. One number is drawn and that person gets a free weekend at some run down hotel like this one."

"That's nice. That they do that. This *dump* is hardly nice." She looked around with a face full of ironic observation. They both laughed.

They idled away in conversation until the sun set out on the balcony, their bodies inches apart. They had two more large tumblers filled to the top with iced booze. Sexual tension was reaching bursting heights. Nick took her hand and walked her back inside. She dropped her tumbler off at the gritty table just inside the sliding doors. Nick placed his glass on the television stand. Neither held any illusions about what was coming next. They kissed passionately once, twice, three times. Both were breathless and filled with desire.

She bent before him, unzipped shorts, reached inside to pull out his manhood and took it fully in her mouth.

Nick moaned, took her head in his hands and eased her off, removing his throbbing member from her passionate oral play. She looked up with a pout. He said, "Wait. Not yet."

They fell onto the bed. Nick tore off her panties. With his hand he stimulated her clitoris. She writhed, crested, and fell. She panted. He panted. They sweated together. He rode her. She rode him. She was an able sexual partner and he was extremely pleased. He came. She came numerous times and begged for more.

"Lady you are on helluva fuck," Nick said, catching his breath on his back with a hand wiping his sweaty forehead.

"I want more." She pulled him to her and began to again massage his semi-limp member back to life.

"You're going to kill me."

"Can you think of a better way to go?" She smiled a wicked smile. "This time let me take the lead."

She rode him every way possible, including upside and going down. She yelled. She writhed. She flung her long auburn tresses into his face. They came together like a great volcano erupting for the first time. Every available bit of love lava having been spilled, they lay crushed together like a two car collision, body parts entangled, energy spent and out of breath.

After regaining their senses they were hungry. They ordered room service, ate like they'd been starved for a month, and within thirty minutes the steam began rising again. They screwed most of the night.

In the wee hours of the morning, as Nick slept, Catherine slipped away and went back to her room, thinking. I need to make some final preparations for the exam. I got a few hours to go, I'll do one last going over the material, make sure I'm in top shape. She visualized all the fun she'd had last night. Damn that was hot. I had a lot of pent up sexual frustrations that Matt and A.J. haven't helped me with one bit on this trip. Not sure I'd want another threesome with those two, but maybe one at a time. She sighed with dreamy pleasure, thankful the last stretch of ten long and lonely days with no sex was over. That fast is oh-ver. Hell, yea. She touched her tender pussy and grinned. Shit that was good.

CHAPTER TWENTY-ONE

When Catherine came downstairs Friday morning at eight o'clock sharp, Randall was already there, waiting and fretting. He was nervous by nature and waiting had never been one of his strong points. He said, "Glad you're on time. Let's get moving."

It sounded like marching orders to Catherine, so she fell in beside Randall as he rushed out the door. Randall had left the Bentley running and was doubly nervous about some thug coming by on his watch and stealing it.

Catherine had never seen a Bentley before – let alone rode in one. She was beyond impressed. Randall did not open her door for her, but instead went to the driver's side and let himself in. Inside, the posh seats and cool air calmed him down.

Catherine nestled in and said, "This is some car."

"Yes, it is. But it makes me nervous to drive it sometimes."

"Oh really. Why?"

"This car cost three hundred and fifty thousand dollars and it's one of Skip's babies. Need I say more?"

As Randall drove, he rested a limp wrist on the smoothly polished sport wheel and tapped his hand on the dash. Catherine noticed his effeminate quality for the first time. How could I have missed that – he's gay as they come. Must've been everything on my mind lately. She suppressed a chuckle. He's acting exactly like some of my drag queen friends in Key West.

Catherine decided to inquire. "What is it that you assist Skip in?"

Randall spoke with his hands accompanying as he drove. He said, "Well, that all depends. I do whatever he wants or needs. Sometimes I pick up his dry-cleaning if the maid doesn't have time. Sometimes I ferry people, like you, around for him. Sometimes I go the bank for deposits or withdrawals."

Catherine gave a quick nod. "So you don't sit in the office much?"

"Oh – no, girl. I'm his roving gopher."

They drove along for the better part of fifteen minutes before Randall saw the sign for the test center. It was a plain two-story building, painted in drab vanilla. A large sign out near the street said, '*SEC Test Site and Administrative Complex*'. Randall wheeled the luxury car into a reserved spot.

Catherine pointed and said, "Did you see the sign said 'reserved'? In Key West they always tow."

Randall placed the gearshift into park and turned off the key. With confidence he said, "Nobody here is going to mess with this car."

"Ahh," she said with her chin and eyebrows rising, "the voice of experience."

He winked. "I am. Now come on – let's get you settled in."

Two men in Government suits stood smoking near the entrance. Catherine noticed Randall looking them over like a hungry dog would a tasty meat bone.

The interior of the structure was as unimpressive as the exterior. The terrazzo tile floors had a dull sheen in need of waxing. The overhead lights were florescent and cast a sickly color onto everyone. The walls were painted the same dumpy beige as the exterior. The only indicators of who was where were small black signs with numbers and short codes above the doors, but they were undecipherable to anyone except governmental officials. Some of the doors were ajar while others were closed. Midway down the hall was a wide, tiled staircase. Randall began his ascent. Catherine followed.

On the second floor Randall turned left and walked down to door number 2208 code SE3. Catherine figured this must be government lingo for the series three exam. An elderly woman was standing just outside of the door holding a clipboard in her arms. Randall appeared to know her. He said, "Mrs. Goodman, this is Catherine O'Reilley for the series three exam."

Mrs. Goodman consulted her list and said, "Ah yes, I have her right here. You know we are very busy this morning. Let me tell Gus that she has arrived and he'll set her up at a computer screen."

Merv and Stanley, two other federal associates of Ray and Nick, were eavesdropping, keeping tabs on which computer Gus set Catherine up at. They both stood behind a half wall/half glass partitioned section of the inner portion of the room. Both Mrs. Goodman and Gus knew that Catherine was one of Skip's potential new hires.

Mrs. Goodman brought Gus out to meet Catherine and she spoke in hushed tones. "Gus here will get you all set up."

Randall patted Catherine's shoulder and said, "Good luck."

"Thanks," Catherine said, and she followed Gus inside.

Mrs. Goodman said, "Don't worry, Randall. I'll call you when she's about done. Go on and have some fun."

Gus reminded Catherine of the Pillsbury Dough Boy. There were no hard edges to him, just rounded and squishy flab that poured out of his frame. His tummy jiggled when he walked, as did his triple jowls. Gus's cheeks quivered as he said, "You can have a seat here. I will need your handbag and please do not talk. If you have any questions, silently raise your hand and the proctor will drop by. You have eight hours to complete this exam from the time the clock starts. On your computer screen you will see the countdown." He pointed to the right top edge of the screen. "Please be cognizant of the time. If you fail to complete the exam in the allocated time you will have to retake it. Retaking requires a three week wait." He handed her three sheets of blank paper. "These are for your mathematical calculations. They will be collected when you complete the test. Any questions before you begin?"

Catherine had never experienced anything quite like this before. She rubbed her hands together, feeling the sweaty dampness. She shook her head no, but thought, God I'm nervous.

Gus held an automatic starter. He clicked the on button with a flourish and said, "Begin."

The clock began ticking. Catherine read through the brief directions about how to ascribe the answers for the questions and then went to page one. A proctor passed by at regular intervals. Wherever the proctor was near or not, cameras watched at all times to ensure nobody was cheating. After a few minutes Catherine caught on to the format and was moving steadily through the exam. Randall left. Merv and Stanley kept tabs on her answers through their computer screen.

Two hours down and counting. Catherine had just come to the most difficult portion for her, the math section. She carefully calculated her answers and then selected the ones on the screen that matched. Occasionally an answer she arrived at was not on the screen and she had to go back and refigure.

Four hours and still counting. Randall called in to see how far along she was. Mrs. Goodman informed him that she was a little more than two thirds through.

Five hours and nearing the end. Thirteen questions to go. Catherine wanted to get this test over and move on, but some of the questions were deceptive and meant to trick the examinee. She wasn't about to be fooled and thought each one through carefully.

Five questions to go. Mrs. Goodman called Randall and said he should come for Catherine. Merv and Stanley figured she had about seventy eight percent so far. Seventy percent was passing.

At 2:54 p.m., Catherine raised her hand. The proctor passed by. She whispered that she was done. The proctor picked up the loose sheets of paper, shut down the clock, and then pointed toward the exit.

Catherine got up without making a noise, feeling stiff. She fought the urge to stretch and bend. The blood on the lower half of her body felt like it had congealed. She tingled. The proctor handed Gus the loose papers and he disposed of them behind the partition.

Gus said in a hushed voice, "You can have a seat over there. We grade the exam right now so you know immediately if you pass or fail."

Catherine was pensive. She also had to use the restroom. She said, "Do you have a ladies room I can use?"

Gus's said, "Out the door, turn left, and about midway down the hall on the left you will see the doors to the restrooms."

"Thank you."

At the door Mrs. Goodman handed Catherine her handbag and said, "Randall should be here shortly."

Catherine went into the bathroom. She splashed her face with cool water and shook her arms at her sides. The feeling was beginning to come back into them. She looked in the mirror. Ugh, my face looks pinched. She fished out some make-up from her bag and applied a fresh layer of color and a little more mascara.

Randall met her in the hallway with a huge smile. "My lady, I must congratulate you on your score. Eighty three!"

Catherine brought one hand to her twins and another to her mouth to muffle a gasp of delight. "Oh my god – you serious?" Her eyes searched his face.

"As a heart attack. And as relieved as I am, I can only imagine your feelings right about now." He bowed while stepping sideways, making a '*this way*' gesture, and said, "Come with me? Skip wants you to see the main office."

Catherine could not contain a delighted giggle. "Okay. Let's go." Thank god the worst is over, she thought, as she fell in stride with her queenly colleague.

CHAPTER TWENTY-TWO

Cars were moving in and out of lanes at speeds that made Catherine cringe and want to cover her eyes. Randall placed the blinker on near the exit for Commercial Boulevard and began to edge in that direction. This was the longer route of many possible ones, but Randall liked to take his time when he ran errands for Skip, plus he wanted to show Catherine the more scenic way. Catherine noticed that Commercial heading west from US1 was nice on the easterly edge of town, but worsened toward the I-95 interchange. Once they crossed the I-95 exchange, the buildings and terrain became pleasant again, but more industrial.

Catherine said, "I'm lost. I don't know how anybody gets around here."

Randall laughed and said, "Skip's office is just ahead on the left." He pointed to a multi-story black-glassed building labeled 'AT & T' up near the roof. "Right here at I-95 and Cypress Creek Boulevard."

Catherine surveyed the surrounding area with its variety of hotels, chain restaurants, and a few more office complexes stretched into the sky on the opposite side of Cypress Creek. She thought, now I see what they mean by the phrase, *concrete jungle.*

Randall eased the Bentley toward an iron gate and up to a card keyed security monitor. He slid his card onto the card reader that in turn opened the gate leading into the multi-story concrete parking garage. He parked on the first floor in the first slot near the door and said, "We're here."

Catherine extracted herself from the luxurious automobile and thought she could get used to this. Randall hit the key fob and the lights and alarm chimed, signaling the doors were locked.

Two large, ten foot high brass and glass doors separated the garage from the lobby. Randall held the door for Catherine to enter first. Inside was a makeshift guard station with computer banks and television monitors. A middle aged man who had been playing solitaire on his computer looked up and said, "Good Morning, Mr. Millhouse." He looked at his watch. "Oops, sorry – I meant good afternoon." Catherine looked around the lobby. It was dark green variegated marble, highly polished, slick, and clean. Sweet, she thought, much better than that grimy HoJo's.

Randall said, "And a good afternoon to you." He smiled at the man and indicated with a nod to Catherine to follow him. They walked over to the bank of five elevators and he punched the up button. Catherine noted and admired the casings, all polished brass.

The center elevator arrived first. Three people disembarked and then Randall and Catherine entered. The elevator interior was comprised of mirrors and chrome. Catherine saw television monitors mounted in each corner and realized the level of surveillance and security in the building. She had never been in a structure like this before, and was in awe. Randall pushed floor nine. This elevator rose like it was floating.

A few short seconds later a soft bell chimed and Randall said, "That's us."

Catherine looked at him, surprised. "So fast? I didn't even feel the elevator moving."

Randall chuckled at her small town girlishness. "Yes. Magic, my dear. Powered by clouds and wind currents."

The doors swept open in one fluid and seamless motion. Directly ahead was a huge etched glass sign for Commonwealth Financial. Again Randall allowed Catherine to exit the elevator first. In the hallway he deftly stepped around her and opened one of the two ornate frosted glass paned doors.

Catherine stepped in, leaving a sandal shaped depression in the plush, navy blue pile carpet. The aroma of fresh cut roses titillated her as she observed the leather tufted furniture on cherry wood bases with glass topped tables and huge ornamental rose floral arrangements accentuating the room, signifying the importance of the space. Top shelf professional interior decorators, Catherine thought, look at the attention to detail. Incredible. Off to the right, near the entry, stood a long, cherry wood reception desk with granite top. Two secretaries managed the phones and people filing in and out. Catherine noticed how courteous and professional they were. Gorgeous, too.

Randall stopped at the front desk to introduce Catherine to both of the receptionists. He gave a saccharine smile and said, "Ylette and Dominique, this is Catherine. She is from Key West where Skip plans to open his next office."

Catherine said, "Very nice to meet you both."

Ylette was about to speak but the ringing phones denied her conversation. Dominique hung up on a line, smiled and said, "Welcome, Catherine. If there is anything we can do for you please let us know."

A FedEx delivery man rushed in, picked up a stack of envelopes from Dominique, turned and trotted out saying, "Hi. Bye. See you tomorrow."

Dominique nodded, looked at Catherine, held her palms in the air and said, "Sorry – as you can see, we stay pretty busy 'round here. But again, so nice to meet you, and if there's anything you need, just let us know, okay?"

She's a sweetie, and such an interesting accent, Catherine thought, and said, "Thank you." Catherine glanced over the top of the reception desk and noticed there were easily sixty phone lines. *Unbelievable.* My office in Key West has two lines, one for the phone and one for the fax.

Randall tapped Catherine's shoulder and said, "Come with me. Skip's office is back here."

Lining the hall were pictures of the various trading boards around the world. Catherine looked at them in wonder. She turned to Randall and said, "Everyone is so nice."

"Skip likes it that way."

Off to their direct left was a conference area. Matthew was standing at an easel with a group of eager people sitting at the large round table. He spotted them as they walked past, waved and said, "Nice to see you again, Catherine."

She waved back. "What's he doing in there?"

"Teaching and training."

"Teaching and training for what?" Catherine said with genuine interest.

"The same thing he did for you. All of those people are studying for their series three licenses. Matt is the best we have at that."

Just in front of Skip's office was another, more intimate, waiting area. The door to it was ajar and Randall motioned for Catherine to stay a moment while he went inside. She leaned against the wall and waited, thinking. Quite remarkable.

Randall tapped the door and walked in, pushing the door nearly closed. Skip was on the phone. Randall took a seat across from the sprawling mahogany and granite desk and waited.

When Skip hung up, Randall said, "She's here." He paused and cracked his knuckles on both hands. "What next?"

"Take her into the bullpen." Skip tipped back in his leather office chair and glanced at his Rolex. "Introduce her around and then I'll decide what comes next. Make sure she meets Ismail, Eddie, Sam, and all the key players."

Randall always watched Skip with interest. He admired him immensely and wished Skip was gay. He stood and said, "Will do."

Skip followed Randall out the door and greeted Catherine with a warm embrace. He said, "Congratulations on the test, good work and I'm very impressed. Knew you had it in you. Randall is going to show you around, acquaint you with our operation and introduce you to all of our key people. I'll meet with you in a little while." He turned and walked back into his office, leaving Catherine thinking, How abrupt. A rather dismissive end to a long-time-no-see and congratulations greeting.

A man carrying a measuring tape, pin cushion with numerous needles, a single piece of chalk, and several swatches of fabric passed them in the hallway.

Catherine said to Randall, "Who is that?"

"Personal tailor. He's measuring Skip for a series of new suits and shirts. When it comes to image, Skip's motto is always dress for success.

"Well it would certainly seem he can afford it."

"Mm*hmm*."

Randall led Catherine to another room. He pointed with a *this way* gesture and said, "This room we fondly refer to as, *the bullpen.*

Catherine looked all around the vast space. Dramatically different than any of the other rooms, it housed more than 100 cubicles. Each cubicle was furnished with a desk, chair, and computer screen. Most of the faces were those of men. All of them were decked out in two or three piece suits with all the accessories of success. On one wall was nothing but clocks, each set to a different country from around the world. A wide screen monitor was tuned to CNBC coverage of the daily market movements and the ticker tapes. One wall was a whiteboard with names and tallies of trades for each person working in the room. Phones lines were ringing and sales people were talking so loud Catherine wondered how they could hear the people on the other end of the line.

Randall smiled to himself as he observed Catherine's obvious dismay. He winked and said, "Relax, darling, I know it can be a bit overwhelming for newcomers. You'll get used to it. Brokers feed on the energy of those around them and it creates a kind of frenzy. The competition level is extremely high and *that* … is the lifeline of this business." As they passed the whiteboard he added, "This is where we tally daily and weekly trades, which equal sales for all intensive purposes. Those names at the top of this list get a bonus of their choosing and the others have to work harder to catch them. If a person fails to perform within a certain time frame they are terminated."

Catherine cringed. Randall let it sink in.

"Okay, next. Come with me," he said with a tug on her elbow. He took Catherine to the trading office and introduced her to Ismail, Sammy, and Mark. Catherine noted this office was smaller than both Skip's and the main reception areas. The walls were solid halfway up and the top portion was glass. She thought, they look like the windows at drive up banks. Kind of bizarre.

Randall explained to Catherine the details of the operation going on. The trays beneath the glass enclosures were where traders placed their triplicate copies of investment trades along with account numbers. The two workmanlike clocks served to time the trades. As each trade was placed it went into a time clock to check against the time the order was filled. At regular intervals traders went back to collect and track their trades and report the numbers to their investors. He pointed to the center of the room where there were four desks with multiple phones on them.

He said, "Ismail, Sammy, and Mark personally call in each trade," and thought but kept to himself for now, if and when any real ones are made, "and they are responsible for the statements given out to traders and their clients each month."

Catherine nodded, looking at everything, silent. Randall mused to himself. *How is Skip planning on breaking her in? When does she learn that these guys are basically gatekeepers, fabricating the statements to reflect what actual trades should reflect. The vast majority of the time there are no real trades. She's so naïve and innocent. God, I hope he doesn't assign me the task of schooling her into the real world. I'd rather eat shit with a spoon.*

Randall led her up to Sammy's desk and said, "Sammy, I know you guys are never still enough to be interrupted, but I'd like to introduce you to Skip's new gal." He waved to Ismail, Mark also, and said, "Guys, please meet Catherine O'Reilly. Catherine, this is Sammy, Ismail, and Mark." Each man took turns greeting her with a welcome and a firm handshake.

Randall said, "Sammy here is the leader in this office. Mark is number two and he has two assistants, both women. And Ismail's family owns the CFM." Catherine took CFM to mean something important, but did not ask what it stood for since Randall didn't offer an explanation. She did not want to seem even more naive.

Sammy approached first. "If you want something done, I'm the guy to get it done right the first time." He formed a thin, wiry smile.

Catherine's eyes glimmered. *He's kind of handsome. All business.*

"Don't let him scare you," Randall said, "He's a real go getter and he can ride your ass if he thinks you've done something wrong. But he is a real good man, too."

"What are you trying to do – ruin my reputation or something?" Sammy said to Randall.

Smart. Intense. Not as showy as Skip, Catherine thought of Sammy, and said to him, "Whatever the case I hope we can be friends."

Mark walked up. "You can't be serious … this guy's got no friends." He slapped Sammy on the back.

Sammy flinched and said, "And you do?" He turned to Catherine and said, "Guess you passed the exam?"

"Yes, it felt touch and go when I was taking it, but I passed. With an eighty three."

"I'm glad we don't have to pass any exams to handle trading," Mark said with a smile.

The phone rang and Sammy stepped over to answer it. "I guess you two can carry on without me."

Gorgeous gray wavy hair, Catherine thought as she watched Sammy walk away.

"We better be moving on. Skip will wonder what's taking us so long," Randall said.

A gorgeous blonde girl in a short skirt and platform shoes walked in as Randall and Catherine were moving on. Sammy walked over and pinched her on the ass. She jumped and squealed, but her beguiling smile urged Sammy to do more.

Randall watched Catherine's reaction and then said, "That's Monika. She's one of Mark's assistants." He continued walking as he spoke. "As you can tell, Sammy loves the ladies, and they love him back."

As if to drive the point home, as Randall and Catherine walked out the door she overheard Sammy promising Monika there was plenty more where that came from, and her flirting back with a sarcastic, "Promises, promises. You never follow through on them."

"Don't keep tempting me."

Good heavens, Catherine thought as Randall led her to another office, passing the test was one good thing, but there are a million things going on here I still don't understand. The pace in this place – I hope in time I'll get comfortable with it.

"Next stop, A.J.'s office," Randall said, sporting a gay grin. "He has an office all to himself. Right here close to the trading room." They both popped their heads in the opened entry and Randall said, tapping the solid oak door, "Knock, knock. A.J.? I'll be right back, good sir. Do you mind entertaining Cat for a few minutes until I get back?"

Catherine checked out the room. "Smaller than Skip's, but still nice," she commented, a bit louder than she had intended.

"Nobody gets an office like Skip's. Come, have a seat." He had a headset on and slipped it down around his neck. "Cat – great to see you." He motioned to a plush leather chair opposite his desk. "So, Catherine, how do you find things here?"

"Is that a loaded question or what?" She giggled. "Just teasing."

"No, really ... what do you think?" He leaned back, bringing his palms together and his fingertips to his lips, curious, sincere.

Catherine sighed. "Well, to be honest? I've never seen *anything* like this place. Ever. Not even in the movies. Well, okay, maybe in the movies, but jee – I don't know *what* I expected, but this is *so* not it."

"Is that a bad thing or a good thing," A.J. asked and cocked his head to the left.

"I really have nothing to base my thoughts or feelings on. Learning the information for the test was one thing. But I have a confession to make." She pointed toward the bullpen. "I have no idea what is going on out there. That is, beyond what Randall has told me, nothing."

A.J. grunted and smiled at her somber tone. He reached across his desk to touch her hand. "Relax, my dear, it's a lot to absorb all at once. And I'm here to help. Ask me anything. Anything at all."

"What's really going on out there?" Catherine said with less enthusiasm than she felt. She pointed at the wall with all the electronics. "And what's all that stuff for?"

"My equipment is used for listening. I can listen to as many as four conversations at one time while recording another four that I'm not listening in on. It's pretty sophisticated, but part of keeping us in compliance with the laws instituted for trading."

"What's the big deal with that?" Nothing makes sense. I am utterly confused here.

"Well, a few years back we had a complaint from the NFA and the CFTC. Those are the governmental agencies that regulate us. We were told to record some of our brokers' conversations to ensure that they were all acting above board and within the law. When that lawsuit was dropped we just kept doing it because it made sense to know more about what each person says from time to time."

Randall walked in and said, "Just a couple of more places I want to show you, Cat, before we meet Skip. Are you joining us, A.J.?"

"Do I ever miss a meeting with the big guy?" He playfully rolled his eyes, lifted the headset back on top of his head and began playing with the dials on the equipment behind him.

Randall turned to Catherine with a wry smile. "His way of saying yes." He motioned her out. "Come. I'll show you the break room."

The room was on the way back out into the main corridor. Randall and Catherine stepped in. He said, "This room is self explanatory. Almost nobody uses it except for coffee, junk food, or soft drinks during the day."

Three vending machines stood lining one wall and the other was outfitted with a refrigerator, sink, counter, coffee maker, and a bank of upper and lower cabinets. In the center of the room were three hard plastic tables and chairs.

"Seems like you've thought ahead and attended to even the smallest details." It was a little drab and sad in Catherine's opinion, especially compared to the rest, but functional.

Over the loudspeaker came a page for Randall to please call the front desk. Randall picked up one of the phones in the break room and said, "Yea, what?" He paused to listen to Ylette on the other end of the line, then said, "Okay, okay, gotcha." He turned to Catherine, "A quick change of plans. We've got to meet Skip over at Gold's Gym."

"Gold's Gym?" She smiled and stared. After a few seconds she said, "You are joking, right?"

"No I'm deadly serious. Ylette said that was Skip's request."

Catherine frowned. "Why does he keep switching things up, ordering you all over here then over there … to continually keep you all on edge?"

Randall clasped his hands together and pursed his lips. "It's just Skip. None of us are put off or feel inconvenienced by anything he asks because he compensates us so well."

"So it's all about money?" Catherine shifted her weight from left to right.

He looked at her in disbelief. "Yea, sure. What else is there?"

They fell into an awkward silence for a few seconds. Randall clucked his tongue and said, "We better be going. Skip hates to wait."

They walked back into the noisy bullpen and crossed into the main reception room where Ylette and Dominique sat. Both ladies were busy on the phones. Randall waved to them both. As they were about to walk out the main door Matt called out from the conference room, "Randall wait." He sounded out of breath. "Can I ride with you two?"

"Sure, but we're leaving right now." Randall tapped his watch. Matt tended to be on the slow-to-get-moving side. Randall did not want to be late meeting Skip just because of his tardy co-worker.

"Okay, just one minute. Let me get my jacket." Matt disappeared into the conference room and within seconds came trotting out. He was winded when he caught up with Randall and Cat.

Ylette spoke up in her rich, exotic island accent. "You'll want to rush, I have alerted A.J., Matt, Ralph, and Sammy and they have left already."

Outside, Catherine said, "That Ylette – what a beautiful black woman. And her accent. Where is she from?"

Randall grunted and nodded in agreement. Matt whistled in the air and shook his head. Randall said, "Yes, stunning she is. Ylette is originally from Jamaica, she's another long term employee. Been here almost as long as Sammy, nearly thirteen years. Want to know more?"

"What else is there?"

"She's a single mother of four. Old man's a real lout. Never pays child support or anything else. She had a rough life, a tough go of it until she hooked up with Skip."

Catherine stopped with a hand in the air as a halt signal. "Hold it right there. Did you say four kids? With a body like that?"

Randall chuckled and motioned for her to continue walking. "Really, dear, we mustn't dally. Skip can be most impatient. Hates to be made to wait. And yes I said four, and yes even with a shape like – *that*." He made an hourglass motion with his hands and continued to explain. "Skip's been very good to Ylette. He helped put three of her four children through college at Nova Southeastern University. And for a secretary she gets paid, as in P. A. I. D. Fifty large a year, plus medical and dental benefits."

"Wow," Catherine said, "and the other girl – at the desk, Dominique, was that her name?"

"Yes. Dominique."

"She's almost as strikingly beautiful as Ylette. She from Jamaica too?"

Matt jumped into the conversation. "No, although to look at and listen to them you could certainly think that. Dominique is from Haiti. She's worked here five years now. Got an idiot mechanic for a husband. Real low life. Says she's saving her money for a divorce."

Catherine said, "Oh, sorry to hear that. Marriage is so … permanent. Scares me, tell the truth. So many jerk-offs that act all nice until they got you hitched to 'em and then you get the shitty side of them to deal with." She thought better about continuing to rant. "Sorry, didn't mean to go off like that. Well, at least she shouldn't have to wait too long to dump him, making that kind of money."

Matt scratched his shoulder and said, "Ah, well, as the number two secretary she doesn't pull down the same dough as Ylette; but still she gets excellent pay. I think around thirty five k a year. Plus all the bennies, of course."

Randall looked at Matt and said, "So, how's it going?"

"Huh?"

Randall jerked a thumb back over his shoulder. "The class. How's it going?"

"Oh that." He bunched his mouth and nodded a few times. "Pretty good so far. There may be a few who can't cut it, but overall they'll be okay."

Catherine walked along, listening. From out of the men's room popped Mark and Monika. Both were straightening their attire. How obvious, Catherine thought. Having a little restroom romp were we? As they turned and saw Matt, Randall, and Catherine, they both reddened and walked the opposite way.

At the elevator banks Matt pushed the down key and waited. With Mark and Monika safely out of earshot, Matt said with a double wink, "Now I wonder what they could have possibly been doing?"

Randall snickered. "Hardly rocket science. You're joking of course. No? Haven't you heard the latest office girl's gossip, that Mark has a giant schlong?"

"No – little Mark has a giant … what did you call it, a schlong?" Matt broke into hysterical, knee-slapping laughter.

Catherine could not believe what she was seeing and hearing. *I've just met these people and already receiving a little too much information.*

Fuck breaks in the John, and now locker room talk right in front of me. Spare me, fellas.

Matt's sides were hurting by the time the elevator rang. Between guffaws and gasps he managed to say to Randall, "Well it makes sense that *you* might know. Maybe even from personal experience or something?" He winked at Catherine with an expression that said, *you know Randall's gay, right?*" A couple small die-down chuckles later he said, "Hoo-boy. This office is a regular Peyton Place."

Randall said with extra sauce in his voice and a faggot hand gesture, "No, silly. I would have tapped that a long time ago if it was possible. Everyone knows Mark digs chicks and not dicks." He swished and strutted a little for extra effect.

Catherine rolled her eyes skyward and shook her head. Too. Much. In. Formation.

The elevator bonged and the doors swept apart. They stepped in and Randall fingered the lobby button. Matt looked into the mirrored walls, pulled a toothpick out of his shirt pocket, picked a small piece of something from his perfect teeth, and smoothed his tousled hair.

At the parking garage Matt said, "Skip took the Bentley. I guess we better take my ride."

Randall said, "Fine with me. Yours is nicer than mine."

CHAPTER TWENTY-THREE

Skip, who had been following a circuit court case with interest, because it related to his business, was speaking to A.J. on the phone. "Have you been following the Judge Sonia Sotomayer case against Merrill?"

"Yes, she is something."

"Interesting case as it does pertain to us."

"It sure is," A.J. said, "and yes it does."

"She ruled for the defendants. That's not good news for us."

"You know they're going to appeal it."

"Yes, yes …" Skip said, tapping his fingers on his desk, "… and I hope it is overturned."

"Ditto."

The second line was blinking on his desk phone. Skip said, "Got another call A.J. We'll catch up more later. If you happen to hear anything more about this case let me know aysap."

"Will do, boss," A.J. said before hanging up.

"Sammy here," Skip heard as he switched the line over.

"Sammy how are we doing? Wasn't this supposed to be a pretty big week?"

"Hold on, let me check my clipboard. Okay, looks like we took in about one million dollars, and that's just today."

"Great news, Sam. What's happening next?"

"Coming soon we expect wire transfers for another two and a half million and by week's end we should have ten million in new accounts."

"Just what I like to hear." Skip thought for a minute and then said, "Let's send two million to me in the Bahamas. Send five million to our account in Grand Cayman and keep the remainder for salaries and operating expenses at your house."

"Roger that," Sammy said, knowing his boss always used 'your house' as code for Skip's main operation.

"Any word from Buckhead?"

"Wait … did you hear that, Skip?"

"The line – it's clicking."

"Oh, that. Yea, it's probably A.J.," Skip said, and thought, better follow up with A.J. just to be sure. He cleared his throat and said, "So – where were we?"

"In Buckhead."

"Right … as you were saying?"

Skip could hear Sammy easing back in his chair. "Man, Deron and Gary are cleaning up. They have convinced several of the Falcons to invest with us and those guys are so loaded they promised to send no less than a million each."

"Great," Skip said, and followed that with a whistle. "How soon do we expect that to happen?"

"Anytime now."

"Keep me posted, Sammy. Gotta go for now." Skip hung up.

The Fed's on the listening end exchanged knowing glances. Merv said, "This guy is clever. Notice how he always stops short of telling us exactly what we want to know? We know nothing about how he conducts his scam."

Stan said, "Yea. It's frustrating. This case is still a big zip where the funds are concerned. If only we could only get someone on the inside."

Merv looked thoughtful. "You know, Stan, if we could find out *exactly* where he holds *all* the funds it might give us some insight as to what he is doing with them. I mean, we just heard in general terms where he's sending several million from one operation and all, but what was that 'your house' business? My bet is that's code for something important. What da-ya think?"

Stan grunted. "Look – if I had all the answers I sure as hell wouldn't be here with you."

Merv rolled his eyes at Stan's insolence. "I thought Ray was going to try to get inside?"

Stan nodded. "He is, but we can't be certain Skip is going to take his bait."

"Marek told Ray to sort of dummy up, which is so not his forte. I hope he can pull it off. That could be the break we've needed."

***

Catherine and Nick had been seeing each other as they could, but her life under Skip's new business was demanding and it was difficult to get much personal time. Nick understood and told her his schedule was somewhat flexible. She hoped that once the interviews were done she might be able to take a couple of days and have fun with him.

Shamus had called Catherine a couple of times, but she was always coming or going with Matt and A.J. He was frustrated, but loved her enough to wait a while longer to see how things turned out. Sports and loose women had kept him relatively busy, but he missed his interactions with Catherine.

Twenty people had called about the positions advertised. Catherine, Matt, And A.J. had tentatively scheduled them at half hour intervals from Thursday through Sunday of the coming weekend. They had kept a close watch on the impending arrival of Tropical Depression Denis. Earlier in the month, the July storm had formed just off the coast of Cuba and appeared to be heading directly for Florida with 35 mile per hour winds and the potential to reach hurricane strength. More recent weather watches had indicated it may abate in strength and do nothing more than create a little rain and light wind in the Keys. They hoped so, not wanting to have to reschedule and hold up the appointment and hiring process.

Matt dialed Skip to tell him how things have shaped up.

"Hi, Matt. How's it going?"

"Well, we've got twenty people scheduled thus far. As is human nature, some of those may be no shows, but we have no way of knowing that until the time comes."

"Yes, the nature of the beast. Good job."

"When do you think you will come down?"

Skip looked at his watch. "Let's see, today is Wednesday. I'm still in Nassau, but I can reschedule my flight to drop me in Key West and be there in time for the interviews in the early portion of the afternoon."

"Should I tell A.J. and Cat?"

"Yes. Anything else?"

"Just keep a watch on the storm, Skip. If Denis continues to slow and weaken we're all good to go. Otherwise we'll have to postpone and reschedule and your early return would be unnecessary."

"Right. Good point, will do. We'll stay in close contact on how it develops. Drop back and punt if need be."

Matt could hear steel drums in the background. He had a small twinge of jealousy. A.J. and I have now worked non-stop for over three weeks. I'm beat and really could use a break. Bring it up to Skip? No – ain't got the balls for that right now. Suck it up.

"Roger, boss. Other than that, everything is status quo."

"Good. I'll see you all tomorrow then, barring any resurgence in the storm's strength." Skip hung up. Matt went to tell A.J. and Cat what the plan was.

In the few days they had been working on setting up interviews, Randall had put together the office. A dozen mahogany desks with black leather chairs were stacked in neat rows in suites 201 and 203. In the right hand corner of suite 203 was a smaller desk that would accommodate their new receptionist. Scandy Systems, a company that dealt in electronic trading systems, had been busy wiring and installing the new FOREX/GLOBEX trading system. Three television monitors were placed at regular intervals along the walls to portray the trades around the world in real time. Sixteen t-100 lines had been installed to handle the calls. A small desk safe was placed in the second drawer of the receptionist's desk along with a clock that marked the trade times on trade slips as they come in. Everything looked official and worked the same as a real commodity trading operation would.

It looked professional and legit to Catherine, who still had no clue.

CHAPTER TWENTY-FOUR

Wednesday evening, Catherine's cell phone rang. Before she could say hello, Nick said, "Hello, sexy."
She perked up. That's Nick. I'd recognize that sexy voice anywhere. She smiled into the phone. "Hello yourself."
"Hey just in case you aren't sure who is calling, it's Nick."
"Oh, Silly." Catherine giggled. "I knew it was you. Great to hear from you. How's Ft. Lauderdale?"
"Well, I've got a bit of a surprise for you." He waited for her reaction, but got none. "Some buddies and I are coming to the Keys for a long weekend. There is some bartender contest at the Schooner Wharf and we want to support our team."
"Super," she said, and she meant it, too. Thinking ahead, she said, "I'm busy with interviews this weekend. Oh …" her voice got excited, "… I passed my exam! But now I'm in the process of helping Skip get his business up and running. Matt, A.J. and I have scheduled people at half hour intervals for most of this weekend, but maybe I can get away to meet you around happy hour one of those evenings." I hope I can anyway, she thought, but from what I'm finding out about Skip that may not become a reality.
"Great news about the exam. Congrats!"
She giggled again. "Thank you."
"Well, try your best. I'd love to see you and introduce you to some of our gang."
"I will. Thanks for understanding." They said goodbye and hung up.
Catherine let her mind wander and play. God I want to see that man this weekend. See him, hell … I want that hunk in my bed again.

***

Thursday morning, Matt, A.J., and Catherine were gathered at the new office in Truman Annex waiting for their first candidate to arrive.
Skip called just as the first interviewee arrived. Matt placed him on the speaker phone and said, "Hi, Boss – got you on speaker phone so Cat and A.J. can hear."
"Good. Hi everyone, hey, sorry I'm running late – had a delayed flight this morning. Just go ahead and get started, I'll be there as soon as I can."
Matt said, "Which of us should take the lead in the interview process?"

Skip considered Matt's question and said, "I'd like all of you to participate. That will provide us with a more balanced perspective. Okay? A.J., you take the lead since you have been with me the longest." Skip clicked his fingers. "Matt, you are the trainer so your input is crucial here. I also appreciate your keen ability to size people up. Catherine, you are going to be placed in the OJT category. I hope you can learn fast. Oops, here's my cab. Gotta go."

The line went dead.

A short, thin girl with mousey blonde hair was the first to be interviewed. A.J. politely said, "What is your name?"

"Toye" She said in a soft voice, her head bowed as if in reverence.

"Toye what?" said Matt, observing she avoided eye contact.

She looked pained and said, "Ah – Toye Darden."

"Okay. Thank you. What kind of experience do you have, Toye?" A.J. said, also noticing she looked around the room rather than directly at the person who was talking to her. He also thought she was kind of cute. Love the green eyes.

"Ah----well, I don't have any experience in the field you are hiring in, but I work at the Casa Marina resort as a waitress on the beach three afternoons per week."

Matt said, "What makes you believe you would be well suited for this job?"

Toye looked nervous – as though she might cry at any moment. "I'm interested in finance and I am a quick learner."

After fifteen minutes of conversation with Toye, Matt was uncertain that she had what it takes. I haven't seen *the eye of the tiger*, he thought, and ended the interview by saying, "Thank you. We will be in touch." When she was out the door he turned to A.J. and said, "Well?" A quick glance to Cat, "Well?"

A.J. said, "Look, I know she was extremely timid and never even looked us once in the eye, but if I was making the decisions I may be willing to give her a shot, depending on how the other candidates turn out. You know this is Key Weird. Actually, she may be able to be trained or coached to come out of the gate as a pretty good broker." Besides, he thought, *she's a looker.*

Catherine asked, "What criteria are you using to gauge what kind of person fits your profile."

"Good question. A.J., do you want to respond or should I?"

A.J. tried to soft pedal his response. He said, "I want people who are hungry for money, for one thing. Skip values that hunger almost above all else. And, someone who is good on the telephone. But those are not the only things that make a good broker."

The next two people interviewed were definite no's. One looked like he had just come off a two month bender even though he said he was gainfully employed as a plumber's assistant for a local company and was vaguely familiar to Catherine. The other was one step above a common street bum living in the bed of his truck and sleeping in parking lots. He claimed he was a busboy for Trader Jack's and that he wanted to move ahead in life. Nothing stood out about either of them as the slightest bit remarkable.

Number four was a burly man of six feet four inches with shiny, raven black hair that flowed just past his chin. His chiseled face was the color of burnished copper. His beak-like, trademark Cherokee nose was enhanced by his piercing dark, almond shaped, intelligent, and inquisitive eyes. He was the first person who had taken care to dress for the interview. Going on gut instincts, Matt's initial assessment was he was a strong possibility.

Matt said, "Your name is R.J. Goldeneye?" He pointed at the paperwork. "Is that right? Not a misprint?"

"Yes, that's correct. I am Running Jackal Goldeneye, from the Cherokee Nation." His voice was steady and gentle, but there was a trace of discontent resonating just below the surface.

"That's quite a mouth full." Matt smiled.

"Yes. I suppose so. You can call me R.J." He was confident.

"Pleased to meet you, R.J." Matt looked over at A.J. trying to read his face, then back at R.J. "Can you tell us what experience you have that may qualify you for a job with us?"

Mr. Goldeneye said, "I've been in sales, mostly. I sold rhino guard to contractors and automobile manufacturers after hurricane Andrew back in 1993. That job lasted until 1997 when the insurance money dried up. I was instrumental in setting up ATM's on the reservation by acting as facilitator between the banks and the office of the Chief. I've worked in the casinos in a variety of capacities. I sat on the advisory board for the last decade for the Cherokee Nation. I am confident that I can sell just about anything." He folded his arms and waited for a reply to his self-promotion, thinking it best to leave out the part about selling pot to his brothers on the reservation. I only do that to subsidize my own habit of toking on the peace pipe. And besides, it's none of their business. As long as it's on the reservation the local or state police have no jurisdiction.

A.J., who had been jotting down some notes, looked up and said, "Interesting. Do you know what commodities are?"

"Yes, I do. The Cherokee Nation works with various brokerage houses in the placement of investment opportunities for our casino profits. It's crucial that we turn a profit even on our profits."

"Don't you guys also have casinos?"

"Yes, we've got it all. Small benefit for all of the land we lost."

"Which brokerage firms do you currently do business with?"

"I can't really go into specifics. We've got long histories and good, steady business relationships."

"Mostly the majors? Or any smaller boutique firms?"

"As I said before, I won't divulge that information."

Matt's mental process was churning. R.J. was proving to be a deft opponent. *He is a worthy player. I enjoy sparring with him. And we might find a way to get R.J. to take a good chunk of those large casino profits – gotta be in the millions, if not billions, and invest them with us.*

A.J., not quite as deceptively clever as Matt, had not yet come to that monetary conclusion. He said, "I like you, Mr. Goldeneye, because you are a well spoken young man who appears to have goals. And it doesn't hurt that you also have some experience in areas relevant to our business."

Matt said, "I agree."

A.J. said, "Tell you what, R.J., we're going to give you a job."

"Thank you. I welcome this opportunity," R.J. said with confidence.

Matt looked surprised that A.J. had done that without consulting him, but if A.J. had not offered him the job, he had planned to himself.

A.J. said, "Is this the number we can reach you at?" He held up the info sheet on R.J. and pointed at the number.

"Yes, you can get me there. That is my cell phone, but you can also get me via e-mail and that address is goldeneye at cherokeenation dot net."

"Goldeneye at cherokeenation dot net," A.J. said, writing it down. He got up and shook R.J.'s hand. "Welcome aboard."

"Thank you, sir. I promise I will exceed your expectations."

When R.J. was down the hall and out of ear shot, Matt said, "Wow, do you believe that? He is an honest to goodness Indian like in the *woo woo* kind." Matt pressed his hand to his mouth and made a loud Native American call.

Catherine did not understand what the big deal about this Native American was. *Never had one as a sexual partner though,* she thought, *and I've heard some pretty astonishing things about them from Connie and Lori. Jesus, Catherine, stop with the banal thinking and get back on point.*

Number five on the list was Ray. Catherine had never seen him in anything except swimming attire. For a moment she thought he was another guy, the way he was dressed – sharp, with blue golf shirt, tan slacks and matching brown belt and sandals. But the fit, yet not overly muscular, physique, and those darling topaz sunset eyes gave him away.

Again Matt took the lead and said, "Welcome, Ray. Can you tell us something about yourself? Catherine tells us that you see her friend Connie from the ice cream shop, but what is there about Ray that's pertinent to this business?"

Ray had known from Catherine that Matt was the trainer for Skip's operations, so he had decided to tread easily and not play all of his cards at once. He said with a steady, unwavering gaze, "I'm a commodity pool operator of sorts. I have fifteen buddies who I invest for and we've managed to do pretty respectable so far. So I guess I understand the basic game."

Matt was wary, A.J. could sense, but also impressed.

A.J. said, "Fifteen is just under the limit for licensure, but I guess you already knew that."

"Yes."

"What do you trade?" Matt said, curious to know at what level he operated.

"Mostly S & P's, but if I see some opportunity in any other industry I may jump in there to test the water. We don't do anything long term. I mostly day trade----easy in, easy out."

"Are you trading options or futures?"

"Futures."

"Ever trade on FOREX or GLOBEX?"

"Yea – depends. I've played all the markets at one time or another."

This Ray guy is cool, Matt thought, rubbing his chin. Perhaps too cool. But I can't really blow him off, either. He leaned forward and said, "Calls? Puts? Straddles?"

Ray was steady, tapping his fingertips together a few times. "As necessary."

"How much do you invest?"

"We're mostly penny ante stuff." Ray was being purposefully vague, but neither Matt nor A.J. was adept enough to get him to be explicit.

Matt leaned back, raised an eyebrow. "Ever do the currencies?"

Ray nodded. "Sure. We did the Yen when the Asian markets were tumbling and looking for support."

"Smart move," Matt said, and thought, *damn smart*. "On the right side of that trade there was serious money to be made."

A.J. had heard enough. He liked Ray, but like Matt, he was also wary of anyone who knew too much. He said, "Okay, Ray. We're going to hire you, but you will need to pass the series three exam and also be able to follow instructions. Fair enough?"

Ray squirmed internally. This was a test of his mettle and commitment. I hate being treated like some underling or subordinate, especially by these thugs. But buck up, buddy, because breaking this requires it. He put on a bright smile and said, "Sure."

A.J. consulted Ray's information sheet and verified all of his contact information before letting him go. "We'll be in touch as soon as we're sure when the classes begin."

Ray and Skip passed in the hall. Neither said anything more than hello, but Ray sized Skip up.

Skip came into the office, looked around, and said, "This looks nice. Randall did a great job. I don't suppose either of you helped him?" He pointed over his shoulder and said, "Was he one of our interviewees?"

A.J. chimed in ahead of Matt. "Yes, he was and we hired him."

"Have you hired anyone else?"

A.J. looked at Matt and then said, "Yes, two others."

Matt looked confused. "Two?"

"Yes, two, Matt. Recall Toye and Goldeneye?"

Matt shook his head. "Toye was weak."

Skip looked at A.J. "Was she?"

"Well sort of, but I think we can bring her along. She has potential."

"Okay, I'm going to trust you on that one. You okay with that, Matt?"

Matt paused, looking down. He bunched his lips, lifted his face with a nod and said, "I guess, but she was sooo mousy."

Skip looked over at A.J. and winked. "Who is this Goldeneye fellow? What a strange name."

"He's the best one so far." Matt rubbed his hands together in excitement. "He's an honest to goodness Indian."

"Me, I thought Ray was the best so far," A.J. said.

Skip was still looking at Matt. "Come again? What kind of Indian?"

"Native American. You know, like Pocahontas."

"Really?" Skip's eyes sparkled. Interesting, he thought, I've never had a Native American in my employ before. "What tribe is he with?"

Matt was beaming, his voice chipper. "The Cherokee Nation. You know they have all of those Planet Hollywood casinos. And anywhere there are casinos there's a lot of money waiting to be taken by us. He also told us – even without our asking, the tribe invests with outside brokers. Man, if we could tap some of that it could be worth millions, maybe billions."

Catherine stayed silent, observing. This talk about casinos and actual investing was way over her head.

Number six on the docket was Tracey Bush. A short and squat woman of forty one, as she shuffled into the room Skip had to stifle a chuckle before he could speak. Good grief what a getup, he thought, observing her multi-colored pantsuit making her appear wider than she already was. And those mammoth wire rim glasses, didn't they go out in the '80s? He put on a professional demeanor, consulted the list of interviewees and said, "Welcome, you must be Ms. Bush?"

"Thank you. And yes, that's me," She said.

Skip was caught off guard by her pleasant, lyrical voice. Doesn't fit with the fat and dumpy look. His jaw dropped open. He closed it quick and continued. "Can you tell us something about yourself?"

Again the most musical voice Skip had ever heard responded. She said, "I was in radio for twenty years. And I plan to continue to do radio, but only two days a week."

Skip looked sincerely interested. "Have you had any sales experience?"

Tracy shook her head. "Mmm, no."

Skip wagged a hand. "Well, that may not matter." He looked back at A.J. and Matt and said, "Are you thinking what I am thinking?"

Both shook their heads in the affirmative.

Love hearing her speak, Skip thought, if I could only blot out her body she'd be a perfect creature, but that's not possible face to face. Fortunately for her and me, this business is conducted at least 98% on the phone. Her voice alone will attract a record number of investors. He leaned back, clasped his hands behind his head, thought for a second, then leaned forward with a hand extended and said, "We will hire you."

She was so pleased she nearly jumped out of her seat. Her eyes dampened and she blotted them with her silken kerchief. "Oh, thank you. I could just give you a hug." She regained her self control. "When do we begin?"

A.J. said, "Most likely next week sometime, but if this information on your contact sheet is correct we will contact you and tell you exactly when, okay?"

"That will be super." She strolled out of the room and down the hall.

Skip said, "Could you believe her voice?"

Matt said in a mocking tone, "Could you believe her name?"

A.J. ignored Matt and said, "No. It sure didn't sound like it should come from *that* body."

"I know," Skip said. "She is going to be great. Does that make four or five?"

Matt looked at his tally and said, "We've got Toye." He frowned. "And Goldeneye, Ray, and now Tracey ... so that's four."

A.J. said, "We're a third of the way there."

Skip said, "Who's next?"

"I rightly suppose that'd be me, mate," a man said as he walked through the door. He looked around and said in a British lilt, "The name's Chris. What's doin'?" He held a long switchblade in his left hand and flicked the blade in and out as he spoke.

Catherine thought, what a whack job. Get a load of those black Army boots and the shaved head. And what's with that switchblade?

A.J. was not deterred by Chris's unorthodox appearance. He said, looking down at his clipboard, "Chris Angleton, I presume."

"That would be me, old chap. And you are?" The blade continued to flick in and out as if it was a life form of its own.

Skip walked between them and said, "I'm Mr. Horowitz, the boss." He extended his hand.

With his right hand Chris shook hands with Skip, then A.J. and then Matt. Catherine kept to the background and watched.

Skip began the interview. "Chris, have a seat. Can you tell us a little bit about yourself?"

Chris sat and began to brush the open blade back and forth on his tan chinos as he spoke. The blade glimmered in the stark lights of the office. "What do you want to know?" His dark eyes became slits.

Menacing, Catherine thought.

Interesting, Skip thought, I wonder what makes this guy tick. He said with an even tone, "Well, Chris – what kind of experience do you have?"

"I am a captain on the Fury."

Skip thought, Fury ... what is that? I can't quite place it, and then said, "Oh – that catamaran, right?"

"Aye."

"How long have you been doing that?"

"For about four years now. Ever since I came here from England."

"Ever done sales before?"

"Well, my parents had a chandlery back in Brighton. I worked there as a young chap."

Skip made a note, then looked up. "I see. Are you working here legally?"

Chris eyed him. "Yes."

"Resident, alien, or otherwise?"

"I'm married to an American. So I can legally use both citizenships," Chris said, his tone rising in harshness along with his dander.

Skip raised a hand, face level, meaning it to be a calming action. "Okay, just checking. You have to pass a federal exam and in order to do that you've got to be a citizen."

"No worries there, old chap." Chris eased back in his chair, the perceived threat having passed.

Skip liked his voice. Not sure why, but I have a hunch it would be a strong selling point if Chris can manage to pass the exam. "Okay, Chris – you're hired. I am giving you a golden shot."

Chris' face lit up with a broad smile. He stood, opened his knife fully and tossed it blade first into the desk top where it stuck with a loud thunk. Leaning forward to rest both hands flanking both sides of the dagger and looking Skip squarely in the eyes, he said, "Solid. When do I start, eh, mate?"

Direct, forceful, uninhibited, Skip thought, I like him. "Probably mid-week. Does that work for you?"

"Bloody good, then." Chris yanked his knife out of the desktop, flipped it closed, then open again, and walked out the room tossing it in the air and catching it with practiced skill.

Matt was at a loss for why Skip would hire this guy and he did not try to hide his dismay. "Skip – are you losing your mind? That guy reminds me of a psycho. Did you notice the way he was fingering that knife? And then he just tossed it into our desk like it was nothing."

Skip's face flared with anger for a second, then relaxed. He shut Matt up with a raised hand in a 'stop right there' signal, and meditated for a calming and centering moment. Father Zeke had taught him this when he had been a guest in the big house back in New Jersey and he had never forgotten it. He breathed out and said, "Matt … it takes all kinds, and just like the fat frump with the lyrical voice, this man has the gift of the English lilt." He patted Matt's shoulder. "Trust me. People, especially investors, are going to love that."

A.J. looked at the appointment schedule, then the clock, and said, "That's it for the day."

Matt said, "Thank God. I was about to slit my wrists."

Skip let Matt's sarcasm roll off, turned to Catherine and said, "Catherine, how did you feel about today?"

"Honestly, I don't know how to feel. All of this is still so new to me."

"Why don't you let me explain some of the finer points of this business to you before we all call it a day."

There was no acceptable way Catherine could get out of it, so she listened to Skip drone on and on for the next hour and a half until she had a raging, skull shattering headache.

CHAPTER TWENTY-FIVE

Friday, after five interviews, they had managed to hire two more brokers. Both were males. The one interview left was with a female. Skip was thinking over the hires as the woman was being asked into the room, reading over their paperwork and his notes.

Lance Lemming, close to fifty. Looks to me like a dead ringer for Jimmy Johnson, the NFL coach, if you took his frame and added an extra thirty pounds, Skip thought. Easygoing mannerisms. He's spent a number of years working for K-Mart in the capacity of merchandiser. He's been around, living and working in thirty of the fifty states including Puerto Rico and, Jesus – been married five times. His latest wife – good grief, this is a bit too much information – was verbally abusive, but smart, working as a legal secretary for the prestigious Spotswood, Spotswood, and Spotswood law firm in Key West. Candid guy, I kind of like him. This Lance appears open in admitting he's trying to decide what direction to move career wise. Also I see he's got some good assets and investments and owns his own home up a canal on Sugarloaf Key.

Skip thought about the other hire that day. A small man, name of Eugene Rappaport, with an interestingly unpleasant odor that nobody could quite pinpoint. Friends call him Gene. Currently working as a pharmacy assistant at the local Walgreens that had just been bought out by CVS, he was concerned he might lose his job. More than concerned, Skip remembered, Gene had been told that he *was* going to be cut. He lives in a tiny hovel of an apartment off Frances street near the cemetery and rides a scooter. In many ways he seems haunted or perhaps scared, but otherwise capable and hard working. Skip felt good about having mercy on him and hiring him.

The last interviewee walked in and, at Skip's request after introductions, had a seat across from him. Kayla Kevlar, Skip thought, most interesting name. Looks to be of Turkish origin. And what a knockout. Less than thirty years old, smoky completion and alluring, dark, wide set eyes with full round lips. Skip's head, both heads in fact, tingled with delight as she nestled her rump into the leather seat and leaned forward enough to tantalize Skip with her deep, wide, and overstuffed cleavage. God, those are the largest breasts anyone in this company has ever seen and a rear end to match. And she flaunts both. She's learned how to use her assets to achieve and possess whatever her heart desires. She's a trained professional, bet on it. Sweet nectar, and I'm going to have a taste of that. Tonight.

Skip shook his head free of his sexual conquest plans and said, "What type of experience do you have that might make you suitable for this job?" Wish I could ask her how many positions she's experienced in screwing in, but stick to business. For now. Sweet Jesus, I've got to get her alone and tear that tiny baby doll dress off of her.

Kayla gave a sexy coo and stood in an ostensible display of needing to straighten her clothes. "Sorry," she said, "need to get more comfy." She smoothed her dress with a caress over her ample thighs, and bent at the waist to tie her calf-high carpenter's style boots. Skip and the guys got the full view of her voluptuous behind and noticed she was wearing no panties. She knew they were watching and she liked it.

The male attention turns her on and gets her motor running, Catherine thought. Bitch, I hate her already. I'll be goddamned if he hires this little frump. She'd be some seriously stiff competition for the affections of Skip.

Kayla ended her staged showing off of sexual assets, sat, and said, "Actually – I am a trained veterinarian by schooling." She toyed with her waist length hair, tossing it over her shoulders so it flowed out across her back. *Damn sexy.* She knew it, all the guys thought it. "I currently work at the Up Stairs Bar on Duval Street." She sucked on her thumb with a pucker and kissy noise. "You know where that is?"

She's reeling them in, Catherine knew. Look at Matt and A.J. – little puppy dogs, lapping her up like bowl of doggie treats. Disgusting.

Matt and A.J. glanced at each other with a knowing look. They had been to the Up Stairs Bar numerous times and had somehow missed seeing the lovely Kayla perform. With a silent wink and nod to each other they vowed they would not make that mistake ever again.

Skip had frozen, mesmerized by her every movement. He snapped out of it and said, "That is perhaps the best sales experience that anyone could ever get. And I mean it." He looked around at the rest of his team, made up his mind, and smiled at Kayla. "I've seen, I mean heard enough. You're on board. Got the job."

Kayla smiled wide, brought a forefinger up to rub across her lower teeth and said with a wink, "Well, thank you, boss man. I appreciate that very much. How can I ever repay you?" She sat up straight with a sly grin, arching her back to prop her rack up and into Skip's full attention.

Catherine could see where this was going and she was getting sick to her stomach. Matt and A.J. are eating this shit like it's candy. And look at Skip. He's buying in with a million.

Skip grinned back at Kayla, leaned forward and said, "Well there is one thing you could do for me."

Kayla purred, "What do you have in mind?" Her dark eyes twinkled as she licked her full lips, a luscious enticement to Skip.

"Have dinner with me?"

Matt and A.J. looked like someone had knocked the wind out of them. Catherine looked away, considering homicide with regard to a certain flagrant coquette and now co-worker, and her prolific whore of a boss.

"What time?" Kayla tossed her dark tresses backward and again and arched her nimble back.

Skip was fighting a trance. "How about six thirty?"

"Fine. Where?" She crossed and uncrossed her legs.

Skip followed every movement and traced the lines of her entire body with his mind. I have to have her. I will have her. I'll savor her like a fine glass of sherry. "Do you want to meet at Louie's Backyard?"

She considered for a moment. Can't tell him about Steve, my husband in our 'seemingly' happy marriage, or our ten year old son, or the fact that the swingers lodge bed and breakfast we run is not too far from Louie's Backyard. What if I get seen? Oh, take a chance. It'll probably be all right. Besides, this guy is wicked good looking, and making him squeal real good will lock in my chances for advancement here.

She said, "That's just fine."

Kayla left. Skip had a satisfied smile as he dismissed everyone early and called it a day. He intended to take his time getting ready for his dinner engagement.

***

Catherine called Connie on her way home from the office to tell her how disgusted she was with the whole Kayla thing. Connie was sympathetic, but realistic, and told Catherine to *let sleeping whores lie*.

Skip and Kayla had a pleasant romantic dinner overlooking the Atlantic Ocean at Louie's Backyard. When the afternoon sun gave way to the striated and colorful sky, dipping into the horizon like a giant orange ball, they headed to Skip's suite. There they had an evening of raw, uninhibited, and passionate sexual delight, the likes of which to Skip was sexually enlightening. She had teased him, pleased him, and left him wanting for more. Kayla had a detached approach to sex. For her it was nothing more than sport, and a game at which she was a skilled instructor.

Skip had never had a woman who had done to him the things she did, they ways she explored his body and sexuality were unparalleled. Part of him wanted to possess her, maybe not for a lifetime, but for a while so he could experience more. The other part was still tied to Frederika and the girls, at least for the time being. Somewhere after three a.m., while he was in a dreamy and sexually overspent slumber, she slipped silently from his room. When the sun began peeping through the curtains in the morning, he was sorry she was no longer there.

CHAPTER TWENTY-SIX

Eight down and four or so to go. Saturday's interviews only netted them one person, and that one was a remote possibility. The morning had begun with fresh steaming cups of Starbuck's coffee and toasted bagels with cream cheese and lox, courtesy of Randall, who had the foresight to think ahead, and to whom everyone was most thankful.

Everyone sat waiting, the clock ticking. Finally Randall said, "Guess we can officially count the first two as no shows."

"I'll say," Catherine said, bored and yawning.

The next two interviewees came and went with not so much as a check mark next to their names.

"Today may be a bust," Matt said, disappointed.

"Are we running out of possibilities?" Skip said.

"Sort of," A.J. said, looking over some paperwork, "but we still have tomorrow and it's a full day. Some people were working today and therefore we had to schedule some for Sunday too."

Catherine thought, Bust. More than a bust. A complete and utter zero.

"Three more are scheduled," Matt said with a meager amount of hope.

In walked the third to the last prospect for the day. "Hi. Am I in the right place?"

"What place are you looking for?" Matt said.

This one looks like an elf, Catherine thought, as she watched him hobble in on his too-small–for-his-frame feet.

Skip was mildly amused.

"I was looking for the new business that was seeking sales persons." His eyes seem more intelligent than his overall looks would indicate, Catherine thought.

"Then you've come to the right place. What's your name," A.J. asked as he looked down at his clipboard.

"Clem. Clem Dekons."

"Why don't you take a seat, Clem," Skip said.

Clem sat. Catherine noticed he was barely as tall as the back of the chair.

"Thank you. Ahm, what kind of sales will you be doing," Clem asked as his unkempt orangey red beard twitched with his facial gestures.

Skip thought, I'd better take the lead or he may think he is the one doing the interview. Jump in now. ""Do you have any experience in sales?"

"Why, yes I do. I work as a bartender for Salute, an Italian restaurant on the beach, and I also work as a server at the Key West Yacht Club."

A.J. made some notes.

Catherine thought, I knew I had seen him before. Now I know it was at Salute.

Clem added, "I am a graduate of Cornell, majored in Italian history, and I speak fluent Italian."

Like that will get you anywhere with us, thought Matt.

Skip asked, "What makes you believe you would be suited for this job."

"Well, I have great people skills. I can sell pretty much anything that I get behind."

He may be small, but he has a big idea of himself, Matt mused.

"What is it you are selling," Clem asked.

"I'll get to that in a minute. Do you have any investment experience?"

"I've got a 401k and I've got some Google and Yahoo stock," Clem said, "Do you sell stocks and bonds?"

"Not exactly," Skip said, "Ever heard of commodities?"

"Oh, sure. Like lumber and coffee and spices."

Matt's expression showed some new interest as he considered Clem's last comment. Intelligent little guy isn't he? He thought, then said, "That's right. That's what we do."

"Way cool."

Skip stirred in his seat, appearing anxious to move on. He said, "Okay, Clem, you've got a chance to make some huge money. We're going to hire you."

Clem smiled so wide his beard parted on his chubby chin. He said, "Oh, thank you. Thank you. You will not be sorry."

The next two were not worthy of notes on the clipboard. One was so hung over he could barely speak and the other was too dumb to comprehend what commodities are.

"That's a wrap for the day, boss," Matt said with a glance at Skip.

And what a grueling day it was, thought Catherine.

Skip said, "Well, we've had a fair run, but we still need to hire at least three or four more. Today was slim pickings. Matt – from the list you have for tomorrow, do you believe that's a realistic goal?"

Matt looked over the list, then up at Skip. "We've got six scheduled for tomorrow, Skip, and I can't imagine that we can't find a few from that stack, but if we need to extend the interview process by a few more days we can do that, too. Your call."

"A.J.?"

"I tend to agree with Matt."

"Catherine?"

"As you know, for the most part I have been an observer in this process, but I also have the inside knowledge of living in Key West for my entire life and, because of that experience and exposure, I know one day is not enough to determine what all days might hold." Brilliant, Catherine, just brilliant. What a pathetic offering. God, I still can't get over Skip throwing himself at that wench Kayla like he did. Get it out of my head. Change the subject.

"Skip, I've been meaning to ask, how will I be compensated?"

"I've been thinking that over, Catherine." Skip looked at his guys, then continued. "I was thinking that one thousand dollars a week would be a good starting place for you."

Oh my God, Catherine thought, fighting to retain a professional demeanor, I've never had it so good. I hope this works out! She smiled and said, "Thank you. That is very generous."

"And that's not all. I will also cover your health insurance." Skip smiled. "And when we get everyone licensed you will all earn commissions, too ... but we'll cross that bridge when we come to it."

"That's awesome, really – thank you."

"Sorry to change the subject back, but *do you* think some of these other candidates may pan out?" Skip looked hopeful.

Catherine brightened, gave a smile and nod of professional confidence. "Yes, I do."

"Okay, let's wait and see. Matt, A.J. – I want you to call back all of the people we have already decided to hire and tell them our classes will begin on Tuesday of this week, got that?"

Matt and A.J. mock saluted.

"I think I'm going to head back to Ft. Lauderdale. This is a big trust, but you have all earned it. You can hire the last few on your own, but I do want a consensus. If there is some dissent then call me. I'll make a valuation based on your notes and opinions. Agreed?"

They all nodded in agreement, and Matt said, "If we start class on Tuesday how long do you want us to drag this out before we begin to schedule these people for the series three? I'll want to gauge my performance timetable based your specific expectations."

Skip held up two fingers. "Do you think two weeks is too optimistic?"

Matt shrugged. "All depends on how fast they can absorb the material."

"Right," Skip said. "Catherine, A.J., and the new guy, Ray, can all help. We will pay a salary of two hundred dollars a week for as long as we need to train them. After that the pay goes to commission alone."

A.J. was marking all of this down, as was Randall.

Catherine smiled, said, "Thank you," and thought, well this new scenario certainly takes some of the bite out of my bitterness. Best I've felt all weekend.

"Randall, you will be coming back with me. There's nothing else you need to do here, and I can think of things at the other offices that need our attention."

"Yes, sir."

Matt, A.J., and Randall conferred for a few minutes, tying up any possible loose ends. Skip took the opportunity to have a word with Catherine.

He sat down beside her, looked deep into her eyes, and said, "There are a few things that I need to say to you."

She was mute, but shook her head.

"I want you to know that from this point forward I will know everything you do. I have eyes and ears all over the place. I do not say this to scare you, but to reinforce my next point. Understand?"

Catherine felt weak and said in a small voice, "Yes."

Skip rested his hand on her thigh and continued. "I try to surround myself with people who I can trust explicitly. Occasionally, I find that I have misplaced that trust and that makes me sad and angry. You see, I pride myself on being able to read people correctly. I have a good feeling about you, but if you should ever be tempted to cross me--you may find yourself in peril."

Catherine felt like Skip's eyes were looking directly into her soul. A dark presence came over her and the hackles on her neck rose. She shivered. "I ... I would never do anything to hurt you."

"I'm going to trust you on that, and to prove to you I'm sincere I've got a couple of gifts for you." Skip handed her two large cardboard boxes wrapped in tissue paper and ribbons. "Here, I hope you enjoy them."

"Thank you." Catherine was now confused, but accepted the two parcels graciously.

"Go ahead – open them." Skip smiled bright.

Catherine carefully unwound the ribbon on the first box and placed it to one side of the desk. Then she undid the tape that held the tissue paper in place, folded it, and placed it next to the ribbons. She lifted the lid and there was more tissue paper inside. She lifted that open and inside was a ruby colored dress with a flowing hemline and an empire waist. She plucked it out and held it up. "It's – it's beautiful. Stunning. Thank you."

"Go try it on. I want to see you in it."

Catherine had not tried on clothing for a man since she was a little girl shopping for Easter clothing with her mom and dad. She was a little giddy, but did as Skip requested. She walked out into the hall and went into the ladies room to change.

Randall, Matt, and A.J. walked over to where Skip sat and Randall said, "Does she like them?"

"I think so. Thank you for picking them out."

Matt chided Randall. "You always did have a good eye for a dress. Golly, could you pick me out one?"

Randall played along. "Oh, I know exactly what would look superb on you, Master Matt." He winked and flipped a limp wrist.

Catherine had taken off her pedal pushers and tank top and slipped into the dress. She noticed the price tag and nearly fell over when she saw it cost $398.00. She had never bought a dress that cost over one hundred dollars and was reluctant to put it on. She made herself do it, and it fit like it was tailor made for her. She spun in front of the mirror. The dress accentuated her bosoms without appearing cheap or too showy and flared over her thighs. She felt like a princess.

When Catherine returned Skip loved the new dress and told Catherine she looked splendid in it. She unpacked the next box with all eyes upon her. It was a dark green and burgundy velvet number with a boat neck and finely pleated drop waist skirt. Again Skip asked her to try it on and she did. This one fit her exquisitely too, and cost even more than the first one – a price tag of five hundred fifty dollars. Catherine almost choked, but it did look so marvelous. *How can I refuse?*

She thanked Skip again, and Skip gave her a warm, "You're welcome, Cat. And welcome to the team." He hugged her and gave her a peck on the cheek. He glanced at his Rolex and said, "Well, best to get moving, five thirty already and our plane departs in one hour. Let's be going, Randall.

Once out of the building, Skip said to Randall, "You did buy a few things for Kayla also, and send them to the address she left on her interview sheet? Some provocative attire befitting her – ahem – seductive and beguiling personality?"

Randall was in rare faggot form, playing with Skip, swishing his behind and doing the limp wrist thing. "Boss man, when you see the little darling in the clothes I picked out for her, you'll bust a good nut just looking at her. Dripping wet salaciousness, I assure you. And whatever do you mean, *did* I? Have I ever failed you in this regard?"

Skip had to laugh. "Of course not, Randall. You do what you do for me well and like clockwork. I can always count on you. Good man." He put a playful punch on Randall's arm. C'mon, we need to hurry it up a bit."

Catherine wanted to meet Nick over at the Schooner Wharf Bar, but didn't know how to do so without inviting Matt and A.J. along.

Matt said, "Cat, are you up for some fun this evening?" Mischief danced in his eyes.

"Yes, I am. Funny thing you asked."

"Why?"

"A friend of mine is here for a bartending competition over at the Schooner Wharf Bar. It should be fun. Do you want to meet me there a little later on?" She was hoping to buy an hour or so alone with Nick before dividing her time with Matt and A.J.

A.J. shrugged. Matt said, "Okay, what time and where is this place?"

Catherine figured if she hurried she could get there by six thirty. She said, "How about seven thirty or so?"

"We'll see you there between seven thirty and eight, okay?"

Matt and A.J. wanted to catch one set of Evie over at the Pirate's Den and then head over to see if they might catch the sumptuous Kayla at the Up Stairs Bar. Skip had told them not to tell Evie that he had been in town. They'd promised. Even eight, all things considered, may be optimistic, but they could always call and cancel since it looked like Catherine had some other friends to hang with. Off they went in search of sexual adventure.

Catherine had not bothered to go home, feeling pressed for time. She drove over to the parking lot behind the Waterfront Market and parked in a vacant space. She rushed over to the Schooner Wharf Bar and could hear the revelry way before she arrived at the entrance. When she stepped under the thatch roofed arbor she was transported into a world where drinking and dancing under the open sky was all that mattered. She scanned the crowd for Nick's head and found him with a group of young men near the right edge of the bar. She threaded her way past people who had had more than their share of alcoholic libations already and squeezed past a couple of drunken hotties practically pasted face down on the bar next to Nick.

The band was breaking down and readying for the new act that would take over for the sunset hour. The local station, 98.6, played oldies but goodies from speakers spread out at regular intervals inside the bar. On the left were six long plastic tables where bartenders were busy mixing their concoctions. Just beyond the bartending tables was a small open air kitchen that served mostly greasy fare and stunk up the air. Opposite from the entrance were floating docks. Sebago catamaran, the Wolf, the Western Union, Appledore, and other charter boats were moored there.

Nick laced his arm around Catherine's waist and gave her a gentle kiss on the mouth when they met. "I'm so glad you could make it."

"Me too." She smiled and kissed him again. "What's a girl got to do to get a drink here?"

Nick reached down and pinched her on her butt. She squirmed. "More of that later."

"Do you promise?" She rubbed her breasts on him.

"That and more. Now what would you like to drink?"

She looked at his cup and said, "What are you having?"

"This is a combination of Rum Runner, Pina Colada, and the Slippery Nipple."

"Sounds good. Can I have a taste?"

Nick handed her his cup and she took a gulp. She grabbed her forehead with a wince. "Ah – brain freeze." She rubbed and rubbed, recovered, chortled and said with a grin, "I guess I better have one of those too."

"With or without the shooter?" He pointed to an empty shot glass. "Hundred fifty one proof rum."

"Definitely with." She regarded his level of inebriation. "Looks like I've got some catching up to do."

Nick flagged down a perky bartender and ordered another round for everyone, including Catherine. He turned around to introduce his friends to her. "Catherine O'Reilley, this is Ray, Sean, Marek, Sal, and Vito."

"I know Ray. How do you know Ray?" Catherine said with surprise. She acknowledged the rest of the men. "Nice to meet you all."

The radio music was as loud or louder as the band had been. Nick had to talk directly into her ear to allow her to hear him correctly. "Ray and I went to college together. We just sort of got back in touch." Cool enough, he thought, she has no idea who these guys really are, and my cover is intact.

Catherine cocked her head to the side. "You didn't tell me you went to college." She took a long pull of her too-cold drink and then a sip of her rum chaser.

"That was a long time ago."

"All of these guys work at your bar?" She waived a hand at all the men in Nick's group.

"Yes. We all, that is everyone except Ray … guess he was the only one to get a serious job – double as bouncers and bartenders, as well as fill in anywhere else the boss needs us."

Catherine said, "Did you know that Ray interviewed with us and Skip hired him?"

"He was just telling us about that. What a coincidence, eh?"

Catherine bent toward Ray. "Is Connie coming here?"

"Yes, she is when she closes up the ice cream shop. You know how she is – always late." He smiled.

She smiled back. "Congrats on coming to work with us. I wish you could've met Skip."

Me too, Ray thought. "Thanks. I hope it's as good as I've made it out to be in my mind. By the way, what is this Skip guy like?"

Leave the dreamy part out. Just the facts, Cat. "Well, he is rich and smart and savvy. He has a lot of businesses. I don't really know about them all yet. He is generous."

"Sounds like you like him quite a bit."

God I hope it doesn't show on my face. "He is a pretty remarkable guy. He came from nothing and look where he is now."

Ray kept his real thoughts to himself. Yeah – look where he is now. I can't wait to get him where he really belongs. He put on a courteous smile and said, "Really. That *is* special." Schmuck! Boy has he ever got her fooled.

"Did I mention that he wants you to help train some of the new people?"

Ray was taken aback. "Really? When did he say this?"

"After Matt and A.J. talked you up to him." She smiled and took a sip of her drink. "God I wish I knew what you know."

"It just takes time. I've been at this for quite a while."

Nick said, "Really? Cool, I guess." He knuckle-bumped Ray. "Way to go, bro. Everything in good time."

Nick and Catherine necked a bit while the guys talked about how much fun it was to be on duty in Key West. Things were getting hot and steamy. Nick was getting a woody. "Cat, you better stop that. What will my buddies think?" He nibbled her nape.

"That you are a horny dog, that's what."

They laughed.

"Look – its Connie," Catherine said in a slur with a frantic wave. The man next to her ducked to miss her flailing arm.

"Looks like you all have a bit of a head start on me," Connie said when she had threaded her way over to where they stood. She pinched Ray on his nipple.

He kissed her on the small of her neck. "What do you say we do some shots. Doubles for you. That ought to even things out." He ordered a couple of rounds.

They started in with shots of one fifty one and moved on to shots of tequila and then jello shots made with pure grain alcohol. They were soon all drunk.

McCloud's band had been setting up and they were now testing the microphones and speakers. A screech came loud into the crowd. Many covered their ears, too late. McCloud said, "One, two, three, four … test." The band began to sing an edited version of one of Jimmy Buffett's songs, *Son of a Sailor----Bitch.*

People moved onto the dance floor where there were only inches between sweating bodies gyrating on the sand. Some sang along with the band.

By eight o'clock Catherine had all but forgotten about Matt and A.J. A chance glance at her watch prompted a thought. They're probably detained at the Up Stairs Bar watching Kayla shake her boobs and booty while kicking off her clothes. The bar was so loud she never heard her cell phone ring at eight thirty, didn't get the message they left, telling her they would catch up with her tomorrow and to have fun.

She did.

CHAPTER TWENTY-SEVEN

Sunday morning back at the resort, Catherine awoke hung-over, with a hideous headache. She pulled the blinds all the way shut to block out the blazing hot sun. *Damn, not so much as a puff of a breeze to cool off with.* She took a shower, but that didn't help much. The alcohol was leaking profusely from her pores. She dressed, resigned to facing the day, and went down to the continental breakfast bar in desperate need of a strong cup of coffee. There she saw Matt and A.J., sitting together drinking java with water chasers. She approached them and said, "Hi, fellas – how we doing today?"

"I feel like shit," Matt said.

"Me too," A.J. said, pressing two fingers to his temple.

"Hm, well join my club. I'm more hung over than a fat man's belly. Here – try these." Catherine passed out a round of aspirins, and took four herself, along with a swig of Matt's water.

Matt accepted his water back from Cat, took his pills, and said, "Sorry we missed you last night, Cat. I hope you managed to have some fun without us."

"No worries there. Between the shots and the testers we had more than our share of drink and fun." She groaned and felt her stomach. "Maybe – check that – definitely, *too* much fun."

"Ha. Yeah, you look like I feel. Jesus, what a bender last night. I'm glad Skip isn't here to witness this."

Catherine looked surprised. "Would he be unhappy?"

"Oh, yea. Especially because we're still in the hiring process – not actually up and making money. This phase of the business just costs him money."

"I see," She said, fighting off a wave of nausea from the extreme heat. "I just sort of assumed he had plenty."

"Oh, he does. But nobody likes to lose money," A.J. said.

***

The air conditioning was struggling to do its job, apparently having been shut off overnight and just recently turned back on, so when Matt, A.J. and Catherine got to the office the oppressive heat did nothing to abate their hung-over doldrums. Matt gave them all a pep talk and they agreed to suck it up and get the job done professionally and efficiently in spite of how they were feeling.

The first person interviewed was Craven Hutchinson. Cray, he liked to be called, was a fifty one year old man who had had a bar up on

Saddlebunch Key. When asked what happened to his business and why he was looking for employment, he said that he had been shut down for serving underage spring breakers this past spring.

Matt eyed the man, thinking how much older than his age he looked with the bulbous red drinker's nose and skin like wrinkled, tanned leather. "So Cray, do you think you would want or plan to leave here to reopen your bar business?" Matt wiped some sweat from his forehead with his linen handkerchief.

"No, the damn Sheriff was firm in that he was taking my license and that is----was----my livelihood." He snorted and shook his head.

Definitely bitter, Matt thought, and that's understandable. His hazel eyes still have a lively mischievous twinkle to them, though. Looks like a fighter. Good. "Do you think this – ahem, *little glitch* would prevent you from obtaining a series three federal license to conduct our business?"

Shaking his head he said, "Well, I don't know about that."

Matt looked over to his left. "A.J., maybe you can find out about this?"

"I'll make a few calls tomorrow. If there's no problem we start class on Tuesday. Can you make that, Cray?"

"Why, yes sir. I sure can. Does that mean I'm hired?" He smiled and his wrinkles multiplied. "I sure could use the money. I've got an ex-wife and three deadbeat kids to take care of and no money coming in."

"Yes, if we get an okay on the license issue you're in," Matt said with an easy smile.

Cray rose and extended his hand. "Thank you very much. I just know I can do this. You won't be sorry."

"Ten down and how many to go?" Matt said when Cray had exited. He paused to notice, "Hey – the air is finally overcoming the heat in here. Damn, feels good to feel some cool, eh?"

A.J. sighed and said, "Got that right. Ah, let me look. We've got another six scheduled for today. Let's see who else comes up and looks good. We know Skip wants at least twelve, but maybe we should take fourteen, if we can, that way we have a cushion in case some fall out later on."

Matt pointed at A.J. with one firm nod. "I like a man with a plan. Okay. Who's next?"

A.J. read the agenda. "Number two is a Dan Akin. Forty three years old."

"Catherine, would you bring him in?" Matt said.

"Right away," Catherine said. She left the room and returned promptly, followed by a gigantic belly that emerged through the doorway with a medium height man attached to it.

Matt had to restrain a laugh. *This guy looks like he swallowed a prize-winning watermelon. Dark intense eyes, though. Give him a fair shot.* He invited the blimp to sit, and after introductions and basic pleasantries, got into the meat of the interview.

"Dan, can you tell us what you were doing just before this."

"I was a maintenance man for the Banyan Resort on Whitehead Street."

Catherine said with a snap of her fingers, "That's where I've seen you before. I knew you looked familiar. Isn't that a timeshare resort?"

Dan turned to her and said, "Yea, you too. Do you own there?"

"No, but two of my good friends own a share there and they love it."

"Who are they?"

"Connie Porter and Lori Katzen."

A squirrelly smile crossed Dan's smooth face. He scratched his chin and said, "That would be Pearl and Battlestar Gallatica."

"None other." Catherine said with a knowing, sly smile. *So he knows the code names for Connie and Lori the Special Forces guys use.*

"Oh, God – can I tell you some wild stories about those two."

Catherine held up her hand and said, "Don't bother. I probably already know." *Like doing an entire battalion of special forces guys in one session. Many times. My, my – their infamy is of considerable proportions.*

"So Dan, why would you leave that job to come to work for us?" Matt said, slightly entertained by the conversation between Catherine and Dan.

"Well our management company has just been taken over by some crazies on the board and I've good reason to believe my job's going to be cut from the new budget."

"Sorry to hear that. How long have you been in their employ?"

"Thirteen years."

Matt paused in thought. *He seems like a nice guy.* A quick glance at Catherine and A.J.'s expressions let him know they felt as he did. Dan was hired.

Number three was a man by the name of Glenn DeRenzo. Once Glenn was seated Matt looked him over. *Not a big man,* he thought, *nicely styled dark hair, stately looking salt and pepper beard.* He said, "Glenn, it says here you are forty six and divorced."

Glenn scratched his thin nose and said, "Yes, that's correct."

"I see. And what is it you did before this or now?"

Glenn was wearing tan chinos and a black, Ralph Lauren polo shirt with tan loafers and belt. He said with a tinge of embarrassment, "I am a hair stylist." His full lips curled into a smile exposing his coffee stained teeth.

"Really?" Matt was amused.

"Yes. Really."

Matt felt playful. See if he's got a sense of humor. "So if we need haircuts you can do that for us?"

"Well, I suppose so," He said in a huff.

Hm, maybe not, Matt thought. "Where did you work?"

"John Santiago on Duval. That queen is impossible. Drama up the ying yang!" He dropped a limp wrist, reminiscent of Randall, Matt noticed.

"Does that mean you're gay?" *Oops, back track, Matt.* "Ah – excuse me … not that that makes a difference."

"Absolutely not! I do have an ex-wife," Glenn said, reddening.

"Good. Well, I mean like I said, it wouldn't matter either way, but …" Matt rose and extended a hand. "… welcome aboard."

The next prospect introduced himself as 'Cooper'. Matt said to Cooper, once he had been seated, "Tell us a little bit about you, your background."

"Well, I attended the University of Miami on a football scholarship that I had hoped would get me into the NFL. Played junior varsity, then varsity. Even made All American my junior year. As luck would have it, my senior year I blew out my knee, third to the last game of the season, and never even got close to warming the bench in the NFL."

"What position did you play?" Matt's love of sports had him interested. *I'm no athlete like Skip or some of the rest of the crew, but athletic prowess is almost as great as a good scam.*

"Quarterback."

Matt's eyes widened. "Really. So what are you doing now?"

"This and that." Cooper's eyes darted here and there.

Evasive, Matt thought, press him a little. "Have you ever had any investments or worked at all in this field?"

"I've an IRA that my parents set up for me along with some CD's, but nothing more. Why?"

"Ever hear of commodities?"

"Like in that movie, *Trading Places?*"

"Yes, but less glamorous." Matt hazarded another quick question. "Do you think you could do it?"

"Absolutely."

Matt looked at A.J. who gave him a thumbs up. Matt said, "Okay, Cooper, we're going to give you an opportunity to move in on the ground floor and prove you're the ace you tell me you are."

"Man, you're gonna make my mama proud." Cooper was beaming. "Thank you."

Barbara Allen was next.

Matt couldn't help but stare. Would you get a load of those tats. And is her hair really pink? Another freak. This place is filled with 'em. Matt desperately needed to use the restroom. He stood and said, "Hello, Ms. Allen. A.J. here will be interviewing you today." He turned to A.J. and said, "I'll be right back."

This was news to A.J. since Matt had been taking the lead in Skip's absence. A.J. looked at Barb. His first impulse was, she seems pushy. Wonder what she'd be like in bed? He opened the interview with a couple typical ice-breaking questions. Barbara's answers were brief, with a flippant attitude. A.J. couldn't stop looking at her hair. He had to ask and said off the cuff, "Barbara, can you tell us about your pink hair?"

"I just felt like fuckin' colorin' it pink, that's all," she said with a palm flipped up and a wide eyed head wag expression that said, duh.

Matt returned just in time to catch her toilet mouth reply. Jeez, did she really say what I thought she said? "A.J. I'll take it from here."

A.J., relieved, thought, does she have a mouth like a drunken sailor or what. Got us a social rebel here. What a contrast to the cute turned up nose and the intelligent looking eyes. And what's with the ridiculous barbed wire fence around her neck?

Matt took the reins. "What's your current occupation?"

A.J. thought, something about her interests me – despite her outward appearance.

"I work for ReMax. Cat knows me." She pushed her chin out toward Catherine.

Catherine nodded and said, "Yes, I know Barbara through the board of realty." She said nothing more, but thought, this girl has a serious drinking problem that interferes with her job performance.

Matt looked at Catherine, seeing her mental wheels turning, then turned back to Barbara. "I see. So, Barbara, what makes you want to do this type of job?"

Barbara popped a bubble gum in her mouth. "Oh, I don't know – something different I guess. The real estate market is beginning to dip and I need to secure some other employment to weather the down times. Know what I mean?" She crossed and uncrossed her legs, treating A.J. to a no panties delta glimpse beneath her spaghetti strapped blue and black sundress. Then she reached down to adjust her sandal strap, giving him his second treat – a nice look at her boobs.

The coquettish display caught A.J. and Matt in a silent trance … and it was followed with an awkward silence. Catherine looked on, aghast at the insipid little tart and her men colleague's easiness.

Barbara broke the spell, saying, "And another thing … I know lots of people who have money." She crossed and re-crossed her slim legs again. "That would be a bonus, right?" She blew a bubble and popped it.

"Yes, that would." Matt said.

A.J. could not get the beaver shot out of his mind. He looked at Matt, then Barbara, and said, "Okay, Barbara we're going to give you a shot."

Barbara popped another bubble and said with a sexy wink, "Well fuckin' allrighty then." She got up and high fived him, then swished and popped her narrow behind out the door.

Number six was a no show.

"Who's up next?" Matt said.

"Sherman Goldman, is that right?" A.J. said as the next man walked through the door.

"Yes, I am he."

Matt said, "Have a seat. Tell us something about yourself, Sherman." At least this one knows how to dress for an interview. Please!

"I've previously worked for Raymond James and T. Rowe Price. I have a series seven license so getting the series three is not a big deal. I've got some clients that I could easily move over into this business. I've managed accounts in excess of thirty million dollars and have had no complaints." His voice was strong and confident, a noticeable contrast to his slight frame.

Matt leaned back, impressed, and tapped his fingers on the desk. "That's quite a resume. Are you unhappy with where you now work?"

"Well, not exactly unhappy. I would say more like looking for something different. Just a lateral change." He stopped for a moment, leaned forward and said, "Can I be totally honest with you?"

"Please do." Matt brought all ten fingertips together and rested his chin on his forefingers.

"I got caught with the boss's wife." He paused, shot a look straight into Matt's eyes. "Yeah. They're getting a divorce and, well – things are just strange if you know what I mean. I never actually thought they'd ever end up this way and I've made no plans to have her in my life more than – well you know what I mean." He shrugged. "She was a great piece of ass. What can I say?"

Catherine could not believe what he was saying. She wondered what kind of woman would actually go for a petite little man like Sherman. Sure as hell not me.

Matt and A.J. were smirking and winking at each other. An unspoken decision was made between them.

A.J. walked forward and said, "Congratulations, Sherman. We think you would be an excellent broker. Welcome aboard. By the way, training begins on Tuesday morning at nine sharp – right here. Don't be late." He whispered in his ear, "You really got to tell us all about this boss and the wife. That is too precious."

Sherman formed a conspiratorial smile and said, "Thank you. I'll see you on Tuesday."

"Well, we've done it!" Matt said with serious pleasure after Sherman had left. "We've hired our crew."

"And a fine bunch of misfits they are, if I do say so myself," A.J. said.

"Boy, I'll say," Catherine said as a matter-of-fact. "Especially that Barbara. You may live to see that one bite you in the ass."

"She's no worse than that English chap, Chris, and Skip hired him. I'll take full responsibility for that one," A.J. said with an evil smile, "And tell ya what – she can bite me anytime, anywhere."

"Got something up your sleeve, don't you?" Matt said with a teasing tone and a playful punch on A.J.'s shoulder.

"I ain't jus talking, pal."

CHAPTER TWENTY-EIGHT

Tuesday early and bright as could be, A.J., Matt, and Catherine set about preparing their new recruits for the days and weeks ahead.

Matt walked to the front of the room and said, "Everyone, please find a seat." After they had all done so he continued. "We've got some paperwork to get out of the way before we begin studying for the exam. I'm going to have each of you come forward and A.J. will fingerprint you and begin your A-211 for registration for the series three license exam. Any questions before we get started?"

Kayla asked, "What if I don't have the original copy of my social security card."

Matt smiled. "Good question. How many of you don't have those with you?"

Four people held up their hands----Kayla, Chris, Goldeneye, and Barbara. Matt addressed them, "Do you think you can manage to bring them with you tomorrow?"

Everyone spoke in near unison, "Yes."

"Okay, we've got a lot to cover and a relatively short time to cover it in." Matt reached into an open cardboard box, drew out several training manuals, and handed them to Catherine. "Catherine, give everyone one of these, a fresh pencil, and a few sheets of blank paper." He waited patiently for them to begin his list of instructions.

Cray said, "I really don't do computers."

"You will when we get through with you." Matt smiled.

A.J. called them one at a time to come forward and be fingerprinted. He filled in all pertinent information on the A-211 sheets and then asked them for a signature. The whole induction and orientation process took the better part of the morning.

Matt had lunch catered in. It arrived at eleven forty five. Sandwiches with a variety of meats and cheeses, chips, apples, oranges, and soda or water were available. He said, "When you have these outlined tasks completed you can feel free to pick up some items for lunch. Paper plates and napkins are on the forward table." Matt picked up a corned beef sandwich and some salt and vinegar chips with a cold bottled water.

***

Back in Sea Ranch Lakes, Skip and Frederika were getting along like two piranha fish sharing a too-small tank. They had been quarrelling and fighting, with more and more frequency and intensity for the past few months. Skip had become distant and spent increasingly extended periods of time away from home and the girls. Frederika was incensed when he finally did come home. More often than not they would fight, and Skip would hit her, even beat her up. Frederika kept notes, documenting the physical abuse. She reported the incidents to her attorney, for use in the eventual divorce she was figuring was the only way out and away from Skip's sorry ass. She still had not filed any police reports – even though her lawyer kept reminding her that was a necessity if and when she needed to press criminal charges. Skip walked nonchalantly into the house on Tuesday morning as if nothing was wrong.

Frederika had her hands on her hips, looking ready to spit at him. "Where've you been? You never even call anymore. What am I supposed to tell the girls when they ask where their Daddy is?" Her face red, she stomped the floor. "If you want to be out fucking your newest little slut then why don't you just move out!"

Skip slammed the front door shut. "You know what your problem is, Frederika? Do you?" He lunged toward her. Veins were sticking out at his temples and his face was blood red.

"Yes – you!" She stepped in to meet him.

"No. Not me. You! You are nothing but a bitter old bitch!" He slapped her across the face.

Frederika clutched her cheek where red welts were already visible. "And who are you – Mr. Perfect?" She sobbed and clenched a fist at him. "You're going to be sorry you miserable bastard!"

"I didn't say I was perfect, but I do better than you." He seethed. "Just look at you. Why you're – you're … pathetic!"

"Like hell you do. If you ever did an honest day's work I don't know when." She was shaking. "You fucking son of a bitch!"

"Don't talk about things that you don't know about, Frederika."

She screamed, "I know a lot more than you think," and ran toward him, fingers clawing at his face. She missed.

He grabbed her wrists and held them tight. "Don't you ever try that again, do you hear me?"

She was shaking and in tears. "Fuck off, Skip!"

He shoved her down on the floor and stormed off to the shower.

The maid had been hiding in her apartment. When Skip stomped off in a huff she went out to attend to Frederika.

Half an hour later, Skip came down stairs looking like his usual million plus dollars. His clothing was pressed, hair combed, and his jewelry the perfect accent to his attire. He was on a mission, previewing a home for sale he had noticed nearby yesterday. Nice property, on the water. He had called and set the appointment with the realtor for this time of morning. He patted his suit pocket where he had stored the note on which he had written the address.

On his way out through the living room he did not bother looking for Frederika. He walked out and jumped into his Bentley turbo. He drove over to the next street, parked, and walked up the sidewalk to meet the realtor, Mrs. Scotsman. He cringed at her getup, featuring a colorful Mumu that hung limply down to her thick ankles and flip flops with layers and layers of bangles lining up each arm. Seventy-two, he guessed her age. *Does she have to wear a bouffant, purple gray do? I hope she doesn't talk much; I just want to see the house.*

Mrs. Scotsman shuffled and clanged as they exchanged greetings and walked the property. The house was a ranch style, stucco exterior, with a slate roof that needed replacing.

Skip said as he perused the show sheet, "The asking price is $1.375 million, right?"

"Yes," Mrs. Scotsman said.

Skip walked around the exterior of the house. *What a view, but the house itself is a piece of shit.* Mrs. Scotsman caught up with him and Skip said, "Tell you what – I will offer eight hundred seventy five thousand, cash, closing in two weeks."

She had to catch herself from falling over. She had never had a cash deal before, in forty five years in the business. She brought a pudgy hand to her breasts, cleared her throat and said with regained composure, "Well, okay. I can't say for certain what the owners are willing to accept, but I will give them your offer."

"Fine, call them now." Skip's expression told her, *right now.*

Flustered, she fished her cell phone out of her Mumu and dialed the seller. "Mr. Fishman, it's Eleanor. I'm at your house on Naraganset Lane and I've a man here offering eight hundred seventy five thousand dollars." She listened to his reply, then said, "Well, it's cash and closing in two weeks. Yes, that is soon." She listened more. "Okay, I'll tell him. One moment please."

She placed her hand over the speaker and said to Skip, "Mr. Fishman said one million even and you have a deal." She was beginning to feel giddy.

Skip frowned and contemplated for a moment, playing the game with practiced skill, and then said, "Nine fifty." She took her hand off the speaker and said, "Well, he said nine fifty." She waited and then said, "Okay, I'll let him know."

She turned to Skip and said, "Well, he said okay. It's a deal."

"Great. Send the contracts to my real estate attorney. His name is Clancy Jacobs. He's over on Commercial." Skip walked off.

Skip called Clancy and told him about the deal. He asked him to send over a contractor to determine how much money it would take to tear it down and build something livable. He needed to get out of his home with Frederika and the sooner the better.

CHAPTER TWENTY-NINE

For two weeks, Matt, A.J., Ray, and Sherman brought the new recruits up to snuff. It had been a considerable challenge, but they felt that everyone, except maybe Eugene, who continued to struggle, was ready for the series three. The A-211's and the fingerprint sheets had come back clean with the exception of a small restraining order that Toni had taken out against English Chris nine months ago. A.J. was in the process of alleviating that so Chris would have no further hitches in the licensing process.

Though the Fed's had overheard every step of the training sessions, they were only able to get fragments of information on how Skip's covert operations worked. They knew, from nightly conversations with Ray, they expected all to pass – with the exception of Eugene. Nick had acted as formal go-between for the daily briefings between Ray and the main office. Ray had just placed his final call from the training portion of the investigation to Nick.

Ray said, "Man, I'm beat. I wanted to squeeze in some trading myself. but by the time I get home the markets here in America will be closed."

"Don't fret, dude. Who ya gonna call?" Nick said, imitating the *Ghostbusters* theme song.

"FOREX. GLOBEX."

"So when do you sit for the exam?"

"Probably Monday or Tuesday depending on when this Sammy guy----he apparently works in the Lauderdale operation----can manage to get thirteen people scheduled."

"I happen to know a thing or two about that."

"I'm sure you do. And so do I, but I'll never tell."

Both Ray and Nick knew that whenever Sammy called, space would be made to accommodate Skip's people. The Fed's were anxious to see them trading.

"I'll call you when I know who is handling the detail tonight," Nick said as he mounted his BMW touring bike and began his ride home.

***

Skip had closed on his property. The old house had been razed and new construction was in full swing. He had hired an architect to design plans for a 10,000 square foot house with a three car garage, swimming pool/Jacuzzi combination, new seawall, and more. Estimates for the new construction had come in between three and four and a half million, depending on the finishes that Skip selected.

The offices in Lauderdale closed at four o'clock every day. On Tuesday and Thursday nights the brokers worked from six until nine at night, in order to connect with potential clients in later time zones such as Alaska, Puerto Rico, Canada, California or west coast US, and Hawaii. Most of the workers had already left for the weekend. Sammy and the guys in trading were the exception. They were working hard at the fabrication of statements that needed to go out over the weekend. Skip sauntered back to the trading room to speak to Sammy before finalizing his weekend plans.

"Sammy. How'd we do this week?"

Sammy had been shuffling paper and tabulating trades to be sent in with certain statements when Skip walked up. He stopped and turned those that were still to be tabulated up-side-down to keep his place.

"Slow week, Boss."

"How slow?"

"Well, we only took in ten million."

Skip looked down, hunched a shoulder. "I'll take ten. How about Buckhead?"

"Let me find those." He lifted another stack of papers and said, "Looks like they took in thirty five million. I tell you they're kicking some ass – thanks to the Falcon's guys."

"That's great news. And Vegas?"

"I thought you were going there this weekend." Sammy shuffled through some more stacks of trade slips.

"I think I am. You know, Natalia came on board with us last month, and she's dynamite."

Sam winked. "I heard she's a great piece of ass, too. Ever tapped that?"

"Sam – do I look like the kind to kiss and tell?" Skip smiled like a snake that just swallowed a rabbit.

"I can't find Vegas right now, but I'll get back to you. Oh, maybe Mark has those."

"That's okay. I'll let you get back to fixing those statements. Have a good weekend."

Finding the spot he'd lost before Skip's interruption, Sam said, "You too, Skip."

Skip settled in behind his spacious mahogany desk in his high-backed leather chair to place a call to the Bahamas and Costa Rica.

Tommy was on his way out to meet his drug dealer for a new week's worth of toot when the phone rang. He saw on the caller ID it was Skip. Shit!

"Hi, Skip. What's doin'?"

"Just getting some weekend tabulations before I head out to Vegas."

Tommy squeezed his lips and one fist tight and shook his head. Mother fucker it must be nice. Shit I miss the days of freedom and travel with the mob. If only I hadn't ratted on … oh what the fuck, this is my pathetic life now. "Well, we took in about twenty mil. Effectuated some trades with that. Everyone lost, naturally."

"Good. That's very good. Now listen to me. I need you to redirect some of those funds to the accounts in Cayman and Costa Rica."

"Why Costa Rica. Why not just leave it right here in the Bahamas?"

"Because I said so----that's why. Now don't ask any more questions. Send ten to Cayman and three to Costa Rica----and do it now."

Now you're pissing me off, Tommy thought. This is cutting into my party time and I'm running late to my hookup. Goddamn dealer always cuts the shit if the time passes away too long. Hate my shit cut, man – hate that shit. Tommy's breathing got huffy. He was becoming enraged and jittery. He said, "Now?"

Hotheaded Italian's got some nerve, Skip thought, and what's with the excited, anxious tone? Almost like what you'd expect from a junkie needing a fix. Need to maybe do some checking up on Tommy. Later. Right now he needs to remember how to follow a direct order. "Yes, Tommy – *now!*"

"Fine!" Tommy slammed the phone down.

Skip was incensed. Fucking asshole is so goddamn ungrateful. I should have left him with the mob. He'd be swimming with the crabs about now. I'll attend to that soon enough. Better call Vegas. He depressed the speed dial on his phone and got Vinnie.

Vinnie was upbeat. "Hey, Skip. We're crankin' out here. I tell you this twenty four seven stuff is hitting heavy."

"Vinnie, can we buy leads for Puerto Rico?"

"What's up in Puerto Rico?"

"I was just thinking maybe we could increase our business if we could tap into Puerto Rico more, too."

"Nah, we don't need no leads for Puerto Rico, Skip. We can use the phone book."

Ever the practical one, Skip thought. "Okay, give it a try and let me know how it pans out."

"You talkin' 'bout my operation here in Vegas? Got me confused."

"Yes, Vinnie. But not only you – all of the rest, too."

"Hey, you still plannin' on coming out here this weekend?"

"Yes, I am. I'll call you when I land."

"Okay, man. See ya then."

***

Costa Rica was purely a gambling and bookmaking operation. The money Skip spent buying the operation from Bob Rolly was more than made back the first week of football season. This was one of Skip's favorite operations. Most of the cash made from it was sent to the Caymans, but thirty percent of the profits were kept in Costa Rica. Skip dialed Natalia there next.

"Hola, mi amor." Skip said in his best, practiced, novice Spanish, when Natalia had come on the line.

"Señor Skip. Se salta, tal placer."

No match for the fluently multi-lingual Natalia, Skip reverted to English. "Natalia, how's it going?" He conjured up a mental picture of voluptuous Natalia. She had originally gone with Rolly to Panama, but decided to come back to Costa Rica. He remembered how he thought it best to take her in because she knew the business inside and out. She made the perfect bookkeeper.

She said, "We did great last week. Fifty two million in and twelve out."

Skip paused. "Twelve million out?"

Natalia had to think quick. If he ever finds out I've been skimming the profits since day one, it's lights out for me. She cleared her throat and said, "Well, remember – you know baseball season does not net us as much money as football does." Buy it. Dear lord, please let him buy that.

Skip said, "Oh, right. Well, that's still very good, Natalia. Give the brokers there a ten percent bonus and tell them I said good job." He paused and then said, "Would you like to join me in Vegas this weekend?"

She said, "Would I – oh, yes. Very much so, papito."

He said, "I'll have Lilly arrange your flight tomorrow, okay?"

"Skip, one thing – about that …" she paused for emphasis, then said, "… I think it is time you buy your own plane." She let that sink in a moment and then continued. "And I know just the plane and the person. We can run the deal out here and that way there is no trace of it in the USA."

Skip chuckled. "I've got to hand it to you, Natalia. You are a resourceful young woman. Send me the details and I'll see if it works out."

Natalia's voice raised in pitch and intensity. "Can't you do it before Vegas? I hate to fly commercially out of Costa Rica. The flights are always getting delayed or cancelled. The seller is highly motivated. He really needs the money now and if we move on the deal now we can probably take his pilot, too."

Anxious, Skip thought of Natalia. Interesting. Does sound like a potentially good deal to look into pronto, though. "Tell you what – I'll send Father Zeke down there tomorrow, and if it all checks out, we'll do it aysap." Skip remembered he had Father Zeke busy blessing the new Key West office. Oh well, he'll just be more busy now, blessing the plane if I buy it, too. Two hundred fifty large a year in compensation buys a hell of a lot of allegiance with no complaining.

Natalia was gushing now. "You're the best, papito!"

Skip's cell phone rang. He looked at the caller ID. Mariela. He said, "Natalia, I've got another call that I've got to take. I'll talk to you later, okay?"

"Si, no es un problemo." They hung up.

"Hello darling." I'm not looking forward to this call, he thought, how am I going to tell her she's not going to Vegas with me like I told her she would?

"Skip, I need some more money to buy some things for Vegas."

"Mariela, settle down. I've got some bad news where Vegas is concerned." Be firm and gentle at the same time, Skip. Mariela is so eager and naïve, sometimes she doesn't quite catch on. He pictured her, twenty years old, dark hair, a body that could stop a clock. He remembered picking her up at a strip club where she worked, how he had put her up in a condo and taken care of her, giving her a better life. In return for some great sex, of course. He smiled at that last thought. But, Natalia is a much better companion where business is involved. I'll soften the blow by sending her some jewelry.

"Don't start with me Skip," Mariela said in a whine, "you promised."

"I'll make it up to you. I promise." She just doesn't get it. She's beautiful arm candy and a great lay, but brainless beyond that.

She sobbed and said, "You promised before."

"Remember that fabulous diamond and sapphire necklace you liked over at H & H Jewelers?"

"Of course I do." She sniffed.

"I'll have that sent over first thing tomorrow. Will *that* make this trip up to you?"

Mariela brushed away her tears with a delicate finger and said, "Oh, I guess so. Do you really mean it? Really?"

"Yes, Mariela, I do." Sometimes she can be so difficult. I hope this is not one of those times.

"Done," she said with a bright chipper voice. "I forgive you."

Well that was easier than I thought it would be. Relieved, he said, "Are we still on for dinner?"

"Yes! What time should I be ready?"

"I'll pick you up at six."

Neither said good bye before hanging up. Mariela was like a child waiting for Christmas. Oh my god – the necklace – I can't *believe* it. She sang happily along with the radio as she tore through her walk-in closet in her spacious apartment trying to decide what to wear for dinner. She looked through the hundreds of dresses and pairs of shoes with matching handbags. Tonight I must be irresistible. I'm going to be the only woman in his life. His one and only, even if that means getting pregnant. God, I don't know if I'm ready to be a mother yet, I'm so young. But I know plenty of girls younger than me who've had babies. If they can do it, so can I. It's worth it. He's going to have to make me his number one when I tell him I'm having his baby. Oh, this is the perfect outfit. Skip will have to screw me real good when he sees me in this tonight.

Finalizing her plan, she laid out her chosen attire of sexual enticement on the bed. With a devilish grin, she took her birth control pills out of the medicine cabinet and flushed them down the toilet.

CHAPTER THIRTY

Matt and A.J. had heard through the office grapevine that Skip just bought a new plane. They decided to ring Skip on the speakerphone from the Key West office Saturday morning. They caught him as he was boarding for Las Vegas with Natalia. Natalia, Father Zeke, and the pilot had come from Costa Rica earlier that morning. Since the deal had been taken at her request, Natalia was anxious to show Skip his new plane. Father Zeke had already christened it, *Traders II*.

"Skip, we heard a rumor this morning," A.J. said, slow, careful not to reveal his sources of information.

"What kind of rumor, guys?" Skip said, smiling to himself. Play along, this is fun.

Matt and A.J. could hear the revving of the engines in the background. Matt played it cool. He ventured to say, "Hey, Skip – what's that sound? Are you already at the airport?"

"Yes, we're at the airport, but don't tell me you called to ask me that."

"No." Matt sighed, knowing the jig was up. "Okay, look – we heard something about a new plane and Costa Rica."

Skip had a good-natured laugh. "My, word travels fast. Yes, I've bought a great new plane and we're headed to Vegas."

"We?"

"Didn't I mention that before?" The part about Vegas, that is.

"Yea, you told us that. But who's with you?"

"Natalia. We've just dropped Father Zeke. Natalia helped me buy the plane."

"An airplane! Get real. You can't be serious," Matt said, impressed.

"I am dead serious. We now have our own aircraft. It can hold ten passengers and fly three thousand miles between refueling."

"Way cool. When do we get to see it?" A.J. had a thumb up to Matt.

"I'll be keeping it in Lauderhill this week after we return. I don't know just where I'll keep it long term, but Natalia has a friend looking for a good deal on a hanger."

Natalia gave Skip a peck on the cheek and walked up the boarding stairs. She felt like she had finally arrived. She recalled that Skip had once told her he met Bernie Madoff and that he felt the power of Bernie the moment they shook hands. She now felt that same power. And it was heady.

"We'll be in Vegas for most of the weekend. I've got to check in with Vinney and Gabe. I'm dropping Natalia back in Costa Rica earlier on Sunday. By Sunday evening I'll be in Ft. Lauderdale. When are you coming back up this way?"

"Did Sammy get us scheduled for Monday, or Tuesday?"

"I believe Tuesday, but call him on that to be sure." Skip inched up the stairs. "What's the game plan for the test?"

A.J. said, "Well, because we are thirteen plus three we decided to rent two Econoline vans and drive everyone up at one time."

"Great. Do you need my credit card to reserve them?"

"I think Randall has already handled that for us."

"All right. See you on Tuesday. Ciao." Skip hung up and walked the remaining stairs into his new King Air.

Matt and A.J. took a few minutes to converse about the new plane after Skip was off the line. Matt said, "Man, I so want *my own plane*." A wistful look came over his eyes. "Can you imagine not having to wait in line with all of the riff raff?" He paused in mid thought and whistled. "Sweet."

"Who ya calling riff raff?" A.J. said with a laugh.

"You, dude," Matt said as he reached over to nudge A.J. in the side.

"Maybe you better look in the mirror, dude," A.J. said, and nudged Matt back with a wink.

On one of the other lines Catherine called Nick.

Nick said, "What a pleasant surprise. How are you? Where are you?"

She smiled into the phone and said, "I'm fine. Still in Key West right now, but I think I'll be back in Ft. Lauderdale sometime this week. At least that's what Matt and A.J. tell me."

"Really. Do you think you can set aside some time to see me?"

"Well, I certainly hope to see you – sometime. I believe we have some unfinished business to conclude."

"What's this trip all about?

"We're bringing the new recruits up to sit for the series three."

NFA agents Dan and Bart looked at each other, and made notes as they listened in.

***

The Las Vegas trip was fast and furious. Skip and Vinney met briefly. They tallied receipts for the offshore funds being sent to their various destinations. Skip said, "Vinney you're doing a great job with the Vegas operation."

Vinney said, "Thanks, boss. Glad you are satisfied." God I hope I've covered my tracks on this one. If Skip ever caught me skimming he would cut off my balls and feed them to Frederika. "How's the new plane?"

"Great. I can't imagine what took me so long. I had no idea how great it would make me feel. Like Natalia said to me on the way over, *it is power personified* – the *only* way to travel.

"When are you leaving?" Vinney couldn't wait for Skip to exit and leave him to his own scam. He shuffled his feet and cleared his throat.

"Natalia is out shopping now. As soon as she gets back we are going to spend the rest of the weekend back in Costa Rica."

Lucky fuck. When I've got all of the money I can spend I'm going to do some traveling, too. "I guess as long as we keep the money flowing in you can keep having fun."

Skip gave him an askance glance. Odd thing to say, do I detect a note of disgruntled jealousy? He made mental note of it, but said nothing.

An hour later Natalia met Skip at Vinney's place. She had her arms full of shopping bags and was panting. "I really got lucky today."

Skip had to tease. "It looks like you bought everything on the strip."

Dames, Vinney thought, wow – can they ever blow the cash.

"This is not all. The rest are being delivered directly to the plane." She was beaming.

"What else could you possibly need?"

"Who said I *needed* anything?" She was serious. "I *wanted* all of this."

The cab arrived. The driver placed all of Natalia's new purchases into his trunk with care as Skip and Natalia took their seats inside. Skip waved to Vinney.

Vinney waved back and said, "See ya next time." Whenever the hell that is.

***

Back in Costa Rica Natalia said, "I've got such a wonderful weekend planned for us."

"Really?"

"Yes, I thought we would dine at the Monestary. It is sooo good."

"The Monestary?"

"Yes, it's up by Lake Arenal. Did you know that Arenal is an active volcano?"

"No, but I bet you can tell me all about it."

"Yes, and we will get into the hot springs after dinner … or before, if that is better for you?"

"Whatever, you decide."

"And tomorrow I've arranged for us to raft the Paquare River. This time of year they may even have some number fours."

"Number fours?" Skips eyebrows went up.

"Yes, that is what they rate the white water. But don't worry, it is quite safe and a guide is in each boat on every trip."

"Oh, I'm not worried. Do I look worried?"

She touched his cheek. "No, not worried."

"Natalia, how long have you lived here?"

"Nine years. Why?"

He leaned in toward her. "Do you ever want ... more?"

"No, I like it here. I've made a lot of friends here. And now with the plane we can go all over the place at a moment's notice." She smiled, a portrait of sweetness.

Both Skip and Natalia had a superlative weekend. Great food, good exercise, and ardent sex.

***

Sunday evening Skip was packing his travel bags to leave. He had just shoved his ditty bag into the larger travel case and called Natalia over. She came, he caressed her and said, "Thank you. I've had a marvelous time. You know I hadn't given much thought about owning my own airplane before you brought it to my attention, but that beauty is the icing on my life's cake." He looked into her dark eyes with love. "I don't know how to thank you."

She made a kissie noise with her full, pouty lips, winked and said, "Oh, I think you do." She grabbed his hand and led him back to her sumptuous bedroom. She gently pushed him back onto the downy bed and said, "No excuses, now. With your own plane now we can go whenever *we* are ready."

"Touché." Skip smiled and pulled her down on top of him. Her long dark hair fell over his face in soft tendrils. He inhaled her sweet perfume and kissed her lightly on the side of her neck.

She purred with delight.

Skip pulled her hair back off her face and kissed her forehead. She began to unbutton his shirt. Skip's body said yes, but his mind said no. He brushed her dark hair from her soft forehead and gave her another kiss. "Sorry, Natalia. I really do need to get back."

"No time for ... just a little bit of fun?" She purred into his ear.

"I would have guessed this past weekend would have sated even you, my little sex fiend." He kissed her, soft and deep. "Your sexual appetite knows no end."

"And yours does?" She said with a fun-loving, easy laugh. "Isn't that a bit – how do you say ... like the kettle calling the potty black?"

Skip laughed at her mixed up example and nibbled her earlobe.

She moaned. "Ah, come on, popitio." She reached for his zipper and tugged. He brushed her hand away, careful to not be too brisk. She said with soft, enticing eyes pleading her case, "Por favor."

"Begging does not suit you." He rolled her off to his side and began to straighten his clothing. Before leaving he reached into his travel bag, pulled out a long, thin jewelry box, and handed it to Natalia.

"For me?" She said in a tease and leaned backward. She held the box in her delicate hands. It was light powder blue with a white satin ribbon. She recognized the label even with no name. She murmured, "Tiffany's?"

"Open it."

"What is it?" Her dark eyes were pools of liquid velvet.

"Open it and see." He loved to watch her open gifts. She was always truly thankful.

Her eyes danced with delight. She removed the white satin ribbon and set it aside, then slowly pried open the lid. Inside was a ten carat tennis bracelet with alternating baguettes and round brilliant stones all set in ... platinum? She squealed, threw her arms around his neck and showered him with kisses. "Gracias. Gracias. Gracias. Oh, mi amour." Tears of happiness streamed down her finely chiseled face. She momentarily lost her voice. When she found it again she said, "Car linda."

Skip smiled, pleased, knowing a happy Natalia equates to more money for him in the long run. The cost of the jewelry was a small price to pay for the net results.

She said, "I will think of you when I wear it. Always. Will you help me put it on?"

Skip took the exquisite diamond bracelet out of the box. Multi-colored rays of light glittered and danced from each facet. He wrapped it around her small wrist. Carefully, he latched the double clasps. Satisfied that the locks had caught, he held her dainty arm out so they could both admire it. He said, "It looks spectacular on you."

"Does the bracelet make me or vice versa?" She asked in a woman's beguiling way.

"Does it matter really?" Skip kissed her again, this time with more force. "Natalia, you are both devastating in your beauty."

She gave him a butterfly wing on his cheek. "You are a magnificent man. I love you."

"Natalia, you deserve nothing but the best ... and that is why you will always have me."

Through fresh tears she formed an appreciative, sweet smile.

"Adios," Skip said. He turned and walked out the door.

Skip had a relaxing flight back to Ft. Lauderdale with none of the usual inconveniences of commercial flight. He felt wonderful, like he had finally arrived. He let his mind wander back to Bernie Madoff. He figured that Bernie was older and had made some shrewd investments, but he also knew Bernie was a scammer just like him. When they had met in Palm Beach three years ago, each had bragged about how much money they had ripped off of unsuspecting investors. Bernie had won by a long shot, but Skip had set some goals at that time and steadily he was achieving them. Skip was not easily impressed, but he was impressed with Bernie Madoff.

And I want the same, Skip thought, as he eased back in his cushy leather chair and looked out the window at the world to be conquered below. I *will* have the same.

CHAPTER THIRTY-ONE

Monday morning before the markets opened Skip always liked to get a reading from Ismail, Mark, or Sammy about what he could expect that week as far as infusions of cash or new accounts were concerned. Skip walked over to the trading windows. He looked right and left. Sammy and Mark were nowhere in sight. He stepped over to the center window where he could have a word with Ismail. "Ismail, do you have the tallies for the day? The account and cash projections for the week?"

Ismail, small and dark, looked down at his clipboard and said, "We should open twenty new accounts this week according to the packages we sent out last week and the brokers' notes. Fourteen new accounts are still pending from last week. I hope to have more information about those later today. Monies being wired will have a twenty-four hour delay unless we want to suspend that house rule." Ismail looked at Skip, but Skip said nothing. He continued, "Thirteen trades have already been transacted this morning and it's not even nine a.m." Ismail winked. "We should generate some four hundred trades by the day's end. We sent out seventy-five statements this weekend and we will have more go out today." He pushed his wire rimmed glasses back up his smallish patrician nose, straightened his posture from bending to read the clipboard, and looked up at Skip again. "Was that all? Is there anything else, Skip?"

"Good. Thank you, Ismail." Skip didn't move. As an afterthought he said, "By the way, Ismail, where's Sammy?"

He's in A.J.'s office. Something with one of the new guys that he wanted to listen in on."

Skip walked off in the direction of A.J.'s office to speak to Sammy.

Nick had called Ray to see if they were still on schedule for the exam on Tuesday. He hadn't had the opportunity of being up close and personal with Skip and wondered just what this man was like. "So tell me, Ray," he said with genuine interest, "What was Skip like?"

"In a word," Ray said, "I'd say – impressive. The guy is a born salesman and leader."

"Seriously?" Nick regarded his partner. "Are you sure you don't mean born scammer?"

"Yes, that too. He was smooth – very smooth, and also extremely knowledgeable." Ray held up his hand and counted three fingers off as he said, "Arrogant, self-serving, and slick."

"So the guy is full of himself, huh?"

"Understatement of the decade," Ray said with a huff and a shake of the head. "This girl, sexy chick – Kayla Kevlar, was interviewed by Skip personally. The way I understand it he took her out that night and knocked a little off. That takes a real pair."

"I would say he knows how to seize the moment." Nick laughed.

"You would. Seize this." Ray grabbed his crotch and did a Michael Jackson pelvic thrust with an *eee hee!* high pitched warble.

"Tell me something we don't already know," Nick said after a good natured chuckle, picturing his partner's antics. "We've followed this Skip guy for eons now. We know he has a stable full of young, brainless beauties. But those chicks aren't what we're after here."

"Right." Ray pulled on his cheek. "But goddamn. This prick is just sooo ballsey. Sort of comes with the turf, I guess."

"Yea, I guess so. Money and power are as addictive as meth or crack."

Ray snorted. "Yeah, right. Like you wouldn't know. Look – we *know* he used to have a license too, but he lost that a long time ago. What's his angle now?"

"He's running a Ponzi scheme. Pure and simple." Nick yawned.

"Do you recall when we broke up Luke's game – what was the name of his scamming circle?" Ray looked up and to the right, then snapped his fingers. "Ah, yes – Credit Swift. He gave us some dirt on Skip. Sad part is, it wasn't enough to put him away."

"Ah, yea – Luke LeBroc. He was another wise guy – thought he was so clever until he got caught. With reference to Skip, LeBroc did point us in the right direction."

Ray's voice elevated. "Oh shit – It's ten a.m. and Marek wanted us all to listen in on the conference briefing regarding Mr. Horowitz. Better wrap things up and dial in."

Ray and Nick hung up and then dialed the conference line. They had missed the first few minutes, but got on in time to hear Marek saying, "Maybe we can insert Daren? Didn't he used to work at the CBOT?"

"Yea," another agent said, "His family owned a seat on the CBOT back in the heyday."

Nick said, "Why don't we see if we can get him into American Futures. That is supposedly Skip's FCM."

Marek said, "Welcome to the briefing, Nick and Ray – glad to see you two clowns could join us. Ahm, we actually audited them a few months back. They seemed to be pretty clean back then, but it would be a big help if we knew something – anything actually, for certain. I'll talk to Aiden about that particular point."

Sampson thought a moment and then said, "I believe last time we checked – and that may have been a while ago, come to think of it … there was no trace of trades for Skip's organization in Lauderdale. We saw some trades for Buckhead, but the only trades on American's books for the Lauderdale operation occurred months ago."

Marek said, "Check again. Does everyone know what is expected of them for the week?"

Each came back with a *yes*, or *affirmative boss*.

"Okay, that's it for today. Ray, let me know the outcome of the testing from your perspective tomorrow evening." Marek disconnected the conference line.

After lunch was a brief study session to ensure that Matt's students were all prepared for the series three in the morning. Skip had called to have a word with them prior to this important next step.

"Put me on the speaker phone," Skip said.

Catherine hit the speaker mode on the phone and adjusted the volume all the way up.

Skip said, "Welcome to Commonwealth Financial. I want to personally congratulate each of you on being selected to work with such a prestigious organization. My organization can reshape the way you previously conducted business and provide you with a plentiful lifestyle." He paused. "This test tomorrow is the first step. The road ahead will not be easy, but because of the excellent tutelage of Matt I feel confident that each of you has learned the required material that will allow you to pass the exam, allowing you to become brokers of commodities." He paused again to take a gulp of cold water. "Are there any questions for me at this time?"

Matt dropped back to have a quiet word with A.J. while Skip rambled on. "A.J. what do you think? Optimistic? Pessimistic?" Matt leaned against the back wall and crossed his arms over his muscular chest.

"Honestly, it's a crap shoot. I know Skip wants to generate lots of increased revenue and he wants to do so a.s.a.p., but some of these people look like they've never handled anything more than a few hundred dollars. I don't really know. Maybe we can press em' into a certain comfort level with their scripts when the testing portion of the enterprise is over?" He did have some other concerns, but wasn't about to voice them. He put a hand on Matt's shoulder. "We'll be just fine."

Ray was wearing a wire for the entire two weeks of training, also calling in to his direct superiors each night to be certain they were getting it all right. Cracking this case was his ticket to a promotion. He assured them he was so far ahead of these bozos they didn't know if he was coming or going. His superiors were pleased, but still needed more solid facts before they could take the evidence to the D.A. and secure an indictment

At the end of the meeting with Skip, Catherine dialed Nick. "Glad I caught you," Catherine said, tired to the bone and bleary from the pace they had been on to train the others.

"What's up?" Nick paused. "You sound tired. Are those guys overworking you?" He smiled through the phone. He knew full well what was going down.

"Sorry." Catherine's tone was apologetic. "The answer to that question is yes. And that's why I'm calling *you*. I could use a little dose of sunshine. Wanna come down next weekend?"

She sounds drained, Nick thought. "Ah, sure, Cat – I think that's doable. Can I let you know for sure in the next day or two?" He was thinking, I'll need to consult with the main office before making any commitments.

"That's fine. Guess I better get back to the grind."

Nick stood still after she hung up, holding his empty phone, deciding what to do. I should call Ray again. I'll ring him now.

Ray answered immediately.

"What's going on," Nick asked.

"Oh, it's you. I thought you were my bookie," Ray said with no enthusiasm. He walked over to his computer screen where he could follow the odds of his most recent bet in real time.

"Sorry to disappoint you. I just got a call from Catherine. She sounded beat. How are things going?"

"Same ol' same ol'." Ray took a sip of his Jack and Coke. "The test's tomorrow and Skip called today." He logged out of his computer and hoped the next call was from his bookie.

Nick asked, "What'd he say."

"Weren't you listening in?"

"Ah no, but I have the transcripts right here. Save me the trouble of having to read each and every page?"

"The long and the short of it is, Skip has invited us up to his office after the test."

Nick slapped his thigh. "That's extraordinary luck."

"Yes, it is. I can hardly wait. This'll be a perfect opportunity to get an inside look."

"Great. Wish I could be there too. Are you taking the camera phone?"

"I'll have everything hooked up in my briefcase. I hope the tour takes us by the trading department." Ray took another sip. "Perhaps – perhaps, I can even get a look at some of their sheets if everything goes my way."

"Be careful."

Ray snorted. "Whaddaya think – I'm an amateur or something? I can more than hold my own with slick dudes like Skip."

Nick said, "Hey on another subject – we got another complaint about that Madoff guy today. This time from an exec at Goldman's. He said that he's had his entire analysis department working on crunching numbers within different sectors and he can't see how this Madoff guy can get the returns his prospectus says he does."

"So what are we going to do?"

"I don't know yet, but Marek thinks he is big – *real big* ... like in the trillions of dollars worth of big."

"I smell a scam brewing bigger than the last hurricane."

"I'll let you know how it goes." Nick paused, lowered his tone some and said, "Another thing. About Catherine. How soon do you think we should try to turn her? Or do *you* even think we should go there?"

Ray took his time answering. "Personally ... I would not – rush that. Most of these people are so green they don't even know how to place an order for a put or a call. Give us a month or two to learn a bit more. These things take time and *we* don't want to blow it. You work on setting the trap and then maybe we can see if she will play with us. Just keep things nice and cool for now, okay?"

"Gotcha." Nick felt relieved that Ray believed they should take a little more time. "That's kind of what I figured, but since *you're* on the inside I thought *you'd* have a better read than the home office on this. Actually, they wanted to do it sooner rather than later."

"One step at a time, my friend." Ray's other line rang. "Hey gotta hop. I think that's my bookie calling. I need to take the call." He rang off.

CHAPTER THIRTY-TWO

Seven o'clock the following morning, a sleepy A.J. and Matt caravanned over to Truman Annex where they picked up their students and shuttled them to Ft. Lauderdale for the exam. They had previously stopped off over at Starbucks to pick up muffins and coffee. They brought enough for everyone to have two muffins and one coffee.

"Hey A.J. – do you think if they all pass Skip would fly them all home instead of making us drive them back?" Matt asked in a grog as he sipped his steaming hot coffee.

"Wouldn't that be nice, but I doubt it."

Before long the large group began to trickle in. They all looked tired. Matt and A.J. offered them fresh coffee and muffins. They waited another few minutes before beginning the head count for the ride.

Matt called out, "We are leaving in fifteen so everyone needs to be ready. That means if you need to use the bathroom, do it now."

Catherine walked alongside Toye. They both stopped for a brief chat with Matt and A.J. before heading for the coffee and muffins.

Toye had a hard time acclimating with the new group of misfits. She felt out of place, but somehow over the past few weeks they had bonded and formed a friendship of sorts. She said, "Good morning," looked around the area with a nervous expression and said, "Is anyone nervous besides me?"

Matt smiled at her and said, "I think everyone is pretty much on the same wave length here." He paused to offer her some encouragement. "Don't worry you'll *all* do just fine."

Catherine counted people and names as each person arrived and checked them off of Matt's list. Matt and A.J. divided the people into groups of seven and six. They separated Catherine and Ray so each could act as proctor in their respective vans. Sherman was in Catherine's van so he could effectively help her help them. At 7:29 a.m. they pulled away from the Truman Annex, headed toward Ft. Lauderdale.

Matt and A.J. stopped twice along US1 for bathroom breaks and junk food before getting on I-95, ending up at a beige, brick, testing structure that looked like it was in desperate need of some love and paint. They parked in two of the wider handicapped slots near the front entrance because those were the only spaces large enough to accommodate the two long vans. Matt figured he would clear this with the attendants once they got inside. The sign out front read simply, *TESTING CENTER*.

Everyone disembarked and walked silently behind Matt and A.J. When they reached the double glass doors Matt stopped to hold one door open for the remainder of their group to pass through.

"Last bathroom break before the test. Any takers?" A.J. pointed toward the men's and women's room doors. Several faces looked confused and scared. He decided to soften his warning by adding, "I was just kidding. If you follow their rules you can use the bathroom once the test begins, but it's a little dicier."

Matt said, "You know they always think you've gone to the John to get some specially hidden cryptic notes or something else that can help you pass the exam. Seriously, they don't trust anyone."

Ray and Lance were the first to enter the men's room. The door opened with a squeak, squeak, and then boomed closed before they were able to get inside. Lance was reminded of the joke about not letting the door hit them in the ass and he retold it to Ray. They both laughed.

The rest of their group filed into the restrooms for a final pee before the grueling test. Matt and A.J. waited for them in the industrial looking hallway outside.

A.J. turned to Matt and said, "I'll go on up and get things moving forward. Bring them up when you have them corralled." He walked to the elevator bank and hit the up button while Matt waited patiently for their group.

Matt looked over the heads and noted each of his flock by name. When the gang was all accounted for Matt led them up the stairwell to the second floor. Catherine had been this way before. Matt said, "I hope none of you mind using the stairs. I felt we could all use a little exercise after the long drive." He was trying to break the ice and get them all to relax a bit.

They got to the second floor landing and Matt turned left heading toward room 203. At the open door to the room, Matt stopped and said, "Well – *this* is it." He pointed inside and spoke softly. "Remember to take your time. Don't rush. And my advice? Do not change the first answer because that's usually the correct one." He looked at each one and then said, "Any questions?" He scanned their haggard faces for questions they were to probably too chicken to ask. Nobody said a word. One by one they gave Matt the thumbs up. He said, "Good luck."

Kayla had purposefully worn a see through dress. Even in the dimly lit hallway it was possible to see everything underneath. A.J. had placed Kayla in his car on the drive up because he felt Matt might have an accident, or at the very least developed a kink in his neck, trying to drive forward while looking in the rearview mirror at her. Both Matt and A.J. eyed her as she walked into the test center. Her breasts were practically falling out of her undersized top. Matt was momentarily distracted by her captivating beauty and found his mind slinking off toward the no-mans-land where he fantasized what kind of lay she would be. She brushed past him when she entered. He could smell her sweet perfume even after she had long since gone inside.

Lance, always the practical joker, noticed Matt gawking at Kayla. He cracked another joke as he walked in, whispering, "Ah Matt. There is something about Kayla that lingers----oh, I mean on your fingers, eh?" He laughed.

Matt and Lance had forged a good understanding, albeit somewhat banal, and appreciation of women since they began on the exam quest. Each man pulled no bull, yet appreciated the other's candor.

When Kayla was safely inside the room Lance nudged Matt in the side and whispered again, "You know those knockers are fake, don't you?"

A smirk crossed Matt's face. "And just how would you know?"

"I can spot them a mile away." Lance gave Matt a sly wink.

"Lance, you got to love you – you're a man after my own heart," Matt said, feeling Kayla's ether. "Now get in there and pass that test." Matt made a whip-cracking motion.

They formed a single file line inside the test center door. One by one the proctor scanned their driver's licenses into her computer's data base and waited for confirmation of their acceptability before handing them off to another proctor who would seat them for the exam. Bush, Banks, DeRenzo, Goldeneye, Angleton, Darden, Allen, Aiken, Hutchinson, Kevlar, Lemming, Pappy, and Rappaport were all present and accounted for. She was thorough because on some occasions people had been rejected by the computer, based on non-matching identification or other criteria. She was aware fingerprint forms and A-211's were now fed into the Federal Crime Lab's data base and shared with the SEC, CFTC, and the NFA as necessary for background checks to be completed.

Each person was handed a rule card along with several sheets of blank paper before the proctors checked their personal items and ensured that their calculators were tamper proof. Handbags were stowed behind the proctors' counter. Seat assignments were made. Timers were set and the exam began. Strategically placed in obvious locations, overhead cameras acted as eyes in the sky.

A mere five hours into the test Kayla stood up and stretched. Her boobs threatened to slip out of her baby doll top. Standing or any other activity was a signal to the proctor that she or he had something that required their help or immediate attention. The elderly proctor woman took her time walking over to Kayla. She was not amused with Kayla. Her expression indicated she considered Kayla and her display to be quite a distraction. Her panty hose made a swishing sound as she ambled along in the otherwise silent room.

Kayla whispered to her, "I'm done." She waited for a reply, but none was forthcoming. "What happens next?"

The officious woman did not smile or utter a word for the next couple of minutes. She logged Kayla out of the computer terminal and pointed in the direction of the white plastic chairs adjacent to the testing area. In a hushed tone she said, "Please wait over there. We grade the test immediately so you know *now* if you pass or fail." She stepped past Kayla and whispered, "This will just take a few minutes, now go on."

Catherine motioned Kayla in her direction. Matt and A.J. magically appeared in the doorway. They met Catherine and Kayla at the white plastic chairs.

Matt looked at Kayla and asked anxiously, "So?"

Kayla fidgeted and said, "I have a good feeling about this." She paused to look at Catherine. "I really think I did okay." She crossed her fingers and held them up for the extra luck. "Excuse me for a moment while I go to the ladies room."

Nine minutes later Ray was finished with the exam. He met with the proctor and then walked over toward Matt and A.J. He had read up on new laws and regulations while everyone, except the proctors who knew he was a mole, thought he was taking the exam. They all whispered a hushed hello to him. He smiled.

A.J. said, "Ray, how'd it go?" He figured he would be an easy pass, but was looking for assurance.

"No worries, man." Ray said with complete confidence. "Aced it, I think." Not wanting to sound too over confident he added, "I honestly thought it was going to be harder than it was."

Lance was next to finish, then Tracey, Goldeneye and Coop. The rest completed the test one or two at a time over the next couple hours. Most seemed pensive as they waited for the proctor to tell them pass or fail. Since so many had finished near the same time the proctor decided to keep grading and then come back with the names of those who either passed or failed all at once. They sat in silent anticipation. After an arduous, lengthy wait, the male proctor came over and announced that all had passed except Eugene Rappaport.

The group went out into the hall to hug and exchange congratulations. Gene was despondent and forlorn. He ran for the men's room as fast as his odiferous body could take him in tears of frustration and embarrassment.

Matt watched him rushing away and said, "Someone should really go after him."

A.J. said, "Okay, I will."

In the bathroom, the overhead lights seemed to have drained the life force out of Gene. His face was ashen and he was shaking and shuddering.

A.J. felt bad for him, but he did not want to approach him too close or offer him a hug. He smelled. With the addition of anxiety sweat his odor was funkier than a skunk. A.J. opted to stand nearby and said, "Gene, Gene ... get a hold of yourself. Don't worry about this – really. We can have you ready for the retake in a week. By law we have to take the week, but we can retake it then, okay?"

Gene, red faced and even more embarrassed, said, "Do you have any idea how I feel?" He sobbed. "I was the only one who didn't pass!" He was crying. His nose was running. He wiped the snot off on the sleeve of his shirt.

A.J. cringed.

Matt had taken the group downstairs where they could converse in a normal tone of voice. While they talked amongst themselves he called Skip.

Skip said, "And the verdict is?"

"Everyone passed except Gene."

"Well didn't we all figure he was the weakest link?" He didn't wait for Matt to reply. He knew the answer. He said matter-of-factly, "Wrap it up and bring them over here. And Matt? By the way, good job."

"Okay, thanks. See ya in about fifteen depending on how traffic is." Matt hung up.

A.J. had finally calmed Gene down enough so they could leave and head over to Skip's office. Gene was still forlorn, but he followed A.J. out to the van. The group was considerate, and refrained from commenting on Gene's failure.

Matt and A.J. corralled everyone back into the vans and headed toward I-95. Everyone was anxious to see Skip's office and to meet some of his other brokers. Catherine told them about her first visit.

A.J. told his group, "Skip is big time. And that's big with a capital B. His operation here is really something. Trust me, this is the major leagues." He stopped for a red light and said, "Right, Catherine?"

"Is it ever."

Matt was telling his group much of the same that A.J. had told his. "If any of you are lucky enough, Skip may invite you to come up here to work a week and then back to the Keys for a week. He calls that flex-time. He uses that in Buckhead and Lauderdale now, just to give everyone a taste of all of his operations." He looked at them in his rear view mirror." Now tell me that isn't the ultimate job."

Ray, who was in Matt's van, hoped he would be selected to pull some of that double city duty, for obvious reasons.

The vans took the Commercial Boulevard exit and turned left onto Cypress Creek Boulevard. Instead of parking inside the parking garage they pulled up and parked out front on the circular driveway at the twenty story, black glass, AT & T building. A guard from inside the building had walked outside to see who was parking in the no parking zone. When he saw it was Matt and A.J. he waved them in.

Matt and A.J. unboarded their respective vans and walked toward the big bronze glass doors that fronted the structure from the street side. The doors were nearly ten feet tall and heavy. Inside the lobby was green marble with shiny, mirror-like walls. From floor level it soared up an imposing two stories. They strode toward the quadruple bank of shiny brass elevators and pushed the up button. One elevator arrived and half of their group got aboard while the remainder waited for the next one.

"Nice," Lance said inside the elevator.

Cooper said, "It sure is. There's nothing like this in the Keys. You know in Miami we had a lot of buildings with this kind of extravagance."

Lance said, "Coop----you may not have noticed, but we're not in Miami anymore." They both laughed at his kidding.

When all the new recruits arrived on the tenth floor, Ylette greeted and welcomed them.

Matt led, with A.J. following along with the group. First, they walked over to trading where Matt introduced them to Sammy, Ismail, and Mark. Ray took a keen interest in this part of Skip's operation and looked for opportunities to get something of use on his camera. When none arose immediately he engaged Mark in conversation about FOREX.

Ray said, "Do you trade on the FOREX too?"

Mark said, "Yes, we trade on any exchange our clients want or need us to."

Ismail stayed away from the discussion and continued to tabulate the pre-arranged trades from the brokers' daily trade slips.

"What do you like the best?" Ray said.

"I've always been one for the S & P's."

"Me too. Nothing quite a fast moving as the SPOO's."

Matt interrupted them to say, "Come on. There is a lot more to see and Skip wants a word with everyone before we head back to the Keys."

Matt introduced them to many of the brokers and showed them how the computers track trades in real time and from exchanges around the world. "Same as they do in the Keys," he said. Ray was impressed at the sheer size of the operation and the volume of brokers who inhabited the space. He was eager to learn more.

Skip came out of A.J.'s office and met them in the hall. He said, "I just want you to know how pleased I am that you all passed." He had completely forgotten Gene who sulked in the corner. Skip smiled again and turned to Matt and A.J. and said, "Good work, men."

A.J. took this opportunity to correct Skip's assumption on all passing. He whispered in Skip's ear, "Ah, remember Gene?"

"The little squirrelly guy?"

"Yes, he's the one. He didn't pass" A.J. paused and then added, "I know what you're thinking. Go easy on him. I don't think we have to worry about him wanting to take the exam again."

Skip excused himself as did A.J. while Matt continued the tour.

Promptly at five minutes of five Skip rejoined the new recruits in the conference room. This time he had also invited his entire brokerage staff. More than eighty people lined the walls and stood in the hall as Skip got ready to speak. Skip had Matt bring in the whiteboard depicting who had traded what the previous week.

Skip spoke loud and clear. "Thank you, Matt." He turned to face the whiteboard. "As you can see this is our whiteboard. On this board are all of last week's trades." Skip was intentionally making a show for the new recruits. "I have in my hand records of the commissions earned by each of you in this office. Once again I want to congratulate Teddy Romeo, Edward LaVant, John DeNofrio, Larry Kent, Tabitha, and Alan Ader. They were our top producers. And *that* ..." he stopped to survey the room of rookies, the silence emphasizing his next words, "... is what each of *you* should shoot for."

Skip put a finger in the air and raised his voice a notch. "Now I want all of you new recruits to listen up. Alan, here ..." he pointed at him, "... earned $22,500 last week." He looked at the whiteboard chart. "Slow week for you, eh?" Alan smiled at Skip's ironic chiding, but said nothing. Skip continued.

"Teddy earned $16,000. Edward earned $9,800. John earned $17,200. And Tabitha earned $6,000." He smiled at each one of them then pointed out Tabitha to the group, "She has only been with us two short months." Tabitha turned red and giggled. Her ginger steps to and from the front of the room to receive her check from Skip were the only sounds in the room full of stunned newbies. Murmurs of amazement ruffled through the room as she sat back down.

Matt and the other veteran brokers knew this was just a big show for Catherine and the Keys recruits. Skip always drove home his and their shared good fortune by showing them the money.

Skip continued until he had named off all who had earned money and then called out those who owed him money for lack of performance in monies he had advanced them. To those he said in a menacing baritone, "Look, *losers* – you've got one more week ... one week, do you understand that – to turn things around. Don't let me down." He looked each one of them directly in the eye. Nobody doubted his sincerity.

Catherine saw a few of them cower.

"I'm going to turn things over to Matt now." Skip smiled at Matt as he came forward and shook his hand.

Matt, in a playful mood now that the test was over with such good results, said, "I've got some fresh leads. Anyone for fresh leads? I'll be bringing them around to each of you shortly." He parted the top seam on a large cardboard box and pulled out a stack of small strips of paper with names and phone numbers. He dropped them back into the box where they fluttered around like confetti.

It was now well past four p.m. and the regular US markets were closed. Because it was Tuesday most of the brokers would stay right through the allotted break and knock off early. Those who traded FOREX or GLOBEX went back to their desks to see where they might finagle some money in trades.

Ray observed that not all of the brokers appeared to be in on the seamier side of Skip's business dealings. The only people privy to the clandestine operations were the few top, key personnel. They knew there were no real accounts or trades being conducted in this office or elsewhere. They knew Skip was dummying up monthly statements and stashing his cash in the Caymans, Costa Rica, Bahamas, or Switzerland. Whenever any clueless employee confronted Skip with why all of their clients lost and nobody ever won, Skip would say, "Did you make money?" And the answer was always yes, they did. Then he would say, "Just be a broker. Do not try to analyze things."

Yes, Ray realized, stroking his chin, I can see how it all operates. But I need proof. Hard evidence.

Matt explained to Catherine and the Key Westers that the more one broker produced the more leads he or she got. Most were still confused, but some things were beginning to make sense. This business was capable of raking in enormous amounts of money. More money than Catherine or any of the others, with the exception of Ray and Sherman, had ever been exposed to before.

A few minutes after the meeting broke up a tall man with a hooked nose approached Catherine and said, "Hello. I don't believe we've met before." His smile reminded Catherine of a weasel. He reached out his immaculately manicured hand to shake hers and said, "My name is Alan Ader."

"Catherine O'Reilley," Catherine said. "I saw you in the meeting just a few minutes ago with Skip. Evidentially you are one of his best producers." She noticed he was wearing a gold toned Rolex with diamonds around the bezel and a pinky ring with a diamond that could have choked a goat.

"I'm usually the top producer in Skip's business. It you need any help finding your way, just ask me." He appeared to be both warm and sincere.

"Nice to meet you, Alan, and thank you for the offer of help. I'm sure I'll need all the help I can get."

Skip noticed Alan engaged in conversation with Catherine. He stopped by to offer his well intentions. "I am glad you two met. Alan is the *best* and he can help you a lot once you get settled in the Keys." He looked around. "Where is Matt? Check you two later, I'm looking for Mathew."

Skip left them to continue his search.

"Well," Alan said with a gentlemanly bow, "It's been a pleasure. I'll see you later." He began to walk back toward his private office.

Catherine nodded and went to catch up with the group.

Skip found Matt and said, "Matt, get the leads handed out and then I need you to get those people back to the Keys."

"I was kind of hoping you might fly them back," Matt said, then felt he should soft peddle by adding, "You know – now that you have the plane and all."

"Actually, that may not be a bad idea." Skip contemplated that. "I still need you to get things moving in the Keys … so that means you need to get back there, too."

"I thought you said that Kevin was going to head up the Keys operation."

"He is … in good time."

"Skip." Matt was stuck on this change of plans.

"Skip nothing, Matt. You've got to go and finish what we started. I'll get Kevin there by week's end, okay?"

"Whatever." Matt was unhappy, but had no alternative except to do as Skip said.

Skip arranged for the new recruits and Matt to fly in his new King Air down to Key West. Ray had been able to get some good inside photos of the Lauderdale operation and even managed to sneak one shot of a trade sheet when he stopped there to speak to Mark. He knew that single trade sheet would not make them a case. He needed more, much more.

CHAPTER THIRTY-THREE

Kevin Halloran had been in place in the Keys for just over a month. He ran the office like a dictator because, in truth, he had a bit of a Napoleon complex. He was a slight man with a huge ego who had come to this job because Skip owed his mother a favor. Kevin regularly stated that his mother was a *big wig* in a regular investment banking corporation by the name of Berkshire Hathaway, headed up by the now infamous Warren Buffett. Even if people were unfamiliar with Berkshire Hathaway they all knew Warren Buffett and his importance to the financial sector.

Kevin said, addressing the Keys' new brokers, "In front of you, you'll see a sales pitch that has been hand crafted by Skip and Matt." He stopped for emphasis and then said, "Please read it each time you are on the phone, verbatim."

It read:

Hello/Good   Morning/Good   Afternoon/Good   Evening   Mr./Mrs. _____(fill in the blank according to the name provided on the lead slip). My name is _____(fill in the blank---broker name) from Island Investments in Key West, Florida. The reason for my call is that you expressed interest in investing. Is that right?

(wait for reply-if yes, continue---if no, either hang up or try to drum up some interest)

Well this is your LUCKY DAY! How much money are you prepared to invest?

(wait for reply and fill in the blank – if under fifty thousand dollars include the next sentence, if over, skip ahead to the next sentence after this)

Well, usually we do not open any accounts smaller than fifty thousand.

(try to get as much as you can regardless of their ability to invest.)

We have an investment vehicle that can triple your investment inside of six to eight weeks. Would that be something that would be of interest to you?

(anyone who says 'no' to that is a loser, get off the line as fast as possible and work a new lead)

Great. Yes, that's what I thought too, when I first heard about this. Let me explain how it works. Get something to take notes with. That way if you have any questions you jot them down and ask me when I'm done, okay?

Take for instance you want to get into oil or natural gas, both are very lucrative deals. One contract in the options of futures market is equal to 42,000 barrels and a one cent move can net you as much as $420.00 profit. So as you can see, the market does not have to move much for you to make a lot of money! Now I also need to tell you that there is a slight risk that you could lose your investment, but any good and honest broker will tell you that if there is no risk there is no reward.

The cost for each of these contracts vary according to where the markets are trading when we get in, but I will use $1,000.00 as a round number to complete this example. Say we pay approximately $1,000.00 per contract and you have invested fifty thousand dollars, that gives you fifty contracts and then a one cent move will net you $21,000.00. That's really something isn't it? (wait for reply)

And another thing – we can make money on a rising or falling market so we can cover both ends. Rising markets are calls or long positions and falling markets are puts or short positions, but let me handle that for you since I am the professional. .

And that is basically all you need to know to get started. It's simple, foolproof in the sense that we can make money on rising and falling markets, and we do all the work for you!

(Now ask this question, word for word)

So tell me Mr./Mrs./Ms. (fill in the blank) – What do you like best about our program?

(Whatever they say they like best, repeat it and agree with them)

Exactly! That's what caught my attention right away. I really like (repeat what they said they liked) – Couldn't agree more.

(Now go for the close)

So. Here's the million dollar question. Are you ready to get started making large profits with us?

(If yes, skip this step. If not right now, maybe, or I'd like some more information, proceed with …)

I can send you out a free information package that includes a video if you like, I'll just need your

Mailing address

(get mail info).

My contact information is in the packet. I would encourage you to not hesitate long. Time is money, and our investors are making a ton of it while you wait. Okay, have a great day!

(hang up on the loser and move on)

(If yes, proceed with)

Great! Smart decision. I can tell a winner when I talk to one. Okay look. I will send you out a free information package that includes a video and all of the account opening information along with my personal profile and our company prospectus. All I need from you is a credit card number so we can send this out FedEx TODAY! There is no time to waste because every minute you are not in the market is a lost opportunity. Now what type of credit card will you be using today?

(take the number down and select M/C, Visa, and Amex)

Please spell your full name and address for me.

(take down all pertinent information)

Thank you! What is the best time for me to call you back?

*(morning, afternoon, evening-select one and be specific to within a half hour)
Great! Let me schedule (whatever was the best time to call them back) so we
can go over all of the information in that package and get you signed up. If you
have any questions please do not hesitate to give me a call. We work Monday
through Friday from nine a.m. until four p.m. and Tuesday and Thursday
evenings from six p.m. until nine p.m. I look forward to getting you into the
markets and helping you to make some serious money. Have a great day!*
Kevin had stated that no broker was to deviate from this plan.
However, Ray and Sherman varied theirs somewhat. To them, with their
particular and considerable experience, it sounded a little hokey. Also,
Ray and Sherman had a bad feeling about pitching such a high and fast
rate of return when they knew the markets could just as easily go against
them.

Ray was still trying to get his hands on the trade slips, but Kevin was
especially secretive about them, so much so that he privated them away
in the second drawer of the secretary's desk where only he and Karen,
the secretary, had a key. Ray had waited for both of them to leave the
office during breaks on Tuesdays or Thursdays, then tried to pick the
lock. Each time he was close to having his hot mitts on them, someone
came back and broke up his venture. He had been wired up until this
point, but there again, there was nothing particularly damaging he'd
gotten that could effectively incriminate Skip.

Things had calmed down between Catherine and Kayla since Skip
was not a regular fixture in the Keys anymore. Toye had opened a series
of very small accounts and Kevin was working with her to build more
confidence toward asking for larger amounts of cash. Lance, Goldeneye,
and English Chris became a clique of their own. Goldeneye was trying to
get his dad to give him some of the reservation's funds to invest, but so
far his dad had selected to be a cautious observer, leaving Goldeneye as a
definite maybe.

Barbara and Kevin had been sleeping together ever since he came
onto the scene. Craven and Tracey hit it off and were toying with an
emerging romance. Frank paired up with Glenn and began to get nicer
looking haircuts. Ray and Sherman went about working what they knew
better than anyone else in the office. They tried to make money for their
clients because that was the right thing to do. Kevin always cautioned
them about being to *analytical*, like he possessed years and years of
experience, which they all knew he did not, and trying to second guess
what a volatile market might do. Largely they blocked his gibberish out.

Hurricane Rita had glanced past Key West in September, but news
reports had stated that the residents of Key West should prepare for the
onslaught of Hurricane Wilma. Kevin said, "In case some of you've not
been following the weather channel, there may be a hurricane coming

our way. I've spoken to Skip and he believes we should close up shop and take care of our homes until or unless we know Wilma has passed us by." He looked around the office. "This will be effective at the end of today. So take the next couple of days off and I'll see you all back in here after the weekend."

Ray intended to heed this warning, but he was also going to trade his clients from his home as long as the markets remained open. Nothing like a little sensationalism to make everyone some money.

Sherman edged over to Ray's desk and said, "So, Ray, what would you place your clients in, in order to make some money out of this possible storm?"

Damn guys got game, Ray thought. "I was thinking lumber for sure."

"Isn't that awfully thinly traded?"

"Yea, but nothing like making your own markets, right?"

"I guess so. Anyway, where would you go and what would you play – up or down?"

"Let me analyze the charts a bit and get back to you on that one."

The storm came and went. Luckily Key West took no real damage past some heavy rains and wind. The office was back in full force the following week. Skip was pleased with their progress and the money he was making.

Thanksgiving was rapidly approaching. Skip didn't know which of his women to spend that holiday with, but he finally decided that for the sake of logic he would invite Evie. He had seen her off and on while getting the office going in the Keys. She had continually pressed him for more of a relationship than he was willing to commit to. He figured this short trip would smooth things out between them.

For Thanksgiving Skip flew himself and Evie over to Paradise Island on his new King Air. They were staying at Atlantis. It was a pleasure trip, but also a working visit. He planned to visit his currency office and snake away a few more million dollars from that profitable enterprise. Unlike the commercial flights that were required to check in with Customs, Skip's new aircraft commanded respect. He paid off the Customs and Immigration people who were more than happy to take his money and not bother him with legalities.

Skip had arranged for the Honeymoon suite. He had stayed there before with either Natalia or Lilly, he couldn't quite recall, anyway he knew it would impress Evie. To Skip impressions were everything and he hadn't seen her in quite some time. The last time was not very pleasant; he had been stiff, aloof, and brutal towards her. He would make that up to her with this lavish trip to the Bahamas.

Skip's voice was soothing as he placed his gentle hand on Evie's shoulder. "Atlantis is a very posh resort. They offer just about every amenity that anyone could want. And if they don't have what you want, they make a concerted effort to get it and please you. So have anything... anything at all."

When the bellman stopped in front of the Honeymoon suite Evie's heart fluttered and her blood pressure rose. He slipped the card key into the slot and opened the door for them to enter ahead of him. Evie rushed in. "Oh, my God – Skip come quickly...look at this view."

Skip paid the bellman and walked over to the balcony that oversaw the pool. He said, "I thought you'd like this."

"Oh, I do. Thank you, Skip." Evie stepped over to Skip and kissed his cheek.

"Is that all I get?" He teased.

"For now, ha ha. I can't wait to see the rest of this place."

The suite was comprised of a sitting area, two large bedrooms, and sweeping balconies on which one could relax or take in some sun. Evie walked from room to room, mesmerized with the entire scheme.

"Oh, Skip – this is the best vacation ever. Thank you so much."

Skip kissed her lightly and said, "Why don't we go out by the pool?"

A tapping came at the door and a woman's voice in a Bohemian accent called out, "Room service."

"Oh, please come in," Evie said like a princess.

The rather large woman stepped in and said, "I'm here to unpack your bags, and – is there anything else I can do for you now?"

"Oh thanks, but no need, we can unpack. That'll be all for now," Skip said as he slipped her a twenty dollar bill.

Skip and Evie headed out by the pool. Evie took a lounge chair and relaxed in the warm sun. Skip said, "I'll be right back, Evie. I want to call Tommy." He walked over to a nearby table for some privacy.

The Fed's had followed him and Evie from the airport to Atlantis. They were listening.

Sheila, the secretary, answered on the second ring. "Good morning, Merritt Currency. Where may I direct your call?"

"Sheila, it's Skip. How ya doing?"

Sheila took on a dreamy look. She loved Skip as a boss. Her tone was warm and friendly. She said, "Jus' fine, boss. Thank you. Guess you probably want to speak to Tommy?"

On the phone tap, Stan said to Ernest, "Ya think maybe she has the hots for him?"

"Don't they all?"

"Shush----here he goes."

"Yes, I do. Thanks again, Sheila."

The line clicked three times before Tommy came on the line. "Hey, Skip. What's doing?"

"Listen, Tommy. I need to have you deposit some money in the numbered account over in Switzerland today. And I need about twenty five thousand in cash for myself. Got that?"

Skip did this on a semi-regular basis, so Tommy was not fazed by this request. "Yea, yea, sure. How much you want again?

"I need one million transferred to Costa Rica. Two million to the Caymans. And ten sent to Switzerland. And another thing … this may not be the final tally." Skip lowered his voice one octave and said, "I've got it on fairly good word that the Fed's are sniffing around again."

"No shit?"

"Yes shit. Should we run into any problems with them I want to ensure that I've got access to some serious funds to weather any shit storm might rise up."

A federal agent dressed like a grounds keeper was catching all this. He was idly trimming a palm tree five feet from where Skip was standing. Skip paid him no attention. Another fed nearby was acting like a guest, lifting his binoculars and pretending to look at an attractive woman with her children beside the pool. But it was Skip he had in focus.

"Okay, boss, but I'm gonna need until the end of the day today." Tommy mopped off the gathering sweat on his brow. "Gordon opened a big fish last week and he's wrung him in for over two fifty large. The wire transfer for that deal came in late yesterday and those funds should be clear to move by this afternoon."

"Great. How many more do we have like him?"

"Without consulting the dailies I can't say for sure, but I'd guess in the area of sixteen or so."

"All for that dollar amount or more?"

"Si, señor."

"Excellent. Later." Skip flipped his cell closed.

Skip rejoined Evie and said, "I've made some plans for this evening." She was busy filing her nails. "What're we doing, sweetest?"

"I'm taking you on a sunset sail. Be ready by five sharp."

"Where are you going?"

"I've got some business to conduct. If you get bored just go shopping. You can charge it to our room."

Shopping was the magic word for Evie. As soon as Skip was gone she paved a road right down to the shopping promenade and proceeded to spend as much money as she could before he got back.

Skip wanted his twenty five g's and confirmation slips from the wire transfers before he set out on pleasure of any sort. Four o'clock sharp he entered Tommy's office over on Ocean Boulevard. He greeted Sheila who was on her way out and went directly to Tommy's private office door. He stepped inside without knocking.

Tommy was high. His face was numb and contorted. His jaw began moving uncontrollably like a steam shovel on high speed. He tried to stand but was unsteady from the rum and coke he took to counteract the cocaine. He knew Skip was coming by, but had no idea it would be now. "Hi, Skip. Come on in." He tried to calm his pounding heart. *Oh shit. What to do now?*

Skip grimaced. He knew what was up. *I've seen these signs so many times in the past on my mother when I was just a kid. He's on something and I'm betting it is coke.* He snarled, "Tommy don't let me catch you tooting. And don't lie to me now! I know the signs and you're as high as a frickin' kite right now." Skip's upper lip twitched. "I have a zero tolerance for drug and alcohol abuse policy, in case you don't happen to recall. If you need help, and I think you do ... let's get it now."

Tommy tried to stifle a sniff, but couldn't. "I don't have a problem. Honest, Skip. It's just ... you know, being a three day weekend and all ... I thought I might have a little fun, ya know, a few laughs and all."

"No, I don't know – and I really don't want to know. So – save it for someone who cares?" His lip curled and he said, "Do you have my confirmations and cash?"

"Chantelle said I could get it all at four thirty."

Skip raised a fist, bit his lip, and caught himself. "You know what? I don't give a flying fuck what she said. It's four o'clock now. I've got a sunset sail scheduled with Evie. I want you to go over and get that cash, *right now!*" Tommy did not immediately move his feet, so Skip said, "Did you hear me? *I said now!*"

Tommy brushed past Skip and flew out the door. The sudden exertion of adrenaline got him panting, heavy with sweat. Not wanting to risk a heart attack; he stopped at the water fountain on Third and took a long pull of cool water before continuing on. *Is the sun suddenly brighter or what?* He reached inside his right jacket pocket, drew out his sunglasses and placed them squarely over his eyes. *That's better.* He trudged toward the Royal Bahamian Bank, thinking, it's about time to get out of this business, run away from Skip and the mob too. A man has got to set his limits and I'm at mine.

Skip paced back and forth until Tommy finally returned. He was pissed that Tommy had lied. He had found Tommy's stash in his desk drawer and had been tempted to flush it down the toilet. Always considering business ahead of all else, he wondered who he might shift over to the Bahamas to replace Tommy if he got too far into the coke.

Maybe send Matt? He would be a good overseer in this place. But if I continue to expand I'll still need Matt to handle the training. Maybe A.J. could work out – he has no family and no life outside me and this business.

The Royal Bahamian Bank was a small concrete block structure with triple plated bulletproof windows that fronted the street. Inside there were only three teller stations, two new account opening desks, and one large vault that held the safety deposit boxes and cash on hand. The door was open and an armed guard stood nearby.

Chantelle saw Tommy when he came in. She intercepted him. "Hi, Tommy – why don't you come into one of the rooms we use for the safety deposit boxes. In there we can be away from prying eyes." She parted the curtain on one vacant stall so Tommy could step inside. Tommy dropped a big leather satchel on the table and waited for Chantelle to return with the cash.

Chantelle came back a few moments later with an arm full of small bills in wrappers. She placed them in front of Tommy and said, "Do you want to count them?"

"No, Doll. Skip's back at my office waiting for me to return. I'm kind of in a hurry." He still wore his sunglasses and sweat was pouring off his pasty face. "And, you know – I trust you and all."

They stuffed the money into the bag and placed a sweater over the top before zipping it closed. As an afterthought he said, "When I said, *small bills*, I meant tens and twenties – or even fifties … not fives or ones. But I guess this will be okay."

"On such short notice that was the best I could do. The armored car has already stopped here for our daily pick-up. Anything else, Tommy?"

Tommy zipped the bag closed. "Did you do that other thing I asked you about?" He looked at her straight on. She knows what I mean – the transfer of one million dollars into my personal account in Switzerland.

"Yes, sorry – in the rush I didn't give this to you before … the receipt is right here." She handed him a stack of wire transfer slips that were dated today, some for Skip or his Bahamian operation and one for him.

Tommy reached into his front breast pocket and drew out a single white envelope. He handed it to Chantelle.

She opened it and scanned its contents. There were neatly packed twenties amounting to five thousand dollars. She chuckled, smiled and said, "Thank you, Tommy. As usual it's always a pleasure doing business with you."

Tommy always took care of Chantelle because she took care of him. But he had other more pressing things on his mind as he hurried to the front doors. Man, I desperately need another bump. Better hurry back and get rid of Skip so the fun can begin. As he exited the coolness of the air conditioned bank, the outside heat and humidity caught him off guard. He felt suddenly weak and dizzy. He walked back down the two plus blocks toward his office, locked into his own thoughts, erratic as they were and seeming to bounce from one topic to the next. He attributed that to the dope. The pressure of sneaking and Skimming off of Skip and now Skip's awareness of his drug use was pummeling his willpower into nothingness. He needed a fix to buck up.

The Fed's were watching. They had court orders to preview the wire transactions from the Royal Bahamian Bank today. One man entered the bank while the other continued to tail Tommy.

Tommy's heavily starched shirt was sticking like wet toilet paper to his sweaty body. He felt like he was going to heave. As he neared his office and opened the door he felt the cool air-conditioning. Coming in from the heat to the cool he felt better. To his left was a large mirror. He glanced into it and caught his reflection. Shit I look awful. Better step into the men's room before meeting Skip. He splashed some cold water on his face and neck and smoothed his ruffled hair back with his shaking hands. He took a deep breath and went out to face the boss.

Tommy walked back to his office thinking about how happy they both were when they first opened this office eight long years ago. They had been on a long weakened junket with a couple of hookers when they happened upon this place. It had been a perfect cover and an excellent place to transact business. Tommy had reluctantly made the Bahamas his new home. Things had come a full circle, they had changed now, for the worst … and Tommy desperately needed a change, too.

Tommy opened his office door and stepped inside. His heart was as fast paced as his face was drained. Skip sat atop the cranberry leather sofa like the hen on her egg. Tommy avoided eye contact and handed Skip the receipts and bag.

The bags handles were soaked with sweat from Tommy's hands. Skip made a face as he touched them, and then said, "Do you happen to have a paper towel or something? These handles are sopped. What – did you take a shower with this bag or something?"

"Sorry about that, Skip, but it's awfully hot out there."

Skip unzipped the bag and peered inside. He asked, "Did you count it."

"Yea, it's all there." Shit – I hope so, anyway. If not I' m fucked.

"Thanks, Tommy. On another topic, I hope you've been shredding on a regular basis. We can't afford to let our business transactions fall into the wrong hands."

Tommy was speechless. He was parched and fatigued from his walk to the bank. All he could think was, *when is Skip going to leave?*

"Yea, we shred. Every Tuesday and Thursday night."

"Good. Keep up the good work." Skip opened the door and left.

Tommy was relieved beyond measure. He made a mock salute and reached for his desk drawer. He muttered to himself and poured another nip of rum before pulling out his bullet and taking a few snorts of coke. He had to plan his exit strategy just right. The time was now.

Outside, the Federal Agent located Skip. He noticed the leather bag and followed him. Agent Donovan was from New Hampshire and unaccustomed to the Island heat. He felt like an oversaturated sponge dripping from every pore. He tried to hop from shade spot to shade spot in order to avoid more overheating. He glanced up and noticed that the fronds from the native palms along the roadway had not moved an inch in the past hour. He cursed. *God I hate the tropics. Not so much as a single fucking cloud to be found in the goddamned blazing blue sky. It's like a desert out here.*

He fell in place behind Skip. He adeptly dodged scooters and local color in his quest to keep pace with Skip who appeared to be in a rush. In his trot he managed to catch a whiff of the freshly baked Biminis Bread and his stomach groaned. He looked at his watch and noted that his last meal was at seven a.m. *Damn – hungry.* The distance between he and Skip was growing. He forced himself to keep moving, keeping his eyes and mind on his quarry. He followed Skip around the back streets, through the bad portions of town where drug dealers operated unhindered, back to Atlantis where he radioed for the next guys to take over. *Now* he figured he would get a bite and hopefully cool off.

Skip's neck hairs raised and began to tingle. He stopped to turn around and glance behind. Something is amiss, he thought. *I'm not alone.* Satisfied somewhat after surveying the area, unable to discern anyone following him, he relaxed and walked on toward the entry of Atlantis where he knew he was safe.

Ah, Atlantis, he thought with a smug smile. *The crown Jewel of Paradise Island, where the rich like me come to play.* Another strange sensation came over him. He stopped and turned around again. Nobody there except a couple of thin and scruffy gardeners trimming the ruby red hibiscus near the fountain. *Why am I having such a hard time shaking this feeling? Relax, you're inside now, and safe.*

He was not.

The Fed's posing as gardeners looked at each other behind Skip's back and nodded, indicating, *that's our man.* One of them pulled out a cell phone and made a call.

A thin, wiry man with a tall, fat wife, dressed as Midwestern tourists, pretended to be looking at the list of activities available to the guests of Atlantis. Both were packing heat and wearing wires. Their ink pens were cameras and they clicked shots of Skip with his stuffed money bag. Skip did not notice. He continued on to the docks to confirm his sunset boat ride.

Skip strode past the tourists and stopped at the concierge desk where a chubby, cherubic young woman greeted him. Her clean scrubbed face and clear complexion reminded Skip of a Dove soap commercial. He dropped his satchel in one of the two chairs opposite her ornately carved, wood and rattan desk and said, "Hello."

"Hello, Mr. Horowitz. Is there something I can do for you?"

It always amazed Skip that these people could recall the names and faces of all of the people who stayed in their resort. "I just wanted to be sure we're scheduled for the sunset sail this evening."

She checked her chart and said, "Yes, you are. Is there a problem?"

"No. What time does it depart?"

"Six o'clock on the dot."

"Thank you." Skip picked up his bag and walked toward the elevator bank.

The Fed's followed a few steps behind.

CHAPTER THIRTY-FOUR

Coming up to the Christmas holidays, Kevin decided to hold a contest for the Keys people. He said, first thing in the morning on the first of December, "I've got a special contest for you this month. The one who opens the most accounts this month will get a free weekend trip to Atlantis in the Bahamas. All expenses paid by Skip."

English Chris said under his breath, *wanker!*

Dan and Sherman snickered.

Lance sought clarification for that statement with, "Would that be a trip for one or two?"

"Two, of course. Any other questions?"

"Does it go by the number of new accounts opened or the dollar value of those accounts?" Kayla said.

"Good question. I would assume the dollar value over the number, but I will verify that with Skip and get back to you. Okay?"

Kevin called Catherine over and said, "I need to have a word with you privately."

"Why?"

"Skip has an offer for you. He wants you to pull the dual duty between Lauderdale and the Keys."

"Why me?" She groaned internally. *Like I need this now. Shit.*

"I don't ask those sorts of questions of Skip." He raised an eyebrow.

Catherine let a small sigh escape. "For how long?"

"At least for the next month." Kevin could tell she was not happy about this development so he tried to soften the blow by saying, "He told me he was very proud of how you've come along, but he wants you to get a taste of the majors. You don't have a problem with that do you?"

Ray had seen Kevin ask Catherine for a private talk. He was milling around just within hearing distance, hoping his new bug was catching this game changer. He wished it were him instead of her. *What I wouldn't give to be the one to break this case wide open. Guess we may have to approach her after all.*

Before Kevin could get a read from Catherine, Kayla paraded by in another of her low cut dresses with ultra short skirts. She could feel Kevin watching her and that excited her. She had never quite gotten over being onstage. She bent over in front of him exposing her breasts nearly down to the nipples. If a gaze could grab and pull he'd have fallen into her shirt.

Whore, Catherine thought. *What she will do for the slightest bit of attention. She doesn't have to make all women look as cheap as she is. And what's the big deal about her anyway?*

Kayla smiled seductively at Kevin even though his eyes were clearly not on her face. "Oops. Sorry to interrupt. I just had another quick question."

Kevin felt her trolling, pushing his buttons, but was powerless to fight off her hyperactive sexuality. He finally managed to say, "Ah – sorry about that." *Focus.* "What was your question?"

"Someone said you mentioned a dress code. Could you please elaborate?"

Kevin looked directly at her boobs as he spoke. God what I wouldn't give to tear that up. Bet she is a regular cougar in the sack. "You, ah … you're dressed just fine."

She loved toying with men and having one on the hook. She spun on her camouflage work boots and her short skirt flared out giving him a good view of her bare rear end as she walked back to her desk.

Ray and Sherman shared a plan-of-attack look. Ray said, "She can be my secret weapon anytime and anyplace."

"I'm just digging the daily show. She really is something."

Ray said, "So, tell me – what do you think of Kevin – really?"

"Napoleon complex – pure and simple. Probably has the teeniest weenie ever."

"Amen, brother." Ray snickered.

Catherine had been watching the entire Kayla show daily now for months. She assumed that whenever Kayla needed an ego boost she would just show off her t and a. They had forged a difficult friendship, if it could be called that. But the longer Catherine was forced to watch her parade around as if she were naked the more she began to begrudge and dislike her. Under her breath she said, "Bitch," and thought, she must be infernally insecure to have to resort to such lowlife tricks. I wouldn't ever stoop so low. She muttered, "What a floozy."

Kevin heard her. "Excuse me?"

Catherine looked over at him, startled and chagrined. "Oh, nothing."

"Well … are you excited about Skip's new plans for you?"

"Yes and no. I've lived in Key West my entire life and I've never once considered living anywhere else. I love it here. My family is here. My friends are here." She stopped herself from rambling further, sighed and said, "Let's just see how it goes."

Kevin said, "Can we talk about this more over lunch?"

"I guess so." She went back to her desk and fielded her first callback for the day. Skip had said not to leave messages, but over the past few weeks she had done so from time to time and about half of those times had panned out by becoming clients.

Kevin had been talking to Karen about the voice mail, messages, and how to manage trading. He looked at his white and yellow gold toned

Rolex and noticed that it was nearly lunchtime. He called out to the office in general, "Let's break for lunch and reconvene at one thirty."

Ray said, "I've got some people to call over the break. Do you mind if I hang back here and take a little later lunch – or none at all?" He had planned this ahead because he wanted to try again to see the documents that Karen had been told to secret away and then later shred. He knew she kept them in her top drawer on the left hand side of her desk and dutifully locked them up at the end of the day and during lunch.

Kevin did not like nor really trust Ray, but he also had no authority to stop him from working over the lunch hour if he wanted to do so. "I guess that'd be all right, but let's not make this a regular thing. Okay?" He turned to Karen and said, "Would you like to join me and Catherine for lunch?"

Karen was not one for fraternizing, but she did find Kevin interesting in a weird way. "I guess so. Just give me a minute to lock up here."

"We'll wait for you by the elevators," Kevin said, and he and Catherine exited the office.

Ray frowned and shook his head. He knew he would now have to pick the lock. Just got to get photographs of those docs. I'm sure that can give us a lead and most likely a major piece or two of hard, incriminating evidence

Once the group had left, Ray snuck out into the hall to listen for the elevator. Satisfied they were indeed on their way to lunch he went back into the office and locked the door. He sped over to Karen's' desk and bent down beside the top drawer on her left hand side. With practiced skill he picked the lock with the tip of his ink pen. Before long it sprung open and he rifled through the file on accounts and trades. He was in the process of photographing them when there was a knock at the door. Concealing his nervousness, he called out, "Ah, yea. Who is it?" He snapped closed the file drawer and locked it in one silent second before walking toward the door.

"Guess?" said the voice.

It sounded vaguely familiar. "Give me a hint."

"Just open the god damned door, you idiot!"

Chris, Ray recognized, but without the British bit. He opened the door to find the Englishman standing there with an amused look on his face.

"How did you lose that English accent so fast? Don't tell me it's a put on from the get go?"

"I've got quite a few tricks up my sleeve," Chris quipped. "What's going on in *here*?" He had moxie and he knew Ray was somehow up to no good. His dark eyes danced.

Ray tried to find a plausible excuse, but none came readily to mind. Finally he muttered, "I was on a call, that's all. I guess Karen or Kevin must have mistakenly locked the door when they left." Ridiculously weak bluff, Ray knew; hope he doesn't call me on it.

"Well, okay mate, good enough." Chris looked around the office trying to size up whether or not Ray had been straight with him. He had an unusually good sixth sense that told him to remain on guard where Ray was concerned.

Ray felt certain Chris did not suspect him of anything illegal or untoward. He needed to call the main office so he said, "I'm just going to go to the men's room. I'll be right back." He padded down the hall and ran down the stairs to the first floor. He went out the exit and found himself by the fountain. He dialed Nick, who answered on the first ring, and said, "Did you catch the conversation between Kevin and Catherine this morning? And for that matter, the one that just occurred between Chris and me?"

Nick was distracted. He said, "What? Sorry about that, I was reading the transcripts from another conversation just now. What did you ask me?" He activated the recording switch.

Ray dropped down into the nearest bench, looked around, and said, "Two things. Apparently Skip wants Catherine in Lauderdale so she can learn from the pros. Learn *what* is still to be determined. Well, *proven* might be a better word. I've got a good handle on what the actual scam is." He looked around again. "I have to speak soft. Not exactly in a private space. Can you hear me okay?"

"Yes. Go ahead."

"I overheard this conversation between her and Kevin. I have it all recorded." He lowered his voice even further. "I got into Karen's desk at lunch, but was interrupted by Chris. I have a few pictures, but not nearly enough. They depict the trades and specific account names. I thought we could check those against the ones that American Futures has to see if there are any missing." He cast a furtive glance around and then said, "If we can catch a slip we might have an entrée into the rest of his business dealings."

"You do realize we can't use that information to help build our case, right?"

"Of course I do. I happen to have the exact same law degree that you have."

"Just a word of caution – whatever you do, be careful. We do *not* want you to blow your cover."

"I know. I know. I've been playing it very low key." He glanced at his watch and noted the time. "I better be getting back before Chris comes looking for me in the men's room." Ray hung up and went back to the office.

Nick clicked off the recording device and wondered when Catherine would call to give him the good news.

Kevin waited for the whole office to come back from lunch before he began his next request. He said, "The play for the afternoon is corn at $2.80. Calls. Place all of your customers into corn."

Kevin was doing this because Skip had told him he had it on good word that one of the other commodities trading houses was about to make a run on corn and he did not want to miss out on the big money to be had. Kevin walked up to Karen's' desk and said, "I want thirty percent of the monies on the sidelines to actually be traded today. The brokers have their instructions."

"What? I've never done that before. How do you want me to do that?" A nervous edge crept into Karen's voice. She hated change and this was decidedly change.

"Just collect all the sheets and give them to me. I'll call them in to Sammy, Mark, or Ismail."

Karen did as she was told, but this was such a stark difference from what she had been doing, she wondered if Skip knew about it. She decided to ring him to ask. Karen was a stickler for details and her loyalty first went to Skip----not Kevin. She phoned him. Missed him, but spoke to Sammy instead. She said, "Sammy do you know what Kevin wants me to do?"

Sammy was feeling playful so he wagered a goofy guess, "Of course I do, Red – mix up an extra batch to match your head and your snatch?"

"Honestly, Sam. Don't you ever take anything seriously?"

He frowned into the phone and said, "Okay, okay, you're wearing me down. What?"

"Kevin wants me to take thirty percent of the monies for the day and actually trade them. Are we authorized to do that?"

Sammy laughed loud and hard. He said, "Those are *my* instructions. Just do as he says. You're such a silly old goose."

"I just wanted to be sure that this order came from *someone* in the main office. You know with Kevin still being green and all." Weak, she thought, but I've got to have some excuse for the call and concern.

"Green … did you say green?" Sammy was doubled over laughing now. "Kevin has been there five or six months now. Thanks for the inquiry, but everything he said is all just fine."

Sammy clicked off and Karen was left with the fading memory of his laughter. She scratched her red colored head, bucked up and did as Kevin said, even though she had no idea of the what or why of such unusual orders.

Sammy knew. Skip had gotten got his tip regarding corn from Shirley, Kevin's mother, at Berkshire Hathaway. She had gotten it from another source and had acted in good conscience by telling Skip so her son's branch of his business could profit. The news had not been publicized yet, but there had been some intense speculation on behalf of several analysts who had the inside track and had let it leak to the press later that same day.

That day corn trades were exacted across the board from all of Skip's operations. They panned out as planned. Skip won a lot of cash and his brokers made some money on the trades because they charged the highest allowable fees under the current laws. They charged $225.00 per trade and counted each contract as a single trade – unlike reputable trading houses who bundled them together as one. He told his brokers to tell their customers that the market had gone against them and in order to recoup those lost funds they should send in some more cash to play again.

Corn contracts were bought at one hundred twenty bushels per contract and each one cent move in that market, up or down, was worth one hundred twenty dollars. Skip grossed twenty five million dollars that day from corn alone, while all of the investors suffered a loss. The official statement to the clients as to why they had lost in this case attributed it to a possible draught across much of America.

Inside trades, Skip smiled and thought to himself, you just gotta love 'em. Having sources from within an organization that knows or has an interest in how the markets might perform. His smile broadened as he considered his leg up on the Fed's by making the most of this kind of insider information. These occasional trades give me a legit edge right when the Fed's least expect it. God I love keeping them dazed and confused … almost as much as I love to make money.

Clayton, Nick, Marek, and the rest of the investigators in the NFA and CFTC working under the SEC were following these corn trades as well. They saw the market open, rise, and close down on corn. A tremendous amount of volume had passed through the exchanges that day buying corn, then selling corn, then leveling out for the day. Perhaps if it had not been for Ray's red-flagging this incident they would not have known at all. They needed to know who had actually made the money---- was it Skip, or his clients. Where had the information come from? Had the clients given authorization to participate in this trading scheme, or did they, as in the brokers, hold proxy or power of attorney over the accounts? Following the paper trail might lead them to something that could be used in a court of law. If that trail turned cold, they were hoping that Ray might be able to ferret that information out of his office and pass it along. Either way they were upbeat because something was finally happening in this long, dragging on case.

The next day in a conference call, Marek said, "There was a run on corn yesterday. It was a market wide corn drive. There was more open interest than we've seen in the corn sector in quite some time. And it had nothing to do with the time of the year either, from what I understand."

Nick said, "Yea, we *all* watched it. It was a good move on the up side and one that surely made some brokerages a lot of money. Obviously a day trade – and one day ahead of the government coming out with the crop report, which is equally as suspicious and unusual given the players. Do we know yet how this guy Skip fared?"

Marek said, "I'm sending a team over to American right after lunch. We should have some definitive information this afternoon at the latest."

Tad, a junior investigator, said, "Any news from Ray?" Tad was a classic brown noser. Most of the guys detested that type of sucking up.

"He's doing what he can, but he tells me the secretary is keeping a pretty tight lid on it," Nick said, flustered. "When will this guy leave us room to jump in?"

Marek came back into the conversation. "Soon I hope, but maybe it's time to contact someone on the inside and let them help us along." His was a rhetorical statement. Everyone on the team was aware that Nick was going to try, at some point, to turn Catherine.

"Ray and I discussed the possibility of using Catherine, again, and I'm going to be seeing her this coming weekend. On a personal note, I think she is still a little too green to really understand how she can help us," Nick said to Marek.

Marek was tempered in his reply. "Let's play that one by ear."

"Gotcha." Nick cocked his head to the side. "But if not *now*, then when?"

Oscar said, "Hey Nick – if you're banging her, and we know you will be, you surely can't wear a wire. Even green as she is she would be suspicious of what that's all about. And then what would you say – I'm just a kinky dude who likes to record my love making sessions?"

Marek rolled his eyes and huffed. "Can we please keep this professional?"

Nick and Oscar did not get along from the moment they had met. Oscar was not a team player and most of these investigations required the people assigned to them to work cohesively. Nick wanted him off the team, but Marek had been reluctant to discharge him when they were so short handed.

Nick roared, "And where is all of this bullshit leading, Oscar? You've got something to say then out with it. Quit this childish beating around the bush!" God I hate this ass.

"Nowhere, really – it's just a statement of fact. You know, you could use a little lightening up yourself." This Nick guy is so straight---everything by the book.

"And the point of this discussion is?" Nick glared at the phone.

"Some guys have all the luck – you know what I mean? You get the girl and we get the bones."

"Actually that does bring up a good point," Marek said, deep in thought. "I guess that means we better redo the wire in your house so we can follow along in your conversations."

Oscar said, "The last time we had to listen in on you it was pretty x-rated. Maybe you can clean it up this time?"

"I guess so, but you know she could have turned out to be some troll or something, too. I'm just an investigator just like *you* – I'm just doing my job. Clean it up. Pathetic. What – you want a PG thirteen fuck scene?"

The meeting broke up a few minutes later, thankfully for Nick. He was glad he had been on the phone and not face to face with Oscar *the wiener*. I'd have busted his chops good.

***

Skip had just completed construction of his new ten thousand square foot home on the Intracoastal Waterway in Sea Ranch Lakes. He had gone through three crews in the process, the first two of which he did not pay because he felt their work was inferior. They had both filed mechanics liens on his new abode to the tune of five hundred thousand dollars for supplies and labor. The third one completed the job, but charged an extra two hundred fifty thousand to go back and redo some of the work that was not completed by the previous two crews. Skip was planning to move in over the course of the next two weeks or as the new furnishings arrived from his interior designer.

Lori Knowles, a well renowned interior decorator in the Ft. Lauderdale area, had been hired by Skip to furnish his new home and she was spending money almost as fast as Skip's office could make it. She charged Skip for trips to New York, Seattle, and Dallas to buy obscure things that would make a big statement about the new occupant of this classic abode. Her tab was upward of three hundred fifty thousand and counting. Because this house was on the water Skip also contracted with Rybovich-Spencer to buy a fifty three foot Rybovich and had Lori redecorate it, too. The total tab on the boat project was over two million dollars, but the outcome was incredible and Skip loved spending every penny of it. He felt it made him the big man on the water, at least in his immediate pond.

Skip was not sending his plane down to bring Catherine up to work in Lauderdale for the week. He spent money like some people saved, but he preferred not to waste it on one person flights and women he was no longer sleeping with. That could better be accomplished with commercial airlines.

In the course of her luncheon conversation with Kevin and Karen, Catherine said she would prefer to drive instead of fly commercially. That way she would have her own transportation and not count on Randall or someone else to take her to and fro. Kevin had concurred and said he would inform Skip.

Later that same afternoon the CFTC and the NFA, under the authority afforded the SEC, did a random audit of American Futures trading operation on the CBOT in Chicago and the COMEX in New York City. They found thousands of trades for Skip's organizations and many more under Berkshire Hathaway on the $2.80 corn calls. They traced them back by account numbers to the people who had opened them in each establishment and planned on asking some serious questions of them.

Berkshire Hathaway had been cleared by the SEC of any wrongdoing, even though their trades remained highly suspect. Warren Buffett had issued scathing memo's to all of his commodities traders telling them that if they ever caused him and his organization to come under the microscope of the SEC, *ever again,* they would all be summarily terminated. He'd see to it that they would never be able to get a job as so much as a lowly *messenger* on Wall Street so long as he lived and breathed.

The impromptu investigation of Skip's organizations at American Futures had revealed that even though this was a winning trade, and a big one at that, the funds earned were still languishing on the sidelines and had not been sent to the people named on those accounts. Even worse, a closer inspection of the trades had shown that those trades had been tabulated as a loss and not the win that they actually were. American Futures tried to explain this away by stating they had a new person in their trading department who had made an error on those alleged trades and that the situation would be remedied in the coming day or days.

After the investigators left, Skip had called American. "I need all of our winnings to be transferred to my numbered account in Switzerland."

Amin on the other end said, "You know that's not going to look very good after the investigators just came knocking."

"Look here, Amin. We've given your organization a lot of money and helped to make you and your family quite rich. Just where are your allegiances?"

Amin wasn't sure how to take that. Should I consider that as a threat? This man can be so difficult. Just maintain your cool. "I didn't say we wouldn't do it. I just think you should perhaps wait a few days or a week before doing so."

"I don't give a god damn what you think. Just do as I say and do it now." Skip was seething. Fucking towel head thinks he can tell me how to run by business.

"As you wish." Amin shook his turbaned head. His dark features hid his fear at being caught in some scam with Skip.

Skip hung up the line. Amin did as Skip requested, but also made available, although not verbally, copies of the transaction should the SEC or the NFA and CFTC come back with more questions.

It being the holiday season, the Fed's were shorter staffed than usual. First came Chanukah, and then Christmas, and then the New Year's celebrations. Not a lot of business was transacted during the month on Wall Street or elsewhere. Had the Fed's had the manpower or resources to complete the audit at this time, they may have found enough dirt to bring Skip down, at least temporarily, and ramp the investigation up to the next level. Since that was not the case, the investigation dragged on into the following year.

CHAPTER THIRTY-FIVE

Catherine had been doing the Keys-Lauderdale shuffle now for over two months and she was tiring of it. She had rented a small studio apartment in a suburb of Lauderdale, called Victoria Park, so she no longer had to stay at the HoJo's. She had been seeing a lot of Nick on her off time. She thought their relationship was beginning to deepen.

From time to time Catherine spoke to Shamus, but not as often as he would have liked. In an effort to forget about her he had taken up with a pretty red haired damsel from Montreal by the name of Danielle St. Luc. She had a charming French accent and a gorgeous shape. They had been dating seriously for going on six months, and at Christmas Shamus planned to propose. He was crestfallen when, on the eve of his proposal, Danielle had told Shamus she was already married and planning to get back together with her husband before the New Year.

Ray had been trying to get his hands on the trade documents from the corn run for over two months. He knew for a fact the entire operation was nothing more than a Ponzi scheme, but he needed proof. The American Futures documents would eventually back up those suspicions and lend credence to the court case against Skip.

One February morning a cheerful Kevin came in and said, "Okay, team. Today's play is heating oil. Calls at a strike price of $1.43. Place *all* of your clients into this trade. And I do mean *all*." Kevin paused and then walked over to the desks in the center of the office. He said, "Lance, Cray, Ray, and Chris – you guys understand the movements of the market far more than the others here. I want you to do some spreads or straddles to balance things out."

Ray said, "Can we buy at the money or into the money more than the dollar forty three?"

"I'm going to give you some latitude on that, okay?" God I hope this doesn't backfire. If it works as planned Skip is so going to give me a raise.

Ray was giddy. Now he could actually put on some of the trades he had been accustomed to before coming to this phony playground.

Chris turned around in his desk and said, "Hey Ray – where are you going to get in?"

"I want to do some dollar forty calls coupled with some dollar thirty six puts." He sat at his computer screen and punched a few buttons that brought up other screens and then said, "I wonder if we can jump over into crude and gas too?"

Lance said, "Better check with Napoleon first. You know how crazed he gets."

Meanwhile Sammy had given the same instructions to the crew in Lauderdale. Catherine had overheard Alan and Jeff Jedlecki talking about the skim or the vig or something. These were things she didn't understand. Then they changed topics and were discussing how to maximize their $225 dollar per trade commission's with today's market challenge set forth by Sam.

Alan told Jeff his plan to maximize this play. "Let's do it like this," he said. "You be my senior, and vice versa. We call all of the others clients and tell them we have it on good information that there is about to be a huge movement in the energy markets, *today*. We try to wrangle as much new cash from them as possible by stating it's necessary in order to maximize the potential returns."

Jeff listened and said, "I like it." He glanced up at the monitors to see what, if anything, was currently going on in the energy markets. "Tell you what, Alan ... why don't we sweeten this deal."

"What'd you have in mind?" A sly smile crossed Alan's smooth, hawkish face.

"The first one to do 1,000 trades today has to wax the other's shoes for a week."

Jeff was one of the younger brokers in Skip's main office. He was tall, thin and barely twenty three, but he was smart, a very fast learner, competitive, and ballsy – which translated into one of the top earners. He was also an immaculate dresser. He broke into a smile, looked absently at his $20,000 watch – gold to match all his other jewelry, brought over a folding chair, stuck in front of Alan and put one foot on it. He pointed at Alan and said, "You got a deal. Take a good look at this soft, buttery leather Italian, cuz you'll be shining these all week, pal."

Alan snorted his disbelief at Jeff's bravado. They shook on it and went about swapping files.

Catherine decided to ask Ted Romeo about the things Alan and Jeff had been discussing. She went into Ted's office door and, feeling a bit timid, tapped on the frame.

Ted bellowed, "Yes – who is it? Come on in."

She slunk in and asked, "Ted, ah ... can I ask you a question." God I hope he doesn't get all nasty with me.

His fingers were like a microprocessor moving in rapid sequence over the keyboard. The computer screen blinked to life and charts and tables depicting oil and gas trades shifted in front of his eyes. He did not look up from the computer, but said, "Sure – shoot. But make it fast, I've got a lot of trades to place today."

"Jeff and Alan are trading clients today. Why would they do something like that?" I hope I don't sound stupid, but I'm so confused.

Teddy laughed to the point of nearly rolled off his rolling chair. He said, "The answer to that is simple. They're loading each other." She really has no clue. What a green, small towner.

"Loading each other? What's that?" Her face was a portrait of naivety.

Teddy was never one to miss a golden opportunity like this. "Tell you what. How many trades have you made this week?"

"Fifty, I think." That's a *good* week in the Keys, she thought, but nothing up here. Anyway, I'm trying as best I can.

Is that all?" Teddy frowned and huffed. "Go now. Bring me your files and let me show you how this loading works. If I'm not mistaken, and I'm usually not, then I'm sure I can rack up a few hundred trades for you – today alone." He rubbed his hands together. Ha – this is going to be fun.

"Really? How?" She was doubtful.

He winked. "Just watch and listen to the master at work. Of course when I do this you split the number of trades with me." He put both hands out, palms up. "What are you waiting for. Time is wasting – get going!"

Her head was swimming; she did not understand one bit what Teddy had just told her. "Ah okay, whatever." She rushed back to her desk to retrieve her files, her head spinning. I hope this isn't a huge mistake. Oh what the hell – I've got to trust someone and nobody else seems willing to help.

That day Alan and Jeff cleaned up on trades. Jeff managed to wrangle 1,012 trades from Alan's book. Jeff had more clients and a little bit smaller dollar base per client, but Alan was also very good and managed to place 998 trades for Jeff.

Alan walked over to Jeff's desk with his head hung and said, "Good job." He dropped a large stack of manila file folders onto his desk. "It was very close, but you managed to eek out slightly more trades than I did." Ouch, this really hurts.

Jeff licked his lips like a cat lapping up milk and said, "Yes, yes I did." His chest inflated. "I'll be bringing in my shoes tomorrow for you to polish." He handed Alan a thick stack of manila file folders and proceeded to tabulate how much money he had made. God I love money. And I am *so* going to enjoy Alan shining my shoes.

For each of the $225 Skip's operation collected per trade, Jeff and Alan were paid $125. Jeff earned $126,500 that day while Alan made $124,750.

Ted was able to pry another 30 trades from Catherine's clients and that meant they each had a show of 15 more that day, too. Catharine topped out at 65 trades, but her pay scale was only $100 per trade. Still, she earned $6,500 – her best day *ever*. Teddy had begun with over 300 trades, so he was ahead of the curve, before he *enhanced* Catherine's accounts. He ended up with 315 trades at the rate of $125 per trade for a total commission of $39,375.

Catherine wanted to celebrate. She decided to call Nick to see if he could join her.

***

At the Key West operation, Kevin was having a huge fight with Ray over how to conduct trading.

"You didn't have authority to place the trades you did. And someone is going to have to account for this."

Ray screamed, *"Bull-shit."* He turned to Chris, Clay, and Lance for verification. "Did you or did you not hear *Napoleon* here, tell us that we had some latitude on our trades today?"

Chris came to Ray's defense. "You know, Kevin …" He flicked his long bow knife open and closed a few times as he watched Kevin approach Ray in the debate. "…we did hear something to that end. So that being the case, I'd not say that Ray and the rest of us were out of line at all in the trades we put on today." He tossed his knife, sticking it into the desk top nearest Kevin.

Kevin jumped back, fear in his eyes. I hope that careless fuck nutcase doesn't ever cut me.

The fight rose to such a timbre that Karen thought they need some intercession from Skip. She speed dialed Skip's cell phone and told him about the heated argument.

Skip said, "Calm down, Karen. Everything's going to be fine. Let me call you back on the main line so we can be on the speaker phone. When you have me on the line please call both of them in."

Karen said with obvious apprehension, "That may be easier said than done."

"Just do it." He rang off.

Skip dialed back and Karen picked up on the first ring. "Yes, Skip … just one moment."

There was shouting and pushing and Lance and Chris had to hold Ray back from throwing a punch at Kevin. Toye, who disliked any show of aggression, had ducked under her desk. Kayla watched with amusement. Tracey, Clem, and Dan went outside to have a smoke. Coop backed up Lane and Chris in defense of Ray. Frank and Barbara were screwing in the ladies room and were missing the entire show. Goldeneye had gone out for a drink and walked in right when Skip came on over the intercom.

"What the hell is going on?" Skip said, his voice firm.

Kevin shouted at the phone, *"Ray* here thinks *he's* the *boss."* Skip could hear hard breathing over the phone. "He – he's …a rogue and I think we should fire him!" His face was bright red, his eyes flickering with rage.

"Ray?" Skip said with an even voice.

"I am not a rogue. I do, however, know trading and I think I know trading better than he does. He has little or no experience and he thinks he calls all the shots." He let out a sigh. "I'd appreciate him letting *me* trade *my* clients however I see fit. As a matter of fact, most of the time *his* trades make *no sense* at all. I don't even know where he comes up with them and then he tries to force feed us some *horseshit* about why the trades he has proposed should make our clients money. It's all a bunch of shit." Ray was becoming calmer on the surface, but still boiling beneath.

Skip hated to admit that Ray may be correct in that assumption, so he sidestepped the direct portion of his statements and said, "Understand that I hate to step on anyone's toes here. I really do. But Kevin, Ray isn't the only one who believes this to be the case." He paused. "I propose the following; Kevin, just let Ray continue to do his own thing and don't question why. Do you think you can manage that?"

"I can't do that, Skip. You are cutting off my authority." Kevin's face looked like it might explode. He slammed a fist onto the desk top. "I refuse to work under those conditions!"

Skip remained calm, his voice steady, even. "Can't – or won't?" He paused for effect. "What's your alternative?"

While Kevin thought how best to answer that, refrain from murdering someone, and manage to keep his job, Skip was considering the history behind this situation. Kayla *has* called me to complain about Kevin on numerous occasions. Lance also called me in confidence to tell me more or less the same. There's no disputing that Kevin has fallen prey to the Napoleon syndrome. And he's playing it to the hilt. I despise anyone trying to usurp me. The Keys operation has made some money, but not as much as I had hoped. Ray and Sherman know too much. They know how to bend the rules and that has become an obstacle in my scheme. Once they even went to the extreme of teaching the other people in the office how to trade and make money for their clients instead of lose. I know Ray did it to help them, but …

Skip's musings were cut off when Kevin blurted out in a crimson-faced rage, "If I can't run this office my way, then … then I quit!"

Karen was looking back and forth between Ray and Kevin for any signs of a truce. None were forthcoming. She shook her head in disgust. Fine, just fine. Why can't anything good last?

Skip took Kevin at his word. He said, "Fine. I accept your resignation, Kevin. That will be effective as of right now. Clean out your desk and get out."

Kevin slammed both fists on the desk. "You can't do that!"

"Last time I checked, that was *my* office, Kevin, not yours. I can and I just did." The click of Skip hanging up punctuated the finality of his statement like a quiet, but giant, exclamation point.

Karen feared another, more brutal, fight might ensue. Ray stormed back to his desk and under his breath said, "Asshole. I guess Skip told you."

Kevin heard him. "What'd you say?"

"You know exactly what I said, you *pathetic little worm*." He shifted in his seat. "I think *you* got exactly what you deserved."

Toye peered out from under her desk. Kayla sat on the edge of hers, and took her phone off the hook so she could watch the fight without being interrupted.

Karen called out to Ray and Kevin to please join her in the adjoining room, adding, "I don't think this is going anywhere. Why don't you both just calm down."

Kevin wasn't going anywhere. He flew into a wild fit. He raked the files and phones off the first two rows of desk tops. Pens, pencils, calculators, and more crashed about. Karen trotted over to Chris and said, "Please … can't you do something." She was near tears.

Lance, Goldeneye, and Clay latched onto Kevin and managed to stop him from inflicting any further damage to the office. Ray stood with his chest puffed out, enjoying the whole scene. He couldn't wait to call Nick and the guys. He really hoped they had been listening in on this one. What a doozy.

***

Father Zeke had come to christen Skip's new Rybovich. He said, "I christen thee *Traders III.*" He then clanked a Champaign bottle over the bow, which crumbled and bubbled all over the dock.

Skip, Ralph, Matt, and Father Zeke toasted to "Traders III". Nobody spoke about what had transpired in the Keys office today.

Later that evening Ray finally had opportunity to call Nick and tell him about what had happened in the office. He was gleeful. He said, "Nick, you know that *asshole, Kevin* … the worm of a guy that Skip sent down here to oversee this office?"

Yea … you've mentioned him before. Not a very good picture you drew of him."

"Well, he and I had a huge blowout today."

"Over?"

"Trading … he's one of the most unethical sons of bitches I've ever come up against."

"One of many in our line of work."

"Yea, well … he is out," Ray said with a smug smile.

"Really? That's a surprise. What happened?"

Ray snorted. "You can get the sordid details on the transcripts, but he basically is an *idiot.*"

"Won't argue that. What now?"

"Well, I thought we might make a mock run at the purchase of this operation. That way we should be able to see the books, get a handle on how these trades are allocated over at American. By the way … how did that investigation of the corn turn out?"

"I can follow that line of logic. That's not a bad plan. But, let's see what Marek thinks about it before we jump … ah, the corn." He thought back and then said, "Well, Berkshire was cleared and we still need to review those documents from American, but those guys were cooperative and I hadn't exactly expected that."

"Okay, get back to me on those points." Ray took a large gulp of his rum and coke, then said, "Got to go. Let me know."

Sean, Marek, Nick, and the other top agents on the case held a round table discussion about Ray's outlandish idea to buy Skip's operation or at least make it look like that was the case. There had been interest and skepticism on all accounts. There did appear to be a possibility that those higher up might buy into it. Nick called Ray back to tell him the deal was being given due consideration, but no word just yet as to if it was a go or not.

While Nick had Ray on the line he got a beep from his call waiting line. Nick said, "Hey Ray, hold on just one minute – my other line is ringing."

The lines did not mute completely because they were tapped. Ray could overhear voices on the other side; they sounded familiar, but he was unable to make out exact conversation.

Nick concluded the other call and switched back to Ray. "Okay, my friend, I've got the good word for you. We've got the green light for your run at Skip's Keys op, but the main office says not to jump in too fast … you know, take your time. Fish a little first."

"Got it. I'll try to get a rough idea of rent and operating expenses and then we can discuss a dollar amount for the accounts sans the name, which probably does not bode well with investors anyway. If the main office is concerned – we never actually have to go through with the deal … just follow up with the due diligence. And in the due diligence he should reveal the books. That's where the real value is to us anyway."

"Right. Make some overtures to Karen first … feel her out. We already know she is Skip's eyes and ears in that office. Whatever *you* say to her will definitely get back to Skip and sooner rather than later."

"Yes, that's good. We can feel them both out at the same time." Ray liked this angle, but on a personal note he would really love to have the Keys office as his own little trading operation and retirement investment.

Nick interrupted Ray's vision. "Hey dreamer boy. You still there? You know … none of this is for real. It's just another one of the games we play to get our way."

"Yes, I know, but part of me would like to venture out from the rigmarole of this undercover investigation work and spread my wings."

"Come on now, *counselor*. Surely you jest. Why toss off the brilliant law degree for a life of trading? Get real. You're a great agent. You'd miss the hunt … not to mention the kill."

Ray clucked his tongue. "Maybe, maybe not. Sometimes I'd like just to be able to settle down here in the Keys and live a quiet life … you know, find and keep me a good woman. Maybe have a passel of kids. Don't you ever want more than what you have now?"

"What – and give up all this?" Nick said with blatant tongue in cheek. They both laughed. "Seriously though, Ray, I've never been one to let the grass grow under my feet. I *love* this job." Nick stopped for a second, then snapped his fingers. "Hey – reminds me. What's the latest with you and Connie?"

"She is a fine woman and would make a good wife."

"Sounds like a marriage proposal to me. Did I hear you right?"

"Maybe."

"You do realize that maybe does not mean no?"

"Yes, I do, but thanks for the not so subtle reminder."

CHAPTER THIRTY-SIX

Ray began his fishing expedition the following week. He had allowed some time to pass since Kevin and he had that ugly outburst. He walked over to Karen's desk and said, "Karen, can I ask you something?"

She looked up from her desk and said, "Yes, what?"

Do you think Skip might sell me this operation?"

Karen was busy readying the day's mail for FedEx. She looked up, startled, and said, "Why on earth would you want to do something like that?"

"I like this game." He rubbed his chin. "A lot, in fact."

"I like my job too, but I'd never want the headache or expense of owning the business," Karen said, shaking her head as she stuck the address/account information into the clear slot on the FedEx envelope and placed it on the right hand corner of her desk for the deliveryman. "Isn't it hard enough just working here? Don't you think this whole office is a little bit like *Romper Room?*"

Ray considered the *Romper Room* image, smiled his sweetest smile and said, "Would you, please ... just ask Skip if he's interested at all in selling?"

"I will, but ..." She regarded him for a second, "...I'm sure the answer's going to be a resounding no. You know Skip is about the money and this little operation has turned out ... despite all of you doing your own things, to be fairly profitable." She met his eye.

"Just do me the favor of checking, okay?" She nodded in skeptical agreement. He walked away.

***

Frederika was giving Skip an ultimatum. Her arms folded over her bust, she said, "We need to talk about a few things."

"Fred, I don't have the time now. Can't you see that I'm moving?"

She reached down and hurled a goose down pillow his way. It missed, but barely. "You rotten son of a bitch! Do you care nothing about your daughters? Do you care so little about me, the mother of your children, that you think you can just move out?"

"Quite frankly, yes – at least about you, anyway." He continued packing.

She grabbed his wrist. "Can you just stop for one moment and listen to me?"

He smacked her across her face. Red finger marks raised immediately along her porcelain cheek. She lunged at him and scratched at his face.

Her caught her and socked her hard in the eye. She blinked and tears streamed down her face. A purple mark began to form a ring around where he hit her. She grabbed one of his trophies and tried to slam him over the head. He side stepped and tripped her. She fell flat on her back – and stayed down. He finished packing, zipped up his bag, and said, "Au Revoir, Fred."

She lay in a heap on the floor, sobbing, her face red, swollen, and bruised. She vowed to get even with him if it was the last thing she did. Next week I'm calling a divorce attorney. That bastard is going to pay for what he's done to me, both now and in the past!

***

Karen had passed the information about Ray being interested in buying the Keys operation to Sammy. She had been unable to get hold of Skip. Sammy promised to discuss it with Skip when he met with him next. That opportunity had just arisen.

Sammy said nonchalantly, when Skip had come in to inquire about the days' and week's trades, "By the way, Skip, Red, ah, I mean Karen – in the Keys, called and she tells me that Ray wants to know if you might want to sell that operation to him."

Skip was momentarily distracted by the trading sheets and tallies. He looked up and said, "Is that so?" He placed the stack of papers neatly back together. "What makes him think he can handle the upfront cost to take over the FCM? You know, Sam, I've got a lot of money wrapped up in those misfits."

"Don't I know?" He chewed on a toothpick wedged between his teeth.

Skip thought for a second. "What did American charge us on that one?"

"We bonded it out – didn't we? I seem to recall."

"Yes, we did, but still that wasn't cheap."

"I know."

Skip brought a forefinger to his lips, then raised it. "Maybe ask Ismail to give Amin a call to check on that before we even consider it a viable option?"

"You're the boss … but you know that office has not exactly turned out how we hoped it would, either. Those people are squirrelly and all." He made a twisty motion beside his head "Bunch of loonies, ya ask me."

"Some of them could actually become pretty good brokers. It's too bad Kevin was such a putz."

Sam spit a small speck of pepper onto the floor. "How much money you figure we really take outta that place anyway?"

"More than you might think. And that's why I don't want to be too rash."

"Like how much?"

"Well, if Ray, Goldeneye, Sherm and Cray would just do as I want and not as they do, we would make millions down there. But no, they want to be some sort of Wall Streeters or something. They have these ideas like they're all big time ... you know what I mean?"

"Yea, true. And I always thought Ray was a kind of know-it-all." He chewed on the toothpick some more. "So whaddaya wanna do?"

"Maybe we can get Gary or De Ron to come head it up."

"No chance of that from what they tell me. I think Gary's exact words were something like, "Buckhead is the pussy capital of the world for affluent black men."

"Okay, so maybe we can rule them both out, but that doesn't mean one of our other men – given the right opportunity, of course ... might not want to take it over ... right?"

"The way I see it that place is just a pain. Why not cut your bait loose?"

"Let me just sleep on this, okay Sam?"

Sam scratched his head. "Is that what I should tell Karen when she calls me back?" He looked straight at Skip. "Which we both know she will."

"Just dodge her calls for the next few days until I can decide one way or the other."

"Okay."

Ray kept pressing Karen to call Sammy back. She tried several times, but Sammy was always evasive. Finally she pinned him down midway through the week.

"Sammy, why do I feel like you're avoiding me?"

"Karen – Karen ... why on earth would I be avoiding you?"

"Cut the crap, Sammy. Have you spoken to Skip or not. Ray keeps asking me and I'm sick and tired of making excuses for you."

"Well, let me put it to you like this – why don't you say this ... tell Ray that there is a *distinct possibility*. You got that?"

"Do I have to use those exact words?"

"Look. Don't be a pain in my ass, okay? Tell him just what I said and then let him come back to you with a number. Okay?"

"Sammy, don't you think that's putting the horse before the cart?"

"No I don't."

"Okay, then what?"

"Let him toss the first test balloons into the air. We will float them by Skip. That way he has the option to either accept or reject Ray's offer. All right?"

"Well I guess that couldn't hurt anything, and we don't have to accept his offer if we don't want to."

"What's this *we* crap, cookie?"

"Sorry, Sam – it was just a manner of speaking. I didn't mean anything by that … honestly."

Karen knew better than to incite the ire of Sammy. She had heard more than one tale about Sammy the hurricane and she did not want to be in his direct path of destruction, now or ever.

"That's okay. Sometimes I can be a little over sensitive, ya know."

"No, Sammy – not you." She was soft pedaling now.

"But let's keep all of our balls in the air." Sam took a big bite of his snickers bar.

The next time Sam saw Skip he changed direction entirely. He side-stepped the issue of selling the Keys operation to Ray and said, "Sam, I've been thinking about gumball machines."

"What on earth for?"

"Something new for Vegas, perhaps."

Sam was beginning to think Skip had a screw loose. "What? Ya losin' it, Skip? You know you can be honest with me." Sam wondered if his boss was on the verge of blacking out with anxiety disorder.

Skip could read Sam's thoughts. He thinks I'm nuts, pretty much. Skip smiled and said in defense of his sanity, "No, listen, Sammy. I was out there a while back with Natalia … and we went to this convention for vending operations. Anyway, you wouldn't believe what a beautiful scam that is."

"What?" Sam smacked his own forehead. "You *can't* be serious."

Skip held both hands out, palms down and made a *calm down* motion. "Yes, I am serious, Sam. Listen. We sell the machines for about fifty percent more than we take them in for – do you follow me here? Apparently there is quite a list for people who want these things. So we sell 'em to them and we offer to help the new clients secure locations, too."

"Locations?" Sam was beyond confused.

"Yes, locations. We charge them a fee for a specific location or locations. I'm telling you this can be nearly as profitable as our Ponzi scheme and gambling business."

"I don't get it."

"It goes like this. First the machine, then the location … so twice we make money on the same person. And then there is the stock and restock. They *have* to buy all of their restock from us and that's another continuous revenue stream."

As Sam allowed that information to settle in he calmed some. "Okay, and then what?"

Skip rubbed his chin and smiled. "This gets even better, Sam. I tell *you* we never produce locations and then continue to look and they continue to pay and we just keep collecting money all along the way."

"Skip to be perfectly honest with you … this sounds like something from Century Village. And another thing … I am *not* ready to be put out to pasture just yet."

"Sam we don't have to decide right now – so take it easy. I just want to keep our options open, that's all."

"Okay, fine." Sam shook his head and flailed an irritated hand in the air. "Whatever you say." He thought, this is maddening. Change – I hate change, and Skip damn well knows that. Oh well, he's the boss. And he's always right. Let it pass for now. Maybe he'll come to his senses and forget this whole thing.

CHAPTER THIRTY-SEVEN

Karen had just told Ray that Skip said, *maybe,* even though that was Sam's line. When Ray went home for the evening he called Nick and the crew to give them the good news.

A buoyant Ray said, "Interesting. So Skip is mulling it over. Karen made it sound like he would be open to an offer. What do we wanna do now?"

Marek said, "I say we finally get a look into his books … that is if he even keeps his books there. I sense he's too smart to leave too much to luck. I bet there are a couple of sets of books. See if you can get a hand on them both."

"Well, under normal circumstances I'd say definitely, but as we know, Skip is anything but predictable. I promise I'll try. I'll press as much as I can without bringing us under any glaring lights or guns. As I've mentioned before, Karen can be a bit of a problem, she's Skip's watch dog on this end. But I think I can get on her good side now, too."

Nick said, "Great news. Let us know how things go."

"Will do."

***

Frederika had arrived at the law firm, Galloway and Skink, to meet with Amy Galloway, *divorce attorney from hell*, or so her reputation went. After introductions and taking a seat, Frederika said, "Well, of course the reason for this visit – my visit … is to see what it takes in this state to get a divorce." She scowled, thinking and fuming. I honestly cannot believe this is what my life has come to. That rotten son of a bitch is ruining my life. Let's see who'll be the most miserable after this.

Amy, who was short and dumpy, but intelligent and had the reputation of being a pit bull in the courtroom, replied from behind an imposing desk in her private and posh office on the second floor of the Dansk building, "Yes, so you said before." Amy had represented hundreds, if not thousands, of unhappy people who had once been blissfully married in their dissolution of said marriage. The grounds for seeking the dissolution changed from person to person or situation to situation, but the end result always boiled down to irreconcilable differences. "Florida is a fifty-fifty state, meaning that most divorce settlements split the communal assets in half."

"Half?" Frederika shrieked. "I'm not sharing one bit of anything with that low down dirty two bit playboy from hell. You've got to do better than that."

"Sorry, but that's the law. Now, there are certain … circumstances, where we may be able to get the judge to allow us some leeway, but for the most part it's an even split down the middle. If there are properties that you held before this union, those remain yours, but all property divined under your current marriage is subject to this stipulation."

Frederika was stewing, restless in her chair and lips drawn tight.

Amy began compiling a list of what she required to effectuate the dissolution. "What I will need from you are appraisals for all of your mutually owned property – and that includes jewelry and automobiles, mortgage information and deeds, if there are any … an estimate of expenses per month for the household, car liens, boat liens, anything else that you can think of. And don't let's forget the bank statements, tax returns, and corporate records … like the P & L's, too."

Amy scratched her mousy head with perfectly manicured nails and white flakes of dandruff fluttered onto her desk. "You got all that?"

Frederika was losing what little patience she had. With a flippant snort she said, "Yes, you *twit*. I've got it. Now is there anything else I can do to expedite this unfortunate process?"

Amy was a good judge of character. Also capable of *handling* all sorts of characters. She let the twit comment roll off her dandruff flaked shoulders. Even snotty-nosed, short tempered bitches pay her fees. "Well, you mentioned that he had been unfaithful. Do you happen to know the names of the women?"

"Not all of them, and believe you me, there have been a steady series of them over the years. Bitches. One thing about Skip is he never keeps the same slut for too long. God forbid – they might form some sort of attachment."

"Oh, you poor thing." Amy tried to sound soothing. Didn't work.

"Don't you poor thing me." She made a white knuckled fist and furrowed her eyebrows. "I want his balls in a vice and his head on a platter. Do you understand that?"

"Yes, I do, and I'll certainly do all I can to see that you have things your way, Mrs. Horowitz."

"Oh, puhleeeeeze … don't use that name."

"Excuse me?"

"Mrs. Horowitz, you shrew." She snapped her fingers. "That reminds me of another thing. Can you change my name back to my maiden name?"

Oh sure. That's the easy part." She took out a note pad, remaining calm, professional. So now I'm a shrew. This uppity cunt is a special case indeed. She gave a curt smile and said, "What would that be – the maiden."

"Hielman. That's h,i,e,l,m,a,n."

"Got it." Amy dotted a loud period on her notes, folded the pad and set it aside. She looked up. "Is that all for today? I've got a pretty heavy schedule and I've got to be in court just after lunch."

"Just one more quick thing. Do you happen to have the name of a good private investigator?"

She punched a key on her computer to pull up a list of contacts from her ACT program and said, "Per chance I do. But you know what? It would be best if you let me … *handle* this, if you know what I mean." She winked.

Frederika put her arms up like a stick-up and said, "*Whatever*, I'm fed up. I don't really give a damn who does it. Just get it done. I want all of the dirt you can possibly dig up on him. I want to see that fucker squirm."

***

Ray had asked Karen about the books. She remained evasive, but said that she would ask Skip and Sam.

Meanwhile the operation on Cypress Creek Boulevard had been embroiled in the SEC's investigation of the corn calls and was being shut down, effective immediately. The NFA and CFTC task force in a joint mission were to swoop into Commonwealth mid-morning and subpoena all files pertinent to those transactions. Skip had been tipped off that there was going to be a bust in his building and he planned to be nowhere close when it went down. He had invited Sammy to help him make it a seamless process. Sammy had told all of the agents to pack up their desks a.s.a.p. and move them over to a new location on Atlantic Avenue in Pompano Beach.

Catherine was beginning to smell a rat. She had gone to Ted Romeo to inquire about this latest move. "Teddy, why are we moving the office? Skip never said anything about this in any of his meetings. I just don't get it. And why so fast?"

Teddy had multiple boxes of manila file folders stacked all around his office, "Actually, this is nothing new. We do this pretty regularly." He seemed nonplussed. "It basically goes down like this – the Fed's come around looking for wrongdoing … they bust one of the other houses either nearby or maybe even in our building. This is getting pretty close. Skip gets wind of it and we move. End of story."

"But I don't get it. Why? If we have nothing to hide why don't we just face them?"

"I don't have time to go into that right now. You're relatively new at this game." He shoved a few more folders into an open box and sealed the top. "I am an old pro. There are some things that we do in this operation that *you* are better off not knowing. Just do your job and don't ask questions." Teddy quit talking and continued packing.

Catherine was concerned that Nick would miss her in the move so she rang him to tell him what was transpiring. "Nick, I just wanted to tell you that things here are changing fast. This morning Sammy comes in to tell us to pack up and move the entire office over to a place on Atlantic Boulevard in Pompano Beach."

Nick was pleased that she had called to alert them to this change in plans, but it meant it would also require a new subpoena – and those things sometimes took time. "That is fast. I wonder what the rush is."

"All I can tell you is Teddy told me this happens often. He mentioned something about the Fed's sniffing around. Do you think this means Skip is doing something illegal?"

If she only knew the half of it. "Hard to tell from where I sit. But something strange certainly is going on."

"Anyway, when I know the new telephone number and address I'll fill you in, okay? I better get back to work."

"Yes, please do. Thanks for calling."

Nick hung up and immediately called Marek. "You are not going to believe this …"

"Calm down, Nick. You're breathing hard. What?"

"That son-of-a-bitch is moving as we speak."

"How could he know what was going down?" Marek's eyes lit up. "Wait – you don't think …"

"Exactly. Do think. Only someone on the inside of our organization could have tipped him off."

"Then I say we move now. Begin the raid."

"I'm in."

"No! You are not in … not this time. You cannot be compromised. Let me call in the Cavalry and see how fast we can rendezvous."

"Gotcha. Good luck."

"Looks like we're going to need it. This *scumbag* is more slippery than fresh snot on a polished mirror. Nick, get the new address in case we miss them. Find Judge Cantor so we can get the new subpoenas. Do it aysap."

"Will do."

Skip's crew worked fast and furious. Most of them had been through this process many times before. The old operation was shut down and the new operation was constructed in one weekend. The name was changed from Commonwealth Financial to Atlantic Financial. Sammy told the brokers that the accounts needed to be transferred over to the new name before any business could be contracted and that needed to be done now.

Marek could not get the court order and the swat team assembled in time to bust Skip on Cypress Creek, but they did get authorization for bugs in the new office on Atlantic Avenue.

These new bugs were of the latest and best technology. According to the equipment liaisons, Skip's regular sweeps for bugs could not detect this new breed of listening devices.

Meanwhile in the Keys, Ray had told his people, on the QT, that there was a possibility he may be taking over Island Investments. The crew was ecstatic. Goldeneye told Ray that he believed his father would go to the tribal elders if the deal between Skip and Ray worked out, and that Ray could count on a large percentage of the reservation's profits becoming an investment vehicle for them. Ray told Sherman that if things worked out he wanted him to head up the stock and bond department and, if he needed help, he could help tutor some of the other people for the series seven exam. Sherman was extremely pleased.

Skip had finally provided Ray with some books on Island Investments, but to the trained eye they had been seriously sanitized. Ray called a buddy in Chicago who worked for another clearing firm and asked what they knew about American Futures.

The guy told Ray that what he knew of them, which granted was not a lot, was that they pretty much operated above the board. He also promised to ask a few of the other FCM's what, if anything, they knew and said he would get back to Ray with that information.

Catherine and Nick spoke at length about the new office move and name change.

"You know this makes me wonder if I should've just stayed put in the Keys."

Nick decided this was the time to turn her and he had to do it right. He said, "Actually, Cat, I've got something to tell you. It is extremely important."

She took a seat on the tiny sofa in his small studio apartment on Second Avenue, feeling apprehensive. "Maybe I should have a glass of wine or an Irish Whiskey?"

"Okay." Nick went to the small alcove that doubled as a kitchen and poured them each a double shot. He handed one to Catherine and took a sip of the other. "I'm really not sure how to begin ... so I'm just going to come out with it."

"What is it, Nick?" Worry seeped into her voice. "Are you in some sort of trouble?"

"No, nothing like that." He took another sip. The golden liquid warmed his throat. He heaved a sigh and gathered himself to the dreaded task. "Cat, look – ahm ... I'm not really a bartender slash bouncer."

"No?" She took a sip. This makes no sense at all. Why has he been dishonest with me?

He stood before her. "No. The truth is …" he sighed again, "… truth is I'm a federal agent working under cover for the SEC, NFA, and CFTC." He didn't have to wait for her reaction. She bolted upright, knocking her glass onto the floor.

"How could you lie to me? I trusted you." She hurried toward the door.

Nick caught her by the arm before she could exit. "Catherine, please hear me out."

She shot him a look, her eyes flashing gray with anger. "Give me one good reason … just one!"

"We have been investigating Skip for at least six years now."

Her hand was on the door handle. "Skip? Why Skip?"

"I don't have all of the facts before me, but he's been defrauding his investors. He's been engaged in racketeering, money laundering, and fraud. Just to name a few of his offenses." He took her free hand in his. "Won't you please listen to the rest of what I have to say? Then if you want to leave, fine. Go if you must, but go knowing the truth."

Reluctantly she followed him back over to the sofa where he retrieved her glass from the floor and poured her another shot, neat, the way she liked it. She took it from him, looking and feeling numb, and downed it in one gulp. She placed the glass onto the coffee table and took a seat. "Okay, go ahead."

For the next two hours he related all of the sordid details of how they were set up to meet and Ray was part of the undercover sting and how they were going to bust Skip on the Cypress Creek operation, but Skip managed to slink away. She listened with rapt attention to each detail.

When all the truth was out, Nick could see Catherine was stunned, but not losing it. She looks rather poised, considering, he thought. He said, "So. There you have it. Do you have some questions for me now?"

Catherine looked him square in the eyes. "Yes. Why me?"

"Well, we were watching Skip when he first walked into your real estate office in Key West and we wanted to know what he had up his sleeve. He is a very crafty man. When we saw that you were getting involved in his new operation we decided to get close to you and the only way we could do that was with me … or one of the other guys."

Another flare of anger bubbled just below her surface composure. "And, have you been listening to my conversations for all this time, too?"

Nick cleared his throat and looked down. "Well, yes."

"And what about all of the things we've done together?"

With a slow, solemn nod, Nick said, "Yes."

Catherine's eyes narrowed. Her lips formed a clenched, thin flat line. "I see." She started to rise. "I don't think there's anything more we can say to each other."

"Catherine – listen … I never wanted to hurt you. Please believe me. That is the honest to goodness truth."

"And why should I believe you?" Fury blazed in her gray-green eyes. What a fuckstick this asshole is, she thought. And what a naïve fool I've been.

Strangely, Nick found that sexy. He continued. "You can still help us. If you choose to."

"How?" She looked at him, dumbfounded. "And why in the hell should I?"

"Cat, you are a good person. I know that, believe that. Do it because it's the right thing to do. Look. Here's how you can help. You can hand over trade sheets and account information that can help us complete the investigation … perhaps even bring the case to trial?"

Catherine softened some, settled back in her seat, curious now. "How can that help?"

"See, we believe that Skip is running a Ponzi scheme, among other things."

"And what, pray tell, is a Ponzi scam…er, scheme, whatever?"

"It works like this. He opens an account here, promises a certain---- usually unheard of high rate of return … that's the sweetener…"

"Sweetener?"

"The enticement to come aboard in his operation versus working for or investing in another."

"Okay, continue." She ran a hand through her unruly hair.

"And then for a certain period of time he actually does pay these returns … from the next accounts he opens. He has to keep the ball rolling in order to continue his scheme. It's like a pyramid scam, same concept … but he is not actually trading. He is pocketing the funds from all of these accounts – and dummying up their monthly statements to portray god knows what." Nick paused to scratch his cheek, looking down. He looked back up, into her eyes. "Anyway, that is why we need this information." He leaned forward in sincerity and took one of her hands in his. "Cat. Will you do it? Will you help?"

Nick could read the 'stop', 'go' urges conflicting inside her head. She said, "I need some time to assimilate what you've told me."

Nick had to win her over. Now. This is all or nothing and the time is now, he knew. Push, Nick, but be gentle with your persuasion. "Certainly I can understand. This all must come as quite a shock. And you have every right to feel duped and taken advantage of, Cat. But I assure you it is for good reason. Look – we've had numerous complaints from his investors over the years. I've even gone so far as to open an account in his Buckhead operation to see what I could glean from that."

Catherine looked away. "Skip has a lot of money. You know he can afford to fight this if it comes to that."

Nick was perplexed. She's almost defending him----*the scumbag liar*. "Catherine. Look at me." She did. "Catherine, we've investigated his trades at American Futures and they always come up as traded, but never divvied up to the investors' accounts that are supposedly being traded. And then there's the small thing about his churning accounts ... and some of the reputable houses have asked him for his trading strategies and they can't even come close to the returns that he is telling investors they can expect in his prospectus." He shook his head and sighed, exasperated.

"Churning? Is that actually illegal?"

"Yes, it is illegal. And so is insider information used to conduct trades before it becomes public knowledge."

Catherine folded her arms. "And you know this how?"

"Because I am an attorney and a federal investigator ... that's how."

"You are an attorney?" She was stupefied.

"Yes----you act like that is unbelievable?"

"Well, it sort of is ... especially when I thought you were a common bartender and bouncer just a few hours ago. You've asked me to digest a lot of things – and I am trying ... really I am, but I can't make a decision like this on the spur of the moment." She stood and stretched her back.

"Damn you are sexy."

"What?" He has the nerve to talk sexy with me? Now?

"I said, damn you are sexy."

She put both hands on her hips. "I heard what you said. I just can't believe you are saying that right after dumping all this rather serious information and allegations on me. Not to mention the fact I've had my privacy invaded." Catherine slammed her eyes shut, horrified at the thought of federal agents having listened in on their lovemaking sessions. Pricks probably had a real good time listening to me getting off. Fuckers. Probably jacked off like losers ogling a Penthouse magazine. Gah.

"Sorry. It was an observation ... that's all." He forced a smile, knowing it would be a miracle if it were received with any genuineness.

Catherine grunted, got up and walked a few steps away. She scratched her forehead, then turned and searched his eyes. "So. Where does this leave ... *us*?"

"Well ... I will admit that I've had a good time with you ..."

Catherine was livid. "A good time. A *good time*?" She flailed both hands in the air. "A fucking *good time*? Is *that* what you would call it?"

"You are a *great* lay!"

"Yea, well don't let that go to your head." She looked at his manly bulge. "Neither one of them."

He walked over to her and placed his arms around her waist. She did not move away. He nuzzled his way to the back of her neck and gently planted one kiss, then two just below her hairline. She groaned. She turned around and they kissed. Long and deep. The stress and strain of their conversation was overcome with the art of sexual enticement. Electricity flowed through them. Nick held her hand and walked her into his bedroom. He began to undress her, but she stopped him.

"Nick?"

"Yes, love?"

She motioned and looked all around the room. "No bugs this time? Promise me?"

Nick raised two fingers to his forehead in a salute and said, "Scouts honor."

That made her giggle. She reached for his belt and unbuckled it. It was on. They spent the next hour and a half having intense make-up sex. At the end of that sizzling session she was on board.

CHAPTER THIRTY-EIGHT

Ray was informed of Catherine's willingness to help. Nick had provided her with a locket – a tiny camera that could either do video or still photographs. Her instructions were to remain cautious and alert them to anything that appeared to be the slightest bit out of the ordinary.

A red flag had just come up on the computer screens for the NFA/CFTC and the SEC. Skip's operation in Buckhead had just placed a twelve million dollar trade for crude through American Futures. Gary had meant for the trade to be a series of puts in the futures market, betting the market would decline. The money hadn't actually been transferred from their clients' accounts into those of American Futures, but Gary didn't want to wait to get them into the trades. He had it on good word there was going to be a large decline in the prices of oil because the supplies were at or above peak capacity and the world economy's consumption was slipping due to a threat of a worldwide recession. Gary had called these trades in such a rush that he had not checked to be certain they were as he had asked them to be. Mistakenly, the trades were placed on the exchange as calls.

Gary had pulled a fast one on American by forcing them to trade without the funds being placed in their account, nor were they sitting on the sidelines in Gary's firm – which presented them with quite a quandary. The markets had fallen as Gary had been forewarned, but because his puts were called in as calls the money necessary to cover the trade had come to the whopping total of twenty four million dollars. Gary's firm had the money to cover it on hand, but it would come close to wiping them out. He was sweating, dreading, and wringing his hands. Oh my God what am I going to do? He slapped himself on the cheek. Try to get straight … think clear.

Gary asked DeRon for some advice. "DeRon – did you see the trade tallies for the day?" Gary winced.

"Yes, I did! How could you let something like that slide?"

"I just didn't check, that's all," he said, his wince turning into a miserable grimace, "Anyone could have made the same mistake."

"Well, you're not just anyone. And when Skip finds out about this … " DeRon shook his head. "… Jesus, Gary – he's going to have your fucking head."

Gary's eyes were wild. "I know, Bro. What am I gonna do?"

DeRon bit his lower lip, tapping his fingers on the desk. He looked up at Gary with a smack of his lips. "If I were you I'd book the first flight out to outer Mongolia."

"Serious?"

"Dead."

Nick and Sean had been listening in. Sean said, "Ouch!"

Nick chuckled. "This is perfect."

"Is it ever. Do you think they will pay up?"

"I don't know how they cannot pay up. It's in the agreement and clearly stated between Skip and the FCM."

Sean nodded. "Right. And if he doesn't?"

"SEC regulations allow us some latitude here, and I believe we can close American until those funds come in. I mean, legally that money belongs to the exchange. The trades were transacted. Where else would that leave us?"

"And if we shut down American we also shut down Skip," Sean said, making a thumbs down gesture with a smug smile.

"Correct, but we also penalize a lot of other organizations doing business through American that may *not* be perpetuating a pyramid scheme."

"One bad apple does spoil the whole bunch."

Nick shrugged. "In this case I suppose that's true."

"Could American plead for an exemption to continue to conduct business with their other customers?"

"Yes, but that would be up to a judge to decide."

***

Gary tried to remedy the horrific situation by calling the trader from American Futures who he felt had made the mistake – hopefully. The gentleman told Gary he was certain there had not been a mistake and even went so far as to replay the tape of the transaction as proof. Gary was aghast. He *had* been the errant one. He slammed the wall with an open palm. A cold sweat trickled down his back. What the hell am I going to do?

Ismail's father, Amin, came on the phone and said in his proper Indian-English voice, "Gary we need those funds transferred within the next twenty four hours."

"Amin, please … can't you give me a little more time?"

"I am sorry, good sir, but those are the rules."

Gary heaved a mighty sigh. "I've haven't told Skip about this yet."

"May I suggest that you do so immediately? Twenty four hours." Amin hung up.

Amin's next call was to the SEC. He related the recent turn of events and told them that as per his agreement he had informed Gary of the twenty four hour compliance obligation that Skip had signed when he became their customer long ago.

The SEC compliance officer, who had immense respect for Amin and his firm, said, "Tell you what, Amin – we will not shut down your entire operation, but we will require that there be no trading from any of Skip's firms allowed until he does come into compliance."

"Thank you, and once again I am most sorry for this unfortunate turn of events."

Amin called Gary to relate to him what the SEC had said. Gary was beside himself with angst. He had no alternative except to face Skip. That was going to be one ugly scene.

Gary convinced DeRon to call Skip. DeRon soft peddled his mistake as much as anyone could play down a twenty four million dollar error. He said, "You know, Skip, mistakes happen – and Gary is, was – mistaken in not rechecking that the trade was as he had called it in. He *never* meant to compromise you or anyone else."

Skip was seething. He had to bite his lip before responding. This is all I need with the Fed's sniffing around. When he did talk, his voice was white hot with anger. "You know it's not about the money, DeRon. I … I *can* pay for this trade." He paused, his mood growing into that of a thunder storm, cracking thunder and lightning. "It pisses me off to no end to pay for this fucking stupidity. And I will *not* sit idly by as the CFTC or NFA come raining down on me."

"I know, boss. Both Gary and I are real sorry."

Skip wanted to kick something. Anything. "Sorry?" He made a voice like a frightened, whining little boy, "I'm *sorry*, Skip." He had to stop for a few seconds and get a grip. "Look, DeRon. Sorry isn't going to cut it. And you can tell Gary this from me … If I go down, he's going down too!" He kicked his desk.

DeRon cowered even though not in the presence of Skip. "I totally – totally understand."

"I hope you've called me the minute this incident occurred," Skip said through clenched teeth, "because otherwise there could be serious repercussions."

DeRon stammered as he said, "Well, em … ah, not – not exactly, boss."

DeRon could hear the sound of something being thrown across Skip's room and slamming against the wall. Skip's voice was now a raging tornado. "Jesus, Mary, mother of god! Are you fucking shitting me? If this leads the Fed's to my operation and fucks it and me up, I swear to god – I'll eat Gary's eyes after plucking them out one by one and I'll have his balls as an appetizer!"

Skip slammed the phone down before DeRon could say anything more to further piss him off. He kicked his desk again, hard enough that he bounced around the room on one foot, holding his other foot and yelping in pain.

Once the pain subsided enough to walk and think straight he went about cutting his losses and working to avert total disaster. He had to transfer money from his account in Costa Rica to cover the screw up. It was already past the end of the day on the east coast of the US. Costa Rica was three hours behind. Praying there was still time, he lifted the phone and dialed. The bank informed Skip that it would be transferred, but wouldn't be tallied until the following day. Because Gary and DeRon didn't have the goddamn balls to tell me immediately, Skip thought, enraged, the transfer will be past the twenty four hour window.

Skip slumped into a chair and cradled his aching head in his hands. He knew American Futures had no alternative except to turn the matter over to the NFA and the CFTC for arbitration. That thought elevated his rage at Gary to monumental proportions. He let the situation sink in, breathing deeply, struggling to get, and finally achieving, a state of mind in which to act – and act swiftly with effectiveness.

After numerous calls back and forth, Skip managed to resolve the matter with the NFA and the CFTA, but Gary was going to have his license suspended for a while. Skip could have cared less about the status of Gary's license, that stupid shit; he was only concerned about covering his own ass.

Skip called DeRon and informed him he was to take over the day-to-day operations in Buckhead until further notice. Screw Gary.

For the Fed's this was a first – a lucky break that allowed them to pursue more broad authority and gave them access into all of Skip's operations from Lauderdale to Buckhead to Vegas. For the time being the Bahamas and Costa Rica were out of the loop because of their limited ability to conduct investigations on foreign soil. In time, if they could prove there was a connection that necessitated the closure of those operations because they presented an eminent threat to the citizens, they could perhaps get the other governments to work with them – even bring some criminal charges against those who had headed up the illegal organizations.

Catherine had been able to provide Nick with some information regarding trading, or the lack thereof, as well as a list of disgruntled clients who might be willing to join in a class action suit against Skip. Nick was thrilled and thanked her profusely.

The Fed's were able to connect Skip to the Bahamas and Costa Rica and had some preliminary conversations with those governments about extradition of certain key personnel in order to cement their case. Marek had contacted Alex and Doug to feel out Tommy in the Bahamas. They were to approach him about considering cooperation in exchange for his continued freedom.

Alex Morales and Doug Walker, both federal agents for the SEC, had approached Tommy, on the fly, with a deal in the Bahamas. Marek had told them to be as persuasive as possible and that did include using any means possible. Tommy had been broken once before and they knew he was at his most vulnerable now because of his addictions.

Alex and Doug were looking forward to roughing up Tommy. They had agreed to play the roles of good cop, bad cop. Alex the good one and Doug the bad one. They caught Tommy at the end of the day when he was alone in the office.

Alex said, "Tommy, we know all about your past." He looked him directly in the eye.

Tommy shifted uncomfortably in his seat, wishing like hell he had a toot and a snort.

Doug stepped in. "There are still certain members of a certain crime family, whom I need not remind you of their names, who are avidly looking for you ... and I don't think it's because they intend to invite you to a garden party."

Tommy avoided his eyes. They bore right into him. He couldn't think under that intensity.

Alex enjoyed watching him squirm. He said, "We've come to offer you a deal."

Tommy kept his head down, looked up sideways with his eyes only. "What kind of deal?"

"You lead us to Skip and we don't turn you over to your friends from Jersey," Doug said with a sneer. "As you know, they have a ... *special* way of making people who have fucked them disappear." His glare pierced Tommy again, this time straight to the heart.

Alex was impatient with the lowlife. "Look. Tommy. It's a no brainer."

Tommy was sweating, despite the cold air conditioning blowing directly across him. He had known that one day it would come to this and he now wondered why he hadn't left, just vanished without a trace, before things came down to this kind of horrible dead end.

Tommy had serious reservations. It showed on his sweat soaked furrowed brow. He said, "Suppose I do this for ya ... and that's just supposin'. What's in it for me? Besides not handin' me over to the mob." Tommy scratched at his arms, feeling jittery. The coke and rum he'd had before these two clowns arrived to ruin his day had worn off. He needed more. He hoped they didn't notice.

Doug, assuming his role as bad cop, said, "Look Tommy, we know you have stashes of coke in your office, in your car ... and at home. We could just as easily bust you for drug possession with the added penalty of perhaps trafficking … and you could go away for, say, twenty or so. It's not like you've got no priors, capish?. Whaddaya got to say about that?" He let that smolder a bit before continuing. "Rather play it that way?" He was bluffing, but only a little. The threat of a bust and doing some hard time was real enough.

Tommy fidgeted with his shirt, scratched at his neck. "You got me on nuttin'. That's just for personal use. I don't deal or anything else."

Alex good cop said, with a hand on Tommy's shoulder, leaning into his face and with a voice so cool it caused Tommy to shiver, "We know that, Tommy. But what will the judge and jury assume with your record? And what're your options? Look – you don't have to decide now, okay? As a matter of good faith …" He patted Tommy's back, "… we'll give you twenty four hours, but that's it. After that?" Alex cocked his head to the side and held up a palm. "Things are out of our hands."

Tommy loosened his tie, struggling to breathe. "And if I *do* decide to help *you* … can you promise that I'll be allowed to go my own way?" I'm up shit creek anyway, he thought, might as well do a little fishing … find out what their intentions really are.

"We'll do what we can," Doug said, deadpan. He held up two fingers on one hand and four on the other. "Twenty four hours. That's what you have. We'll be in touch – and another thing … until then, don't do anything stupid. We are watching." They both left.

Tommy was badly shaken. He opened his desk drawer, pulled out his trusty mirror and laid out three thick lines. He rolled up a hundred dollar bill, stuffed one end up his nose, bent over and snorted them all, loudly, in under fifteen seconds. He felt a little better. He placed his works back into the drawer, drew out his bottle of rum and twisted off the cap. He raised the bottle to his lips and chugged down a giant gulp. The fast induced euphoric stupor helped, but not enough to eradicate his hellish and self-pitying thoughts. How could I have let my life get so fucked up? What the hell do I do now?

*****

Catherine and Nick were enjoying a romantic dinner at his studio. They were having Maine lobster, creamed spinach, and sweet potato fries with Pinot Gringo. Dessert would be flan and sherry. Catherine said, "This is spectacular."

"I'm glad you're enjoying it." Nick became quiet and somber. He said, "Catherine, you've done a great job helping us. We're closing in on Skip."

"And?" She took another bite of lobster.

"Well …" He hesitated for a second, reading her, "… would you be willing to testify in court?"

She stopped short of taking another bite and set her fork down, still holding it. "I hadn't really thought about that. I guess so, if you need me, but Skip told me once when I first came on board with him that if I ever crossed him he would …" She looked down, put her lower lip between her teeth, lifted her eyes back to him, "… he said he'd see to it that I met my demise."

"He actually said that to you face to face?"

"Yep." She let go of her fork and finger tapped the linen covered table a few times.

Nick scratched his shoulder, considering. "Was anyone else there who may have heard the threat?"

"No. Why?"

"Threats of bodily harm can also be used as evidence in a criminal hearing, but unless you have a witness it's considered hearsay and not admissible."

Catherine lifted her fork and looked at her plate, deciding which tasty morsel to have next. She re-stabbed the piece of lobster. "Isn't that the least of his crimes? Mmm, this lobster is exquisite."

"I suppose so, but we're ramping up the charges as we go along."

"For instance?" Creamed spinach, she decided to have next.

"Well, we can charge him with fraud and the intent to defraud his investors. There appears to be a lot of history to draw upon for that one charge alone."

Catherine chewed, a wrinkle on her forehead. "This is getting even more serious than I thought."

Nick cut off and stabbed a chunk of lobster. "Do you think we would've asked for your help if this was not a very serious and complex case?"

"I guess not." Catherine looked at him, taking a bite, thinking. The dinner is great, and Nick is a good man, but what has happened the past few months in my life is a helluva lot more to chew on than this mouthful of sweet potato fries.

CHAPTER THIRTY-NINE

Skip had always kept a staff of capable and crooked attorneys on retainer, as well as various and sundry other people who operated outside of the law, should the day come when he needed their skills. That day had come. He engaged all of them in keeping his adversaries at bay – not only the Fed's, including the SEC, NFA, and CFTC, but also Frederika.

Amy, Fredericka's attorney, had served Skip with papers for divorce. Skip had gone to Father Zeke and said, "Zeke, the time has come to …" he rubbed his chin, "… ahm – *remove* Fred. That miserable no-good bitch has actually served me with divorce papers. And that's not all – the wench is going after everything I got, too."

Zeke appeared surprised. "Really, why on earth would she ruin a good thing?"

"Beats the hell outta me, but she's got to be out of my life, and I mean *now*." Skip slammed his fist into an open palm.

"Skip, don't you think you can talk to her – smooth things over? I've never found her to be an overbearing woman." He straightened his faux collar.

Skip rolled his eyes and huffed. "Don't you think I've tried that?" Skip's eyes and tone became imploring. "You know, Zeke, we go way back."

Zeke thought back, yes we do. I was lucky that I never got caught for assisting in the whacking Stu and Mick for Skip. They were louts anyway, headed for hell. Just sped up the process, that's all. When was that? Like 1988 or something? Skip is asking an awful lot of me, but he has also been very good to me over the years. Guess I owe it to him. Certainly he doesn't mean murdering Fred, of course. That would be rather extreme. He must mean intimidate her into leaving quietly out of his life. Has to be.

Skip continued, "It's not like this is your first time helping me out this way."

He's being vague, Zeke thought. Very vague. God I hope he doesn't …

"Please," Skip said with a hand to his mouth and a steely gaze. Maybe Ralph can help you."

"Skip, quit begging." He rubbed his temple which had begun to throb. "I'm just trying to get my thoughts in order, okay? Give me a minute."

"Okay, but make it fast. I can't have that fucking cunt ruining me any more than she already has. God knows who she's spoken to. She's got to be axed and I mean *immediately*."

Father Zeke was shaken. Jesus – I think he *does* mean kill her. I like and respected Fred. Killing her ... that's a far different thing than those other losers. He said, stammering, "Well, uhm, ah – if you say so ... so what is it you ah – want me to do, exactly?"

"Why don't you take her out, ah ..." he winked, "... *fishing* – on Traders Three. Pretend you want to talk with her about this divorce thing. Play nice. She loves fishing and she trusts you – at least I think she trusts you."

Zeke's eyes shot a mile wide as the full horrible intent of Skip's orders sank in. Get rid of her. Have her killed. He gulped and blew out a long breath. "Okay. Sure. Okay. Me and who else?" I sure as hell don't want murder on my hands alone.

"It doesn't have to be you *exactly*. You can have Ralph, as I mentioned before ..." he gave a devilish wink, "... *help* you. He is capable, but then again so are you. Don't play the pansy with me now, Zeke. I need you to do this for me." Skip's look was menacing. Zeke knew if he did not do as Skip asked, *he* could be the next to turn up dead.

Zeke hung his head and thought back to the days when he had been a real man of the cloth. When he would have never given a fleeting thought to harming anyone, let alone be an accomplice to or commit murder. He didn't let Skip see his face, which was temporarily riddled with shame over what he had become. He shook it off. Too late to turn back now. Life is what it is, and I'm in far too deep with Skip now, anyway. God help us all. I owe my lavish lifestyle to this man and now I have to pay for his good favors.

Zeke looked up to meet his benefactor's anxious gaze and said with a forced, committed smile, "Okay, Skip. Like I said, I'll do it. For you. What's the timetable?"

"Try yesterday ... actually the sooner the better, okay? I've got enough problems without her adding to the rue."

"Consider it done, Skip."

***

Catherine had taken to calling Shamus with more regularity since she no longer held out hope that she and Nick would have any real relationship after Skip's being tossed behind bars. Shamus had told her about Danielle, and Connie had told her about another woman before her, but Catherine pretended to hear it for the first time from Shamus now.

"Shamus, I am sorry. Really I am. You must've cared for her a great deal if you asked her to marry you?"

"Yes, what a fool I am."

"Don't be silly. Everyone makes mistakes."

He stopped, sighed. "So Cat – do you miss being in the Keys?"

Yes, I sure do – and I hope that in the not too distant future I can move back there and resume a calmer, more normal life?"

"I thought you loved the new job?"

"In some ways I do. Did, anyway. It is, how can I put it … *dreadfully* exciting. But there is a lot about this business that I've yet to understand and well, the more I learn about what's really going down …" she blew out a long breath, "… maybe I'm not suited for this type of work?"

"Ray said you were a natural."

"Did he?" That's surprising, she thought as she held out the receiver and looked at it in disbelief.

"Well, if you come back here …" Shamus hesitated, "… if you come back here … would you think about seeing me again?"

Catherine nearly gasped. "Shamus, dear Shamus. How nice of you to ask that. But … I said such awful things to you and about you – can you forgive me?"

"I already have." Shamus' heart was in his voice, so obvious.

He's such a shirtsleeve emotionalist, Catherine thought, admiring his candid and transparent nature. "Of course I'll see you Shamus, and often, too."

His heart leaped with joy. Oh, to have Catherine back in my life! This time I'll be everything she had told me, so long ago, that she wanted in her man. I'll be her *only* man!

***

The following week Skip moved his offices on Atlantic boulevard again. This time they split the move. Half of the office was stationed over to Las Olas Boulevard and the remainder over to an abandoned bank building on Third Avenue, downtown. Las Olas became Guardian Investments and Third Avenue was Colonial Finance.

Catherine had been filling Nick in regularly and he was getting some valuable information from her. They continued to have sex from time to time because they both enjoyed it, but their relationship had changed, cooling off to a level of understanding that their sex was only for fun and relief, nothing more.

Tommy had agreed to cooperate with the Fed's in exchange for his freedom. He provided them with numbers for corresponding accounts in Switzerland, Grand Cayman, and Costa Rica. He gave them details of how his currency operation operated, including the dummying up of accounts. The Fed's even agreed to allow him to continue to use the coke and rum so long as he continued to provide them with irrefutable information.

Gary Brown, from the Buckhead office, had also agreed to cooperate now that he had nothing further to lose. His license and livelihood were gone forever. Skip had made him the scapegoat. He felt cheated by fate, and betrayed by Skip. The Fed's, in order to sweeten his deal, agreed to reinstate his license if he helped them. But Gary would have to keep his nose clean, and he would have to promise to go to work for a reputable trading firm in the future.

Ismail, Skip's mole between the Fed's and American Futures, had told Skip each time the Fed's had come sniffing around. Ismail was about to find himself in a compromising position. The information provided to Fed's from the Buckhead debacle did not jive with that of the SEC, NFA, or CFTC. Shareed Vorhee, an Indian born American with legal training from Harvard Law, was instated to help the Fed's bring Ismail and his father over to their side.

Shareed had phoned Ismail a few days before the due date to schedule a meeting face to face. They had arranged to meet at the main office for American Futures in Chicago near the CBOT. Ismail fretted. What have I done? What to do now? Finally he had called his father, Amin, to help him determine what course of action to take.

On a cold, dreary December day, Shareed, Ismail, and Amin were seated in the small, but lavishly decorated conference room of American Futures adjacent to the main trading floor of the CBOT. Mrs. Singh served them ginger tea from an immaculate, silver platter.

Shareed said, "Mr. Singh, we know that Skip, from Commonwealth, or Merritt, or whatever he calls his company now, is not your only client in this FCM. Therefore, if you come clean with us we will not cut you off from your other lucrative … let us assume, legally, operating clients."

Amin, always thoughtful in his decision making, paused to choose his words and said, "Our hands are clean. Our firm has not, and will not, ever compromise our reputation by acting in an illegal or otherwise compromising fashion."

Shareed regarded him for a second. He made a small grunt of agreement and said, "We are aware of that. But this is quite a serious matter between you and this Horowitz gentleman."

"I'll be the first to admit … from the very beginning of this relationship with Mr. Horowitz I had some bad feelings and lingering doubts as to the transparency of his operation. However, he was willing to take Ismail into his inner workings … and I might add that he paid him quite well."

Amin looked over and produced a comforting smile. "Over a period of time and with the steady flow of funding from his operation, I suppose I softened my stance and accepted him for who and what he is … so let's assume this was all my mistake. We can leave my son Ismail out of this can't we? What is it you want more from us at this time?"

Ismail was immensely grateful that his father had taken the lead and spoke so candidly with Shareed. He had mixed feelings about double crossing Skip. Skip had threatened all of his employees at one time or another, and Ismail did not question Skip's sincerity. He kept his mouth shut and listened.

Shareed said, "We happen to know for a fact that the trades called in a few months back between his operations in Buckhead … did not jive with those of the SEC. When we first called American out on this, your manager said, and I quote, "It was an honest mistake."

"Who in my employ would have said such a thing?" Amin was aghast, eyes wide.

"No time to worry about the who's … the upshot of this whole thing, my dear man, is that twenty four million dollars is quite a large mistake, especially for an experienced trading firm such as yours … if indeed it *was* a mistake and – well, to be quite honest … we don't think it was a mistake at all. More likely a well contrived cover up to keep Skip's operations afloat … and if that is the case, you would be considered an accomplice in his crimes." He reached into his briefcase, drew out a thick document and handed it to Amin. "I have here a subpoena to compel your organization to hand over those documents and more."

Amin swallowed hard and said, "Where is all of this heading?"

"That depends a lot on you and your willingness to cooperate … and on the information that you willfully provide us." He leaned forward. "Today."

"Today … did you say today?" Amin choked on his breath.

"Indeed I did."

Amin blew through tight lips making a fluttering raspy noise. He wrung his hands in frustration. "Look – that's impossible. We don't have those documents readily available. That incident happened quite some time ago. Those trade slips would be in storage. This – this …" he looked at the floor, running his hand through his thick dark hair falling from beneath his turban, then shot his gaze back up, "… this is going to take some time."

Shareed bunched his lips and wagged his head in a slow 'no' motion. "*Time* is something, I am afraid, you do not have. I can call in some help – if you need some help. Do you understand me? We will be *happy* to locate them if you do not have the time or inclination. Take that as a promise, not some idle threat."

Amin was red faced flustered. The way Shareed said *happy* did nothing to comfort him. He turned to Ismail and said, "Ismail, go now. Go find those documents in question. Prove our innocence in this farfetched fiasco."

Ismail was thankful for the reprieve from the contentious meeting. He rushed out the door and kept running until he reached their storage facility a couple of blocks away. Diligent as ever, and mindful of his father's now compromised position, he set about his assignment with focused speed. A few hours later Shareed had all of the documents he needed.

At the end of the day Ismail called Skip to inform him of the unfortunate turn of events. Skip said he totally understood, but also vowed to fight it with everything he had.

CHAPTER FORTY

Skip called in the tigers. He'd use his ball busters to help save him from the Fed's. He hired Roy Blackman, generally regarded as a vulture amongst friends, as his lead defense counsel. Skip wanted him to yank the bones out of those prick investigators.

Roy was honest and frank with Skip. "Quite honestly, Skip, this is not a little matter that we can easily pay our way out of ... oh, no – not this time." He took a sip of whiskey from the crystal tumbler on his leather topped mahogany desk.

The gravity of the dire situation was all over Skip's face. "I can't believe this is all over the matter of twenty four stinking million dollars lost on a wrong way trade."

"Maybe we can cut a deal," Roy said after another sip.

"What kind of deal." Skip seemed a small version of himself.

"Let's wait to see what kind of information they come forward with, shall we? See just what they've got. Right now we're really getting the egg before the chicken."

Skip silently agreed with a nod and a sigh. They concluded the meeting making arrangements for weekly meeting to determine best way to proceed as events unfolded.

*****

Vinney, in Las Vegas, got the fast traveling word of Skip's newest investigation. He had not been approached yet by the Fed's, but knew that was just a matter of time. He had now ventured into the gumball vending business Skip had been so keen on to provide himself with a legitimate disguise. He still did the bookmaking, he loved the bookmaking, but he had the legit business to fall back on if things got too hot with Skip.

Another thing had helped to drive the gumball thing home. Artie, Vinnie's buddy at the CFTC, had said, "Vinnie, you and I go way back and I say this as your friend first and foremost ... do something to save your own ass. I'm certain it's just a matter of time before Skip is caught and tried."

"Artie," Vinney had told him, "as you know I can't be one hundred percent legit, not my style. But I have taken some measures to ensure my safety."

"Like?"

"Skip was keen on this gumball business a few months back. I was not---at least not at that time, but the more I thought about it the more perfect it sounded."

"Gumball, you've *got to be kidding.*" Artie had laughed out loud.

"Artie, listen to me," Vinney had said, "This gumball racket is something else."

"Yea, right. Save it for someone who cares." Artie had not been able to wait to tell the other investigators about this one.

***

Skip still believed his crew would remain loyal. He called another of his roundtable discussions in the vacant office on Atlantic Boulevard. All of Skip's top men were in attendance, including Vinnie, Gabe, Tommy, Sammy, Ismail, Mark, Matt, and DeRon. The tone of the meeting was uncharacteristically somber. None of the attendees knew that most all of the others had decided to work with, not against, the Fed's.

Skip began the meeting with, "Thank you all for meeting me here on such short notice. I'm sure you are aware of the bust on Mel and Ned's operation, as well as the fact that the Buckhead debacle has caused me a lot of legal pain." He looked at DeRon. Mel and Ned ran a similar operation to Skip's in a building directly across the street from this one. They were baited by Fed's posing as investors and summarily busted. Skip looked around the bare room. His voice tinged with nervousness. "I've heard that *we* may be next." His tone was like a preacher delivering a eulogy for dead soldiers.

Sammy raised a hand and said, "Skip, we've heard that same record playing for decades now. They – Mel and Ned, were strictly small fries. Bozos to the max. Don't let that shit get you down. We're the big time, man. What's a little pain … we're flexible and stand with you. We know the drill." He shot two thumbs up.

Skip forced a slight smile at Sammy's cheerleading pep talk. "I know, Sam, and thank you, but it appears that our federal friends are a little more persistent than they've been in the past. I don't know if they now have more funding, or more manpower, or both. Whatever it is … in order to keep them off our asses we've separated the offices into two entities. One will become Guardian Investments and the other will take the name of Colonial Finance. I want Sam to go on record as the owner and operator for that corporation on Las Olas. Matt will do the same with the one on Third … Colonial Finance."

Matt was suddenly confused about the apparent seriousness of the situation. He scratched his head and said, "Skip – these are serious changes, but – do you really think something this drastic is necessary?"

He looked at his partners for confirmation or dissention. "Skip, you know we are *all* here for you." He looked around the room. "Right guys?"

His question evoked a varied range of silent and dared-not-to-be-let-known emotions within the group.

Skip sensed something wrong, but couldn't identify it. He smiled, but again it looked out of place. "I know, Matt, and I appreciate your loyalty. I really do. But, I've got to go to the mats now. My attorney, Roy Blackman – many of you know him … has advised me to distance myself from the daily operations. He feels this's the best move at this time – so I feel obligated to do what he says." Skip looked and felt drained. He said with a deadpan expression, "I will no longer be in the office every day. Instead we'll hold weekly meetings and we'll talk *often* by phone."

Ralph, the eternal worrier of the group, said, "Look Skip – we can handle the day to day operations just fine, but what good does it serve for you to just be out of sight? I mean won't the Fed's – if they are as close as you think they are … find that out too?"

"My attorney thinks this is our best tact. This is not the long term plan that I foresee for us. Just bear with me in the interim. I see us growing even stronger from these forced changes." He was trying to convince himself. "I'm just doing this for a short while … honestly. I promise just a short while – a very short while, I hope. Just until things cool off a bit."

"Look," Skip said with a glance at his watch and a short sigh, "I have to wrap things up. I don't want a word of this getting out to the other brokers in our firm. I need them united under your leadership … now more than ever before. I need each of them to strive to open more accounts, and larger accounts. I can't stress the *importance* of this enough."

Mark said, "What about the leads? If Matt is heading up the office on Third who'll handle the leads?"

Gabe was fast to say, "Skip – I can manage the leads. I've got a lot of good contacts out in Vegas. At least from the lead generation standpoint. We can get some primo stuff too. That'll free up Matt to run Third Avenue."

Skip eyed Gabe skeptically. "Okay." He was trying to get his mind around it. "That's right. As I recall, you have some experience in that area." He focused on Matt. "Matt, you have no problems with that, do you? Guys – if anyone dissents or disagrees, I want to hear it now. The last thing I or any of us need is problems simmering and boiling out of control."

"No Sir," Matt said like the loyal legion he was, but he was not 100% sold on Gabe's lead generation abilities.

Skip looked to Sammy. "Sammy, the funds from all the accounts here in Lauderdale will be handled by you … and you alone. I need you to send most of it to either the Caymans or Switzerland for safe keeping – maybe a little to the Bahamas." He made solid eye contact with Sammy. "Actually – I may need some of those monies for legal costs. Natalia – you are keeping your share from the booking business in Costa Rica, right?" He looked at her. "I may expand her operation to handle some currencies, too." Skip stopped for a short pause, then said, "At least this way we are diversified. Vinney will send his Vegas money to Natalia and Tommy will continue to push his earnings into the Royal Bahamian Bank and Switzerland." He glanced around the table. "I think that about covers it. Any questions?" He looked around the room again and said, "Ah, and just one more thing ... shred! Anything that looks the slightest bit incriminating has to be shred immediately."

No questions were asked and the meeting broke up. Nobody wanted to hang around, especially not the new converts for the Fed's ... who were wired.

CHAPTER FORTY-ONE

Considering how rapidly things were moving with their investigation, Ray thought his best opportunity to make a deal with Skip was at hand. He contacted Sammy, the new boss at the Lauderdale office. Sammy was in good spirits, considering.

Ray jumped right in. "Sammy, I know the SOP is to run things past you and you will hand them off to Skip for consideration. So what I'd like to do is to make an offer to Skip for the Key's operation only. And that includes the furnishing, rent, everything that he did originally to get it up and running."

Sammy mulled that over and then said, "What'd ya have in mind?"

"I don't plan on keeping his name, so let's cut that off the top. The desks are used, but adequate. The computers are used, but also good enough for our needs. We both know the rent is $2,500 per month and that the feeds for FOREX, GLOBEX, and real time trades are in the area of $600 per month. I am willing to offer him two and a half million dollars."

Sammy had to hand it to Ray. He had balls to offer that pittance on this lucrative operation. Sammy thought it was easily worth five mil. He was slow in saying, "I'll pass it by Skip and get back to you."

"How long do you think before you'll have an answer?"

Sam bit his cuticle. "I dunno. Probably in the next few days. That okay with you?"

"Yes, fine. Thank you, Sam."

"No worries." Sam spit out a small piece of skin and went on about his business.

***

Skip was feeling exhausted. The early anticipated skirmish between him and the Fed's, as well as thoughts of the fight dragging on and on, costing him lots of money in the end, was wearing on him. He decided he needed a break. He flew off in his plane to the Dominican Republic for a long week of fun in the sun. He was hoping that while he was away Father Zeke would take care of the Frederika thing. That would kill two birds with one large stone; some much needed R & R, doubling as the perfect alibi against being tied to her death or disappearance.

The Fed's followed both Skip and Father Zeke and listened in to conversations between Skip's many capos. Ray kept them up-to-date with his offer in progress for the Keys office and Catherine steadily snapped videos and stills as opportunity afforded. The information subpoenaed from American Futures was some of the most helpful to date in piecing together timelines and trades and account information so that it would flow cohesively in the court room and, beforehand with hearings before the judge. Nick was still the go-between for Catherine and the Fed's, but he had also been bumped up. Because of his law degree and expertise in interpretation of financial legal briefs, past and present, he could help in sifting through the legal documentation, discovery, and brief writing stages of the investigation.

Catherine was assigned to the Las Olas office working under Sammy's direction. It was much smaller and the atmosphere was more intimate, but less private. There were thirty five brokers squeezed into the suite which consisted of four rooms that opened out onto a small canal that linked up to the Intercostal Waterway. Sammy was a tireless taskmaster.

Ismail had gone with Matt. Mark had been assigned to Sammy. The girls who worked with them previously had been let go to save overhead. Matt and Sammy had taken great pains to assure the brokers this was merely a cost saving measure because these new offices were much smaller. They could function effectively and efficiently with a skeleton staff.

Catherine regularly reported what she knew or saw to Nick, who passed it along to the rest of the investigators. She felt bad about it in a way, but Nick kept assuring her it was the right thing to do. Deep down she knew it was. From the information provided thus far, the Fed's were able to exact numerous official charges against Skip with more coming down the pike.

Skip's attorneys felt confident they could get the judges to buy, if it came to that, a variety of trumped up, but plausible, counter charges or loopholes for months to come. Skip was somewhat relieved at their assurances, but still his nerves were frazzled and his patience spread thin to the point of splitting apart. He needed an escape. Dominica Republic, he thought with a smile.

***

Father Zeke had taken Ralph White and Frederika out as instructed, on *Traders III*, before Skip left for his trip. Ralph had killed before and had no qualms about doing so again. Doing Frederika was not going to be any problem. Ralph dismissed the boat's captain. He wanted no witnesses, and would pilot the boat himself.

Before Frederika arrived Zeke inquired about how the hit was to unfold. "Ralph, I agree that the fewer involved the better off we are, but what do you specifically have in mind?"

Ralph hit the starter buttons and the MTU engines roared to life. "Zeke, I've done this numerous times before." He checked the fuel gauges to ensure they had enough to get out to the Gulfstream and back. "Fred is a small woman in stature, but she can be a handful. The first thing we will do is dope up her Bloody Mary----and we know how much she likes her Bloodies. Then when she begins to get sleepy we put her in the bunk, tie her up, and I get one clean shot to the forehead----*blam*, she's dead."

Zeke crossed himself, disbelieving everything. "Skip said he didn't want anything too messy ... whadda we gonna do with all the blood? You know how anal Skip is about keeping things neat and tidy."

"Leave that to me, Zeke. I've already got a tarp and several cinder blocks and chains we're going to use when she's dead to toss her overboard."

Zeke was biting his lip, fidgeting and shifting his weight from side to side. I've done a lot of bad things in my life, but never murdered a friend. He pointed, numb. "Here she comes."

"Great – when she gets aboard you take off the lines. Leave them on the dock so they're there when we get back."

Frederika looked like she had stepped off one of the pages of *Yachting Magazine*. She wore white pedal pushers and a navy and white striped boat necked shirt. She had purposefully selected to wear her strand of pearls enhanced with Lapis Lazuli and little gold balls with earrings and bracelet to match. They were the perfect accents to her outfit. Her handbag and shoes were red Pradas. She handed Zeke her handbag and slipped off her shoes.

Zeke forced a sweet smile, attempting to appear casual. "Hello, Fred – so good to see you." He offered his hand to help her aboard.

"Thank you, Zeke." She glanced at the bright blue sky, dotted with cumulous clouds. "It looks like we'll have a perfect day for fishing." She retrieved her handbags and shoes and went inside to place them in the cabin.

Zeke loosened the lines. Ralph nudged the boat away from the dock. Zeke tossed the lines onto the dock and away they went. Seas were only forecasted to be a moderate chop. And the radio said that the Snapper were running. Zeke busied himself rigging some lines to support their story of fishing. Ralph navigated them out of the Lake Worth Inlet and then hung a left heading north and east out toward the color change. He set the autopilot and came down from the fly bridge to toast Bloody Marys to a fruitful fishing trip.

Fred took up residence in the fighting chair on the aft deck with the sun dancing off the water and onto her face. "What a marvelous day ... thank you so much for inviting me out. God knows I surely needed a break. I know you're both in tight with Skip, but *that* man is being so difficult.

Why won't he just give me the damn divorce and let me get on with my life?" She reached for her straw hat and placed it atop her head.

Ralph came out with three tumblers filled nearly to the brim with fresh Bloody Marys. He passed them around, making sure Frederika got the drugged one. "Let me propose a toast. A toast, to ... freedom!"

"To Freedom!" they all said in unison. They clinked glasses and took their first drink of the refreshing concoction. The boat was moving along leisurely at twelve knots in the lightly choppy seas. Weed lines could be seen as they moved further offshore.

A few minutes later Frederika yawned and said, "Wow, it must be the ocean air, or the rocking motion ... all of the sudden I feel a little groggy."

Zeke said, "Why don't you go and lie down. When we get to the color change I'll come down and wake you for the fishing."

Frederika did so. Zeke and Ralph finished their drinks and decided to check on her. Ralph took a .357 magnum from his duffle bag, screwed on the silencer and stuffed it in the small of his back. He handed a fresh nylon tarp to Zeke who opened it and they both walked into the forward cabin. Frederika was indeed asleep. Zeke rolled her gently from one side to the other so they could get the tarp settled underneath her. Ralph leveled the gun to her forehead. Zeke closed his eyes, as if drawing the final curtain on the last scene in his tragic play of forever-lost good conscience.

Ralph pulled the trigger.   Zeke heard *thwack-thwack* ... and knew it was done

Zeke opened his eyes. He marveled at how small the entry wound was. "Somehow I figured it would be much messier."

Ralph let out a sardonic. "Like I told you, Zeke ... I've done these lots of times before."

Zeke shuddered at the thought of his present company. He bent to touch the wound on her forehead. "It's just so small."

Ralph snatched his hand away. "Jesus, Zeke – don't touch anything. As a matter of fact, I want you to wipe every place you've touched here with those Clorox wipes." He began to unscrew the silencer. "And wipe down the tarp, too." He handed Zeke a pair of rubber gloves. "Put these on. Then wipe down the gun and silencer and put them away."

Zeke did as told and then went topside to check on their progress toward the color change. About two hundred meters ahead he saw where the green-blue water changed and turned a deep, sapphire blue. Weed lines marked the change from hundreds of feet of water turned to thousands of feet of water. There were no other boats in sight.

Zeke cleaned things up exactly as Ralph had told him. Frederika was dead. And he was now an accomplice to first degree, pre-meditated, cold-blooded murder. As that condemning and hideous thought penetrated his psyche, he experienced a sudden intense wave of nausea. A caustic chill crept into his joints and overwhelmed his mind. Standing numb in the punishing heat, he shivered.

Ralph came back inside and saw the job Zeke had done. "Nice, Zeke," he said with a smirk and a nod. He fished in his duffle bag and came out with two big spools of three quarter inch line. He placed a set of rubber gloves onto his large hands. "Okay. We've got to roll her up inside the tarp and tie these lines around to keep it closed."

They went about rolling Frederika up in the tarp. Zeke held it closed, holding back the impulse to vomit, while Ralph tied her up. He finished the last knot with a satisfied flourish and said, "Okay, let's get her outside."

They took her as far as the cockpit, Ralph opened the fish door, and Ralph stopped Zeke with a one-hand signal and a grunt. He said, "Drop her here for a minute ... and let me get the cinder blocks."

Zeke stood dumb and mute as Ralph went inside the cabin. One by one Ralph hefted the blocks out and stacked them near the dead body. He looped the line between them and tied it secure. "Okay, Zeke." Ralph motioned overboard. "Help me toss her."

Zeke complied, feeling nothing, incapable of allowing his emotions and thoughts to exist. They flung her out the fish door. She floated a few moments and then began to sink rapidly. When they were certain she was down for good Ralph pointed and said, "Wrap these things up in a trash bag. When we get back to shore you take them down to Miami and put then in a dumpster."

Ralph went back to the fly bridge and disengaged the autopilot. He turned the boat toward the shore being careful not to buck the Gulfstream which kept wanting to push them further north.

***

Skip had found a new playmate. Veronika was from the Dominican Republic where they had met on his last trip. He had brought her with him when he returned to Ft. Lauderdale. Having an exciting, fresh, new lay helped to relieve the stress of his mounting troubles with the Fed's.

When they got back Skip called Zeke and Ralph on a three-way line to see if the caper had come off as planned.

"So how was your fishing trip?" Skip said.

Ralph knew the game; Skip was speaking in code for obvious reasons. "Great. We caught a few Snappers ... they were running offshore."

"The big one got away," Zeke said.

"Sorry to hear that." Skip smiled, pleased. "And the boat?"

"Ran fine," Ralph said.

"Glad to hear it. So, should I count on Snapper for dinner?"

"Yes – what time," Zeke asked, according to the script.

Skip was happy to know there was one less headache to keep him awake at night. He had sent the girls to Germany to spend some time with their grandparents. When they had inquired about Frederika, he had told them that she had a new lover and was in South America until further notice. Apparently this did not create any undue suspicions on their behalf and they all went about business as usual. Skip planned on selling the house they had lived in soon and using those funds to create an irrevocable trust for the girls.

***

Several weeks had passed since Amy Galloway had heard anything from her client. Amy had called Frederika's home numerous time and left messages. She called Fredericka's cell phone and got the same standard messages about being *out of range or on another call*. She was beginning to smell foul play. She decided to look back over the volumes of documents that Frederika had given her to help convince the divorce judge that their properties should not be divided as fifty-fifty, but more in favor of her and the girls. She found a series of ledgers that depicted offshore banking accounts and large amounts of money that had regularly flowed to them from points across America. Amy decided to give her good friend, Marek Andropov, a call to see what he could make of them.

Marek had met Amy years ago when she and a group of young and impressionable attorneys had come for a visit to the offices of the SEC, CFTC, and the NFA. Amy had been one of twenty or so who had made that trip prior to deciding what law to specialize in. Amy had never seriously considered working for the federal agencies. However, she had been impressed with the breadth and depth of the level of their investigative skills. She had pressed a few questions and Marek was the agent who had responded. He was kind, spoke at her level, and was patient and informative in his replies.

"Marek, its Amy Galloway in Pompano Beach, Florida."

"Ah, Amy … I remember you----how long has it been?"

"At least a decade, no … more. Anyway, I've got some documents that I think may be of interest to you and the SEC."

"Amy, as you are aware … we do not investigate divorces." They both laughed at Marek's little joke.

"Actually, this fellow seems to be right up your alleyway."

"Please go on."

"His name is Charles Horowitz and he has numerous commodities and currently trading firms."

"Yes, we know him well. What's your connection to him?"

"His wife. She came to me a little over a month ago now … for a divorce."

"Really? On what grounds?"

"Yes. Basically she wants to have him out of her life for reasons of prolific infidelity. She is a woman of considerable means herself so she doesn't *need* his money, but she wants to ream the cheating – scum, she would call him, or worse … clean him out for all he's worth if she can. Anyway I've not been able to speak to her since, but she left me a considerable quantity of documents that connect her and this man to offshore and numbered accounts."

"Really?" Marek's interest rose with his voice.

"Yes, really. So, would you care to help me understand how I can help her recover more than the standard fifty percent of those assets in this case? Might be a win-win for both of us."

"I'd be happy to do that and much more."

It was Amy's turn to be intrigued. "Why is it exactly, might I ask, that this is of any interest to you and the SEC?"

"It's an ongoing investigation, but we have a lot of information that Nick has been working on – writing briefs for – so we can take it to the judges and hopefully press some charges against this nefarious man."

"Nefarious, eh? Well, when can we get together?"

"I can manage to be in your area at the end of the week … will that suffice?"

"Yes, that'd be fine. Thank you, Marek."

"No – thank you, Amy. This may be exactly what we need to move this case forward."

They rang off, both looking forward to their meeting.

CHAPTER FORTY-TWO

A few months passed and nothing eventful happened. Skip arrived home one day, just shortly after six p.m., having been to the gym and then having his weekly meeting with his men. Veronika was waiting for him with a romantic dinner prepared and set. Not much of a cook herself, she had gotten catered food that she knew Skip would like. This had to be special. She had selected a revealing and enchanting dress that flattered her hourglass figure and that did not reveal her little secret. Skip believed she was on birth control, but she intentionally was not. They had been screwing like rabbits on amphetamines, and now she was pregnant and delighted. When Skip walked through the front door she rushed at him and greeted him with a smile and a kiss.

"Welcome home, poppy."

Skip had had a hard day. He looked at his petite, dark, and beautiful lover with a tired but appreciative smile. "Veronika, you look lovely ... do we have some plans this evening that I forgot about?" He racked his memory. Nothing. He thought back to his meeting her, just twenty years old and having been married twice already. He'd had the second marriage annulled; something easy enough to do in the Republic.

She grabbed his hand and walked with him toward the back patio. She had taken care to have his favorite green tea with ginger ready for this special moment. She poured them each a glass while Skip took a seat on one of the fluffy lounge chairs near the pool that overlooked the Intercostal Waterway and his boat. The gentle splashing and trickling of water from the waterfall in the Jacuzzi and the pool always helped to relax Skip after a hard day. He let his head rest on the fluffy pillows and closed his eyes. Veronika brought the glasses of cool tea over to where Skip sat and took the chaise next to him. The sun was just beginning to dip down in the evening sky and solar powered lights around the patio area had just come to life.

"Skip ... my darling ... I need to talk to you?"

Skip sipped his tea. What, he thought, does she want to buy now? She's worth indulging in her voracious appetite for spending, and god knows I do indulge her, but ... oh, just ask. He said, "If it's about money, Veronika ... just go to the safe. There should be more than enough in there to satisfy even you for a while." He always kept a few hundred thousand in the house safe. These days he had upped that to closer to a million.

"That is very generous of you." She gently stroked his forehead. "But that's not what I need to talk to you about." She was nervous; she took a deep breath before proceeding. "I've got some wonderful news to tell you."

Skip needed some good news. He opened his eyes wide and looked her in the face. "And?"

She did not know how to tell Skip delicately so she just came out with it. "Skip *we* are pregnant!" She beamed and touched her tiny and slightly protruding belly.

Skip's jaw fell open. "This cannot be happening! Are you serious? No, of course you're not serious. Please don't play games with me, Veronika. That's the last thing I need. I've already had a very difficult day."

She took his hand, looked deeply into his eyes. "Skippie I'm serious." She then placed his hand on her tummy.

Skip could feel nothing, but he rubbed her to be sensitive. "How far along?"

"About eight and a half weeks."

Skip nodded, slow, thinking. He made a cluck noise with his tongue. "Would you consider having an abortion?"

Veronika, born and raised Catholic, could not believe she was hearing this from Skip. She began to sob. Huge crocodile tears dripped down her smooth face. "Absolutely not!" she managed between sobs. "I'm having your baby and that's final."

Skip pulled her to him, hugged her, then lifted her face up to his. "Veronika – I didn't mean to suggest that is necessarily what I want. I just wanted *you* to know that the option is there for you."

Her youth and inexperience showed. She didn't know whether to be pleased or feel more foolish. "Thank you, Skip, but there is *nothing* more that I want than a family and life with you."

***

The confrontational situation between Skip and the Fed's was intensifying. Skip's lead attorney believed an indictment was imminent and warned him again to have any and all information that could be further incriminating disposed of.

When the brokers at the Third Avenue operation came to work that morning Matt greeted them looking like he had not slept in a week. Brownish black rings encircled his usually handsome eyes and his ragged face sported a day old beard. He had spent the entire weekend shredding documents.

Matt said, "I've some news and I'll need all of your help. There are documents that I need to have on my desk no later than this afternoon."

One of the brokers said, "What documents, Matt? And what the hell happened to you? You look like you've had no sleep in weeks."

Matt grunted, went over exactly the documents he needed and then went to the sofa in the lobby and fell asleep.

Sammy had not wanted to spend his weekend shredding so he had hired an outside company that, according to their ad, said they were *reliable, honest, and quick.* Sammy valued all three of those attributes and had hired them with no hesitation. He had paid them ten thousand dollars for the work. Unbeknownst to Sammy, the shredding company he hired was a front, operating in concert with the Fed's. The sensitive and possibly incriminating documents had not been shred. Over the weekend the Fed's had managed to collect enough data that, if used correctly, could account for at least fifty charges under Rico and/or extortion, money laundering, fraud or an array of other possible classifications of illegal misconduct in the investment world.

Chuck, Nick, Marek, and Ray were pulled in to work overtime in siphoning through these and other documents. The atmosphere became more jubilant as additional damning documents were discovered.

The cataloging of information and determination of how best to use it had now moved into its seventh year. It had been two months since the Fed's were able to first collect documents from Sammy's operation.

Sammy had been using the federal outfit posing as a shredding company with regularity and, after seeing what a sad, overworked state Matt was in, he pushed Matt to do the same. With a continuous flood of documents coming in from both offices and those that Amy Galloway had provided to Marek a short time back, the Fed's had now managed to effectively piece together a damaging case against Skip. They were ready to pounce.

Nick met with Catherine to tell her to be scarce on the day of the bust. "Catherine, I want you to be as far away from this bust as you can when it comes down. Fade back to the Keys and go back to your real estate business if you can."

"How soon should I be doing this?" She said with a concerned frown.

Nick tapped his watch. "Now. There's no time to waste. Pack up your things and shamoosh."

"Wow, I'm amazed at how fast things are happening. I didn't think you had enough on Skip to move in quite this fast."

"We've had some lucky breaks – very lucky breaks. I can tell you that I've been busy as hell these past couple of months. We were able to infiltrate Skip's operations on Las Olas and Third. I won't go into the details about how that was done at this time because the less you know the better. We may need to call you back to testify for the trial. Are you okay with that?"

Catherine bunched her lips to one side and nodded. "I'll do what I can to help you. I think you know that. I've already compromised myself enough, but if you need me just say the word. All right?"

Nick smiled. "Thanks. We really did and do appreciate all you've done to help us. Your assistance was invaluable. I can say with certainty that we now have the goods on him and believe you me – this is a real doozy."

"How on earth did you manage to infiltrate his organizations? I happen to know he takes a lot of precautions – especially now that he knows you have been sniffing around." Catherine's expression indicated she was intrigued, wanting more information.

Nick paused, considering. He huffed in resignation and said, "Okay look. And this is strictly on the QT, got it?"

Catherine shook her red tresses.

"I could be in a world of shit if anyone knew I was telling you this. It's a need to know only basis and very sensitive situation. Since you've provided so much help and been such a team player for us, I'll … I can tell you this much, okay?"

"Yessir." She saluted.

"But promise you will not breathe a word of it to anyone else." He looked her straight in the eyes.

She crossed her heart.

He said, "We managed to get a job. A phony shredding company that was in fact a front for a federal agent operation. A couple of Skip's lead guys hired them to do the shredding of documents that Skip didn't want us to see."

Catherine's jaw dropped. "Really? That is super!"

"Yes. It was and it is. Sammy – the lazy *fazoo* …" Nick couldn't restrain a chuckle, "… he hired us first because he didn't want to take the time to do it himself. He's basically a conceited and lazy guy. Conversely, Matt had been doing the shredding himself, and get *this* … every weekend all alone. And I might add he was barely able to make a dent in the volumes of stuff he needed to shred. So naturally, when Sammy told Matt about us, Matt decided to use us too."

Catherine leaned back, taking in the gravity of Nick's statements. She got solemn. "When Skip finds out he'll kill them."

"We know he's capable of doing just about anything to save his own hide and we'll be watching. If he does …" he gave a sly wink and smile, "… we can add murder to his lengthy list of charges."

"When will all of this go down?"

"A couple more days. We have filed the preliminary briefs … and the judges have processed the subpoenas so we can begin to see some of the stuff he's been hiding. That is if – he comes clean with what we've asked for, and that may be a very big if. Our legal team, including me, is working overtime to draft up the lengthy list of alleged charges. If everything goes as well now as it has lately ... I'd say by Friday."

Catherine furrowed her forehead. "Shouldn't I stay until then? I mean, I don't wanna look or act suspicious in any way. And I wouldn't want to do anything that might jeopardize your case."

"Catherine ..." Nick leaned in and tapped a forefinger on her forehead, "... wake up here. What's the matter, girl? You got a guilty conscience or something?" Nick smacked his forehead with the palm of his head in a *what're ya stupid?* gesture. "No. You don't stick around at all. Call in sick or don't call at all. It doesn't really matter at this point. Just don't be in the office on Friday – under any circumstances."

Catherine's eyes went up and to the left. She thought the situation over for a few seconds and said, "I've made some friends here. How do I explain my disappearance to them?"

Nick gave a small sigh of exasperation. "Cat. Those people in Skip's employ are *not* your friends. Don't you think that if you were the one in trouble they'd walk the other way and pretend they never even knew you?" He put his hand on hers. "Come on, Catherine ... forget about them and forget about this place. I'm telling you this for your own good." He reached across the table and took both her hands in his.

"I know, but it just happened so fast."

Nick could read her reluctance, her indecisiveness. "Maybe for you ... I'm sure it has. But for us this has been seven plus long years in the making." He squeezed her hands and then patted them. "Look at me, Cat."

She did, without words. She knew it was the end of a chapter in her life and the imminent downfall for Skip when Nick said, his expression grim and his eyes like steel, "*Judgment day* is just around the corner."

CHAPTER FORTY-THREE

In the meeting between Amy Galloway and Marek, Amy had provided links to all of Skip's offshore bank accounts. She also provided appraisals of their collective assets, including the airplane, and the new home, including the millions of dollars for renovation and decoration, the fancy cars, jewelry, and the yachts, as well as proof of his operations in Costa Rica, the Bahamas, and Vegas.

Amy was standing ankle deep in files. "When I first asked Frederika to bring me documentation of their assets I never expected all this. And she was adamant about not settling the divorce with the usual fifty-fifty split."

"This guy must have at least eight hundred million in assets alone."

"And where there is a known quantity of money or other possessions we can assume there is an equal amount that we do not yet know about." She arched an eyebrow. "According to Frederika he is a crafty man."

Marek unconsciously tugged at an earlobe. "Do you know how long we have been investigating this guy?"

"No idea. Try me."

"Try seven years."

"Wow – that is a long time. Looks like this should help you locate all of the buried assets." She spread her arms out to depict the enormity of the documentation.

Marek pointed at one of the documents. "Can you imagine driving a Turbo Bentley?'

"I wish."

"He has that *and* a Rolls Royce Corniche."

Amy flipped a hand open and shook her head. "I could only dream of such luxury."

"Me too. That's more money than I've made in my entire career."

"Little wonder – that's government work for you." She winked.

"Indeed. My god, Amy ... I don't know how to thank you." He began stuffing folders into boxes and labeling them for the legal staff. "This stuff certainly shines a new light on how widespread his operations are and were. In order to acquire such expensive assets he had to rip people off into the billions of dollars."

"Yes, I know ... and that's a major concern for you, but – money aside ... there's still the nagging concern I have about where Frederika is." She rubbed her temples and leaned back from her desk. "I mean, I don't know her well, but from our brief encounter she appears to be a pretty straight forward woman. Caustic, but not the type to beat around the bush or be evasive, trust me."

"That is strange." Marek continued packing and labeling. "Have you checked around to see if anyone in her family or neighborhood has seen or heard from her?"

"Yes ... and it's all a dead end. I am concerned that something bad may have happened to her. Do you think I should contact the police?"

"Why don't you give it another week and if she still doesn't come around ... then call the police, and if they don't give you the response or attention that you want – contact Herb with the FBI." He jotted down a number and name and handed it to her. "Tell him that I sent you and he'll move heaven and earth to see what has happened, if indeed anything has happened."

"Thank you, Marek. I hope that you're able to bring this evil son-of-a-bitch down."

"All things in due time ... but I think we finally see the light brighter at the end of the hallway."

"Let me know if there's anything else I can do for you."

"Will do, and if Frederika shows please tell her to stick around. She would make a great witness for the prosecution." Marek made a call and scheduled to have the boxes of documents picked up and delivered to the main office in New Haven.

"You know that a wife cannot be forced to testify against her husband?"

"Yes, of course, but if she wants a divorce from him so bad she may decide to help us."

***

Noon Friday had turned dark and rainy, a prelude to what was about to transpire between the Fed's and Skip's insidious operations. Rain fell steadily, streaking the sidewalks, buildings, and people. The layers of dark clouds made the day appear ominous and other worldly.

Just after three p.m., the Fed's descended upon Skip's commodities complexes, both Las Olas and Third Avenue, without lights or sirens. A collection of navy colored Crown Victoria's converged at the front and back entrances of both buildings. Twenty officers per location, dressed in navy blue slickers, t-shirts and trousers with bold white letters on their jacket backs that read *Federal Agents*, were poised to strike. Car doors opened and agents silently leaped out. One agent per location stayed back, manning the radio with an assigned car. The point man signaled for the buildings to be surrounded.

The Las Olas office was on one floor. As most of the agents flanked the building's exterior four agents went inside. There was a small lobby and then double wooden doors that demarked Skip's operation from the rest of the structure. The point man opened one office door and the four agents ran in. When all five were inside, the point man called out, "Nobody move. You're all under arrest."

The same scenario was played out on Third Avenue.

The brokers, many of them in mid-conversation with clients, were stunned. Sammy, his face and demeanor stern and forceful, walked toward the dark agents and said, "What's going on here … what's all of this about? This is a private business. *Who* is under arrest?" His eyes flashed anger. He knew his rights. "And furthermore, do you even have a warrant or anything that gives you the authority to be here?"

The point man took charge, approached Sammy and handed him a thick document. He said, "Just do as I've asked." He pointed for his agents to move about and cuff everyone in the office. They began tagging them in place and giving them all their Miranda rights.

"*Stop* … stop this right now," Sammy said. "We've a right to an attorney."

"So call one," the point man said, spitting his words out with a sneer. "But make it fast. You can tell him or her to meet you at the federal building downtown."

Sam had to think fast. *Who to call, Skip or an attorney? Skip.* He speed dialed. When Skip came on the line he said in a panic, "We've got trouble boss and I mean big trouble this time."

"Just settle down Sammy. What type of trouble?" Skip was remaining calm.

"The Fed's are here … and they're *arresting* the entire office. You've got to do something and I mean now."

"On what basis are they arresting anyone?"

"Fuck if I know. They have a warrant for our arrest. Won't fill us in on the details at this time. What am I supposed to do?"

"Calm down, Sam. Where are they taking you?"

"He said the federal building downtown, whatever the fuck he means by that."

"Okay, fine." Skip grabbed his head. *Think fast.* "Let me get Roy Blackman on the line. Don't say or do anything until we get there."

"Will do."

"We'll meet you down there as soon as we can." Skip hung up.

A paddy wagon had been brought to contain the thirty plus brokers. Two of the agents were busy taking names and ID's of the brokers and stacking them into the vehicle.

Matt and his crew on Third Avenue were equally taken by surprise. Matt, in a panic, tried to reach Sammy, but there was no answer. Matt then called Skip and blurted out the events taking place.

"I know, Matt. Sammy just called me. Give me some time, I've a call into Roy's office, but his bitch secretary said he's busy in a trial. I assume that means he's downtown, too. As soon as the trial breaks one of his assistants has promised me to get him my urgent message."

"Whaddaya want us to do?"

"Just go along with them for now. Sit tight. Don't say anything. That is most important, Matt. You say no-thing. At all. Got it? We'll be there as soon as we can."

"Check. Ah, Skip ... do you think it's necessary for each of us to retain counsel of our own, or can we all use Roy, too?"

"Let's wait to see what Roy says is best. He's the professional. There may be some advantage to all of us using the same guy, or maybe not. I'll ask." Skip tried to sound brave for the sake of Matt who he knew was jumpy, but he was not feeling all that certain of himself.

"Okay, they want to take me now ... gotta go. I'll see you soon ... I hope." Matt's line went silent.

Skip considered taking his plane with Veronika and heading down to the Dominican Republic. He believed he might be able to escape extradition there under certain circumstances, but that plan was foiled when Roy's assistant, Jacob, called him back.

Jacob was solemn and resolute, "While Roy was in court our office got notice of the arrest warrants these wise guys have against you and your organization. I don't know yet what information they are basing this arrest on, but the judge will have the final decision there."

"Does this mean that I'm going to be arrested too?"

"Yes, most likely, anyway. There is a warrant for your arrest and the bail is set at two million for you alone. There are slightly smaller bails being set for the top staff of your organization. All in all they amount to a little under four million."

"Four million? This is outrageous. Isn't there something we can do about that?" *The fuckers just blindsided me and now this! What next?*

"Look, Skip – the four million is not all due and payable at this time. We can bond you all out for about four hundred thousand. Can you make good on that?"

"Yes, I guess." Skip was depressed. Not so much over the money, four hundred thousand he could pull out of his hip pocket or wall safe. But he didn't want to let anyone know it was easy money for him. The angst was over the fact of his impending arrest. There was no price for freedom – which he valued most in life.

"Time is something we don't have a lot of – unless you want to spend some time in jail ... and your men will sit there with you unless we bail them out. I'm just stating the facts, Skip. Can you come up with the four hundred large or not?"

Skip thought it over. Best to pony up. For now. Fucksticks. "Yeah. Sure. I'll get my hands on it right away. So what happens next?" Skip's mind was racing. What the hell – how can this be happening so fast? How do I get out of this mess?

"The judge will make a decision in our pre-trial hearing."

"What decision … what judge?" Skip was in full panic mode now. His mind skittered about as Jacob continued.

"According to federal courtroom protocol we are allowed a pre-trial hearing. At that time the judge will hear what the SEC, NFA, and CFTC have compiled evidence-wise and make a valuation as to its relevance and its substantive merits of warranting, or not, a court trial."

"How long will that take?"

"Usually we can get a hearing within a couple of week's time."

"And in the meantime?"

"We need to at least prepare for the basics so we can adequately rebut what evidence the prosecution may have or feel is worthy of a court trial. This will lend credence to why we believe this case should not go to trial." Jacob said those things to Skip, but in private he thought, we'll do the best we can. This isn't going to be our easiest trial, by a long shot.

"Do you think they have a lot of information against me?" Skip's throat was so dry he almost couldn't speak. He said in a croak, "What about my managers and brokers?"

"We'll take care of one thing at a time." He really doesn't get it. I can almost smell the money flowing into our coffers for his defense. This trial could net us hundreds of thousands of dollars if not millions and it may take quite a while, too.

"When. Damn it … when?"

"As soon as I speak to Roy."

Skip's breath was in a pant. "How much longer do you think that'll be?"

"I don't have a crystal ball, Skip. But look at it this way. We will manage to keep your ass out of jail, at least for now. But … your passport has been suspended."

Skip pounded a fist onto his thigh. "What the fuck. How can they do that?"

"Skip, all I can say is that these allegations, and there are at least twelve of them, are quite serious and will have to be tackled one at a time." And each one will rack us up more money to defend, he thought. "The passport should be the least of your concerns. All it means is that international travel is impossible."

Skip let that smolder in his pained skull, dealing with it. He said, "What about the rest of my money?"

"All bank accounts, in the USA anyway, have been seized. I think we can expect more of the same if they are able to identify any of your other accounts."

Skip's head was frying like an egg in a hot skillet. "How can they do this to me? I didn't even have any notice?"

"Unfortunately, Skip, they do not have to notify us until they have the subpoenas and warrants for arrest."

Skip let out a long, painful sounding breath. "So. What ... do we do next?"

"Listen to me and wait for further instructions."

"I'm going to need some money. Four hundred thousand bail will cut down on my readily available capital." I've got hundreds of millions, on the conservative side, stashed away. *Think fast.* "Do you think I should have some cash flown in from Switzerland or the Bahamas?"

"I wouldn't do that. Not now, anyway. If they get wind of those accounts they could attach them all until there is a decision from the court."

"How am I supposed to live?" Skip said, whining like a child in pain.

"Well, Skip, Roy tells me you are a clever man. I'm sure you have some monies stashed away for such a rainy day. Use them for the time being. If you can easily get your hands on some of the other stuff before it has been seized I'd do it ... and the sooner the better. But, Skip? Be wise about it. Don't leave a trail."

The Fed's had anticipated the possibility of Skip being a flight risk and had seized his King Air, his Rybovich, and his Contender. The only way Skip could try to leave the country was to drive across the border to Mexico or Canada and they were having that possibility eliminated in short order. All border patrol agents would receive a recent passport photo of Skip in the event that he tried, with orders to deny passage and report his whereabouts immediately.

Later that day Roy and Jacob met Skip at the Federal Building on Second Avenue in Ft. Lauderdale. Roy had arranged bond for all of Skip's crew. Their movement was restricted to house arrest. Everyone was fitted with ankle bracelets that told the police and Fed's where they were at all times. Even Skip got one.

When the police officer clipped the bracelet onto Skip's ankle he said, "Roy – do you really think this is necessary?"

"Skip, consider this a blessing. They wanted your ass in jail. They consider you a high flight risk."

"This is an embarrassment. Don't they know who I am?"

"Apparently they do, Skip. Look – at the preliminary hearing I can ask the judge to remand you into my custody and he or she may allow that anklet to come off, but until then you're just going to have to persevere."

Outside the Federal Building the media assembled and jockeyed for positions. The rain did little to dampen their dogged efforts. Questions were compiled from data that had become public knowledge earlier that day. Skip and his organization were about to experience their fifteen minutes of fame.

Roy said to Nick, "Of course you will be providing me copies of the information you compiled in order to effectuate these arrests." It was a statement and not a question. Roy was always smooth under pressure.

Nick formed a sly smile that caused Roy to wonder what sort of juicy tidbit he had up his sleeve. "You know, Roy, we've got that and more. And we'll be happy to share." He jutted his chin and nodded toward Skip. "You know even Skip's wife wants him brought to justice."

"You cannot compel a wife to testify against her husband."

"Of course not, we know that. But if she wants to do so of her own accord … then so be it."

"We'll see about that," Roy said in a snarl.

Skip kept quiet, smug in the knowledge of the impossibility of Frederika being in court to testify against him – or anywhere, for that matter.

***

"The way she tells it, she's hardly his wife. She said he ran out on her years ago and that a divorce is merely a formality," Marek shared in private with Roy, days before they were scheduled to meet with Judge Schram. "She gave us names of women who Skip presumably had affairs with. She gave us dates, times, and dollar amounts for monies transferred out of the USA into Switzerland, the Bahamas, or Costa Rica. In fact, she has been our most helpful informant."

Roy had not expected this behavior from Frederika and he did not relish telling Skip. He decided his client had had enough for one day. He would save it for another, hopefully better, day … if indeed a better day would come.

CHAPTER FORTY-FOUR

Long liners from Savannah, Georgia, had been fishing offshore about fifty miles from the entrance to the Savannah River. The *Gloria Dorothy* crew was surprised when their bail line caught on something definitely not a fish. The huge dragnets, fitted with hooks, had come up with a bluish green tarp. The tarp was not empty, although shredded in spots. It was lashed together with three-quarter-inch nylon line.

The captain said above the murmuring of the befuddled fishing crew, "Well, bring it down, cut it loose and open it up."

The deck crew carefully lowered the tarp to the deck. "Christ, look," one crewmember said, "there's blood stains all over it."

One of the other sailors unlashed the tarp from their hooks. "It's free."

Still another deckhand drew up the nets onto the coil. "All clear."

A scrappy young deckhand unlashed and opened the tarp. "Jeeezus!" He jumped back with a hand over his nose and mouth and gagged back a barf.

Another, more seasoned, crewmember walked forward and took a gander, "Well, I'll be god-damned. It's a body."

The captain placed his vessel on auto-pilot and walked down toward the aft deck. The one young deckhand who had opened the tarp first finally lost it and puked over the side.

"It's a woman," the captain said.

"What're ya gonna do, boss?"

The captain removed his ball cap and scratched his matted, oily hair. "In all my years of fishin' I ain't never seen nothin' like this." He sucked on his soiled toothpick and then said, "Guess I better radio this in to the coast guard."

"What should we do with … ah, the body?"

"Wrap it back up and put it on ice. If she stays out here in this heat we can be certain the gulls will nibble and she'll begin to stink."

The young puker said, "*Begin* to stink? That's a bloody understatement."

"Get ahold of yerself, son."

"I'll be just fine." He wiped the spittle from his puke on his shirtsleeve.

"Soon as you two get everything stowed we'll be on our way."

"Roger that, Captain."

At the dock they were greeted by the coast guard, the medical examiner, the local police, and the CSI team of forensic experts. Many questions were asked of the captain and his crew. The tarp and nylon ropes were placed in an evidence container by one of the CSI and labeled with the time, date, and GPS coordinates the captain provided. The same was done to the bluish green tarp.

The ME said, "Upon initial investigation I might hazard that she was killed by the bullet that went through her forehead." He pointed to the bloody indentation.

One police officer was taking copious notes. He said, "I'd reckon that might make this here a homicide."

The ME said, "It does appear so, but please wait for my final analysis." He spoke into his recorder, "Both legs have been severed. One at the knee and the other at the hip joint. Possible evidence of shark or other maritime activity." He broke for a moment and then continued, "The skin on her body is waterlogged and so thin that it is peeling off in places. She obviously spent some time in the water. How long is not entirely discernable because anything after seventy two hours cannot be body temped and she's clearly way past that."

"She still has some of her clothing on. Maybe we can get some clues from that."

The ME cut off her blue and white shirt and handed it to an officious CSI man who said, "Well, she certainly had expensive taste ... just look at the labels on her clothing." He carefully folded them. "Prada. That's very expensive."

"And her jewelry, too," The ME said as he deftly removed them from her bloated body.

A rookie CSI had been too grossed out by the bloated and peeling body. He was near the edge of the road vomiting. The ME said, pointing, with a knowing grin, "New guy, huh?'

"You can always tell." He continued packaging and labeling what the ME handed his way. "Besides the obvious, is there anything else that could qualify as the cause of death?"

"The gunshot wound was point blank and through and through. If she were fresh we could get some powder burns from her flesh, but she's far past that. That gunshot wound was fatal. Until I pull the tox report and complete the autopsy I can't be certain if that was the only or initial cause of death."

"She's is rough shape. Do you think it will be a problem getting an ID?"

"Her fingerprints will never pass the muster, but maybe I can match her dental records and find out who she was. However, maybe a better question might be what was she doing out there?"

"Once we find out who she is we can begin to compile some information as to who may have wanted her harmed or dead. We can send out a BOLO for missing persons, etcetera."

"Since I don't have the bullet I'll have to guestimate what gun may have caused the wound. Finding out the gun may also provide you with some leads. Maybe forensics can get some skin residue from the tarp and ropes?"

"At this point everything----anything, really, would be helpful."

"Wrap her up."

***

Back in Ft. Lauderdale, Roy, Jacob, and Skip gathered for their first hearing before the Honorable Judge Schram in the Federal Courthouse and the hungry alligators from the SEC, NFA, and the CFTC. Judge Schram was known for running a strict, by-the-book courtroom. Roy had hoped they would be heard by Judge Margaret Allenby instead. Judge Allenby was his friend and he felt she might be persuaded to be sympathetic to their cause. But that had not come to pass; today they would have to deal with Judge Schram.

Roy said to Jacob for the third time, "Jacob, you have our pre-trial stipulations, right?"

I've never seen Roy nervous before. Wonder why he is so anxious today. "Yes, of course, Roy. Everything is packed into your attaché."

Skip fidgeted. "What's going to happen today, Roy?"

"In our stipulation agreement we present the issues, witnesses, and evidence we've collected to refute this case in trial. We also clarify any undisputed and disputed areas there are currently and/or to be resolved by the trial."

Skip shut his eyes and grabbed his temples in a wince. He looked scared and dumbfounded. "Roy. In English, please?"

Roy repressed a chuckle and patted Skip's shoulder. "We basically set the stage for the trial."

"And does this take very long?"

"Depends." Roy smoothed his suit jacket and said, "Come on."

Again the media was waiting outside of the courthouse like panthers about to pounce. Cameras were rolling and newscasters were busily providing background details to their various audiences and studio crews. One anchor man was taping his report:

"Forty two year old commodities guru and mega-millionaire, Mr. Skip Horowitz, is being arraigned today for the first hearing before Federal Judge Schram, who is best known for his no-nonsense dealing in the courtroom. Mr. Horowitz has been accused by the SEC, NFA, and CFTC of investment and securities fraud, wire fraud, mail fraud, money laundering, making false statements, perjury, filing false invoices for the SEC, NFA, and CFTC, and theft from investors funds. According to the

Department of Justice they are also seeking relief for investors and have frozen his assets pending appointment of a receiver for his firm. Here they come now. Let's see if we can get a comment from his esteemed counsel, Roy Blackman. Ah – Mr. Blackman do you have a moment? Would you care to make a statement before meeting with the judge this morning?"

Roy held up a hand and said, "I've no comment at this time. Thank you." He kept moving, with Skip's arm in his grip.

The newscaster turned back to the camera. "And there you have it. No comment from the defense. More details on this hot topic coming up at our four o'clock news broadcast. Back to Jeremy Slocum and the weather for this week in Florida."

While Skip, Jacob, and Roy threaded their way toward the front entrance to the Federal Building, Channel 7, 10, 6, and 4 newscasters called out questions and were promptly told, "No comment," by the stone-faced Mr. Blackman. The newscasters were not to be deterred; they continued to dog them until they were secreted safely inside the lobby.

Inside, a security officer said, "Please empty your pockets into these bins and then proceed single file through the scanner."

Everyone did as asked.

"Mr. Blackman, can you please open your attaché?"

Roy dutifully opened his attaché and let the security personnel dig through it while he waited for their final okay. Once they passed through the security check point, they headed to the second floor, court room 202. The corridors and hallways were a beehive of activity. Court reporters, clerks, convicts, bailiffs, witnesses, and their attorneys were combing the halls leading up to the various courtrooms. Skip had not been to the Federal courthouse before. He, who was not easily intimidated, was nervous and fearful now about an encounter with Judge Schram – after what Roy had told him. Would you look at all of these blue-collar people. I feel so out of place. I hope this Judge Schram is not quite the hard ass Roy says he is.

On Judge Schram's docket this morning were several cases, the first being a high profile child molestation case that spanned three states. Next was a case of simple battery against a federal officer of the court, followed by a restraining order that was to be rescinded because the woman who had started it wanted the man, who was a local attorney, and whom the order was against back into her life. There was also a bankruptcy hearing for a nationwide hi-fi business, and last was Skip's preliminary hearing. The mood in the room was one of seriousness and gloom.

Judge Schram had spent a restless night because his beloved Dolphins had lost their Sunday game to the worst team in the NFL, the Tigers. He had a box seat for all of the home games and he usually invited some of his colleagues or good chums along to watch Zack Thomas dazzle the fans. And if the Dolphins lost, the hot babe cheerleaders provided enough eye candy for a pleasant consolation prize. Oftentimes, he invited some of those leggy lovelies up to his box to taste the appetizers or to have a drink. He was a harmless flirt, and they indulged him playfully. But the Dolphins' play that day had been atrocious, and even a playful toying around with gorgeous young cheerleaders had not been enough to assuage his spirits. He was feeling tired, moody, and irritable.

It was an informal hearing. There were no jurors, just the bailiff, judge, a court reporter, and the defendants/plaintiffs and his/her counsel.

The bailiff stood and called, "Will the court come to order for honorable Judge Schram."

Attendants found seats. The clock on the wall said it was precisely nine o'clock.

Judge Schram was a stickler for sticking to a firm timetable. A seasoned middle aged court reporter was poised to take down all of the conversations.

"All rise."

The court rose. Judge Schram entered, scanned the courtroom and took his seat. His robe was pressed and flowing, as immaculate as his mood was foul. He sneezed as he sat. *As if the Dolphin's losing was not enough, I've got my damn sinusitis again.* He rapped his gavel as gently as possible but still winced in sinus pain at the sharp sound. He said, "This court is called to order."

The room became silent. The bailiff said, "The Honorable Judge Schram will hear preliminary findings at this time for the United States of America v. Radio Rama."

Are you prepared to argue your brief?" Judge Schram said to nobody in particular.

A young, unkempt, somber male attorney rose and said, "Yes, Your Honor – if I might proceed to the bench, please?"

Judge Schram motioned him to come forward.

"As you know, Radio Rama has filed for chapter eleven bankruptcy protection. We have no need to call any witnesses as I believe these financial statements and testimony should suffice for evidence in this case." He handed over a stack of documents for the judge to peruse.

Judge Schram looked them over thoughtfully and then said, "Everything looks in order. As you know we need to do a public announcement for any and all creditors to come forward."

"Yes, Your Honor. We plan to submit those announcements to the Sun Times and the Herald tomorrow as well as similar news reels across this country."

"Fine. Pending no unforeseen changes we can render a judgment in two weeks." He then turned to the bailiff and said, "Reschedule this continuation for two weeks from today." He shuffled the papers off to the side and then said, "Next case"

The bailiff stepped to the judge's box and said, "The next case was a restraining order, but it has been rescinded."

"Fine. The next case, please."

In a clear voice the bailiff said, "Court calls The United States of America v. Charles Horowitz."

Judge Schram leaned back in his chair and said, "Are the prosecution and the defense both present?"

Both stood and said, "Yes, Your Honor."

"Come forward, please?"

Both parties walked to the front of the courtroom and had a sidebar with the judge.

"Do both of you have all issues that pertain to this case researched and prepared to litigate? Are you witness lists complete? Is all of the evidence compiled and ready for presentation before the court?"

"Yes, Your Honor," said the prosecution. She handed a thick file over to the judge.

"Yes, Your Honor," said Roy. He also handed over a heavy, stuffed manila file to the judge.

Judge Schram said, "Are there any undisputed areas in this case?"

"No, Your Honor. My client is pleading not guilty."

Judge Schram looked at the mountain of evidence presented by the prosecution and shook his head. "Then I assume that all disputed areas will be adequately addressed at trial?"

"That is, if there *is* to be a trail, Your Honor," Roy said with more confidence than he felt.

Judge Schram gave Roy an askance glance. "Yes – well, we'll have to see about that now, hmm?" He motioned them away with a finger wag. "All right, you can both take your seats now."

Judge Schram peered over his reading glasses and rested his hand on the two substantial files. His voice contained a hint of accusation as he addressed Skip. "Mr. Horowitz, the accusations against you are very serious indeed." He glanced back at the SEC's complaint. "I see here investment and securities fraud, running a criminal enterprise, racketeering and corruption, mail fraud, investment advisor fraud, money laundering, making false statements, perjury, false filing with the SEC, NFA, and CFTC, and theft from investor funds." *That's quite a list. Should make for an interesting and highbrow case.* "If found guilty, the maximum penalty could be as much as life in prison. Do you understand the gravity of this case and the allegations against you, as well as the full potential penalty if found guilty, Mr. Horowitz?"

Roy Blackman stood and spoke for Skip. "Yes, Your Honor. My client understands fully the seriousness of these allegations and is well aware of the maximum penalty allowed by law."

Judge Schram pushed his readers down to the lower bridge of his broad nose, looked Roy over and then Skip. If his eyes had been lightning bolts they would have seared them in half. Thunder cracked outside and shook the inner walls of the courtroom. Roy had a bad feeling. Judge Schram leaned back in his chair and placed his index finger and thumbs beside his aching nose and rubbed.

Oh my god, Roy thought, the judge is not feeling well. He's in pain. Shit.

"Court accepts the plea of not guilty," Judge Schram said with a weighty heave of breath. "The prosecution may now present its argument and evidence."

The case against Skip had been well prepared. The lead counsel for the prosecution was no rookie; she knew the laws regarding the workings of the SEC, NFA, and CFTC. Her pre-trial brief launched into a perfect textbook analysis of the charges alleged against Skip. She also established precedence by citing recent cases of similar nature.

Judge Schram thumbed through the prosecution's file. He said, "I see the prosecution is asking that Mr. Horowitz be remanded into custody until the trial date. What reasoning is provided for such request?" He looked at the prosecutor.

She stood and replied, "We believe he is a flight risk and as such should await his trail in custody."

"Objection," shouted Roy. He stood. "Judge Schram, I'll accept responsibility for Mr. Horowitz, if you will kindly remand him into my custody."

Judge Schram, while prone to moodiness, was still fair. He said, "Very well. I'll allow the defendant to be remanded into your custody, but placed under house arrest and fitted with an ankle bracelet. And understand, counselor," Schram gave Roy a stern, no-nonsense look, "Make no mistake; I will hold you accountable, with severe repercussions coming your way, should your client violate this trust. Do you understand me? Is that acceptable?"

"Thank you, Your Honor, yes – I understand, and that is acceptable."

Judge Schram grunted, rubbed his nose again and said, "Prosecution, continue."

Skip was sweating despite the air conditioning. He tugged on Roy's jacket. "Does this mean I'll stay in jail?"

"No, house arrest." Roy was concentrating on the judge's mannerisms and line of logic.

"Roy, I can't survive like this. I feel like an animal stuffed in a cage."

"Shhuuuh." Roy motioned with his hand. "Let's see what else the prosecution and judge have in store."

Judge Schram asked the prosecutor a few questions about the voluminous collection of information. The prosecutor ticked off each piece that the SEC, NFA, and CFTC currently had in their possession and then said, "What I've just given you is merely an overview. There will be many firsthand testimonies given, as well as a possible testimony from the defendant's wife, if she agrees."

Roy again bolted to his feet and said, "Your honor, I object to the allowing of my client's wife to bring testimony. Her testimony could be prejudicial to this case. I therefore motion in limine, the right to...."

"Counselor, shut it." Schram said with a scowl and a hand in the air. The judge's sinus cavities were filling with goo. He was getting crankier by the moment. He wanted more than anything to blow his nose and rest. "Mr. Blackman," he said in a fatigued, whine of irritation, "I am aware what the motion in limine is. There is no need to explain it to me now."

"Sorry, Judge. As I know you are aware, she cannot be compelled to testify against my defendant."

Skip scratched his head and made a mental note to check again with Zeke and Ralph about the Fred job. Those two better not've been lying to me. I'll tear their eyes out and piss in their skulls.

"As I understood it from the prosecution," Judge Schram continued, "that testimony would only be given if Mrs. Horowitz agreed." He looked at the prosecution for confirmation.

The lead prosecutor concurred. "They are in the process of divorcing, Judge. She expressed her willingness to cooperate with us... actually, via her divorce attorney, Amy Galloway – I believe you are familiar with Ms. Galloway – in any way she could. However, we have been unable to locate her to confirm this testimony as of yet."

Unable to locate her, Skip thought. Good. Very good. Maybe Zeke and Ralph didn't fuck the op up after all.

The judge eyed Roy. "Over-ruled, Mr. Blackman." He turned to the prosecutor. "Under these portentous circumstances I will allow her testimony with the express prerequisite that they are in the process of divorcing, and that she does so under signed statement that her testimony is given freely under her own volition, with no pressure from any outside force, or agency, or special interest group involved directly or indirectly with this case. Is that understood?" He eyed each counselor.

"Yes, Your Honor... of course, Your Honor," the prosecutor said with a bow of the chin. Roy nodded and also said, "Yes, Your Honor."

Judge Schram turned his attention to Roy. "Mr. Blackman, I assume that everything is in order for you to argue your client's innocence?

Roy began with, "Your Honor … It is our firm belief that much of the evidence that the prosecution is going to present in their case against Mr. Horowitz has been obtained through the use of illegal procedures. Therefore, we are stating for the record that we do reserve the right to request stricken from the record and/or admissible evidence, be it now or at any future date, during the due course of these trial proceedings, the use of *anything* …" he paused for emphasis and to take a quick breath, "… be it hard copy or e-file documentation, or testimony, that we can show have been obtained without adherence to the due process of law and the parameters of a legally conducted investigation."

Judge Schram was annoyed by Roy's snotty-nosed and overdone tirade, given this was merely an informal hearing. "Save it for the trial, Mr. Blackman," he said with a wave of a hand and a roll of his bloodshot eyes. "I'll evaluate the evidence as it is presented. Do you happen to have anything of *substance* to add at this time?"

Clearly his patience was being tried and Roy did not want to ruin his chances for a good defense before the case was even brought to trial. He cleared his throat, adjusted his tie and said, "Your Honor, let the record show that Mr. Horowitz has been a stand-up model citizen of this community. He has generously given monies to numerous charitable causes that benefit the 'at risk' youth programs, especially those with sports programs, that this court is so fond of supporting."

"And the purpose of this exchange is?"

"To show the court that Mr. Horowitz is no common street thug bent on not giving back to his community. As a matter of fact, he has not had even so much as a parking ticket before this incident."

"Incident?" Judge Schram's eyebrows went up. He looked directly at Roy. "Is that what you call this, Mr. Blackman, an *incident*?"

"I did not mean any disrespect, Your Honor."

"Enough already." Judge Schram winced and rubbed above his eye again. "I expect that two weeks will be time enough for each side to complete their voir dire for the trial." He did not wait for a reply, but went on to say, "I am going to table this case and any further arguments until the official trial date which will begin on the sixth Tuesday from today." He rapped his gavel and briefly consulted his calendar to ensure the time frame was as he intended it to be.

Roy tried to interject. "But Judge …"

"But nothing, Mr. Blackburn. I will hear your arguments when this court reconvenes in six weeks. Until then I suggest you get prepared. Court dismissed." Schram banged his gavel with a finality that caused pain.

A disgruntled Roy took his seat and began gathering up his documents. He stuffed them into his attaché.

"What now?" Skip said, his eyes narrowed, his features contorted as if in pain.

"Well, we better do all we can in the six weeks before this trial begins. We've got to pour over the evidence piece by piece looking for loopholes or inconsistencies, review witness testimony, etcetera, before we can adequately prove to a jury that you are innocent."

"So is this going to be a trial with a jury?" Skip sounded dubious.

"Yes, that is what the 'voir dire' is. Jury selection."

Skip sighed, resigned. "When do we begin jury selection?" He caught himself. "Oh, right – two weeks. Well, do you believe there's any chance we can, you know ..." he winked, "... *influence* them to side with us?"

Roy grabbed Skip's shoulder and said in a firm whisper, "Not here, Skip, Jesus ..." He looked around in swift desperation, "... we'll talk about this later – in my office, understood?"

Six weeks was going to be an ambitious timetable for his for trial preparation, Roy knew. He had to manage transcription of thirty or so depositions from key people who might help support an innocent vote from jurors, analyze and provide arguments for the evidence that the prosecution had produced thus far, pony up for jury selection, and more.

The court reporter reported the scheduled case date and time and Judge Schram penciled it into his calendar. "Case is adjourned until nine a.m. on Monday, April the twelfth." He banged his gavel again, rubbed his temples, and said, "Next."

Outside there were more television stations waiting for breaking news. A well-dressed reporter from MSNBC was speaking into the camera.

"We understand that Mr. Horowitz has pled not guilty to the numerous charges brought against him by the SEC, NFA, CFTC this morning. The Department of Justice has set up an investor hotline for any clients who believe they have been defrauded by this man. We also heard that he has been remanded into house arrest. That's all for now. More on this hot topic at noon."

News stations around the world had picked up the story by noon. GMT, and newscasters were debating the outcome even before it had been brought to trial.

***

Veronika was getting more and more pregnant each day. Skip was increasingly pensive because he had to stay pent up in the house for the next six weeks. Sammy and Matt were shut down cold. Vegas had been allowed to operate on a restricted basis since the laws there were less clear, but the casino honchos who had been scammed were joining the other people, who now totaled into the hundreds, in a class action suit against Skip and his captains. Phone lines for Costa Rica and the Bahamas had been permanently shut down and the people let go.

Ray resigned his official investigation obligations on the job under the federal government, but made a deal with the Fed's and the SEC, NFA/CFTC to officially take over Skip's operation in Key West. When that office was raided, he had taken care to prepare the brokers for the eventuality and that preparation had panned out well for them. As it turned out, most of those people were too far removed from Skip's scams to be of much benefit to this case or the upcoming trial. Ray began in earnest to teach them some of the more technical ways to put on a trade and helped them to research and analyze which ones would work best for their clients depending on their tolerance for risk and amount invested. He had Sherman trading stocks, bonds, and other investment instruments that helped to offset potential risk from the commodities side. He loved this new enterprise.

Nick remained second in line for the legal team presenting for the prosecution in Skip's trial, but had been promoted and was now the lead investigator in the Bernie Madoff scandal as well. According to preliminary evidence attached to the Madoff case it promised to be more spectacular than even Skip's. He was looking forward to the new challenge.

CHAPTER FORTY-FIVE

Sammy, Matt, Father Zeke, and Ralph came to visit Skip regularly at home during his containment. They also continued to support his innocent claim in public and private. Zeke and Ralph had been secretive to the extent of paranoid.

Father Zeke said, "Ralph, you don't think there's any way the Fed's can nab us for anything in their case against Skip, do you?"

Ralph said, "I dunno, Zeke." He scratched his head. "Honestly, the thing that worries me most is the Fred thing."

They were speaking outside and at a public park, but both still worried about the Fed's listening in. Off in the distance they could hear the playful screams of children on the playground equipment.

"Mums the word there." Zeke made a zipper motion across his mouth.

"Gotcha, Zeke, but still I'm worried."

***

The authorities in Savannah had been able to identify Frederika only by her dental work. Obviously she had been murdered, but leads on who and what happened remained non-existent. She had been a *Jane Doe* for over two long months now. One day while sifting through some missing persons reports from Florida, one of the detectives had a twinge of insight.

Detective McGhee went to the captain's office and tapped on his door. "Excuse me, sir," He said with the missing person report in his hand, "I just thought you might want to take a look at this." He placed it in front of the captain.

Captain Hinkey looked at the description and picture of a good-looking woman who was said to have two daughters and an estranged husband back in Florida. "It *could* be her, but it's hard to tell from what I remember of her remains." He continued to look at the picture, trying to draw her face in his minds eye. "Maybe you're onto something here, McGhee. Why don't you get one of our sketch people or a computer tech up here right away to see if they can prepare a drawing or computer image based on what little we have from the ME's office. If it comes up fairly close we'll make a few calls."

A half hour later, the sketch artist came up to the detectives floor and sifted through the images taken at the Frederika crime scene. From dental records and images of skull shape and size, he came back with a drawing that bore a distinct likeness to the one on the missing person's report.

Detective McGhee rushed to the captain to show him the results. "Capt'n you've gotta take a look at this." He dropped the sketch and the missing person report side by side in front of him and waited for his reaction.

Captain Hinkey looked back and forth between the two and said, "It does look like it could be the same woman. Damn fine job, McGhee!"

"I thought so too. Whaddaya wanna do?"

"Contact the Ft. Lauderdale police aysap and tell them we believe we may have found their *Jane Doe*, Mrs. Frederika Horowitz." He clicked his fingers a couple times trying to jar his memory. "Didn't I hear something on the news about a Mr. Horowitz from Ft. Lauderdale being tied up in some fraud investigation and trial?"

Detective McGhee loved the news and almost never missed it unless he was out investigating a case. He replayed in his mind some of the higher brow cases over the past few months and then said, "Ah yes, I think he was the guy I saw on CNN, FOX, and MSNBC too. Something about investment fraud if memory serves me."

The Captain looked dubious, but played along, "And you know this how?"

McGhee said, "Cap'n I love the news. I almost never miss it – that is when I am off duty." He didn't want the captain to think he watched television during his work hours. "You know, maybe … she found out about his problems and she threatened him? Then he decided to off her or something like that?"

"Maybe. One thing's for damn sure, McGhee. Her death was no accident according to the ME." The Captain brought a forefinger to his lips, then pointed it at McGhee. "Make some calls. Let me know what you find out."

***

There were seventy-five boxes of files affiliated with Skip's case. The prosecution judiciously shared all of this with the defense who was rapidly becoming overwhelmed. Roy had hired a team of students and adjunct professors from Nova Southeastern Universities Law School to help collate what information was pertinent to the case and toss out what was not. They all worked tirelessly seven days a week.

Meanwhile Skip's depression deepened. Staying in one house, even if it was his home, day in and day out, was seriously curtailing his lifestyle. Veronika was growing larger and crankier each day.

"Veronika, why don't you go visit your mother back in the Dominican Republic?"

"Skip, I'm so miserable with this pregnancy. Just look at my feet." She looked down as best she could over her swollen belly. "Anyway, I'm way too pregnant to fly. I'll be right here with you."

God, she's getting on my nerves. I know she is well intending, but shit she is driving me nuts. If it weren't for this goddamned bracelet we'd both be in the DR now.

***

The authorities from Ft. Lauderdale had asked Captain Hinkey to transport their *Jane Doe*, a.k.a. Frederika Horowitz, to Ft. Lauderdale for positive identification. They had. Skip was the next of kin since the divorce between he and Frederika had never been finalized. Sheriff Jenner called Roy Blackman's office because he knew he was Skip's defense attorney.

"Roy, I know you are defending Mr. Horowitz. We have a body that bears an uncanny resemblance to his missing and estranged wife."

Roy was shell-shocked. "Ah … I see."

"We'd like you to bring Mr. Horowitz down to the morgue for positive identification."

"Sheriff Jenner … I'm really pressed in defending his case with the trial a mere four weeks off and all … couldn't we do this after that's over and done with?" The hairs on the back of his neck rose and he felt his sphincter muscles open and close. God I hope I don't get the shits. What has Skip done now? He fought the urge to hang up and rush to the restroom.

"I'm afraid this can't wait. We've had an ongoing investigation and we really need closure."

"Let me see what I can do." Roy shifted in his seat and tried to quell his mounting horror at the possibility that this really was Fred.

"Make it today, okay? We'll be waiting for you."

Roy sat stunned as the sheriff's line clicked off. His bowels were rapidly turning to liquid. He jumped up and ran to the nearest bathroom.

Roy called Skip with his stomach in his throat and said, "Skip … I've got some good news and some bad news."

Skip said with a weary voice, "What … now, Roy?"

"Which do you want first?" Roy's flesh was goose dimpling.

"Give me the good. That way the bad will hopefully not seem so bad."

"Well, Sheriff Jenner just called …"

"And?"

"He said they may have found Frederika."

Skip swallowed hard. "Ah – ah … really?" He was having a difficult time breathing. *Fuck! What next?*

"Yes, he wants us to come down to the ME's office for a positive ID."

Skip paused, catching his breath before answering. "When----how?"

"Today, he said. In fact, he was downright adamant that we do this today."

Skip ran his hand through his hair and tried to think. *I've got to contact Zeke or Ralph, but how? I know the fucking Fed's are still listening in. Danmit!*

"When can you be ready, Skip?"

"Give me – give me an hour." Skip had to call Father Zeke and Ralph to find out exactly what they had done and where they had gone wrong. He knew it was ultra risky, but he had to know. Now. He resigned himself to the inevitable and said, "I'll see you in an hour."

Skip pulled out the GoPhone he had asked Veronika to get for him at the local CVS. He had secreted it away for times when he could not afford to have the Fed's overhear his conversations. He dialed Ralph first since he was the one in charge of the disposal – according to Zeke. "Ralph … listen to me very carefully."

"Sure, what's up boss?"

"I need to know what happened----and I mean *exactly* what happened the day you and Zeke took Frederika fishing."

"Gosh, Skip … that was quite some time ago now. I dunno if I can recall exactly how things happened … why?"

"Roy just called me. Apparently Sheriff Jenner thinks he may've found her body. They want me to come down there in an hour for a positive identification."

"Wow – that's really something considering how we tied her legs to cinder blocks and dumped her … god it must've been – what … thirty or more miles off shore."

"Why didn't you cut her up?" Skip was getting desperate.

"That would've been kinda messy, boss. We were doing it like real neat."

"Neat my ass. This is the *last* thing that I need right now."

"Yea, right … you want me to go with ya?"

"No that won't be necessary, but why don't you go on a little vacation?"

"Like where ya want me to go?"

"I don't really give a damn where! Just disappear and take Zeke with you." He dropped the call.

An hour later Roy drove up in his Lexus sedan and honked for Skip to come outside. "I know this may be unpleasant and I'm sorry we've got to do it now," Roy said as he backed out of Skip's drive. He looked both ways and moved onto the road.

"More than unpleasant, Roy. I feel like the whole house is falling in on me."

"Try to keep your spirits up. You will need your energy for the trial."

"Speaking of the trial, how's my defense going?"

"We're working hard on it … seven days a week. I can't promise anything spectacular because the jury is not in front of us at this time, but as we begin the trial we can see how they are generally taking to the facts and information presented by us and the prosecution."

"Do you think we can infiltrate the jury and pay them off to vote our way? Roy, I can't go back to prison. Not even for a day. I'll do anything."

"Now that all depends. Give me some time to see how that might play out. Judge Schram is a curmudgeon, but I know the bailiff fairly well and perhaps we can arrange something. Let me broach that with him and see how he responds." He made a note of it in his day-timer on his cell phone. "If the bailiff is willing to play ball we will pay him handsomely to bug the jury room. And if we can hear their daily deliberations then we might be able to ascertain the weak links and pay them off, too."

Skip seemed buoyed by this possibility, but left the details up to Roy. He wasn't up to planning anything more than where to order dinner out.

"Now is there *anything* you should be telling me about Frederika, Skip?" Roy's tone was monotone and flat.

Skip blanched. "No, ah … nothing at all. Why would you ask? You know Fred and I weren't exactly chummy toward the end of our relationship."

"Skip, if I don't know *everything* then I cannot effectively defend you."

Skip considered this, but was not ready to divulge anything. They drove in silence to the morgue where they got out and walked inside. The morgue was a dank, dark place. Skip could picture the cockroaches scratching around the shadowy hallways. Disinfectants did little to cover up the smell of serious decomposition and Skip felt lightheaded as they approached the viewing chamber.

A somber little clerk dressed in blue surgical attire ushered them into the viewing room and drew open the curtains. Below them was a partial body on a silver cart. The features were badly bloated and nearly unrecognizable. One leg was severed at the hip with severe gnaw marks on it. The other was torn off just below the knee. Skip recoiled and almost heaved when he saw her. The clerk handed him some smelling salts.

"Is that her," the clerk asked Skip without emotion.

Skip steadied himself on the railing. "Yes." He said, barely audible.

Roy asked, horrified, "Do we know what happened to her."

The clerk looked at the ME's report and said in a clinical, matter-of-fact tone, "She was shot in the forehead, died immediately. She must have been thrown overboard, since she was found tied up in a tarp." He pointed to the bite wounds and severed legs. "Looks like sharks bit at her, right through the tarp. Surprised they didn't consume her altogether. Quite fortunate to have a body at all. And she was underwater for we figure at least three days. That's why she's so bloated and disfigured."

"How? Where? A concerned husband Skip was not, but his interest in knowing the details made him sound like one.

"I don't know all the facts, but she was picked up by some long liners off of Savannah, Georgia."

"Savannah? You don't know anything more?" Skip took another whiff of the salts.

"Well, we are waiting for the tox report and some tissue analysis, but basically that's it."

"I assume you will let us know if something else turns up?"

"You can learn more from Sheriff Jenner's office who is officially handing the investigation."

"Investigation?" Roy and Skip said in unison.

"Yes, you know like in homicide?" The clerk's voice and face were deadpan. "Look at the shot to the forehead. It is quite obviously murder, execution style."

***

Eventually Roy found the right time to test the bailiff on the topic of bugging the jury room and being amenable to bribes. He said, approaching the subject with caution, "You know, Jack, do you ever *listen* in on the jury deliberations … I don't mean *listen* really, but sort of let the judge know where you think they are going in the decision making process of any given trial?"

This was a regular sticky wicket and Jack was uncertain just how to reply. He treaded lightly, saying, "I sometimes overhear things. You know the rooms are not sound proof … so we can hear things when we are standing guard or when we let them out for the bathroom or bring in food and drinks." He shrugged, nonchalant. "Ah … why do you ask?"

"I just thought that maybe … just *maybe* you might be able to do me a favor."

Jack's eyes lit up some. "Like what?"

"Let's just call it a little insurance policy."

"You and I both know we are not supposed to pass any information of that nature along to anybody." He paused, rubbed his chin. "But, there have been times when I gave one of the judges a little heads up in what direction I felt a jury might vote. You know, just so he or she was not all surprised when it was read." He stopped again and then added, "I guess that doesn't do anyone any real harm, now does it? And it's not like I do that *all* the time. There are some trials that just drag on and on. And sometimes we need to have a little idea about is what is inside the heads of those jurors. You know what I mean?" A certain look was exchanged between them that gave unspoken credence to the game they both knew was being played.

"Yes, I do … and you've been very helpful, Jack. Depending on how things progress I might be interested in some of that information you sometimes overhear," Roy said with a wink. "Of course this would be *strictly* between you and me. And of course, I could give you a little something for passing that information on to me."

"How much we talking about," Jack asked a little too quickly to play totally innocent.

"This is a very – very important trial, and because it *is* so important … I would be willing to give you, say … twenty five thousand up front – and twenty five later, *but* that would mean we might also need some innocent votes from a few jurors." He let that sink in a moment.

"Okay. Let's see what happens when the trial opens. Usually, in a day or two, we can see how some of the jurors are siding. Of course, nothing is etched in stone because they have to hear all of the information. Nor does that mean that they'll not change their minds down the road." He chewed the inside of his cheek. "In my experience jurors are finicky. Now, some of 'em can be persuaded by cash. You know they only get fifteen measly dollars a day and if they're not being paid on their jobs. That tends to make 'em want to rush through the trial and get back to earning the wages they's lost."

The door was open, Roy knew.

CHAPTER FORTY-SIX

Jury selection took two weeks and took place during the defense team's scramble of trying to tie up loose ends. It seemed like there was no one in the entire county who had not heard something about Skip and his unsavory investment operation. Most of them had an opinion of Skip that ranged from unfavorable to detestable.

Judge Schram cautioned them about coloring their judgment or coming to conclusions about the defendant before hearing all of the evidence. He told them time and again, "If anyone here believes they cannot render an impartial judgment of this man, please step forward."

Nobody had stepped forward and been unseated, but the looks on their faces were not at all what Roy had hoped for. Roy knew it would be a daunting uphill climb – even with the bailiff on their side.

***

Sheriff Jenner could only think of one person who would logically have a motive to kill Frederika. That person was Skip. He spoke to both Roy and the judge about his suspicions.

"Skip had the motive, the means, and the opportunity to kill her," he said, with arms folded.

Roy was flustered. "That's rubbish and you know it. My client wasn't even in the country when this killing took place." He glared at Sheriff Jenner. "The real killer is someone else, someone who is now running loose while my client sits at home awaiting his trail."

Sheriff Jenner looked down his elongated nose at Roy and said, "Quite frankly, we find that unlikely."

"But not impossible, correct?"

Sheriff Jenner was not to be deterred. "No, not impossible." I hope like hell we can find something undeniable to tie this SOB to her death. I just know he has to have something to do with it. Patience.

***

During the six weeks of preparation for the trial, close to a hundred depositions were taken. A web site was established by the Department of Justice for clients of Skip's operations who felt that they had been ripped off or misled, linking them to the class action suit; more of Skip's assets had been seized and more bank accounts located and frozen. Deep down Roy knew he might also eventually have to defend Skip against one count of first degree murder, but one trial at a time.

Most of Skip's brokers were given sanctuary or immunity in exchange for incriminating information against Skip, as well as convincing proof that they were merely acting on his instructions or orders. Four men held out: Matt, Zeke, Sammy, and Ralph. All of them had admired Skip for a long time and had been so wrapped up in his tangled web of deceit that making a deal for them *against* him was not going to seriously discount or offset any jail time they might incur. Ralph and Zeke had so far escaped any culpability in the murder of Frederika, but they knew eventually Skip would give them up to lessen his jail time as well.

Roy dressed in his slate blue, double-breasted suit with a crisp white shirt and red striped tie for the first day of the trial. Skip wore a pinstriped gray suit with a light pink shirt and paisley tie. The gray of his suit matched his mood. Roy hoped to make a lasting impression on the jury by presenting an imposing legal team. Skip walked in with Roy. Behind them were a half dozen of their hired law students and professors, as well as Roy's paralegal, Jacob. As they ascended the lengthy steps to the courthouse, cameras clicked picture after picture and anxious newscasters shoved microphones in their faces asking for a comment on anything. They got nothing. The mood was somber and business-like.

Inside they had to pass through metal detection devices and scanners before making their way down the long hallway toward courtroom number three. More reporters greeted them there. No one got a comment. Hushed voices spoke about the upcoming trial and all who were present to preview its proceeding today. Two guards stood at the double doors separating the courtroom from the hallway. They passed them with a grim demeanor and went inside to the assigned defense table on the left.

The prosecuting attorneys were already seated, having a mini conference. Directly behind them sat Nick, Ray, Sean, Earl, and Marek. The rows of benches behind them were quickly filling in with anxious spectators and media members.

Three minutes before nine, the bailiff came into the courtroom and said, "All rise. The court will come to order for the honorable Judge Schram."

Judge Schram entered from the rear of the chamber and took his seat. "You may be seated," he said, "Bailiff, bring in the jury." The jurors were paraded in and seated in the jury box off to the right. A commotion of excitement and hushed but still loud gossiping wafted through the room.

Judge Schram rapped his gavel and in a booming voice gave the command, "Silence in this courtroom! The court will come to order." All complied, in quick fashion. No one wanted to incur his wrath, and all shut up.

The court reporter steadily typed as the proceedings began to unfold. Jack introduced the case. "The Court will now hear The United States of America versus Charles 'Skip' Horowitz, case number two three two four five."

Skip's guts wrenched when he heard those words. *The whole fucking country is against me. Jesus, I feel alone. And scared.*

Judge Schram turned to instruct the jurors. "It is your duty as jurors to follow the law as I outline it for you, and to apply the law to the facts from the evidence presented in this case as you find them. Do not single out any one instruction as the law, but consider them as a whole. Nothing I say in these instructions should be perceived or construed as my having an opinion about the facts of this case. It is your function to consider and weigh the facts of this case, not mine. Your duties as jurors should be performed without bias or prejudice to any party. The law prohibits you from considering public opinion, sympathy, or prejudice. Therefore, each of you must carefully and impartially consider the evidence as it is presented to you, follow the law as it is given to you by me, and to reach a verdict regardless of the consequences."

Whiteboards, overhead projectors, and other props were brought in and set up. Sketch artists, assigned to compose graphic depictions of all the various key witnesses, legal representatives, jurors, defendant, and important juncture scenes during the trial, began working their craft with silent skill.

Judge Schram said, "The prosecution will now present its opening arguments."

Bob Hawthorne rose to do the presentation. Nick was second counsel, but Bob had a superlative reputation for his opening arguments and Nick gladly allowed him to step in front of the courtroom. Bob was known throughout the various branches of the government as a well-spoken and amicable guy – until or unless he was crossed or cornered … then he was not so likable – if you were in his cross-hairs. He lifted his hulking self from the chair, tipped his reading glasses onto his forehead and sauntered toward the jury box.

Bob smiled and introduced himself. "Good morning, ladies and gentlemen. My name is Bob Hawthorne and I am working with the prosecution in this important case. Before we get started, I would like to thank you for taking the time out of your hectic lives to perform your civic and patriotic duties." He smiled again and took a moment to look each member of the jury directly in the eye. He began again. "It is my duty as a servant of the court to uphold the laws set forth in our great land. To present the facts in this case so that *you* can make a decision as to the guilt or innocence of this man." He pointed toward Skip. "Mr. Horowitz has been charged with some very serious crimes, which we will get into as the trial progresses. It is your job to determine if he is guilty or innocent. His freedom hangs in the balance of your decision. Therefore, you should not make your decision lightly, but cast judgment according to the facts and evidence presented. If you feel that the prosecution has adequately presented the facts to substantiate his guilt, then it will be your responsibility to vote in good conscience and to exact punishment that is equal to the injustices that he is found guilty of. Conversely, if you are not *one hundred percent* certain of those facts, it is your duty to seek clarification so that you can effectively render a judgment in this difficult case. Do you understand?"

His tone forebode the seriousness and gravity of the trial as he again looked them in the eyes and said, "The State, vis a vis, myself and the other members of the prosecutorial team, are going to present evidence that proves that Mr. Horowitz *willfully and wantonly* set out to *deceive* his clients and investors. That he did so with *forethought and malice*. To swindle them for hundreds of millions, perhaps billions, of dollars ... and, I might add, that Mr. Horowitz has profited *mightily* from this racketeering and money laundering scam. So much so that he has plunged some of his clients and investors into a state of bankruptcy or worse."

He paused.

Judge Schram was impatient as usual. "Will you get on with it, Mr. Hawthorne."

Bob continued. His voice steady and unwavering, "Mr. Horowitz created urgency, where none actually existed, in order that his unsuspecting investors would open their wallets and bank accounts to him without taking the time to further research his corporation or the investments he urgently pressed them to partake in. We will prove that he and his brokers had unscrupulous intent from the onset and that he ...," he pointed again to Skip. "... created fictitious firms to thwart detection from the regulatory bodies that exist to protect you and other consumers from predatory investments scandals such as this one."

His timber rose to a crescendo as he strutted back and forth and made flaring arm and hand gestures. "He even went so far as to promise unlikely and very high rates of return to those who had the misguided temerity to invest with his firms, You may recall the old adage, 'if it sounds too good to be true'? Well, in this case, it was too good to be true." He leaned into the railing. "The overwhelming majority of those promised returns never came to fruition. Instead, Mr. Horowitz pocketed their hard-earned money and bought airplanes, boats, vacation properties, jewelry, and more. On the backs of those trusting investors he opened more businesses to scam more people into his illicit business ventures and continued to profit from their ignorance and misguided trust."

Bob stood back from the rail, building more momentum as he spoke. "He has shown a *disgusting pattern* in his *inexcusable and reprehensible behavior*. He must not be allowed to get off Scott free in these transgressions ... no! He must be held liable for these premeditated transgressions against innocent, law abiding, and trusting people. It is my earnest belief that the evidence that my legal team and I will present will lead you to no other conclusion, except ... guilty." He tipped his glasses back atop his broad beak and walked back to the table for the prosecution.

Roy could tell the jury had clung to his every word, and he was more uncertain now than he had been before. That was a world-class opening argument, damn it. I'm up against a saber-toothed tiger.

Judge Schram looked at the defense table, expecting some movement. "Is the defense ready to present its opening arguments?"

Roy consulted his notepad and said, "Yes." His stomach was in his throat. He sucked in and pressed onward. Roy walked over to the jury box, thinking it best to sound humble and friendly. He smiled, clasped his hands together below his chin and said, "Good morning. I am Roy Blackman and I represent Mr. Horowitz in these horrendous and false accusations by the state. The prosecution would like you to believe that Mr. Horowitz is a *very* bad man. But I can assure you that is not the case. In fact, he follows the laws, he gives to charity, he goes to church, he has a family, and he was merely trying to make an honest living." The words rang hollow even to him. He did not believe the jurors were buying it, judging by the blank looks on their faces, but he continued anyway.

"The prosecution has rushed to judgment where none is required. Capitalism, which is the backbone of this great country, does not promise that every investor will profit from their investments. The SEC, NFA, and CFTC have hastily and falsely implicated my client as a man who has acted unscrupulously or unethically and, in so doing, have brought bogus charges against him and his firm. But I assure you he is not an unscrupulous or unsavory man. He has been the poster boy for what successful businesses embody and exude. He and his brokers have always tried to make money as best they could for his many clients. However, there were times when the market went against his decisions and that cannot be helped by him nor blamed on him. There is no such thing as *no risk* when it comes to investments. Mr. Horowitz was a *victim* of bad market conditions and poor economic circumstances – and that is all. The clients that the prosecution will use, to support their frivolous claims against Mr. Horowitz, are all seeking monetary compensation in excess of what they even invested. Where money is the end result, or ultimate desire, how can people be trusted to give an honest testimony?" He was planting seeds of doubt---he hoped.

"When you have had time to hear and review the facts as we present them to you in this case, you will find that the only unbiased and fair decision is to acquit. Because the evidence in defense of this case is so persuasive ... and *so* overwhelming that, *you* will be forced to render a judgment of not guilty on all charges. Thank you for your time." Roy forced a perfunctory smile and walked back to his table reminding himself to hold his head up and shoulders straight.

Judge Schram declared recess for lunch and had the jurors sequestered in the special jury room at the rear of the courthouse annex under uniformed guard.

Skip said to Roy, with creases of anxiety on his forehead, "Well – how do you think it's going?"

"Skip – understand that we've just begun. This is just the first day, opening arguments, one initial morning round. This afternoon they will hear more from the prosecution and perhaps as they get into their presentations we can get a better read from some of the juror's faces. I will say that I think we have at least placed some fertile seeds of doubt that can be nurtured along to eventually persuade them that you are not guilty." Like hell, he thought, unless I can do a lot better than that weak bit of lawyering I just threw up all over the room.

"What ever happened with Jack, the bailiff?" Skip's expression was one of a drowning man grasping for any kind of rope that could be found.

"Jack doesn't believe this jury is open to tampering ... at least not at this time. Now those things can change down the road, too ... so don't worry just yet." Roy unconsciously bit his lower lip. Try and stay positive, he thought, even though you're not very.

Court reconvened at one fifteen.

The prosecution opened with documents collected from the busts on Las Olas and Third Avenue as well as documents that had been secreted away during the alleged shredding episodes.

When the prosecution presented the documents indicating shredding on the part of the defendant, Roy bolted upright. "Objection! Materiality. Those documents were illegally obtained."

Judge Schram looked to Bob before replying. "Have we documentation that these were obtained legally and as such are admissible?"

"Judge Schram," Bob said, "I do have such documentation. One minute, please." He rummaged through a large stack of labeled folders and came out with a signed document in a clear sheath that he presented to the Judge. He said in his smug, nasal voice, "This is a duplication of the one we presented the court prior to the onset of this trial. For purposes of expediency I again present the following, example A-2, a signed contract or obligation between our agents and Skip's two office managers, agreeing to this shredding of evidence, further documenting their willful and negligent wrongdoing."

He handed the contracts to the Judge who looked them over. It took him less than a minute before he looked up and said, "Over-ruled. I'm going to allow this." He then gave them to the bailiff who handed them to the jury foreman.

Bob, setting the stage for a key testimony to follow, produced the new account forms, prospectus' from Skip's many and varied firms, and the disclosure of risk forms. "I now produce Exhibit B-12. I think you will see from these documents that there was clear intent to defraud investors across state and national lines. His investment advisors tried to pass off extremely high risk investments as little more than simple savings accounts." Next he passed around trade slips, both falsified and real.

"These are lengthy, and difficult to decipher if one is not familiar with this particular line of business," Bob said as he strolled toward the whiteboard a projector, "but they are complete. I will simplify things by offering a brief explanation in non-technical language on the whiteboard and overhead projector. Exhibit C-4. As you can see, these trade invoices do not match up with the client accounts and tallies, proving that Mr. Horowitz was intentionally filing false statements with the SEC, NFA, and CFTC." Bob drew circles around the erroneous and conflicting information so the jurors could understand what he was talking about. Murmurs wafted through the jury box and throughout the courtroom.

"And with those purloined monies … the monies stolen from his hapless investors … he enjoyed a fabulous lifestyle. One that few people outside of his realm could imagine. Even when he had amassed hundreds of millions of dollars his thirst was never quenched."

He passed around bank statements and pictures of Skip's various assets and placed them on the overhead again to impress upon them how much he stole from his unsuspecting investors. With his pointer he proceeded. "Theft from his investors' accounts allowed Mr. Horowitz to purchase a three and a half million dollar airplane." He stopped the pointer at a full color picture of the King Air, then moved on. "Here we see a three million dollar plus boat, a two hundred fifty thousand dollar boat," he moved his pointer again, "and two luxurious homes in the Sea Ranch Lakes section of Lauderdale by the Sea." Tapping his pointer on the collective bank tallies, he said, "And from his various bank accounts we can see that he has amassed nearly a *billion dollars of cash*."

The jurors are lapping this up like dogs eating gravy, Roy thought with a sigh. At four o'clock, the prosecution began to display testimony from their first witnesses.

Ray was called first. Ray stated his worthy credentials. His diction was clear and concise. When he responded he occasionally looked toward the jury. Bob led him through the entire start up of the Keys operation and up to the seizure and transfer of the office this past spring. From the looks on their faces, the jurors were following and swallowing the amicable and convincing dialogue word for word.

Roy was unable to refute the testimony that Ray had given or his credentials. He tried to use the angle of entrapment, but it did not fly with Judge Schram who now eyed him with more skepticism and increased impatience.

Catherine was second under direct examination. Bob walked her though her first meetings with Skip and how she had come to be an unwitting and naive player in his illicit businesses. In support of those and other conversations, he presented tapes the federal investigators had compiled. The bailiff took them at Judge Schram's orders, with instructions to give them later to the jurors to replay for review.

"Did you ever know for certain that Mr. Horowitz was intentionally scamming these unsuspecting investors?" Bob said, leaning in to Catherine with one hand on the witness stand's rail.

"I suspected ..."

"Objection!" Roy's voice boomed out. "Improper Predicate ... she was and is a lover of the defendant whose only motive in this whole farce is seeking revenge. Your Honor, this is preposterous – nothing more than a classic case of the jilted lover. Her testimony should be stricken from the record." Weak, he thought, but that's all I've got.

"Is that true?" Asked Judge Schram with a heavy dose of caution.

Bob nodded at Catherine, who had looked to him with question in her expression, and said, "You can reply."

Catherine licked her upper lip and clucked her tongue. She folded her arms. "Actually, yes. Well, yes and no. We *did* have a *singular* sexual encounter, Your Honor, but I assure you that brief session could not be construed as a relationship by any stretch, and has not clouded my judgment in this case."

Judge Schram considered for a few seconds, tapping his pen on his notes. "Over-ruled. I'm going to take her at her word at this time. Please proceed, but stick to the essentials, counsel."

Roy sat, incensed. God damned Schram has not once ruled in my favor. If this is not a clear case of judicial prejudice, I don't know what the hell is.

"Thank you, Your Honor," Bob said with a courteous nod, his tone of voice sounding to Roy like an insipid tune of triumph blown through a snot rag. He focused back on Catherine. "Can you tell us when you first learned that Mr. Horowitz was not dealing above board?"

"Yes, when I was told so by Nick."

"Objection----Improper expert testimony!"

"She was actually in his employ, Judge," Bob said, and directed a scowl at Roy. He turned back to Judge Schram with a respectful demeanor. "She does have some idea of his business dealings, after all. And, we are not using her testimony as *expert*."

"Over-ruled."

"Can you point out Nick," Bob asked Catherine.

She pointed to one of the handsome young men on the table with the defense. "That's him."

"Let the record show the witness has indicated – Nick Craig, will you please stand for the jurors?" As Nick complied Bob went on to state, "Let the record also show that Mr. Craig is and was a federal agent working undercover in this case."

He said to Nick, "Thank you, sir." Nick resumed his seat.

Bob said, "And Ms. O'Reilly – what, exactly, did he tell you and when?"

Catherine went into detail about the things Nick told her and how she initially did not believe what he said, but how he was convincing and provided her with concrete evidence. The evidence was so compelling, she testified, that afterward she could clearly see Skip and his operations for what they were----scams.

Bob asked her, "And were you a willing helper in the federal agents' plan."

She said without hesitation and with her eyes showing sincerity, "Yes."

Bob led her through a serious of questions about compensation and other relevant things. Catherine's responses were honest sounding and believable.

Skip sat at his table with his hands folded under his chin. I can't believe I trusted that little bitch. I paid her way more than she was worth and this is the thanks I get. His eyes fired laser beams at her.

At five o'clock the court recessed for the evening.

Roy was depressed. The first day had gone poorly. He went home and instead of boning up for the case tomorrow, he drank himself into a welcomed stupor.

***

At home, Veronika was having contractions. "Skippie I think the baby is coming." She winced. Neither she nor Skip knew for certain if they were false contractions or the real thing.

Skip said, "How far apart are they?"

She replied holding her protruding belly, "Close enough."

"I'll call nine one one and have the ambulance come for you. Just sit down and breathe deeply."

She did as Skip said. He was frustrated that under court order he couldn't escort her to the doctor. As Veronika was whisked away in the ambulance he sat at home with Ralph, Zeke, Matt, and Sammy, pouring over the testimony and evidence that was given against him today.

"I still can't get over Catherine. I so thought she was one of us," Ralph said, dismayed.

"She's nothing but a two bit whore. I hope she gets some venereal disease." Skip spit air.

Hours later, Veronica came back home. She walked in the door and said, "Well the baby's not coming today. The doctors said it was nothing more than gas pains."

"Soon enough," Skip said as he smoothed her hair and patted her fanny.

"Look – he even gave me an anti-acid. I've never needed an anti-acid before."

Veronika spent the night moaning over her gas pains. Their guests finally went home well after midnight, but sleep eluded them until the early morning hours. They awakened ragged and tired.

CHAPTER FORTY-SEVEN

The first witness for the prosecution the following day was Tommy Fachuli. Tommy was a reluctant witness. Being seen in court was a perilous venture. He feared for his life if Skip or the mob knew he was back in the USA.

After Tommy was sworn in and seated, Bob asked him how long he had been in Skip's employ, about specific dealings with Skip's operation in the Bahamas, and where the money was sent when it left the Bahamas.

Tommy was jumpy. He had been coking up and drinking for two days – his way of coping with such an untimely, fearful situation. He avoided eye contact with anyone except Bob, even though he felt Skip's eyes boring into him.

Shortly into the questioning, Roy rose and said, "Judge Schram, I object to this man's testimony entirely. His testimony, if allowed, sets an improper precedent. This witness cannot be considered trustworthy to give cogent testimony. This … this man is a convicted criminal. It is well documented all of his involvement with and what all he has done for the mob." He pointed at Tommy. "His words should not be taken seriously. Your Honor, may I approach the bench?"

Judge Schram made a weary, indulgent hand motion and said, "You may, make it quick, counsel."

Roy walked a document up to the judge that proved that Tommy had been an informant for the mob and had been given his freedom in exchange for this information.

Judge Schram looked it over thoroughly and then said, "I am well aware of the witness' criminal past, Mr. Blackman. Mr. Fachuli is not on trial here, may I remind you. His past has no bearing on his testimony in this case, and all records of previous troubles he's had have been expunged because of his continued cooperation with this and other cases. You can save your comments for cross examination." He grunted as punctuation to his remarks, turned to the jury and said, "You will disregard those last statements from the defense, please." He motioned to Bob. "Please continue."

Bob said, "His industry invested and traded in currencies and international markets, isn't that right, Mr. Fachuli?"

"Yes, that's right." Extracting much from Tommy after Roy's comments was like pulling framing nails out with tweezers. Tommy finally and reluctantly admitted that the entire operation was a scam and a pyramid scheme. "Yes, I knew it was wrong, but I was paid a lot of money to keep my mouth shut. I was just doin' my job."

"And how much money would you say Mr. Horowitz took out of your business?"

Tommy scratched his head, squirmed around in his seat. *God damned hemorrhoids are acting up again. Must be the stress. Just get through this,* he thought. *Jesus I need another bump.* "It's kinda hard to say."

"Can you give us an estimate?" Bob leaned in, pressing him.

"Like maybe a hundred million or so." Tommy's eyes were glassing over. *More like five hundred million, but who am I to rat that out. I've got mine stashed safely away in the Turks and Caicos, just waiting for this trial to get over.* He squirmed again. *Fucking hemorrhoids.*

Bob eyed him and leaned in further. "And you kept this money in the Bahamas or did you transfer it elsewhere?"

"Objection Judge---relevance!" Roy said in exasperation.

"Judge, please," Roy said, "This line of questioning is leading the witness to set a false precedent in efforts to show that Mr. Horowitz intended to abscond with those funds."

"Over-ruled."

"Can you repeat the question?" Tommy said with a fatigued sigh. *I should've ran. This is Bullshit! Man I've gotta scratch my ass. It's driving me nuts. Shit I itch all over.* Tommy squirmed some more in his chair.

Bob repeated the question. Tommy blew out a long breath and said, "We kept some money in the Bahamas, some in the Caymans, some in Costa Rica, and some in Switzerland. Okay?"

More questions were asked and answered regarding the dealings with clients and how their monies were transferred, on whose authority the funds had been transferred, who controlled them, and how statements were dummied up and never traded.

"So, Skip was the one who directed all of your activities?"

"Yes, Skip alone."

Bob turned to the judge and said, "No further questions." He looked at Roy and said, "Your witness," then walked back to his table and took a seat.

Roy was at near boiling point, but kept his rising rage under control. He said, "No questions, but I reserve the right to recall this witness at a later time." *I need some time,* he thought, *time to formulate some damage control.*

"As you wish," Judge Schram said. "Mr. Fachuli you may be excused, but you will remain under oath in the event there is further questioning."

Tommy stood, walked straight out the courtroom doors and directly into the nearest men's room where he proceeded to take a nice, long toot and scratch his ass, gently, so as not to further aggravate this hemorrhoids. He wished he could go to the nearest bar and relax with a few cold ones, but knew better. The mob had him marked. He'd make himself scarce, available for recall only by the unlisted cell phone he'd given the number of to the prosecution.

Gary Brown was called next. He was sworn in and seated.

Gary was nervous, Bob could tell, so he began with easy questions leading up to those more difficult and damaging. "Mr. Brown, can you please tell the court how long you were in Mr. Horowitz's employ and what abruptly ended that affiliation?"

Gary stated in clear voice, "I worked on and off for Skip – I mean, Mr. Horowitz … seven years. I was a manager in our Buckhead operation." Gary looked at Bob before continuing. Bob nodded. Gary held his head down as he spoke. "We had a lot of wealthy sports personalities who invested with us. One day, when I called in a trade, it – was not traded as called." He looked up and said, "If you can follow me there." He looked back down. "Anyway, there was a huge loss and the money was not sent up to our clearing firm and the clearing firm shut us down and I lost my job and my license in the process."

"Was this an honest mistake?"

"I'm not …" he frowned, "… not sure anymore. But I didn't mean for us to lose the money – if that's what you mean."

Bob led Gary through a series of investor trust and broker scam scenarios that had occurred over the years, all of which depicted a clear picture of Skip's organizational impact on unsuspecting investors. At each interval the impact was more and more damaging to the investor, but more and more profitable to Skip.

Toward the end of Bob's inquisition and Gary's damaging admissions, Skip jumped out of his seat, toppling it over, and screamed, "He is lying!"

"Order in this court!" Judge Schram pounded his gavel three times. "Do you understand that, Mr. Horowitz?" The judge glared at him and banged his gavel twice more. "I will not tolerate any further outbursts."

Skip shrunk back into his chair and simmered in silent rage. The indignant son-of-a-bitch. I gave him a golden chance and he blew it. He's lucky he's still alive.

Bob turned Gary over to Roy for cross-examination.

Roy grilled Gary, but got little information that could help to exonerate Skip.

Lunch came and went and court resumed.

The afternoon's witnesses were comprised of Evie, Mariela, Skip's travel agent, Lilly, and Kevin Halloran. Bob walked them through a variety of circumstances and their affiliations with Skip and his firm. Both Evie and Mariela were semi-hostile and somewhat unforgiving in their portrayal of Skip, still harboring resentment at having been jilted by him. Each young lady described her life before and during their relationships with Skip. Their testimonies and stories began to show a pattern with regard to the kinds of women and relationships he engaged in. In each instance, the women were from low class backgrounds, undereducated, and inexperienced in many facets of life. Both felt preyed upon and victimized by Skip.

Lilly provided details of trips that Skip and his crew made prior to his purchasing the King Air as well as some of her own romantic involvements from years gone by with Skip. She was careful not to state more than was asked in the question because, although she was a witness for the prosecution, her alliances and allegiances still ran deep with Skip. She hadn't forgotten all that Skip had done for her.

Roy objected a series of times while the ladies were in the process of testifying on various grounds, from leading the witnesses to each woman having an axe to grind with his client. All objections were over-ruled.

Kevin's testimony was the most enlightening of the afternoon because he provided direct information as it related to opening accounts along with supporting data as far as anticipated or projected returns stated by brokers in Skip's employ. He also provided testimony that none of the accounts had been actually traded, but the statements had instead been dummied up to support a loss that was non-existent.

Bob Hawthorne judiciously used his props so that the jury could follow what had transpired step by step. He passed the documentation along to the bailiff so the jury could view it close up. He was racking up huge points with the jury. He said to Kevin, "Who else would be party to this trade that was not a real trade … or who would have been in charge of dummying up these accounts for the investors?"

Kevin folded his hands. "Directly Skip, and then under him were Ismail, Mark, Sammy, and some girls----I've forgotten their names."

"Was everything always approved by Skip first?"

"Oh yes, Skip is a micromanager to the max."

"So Skip was the person who would have authorized these illegal and unethical acts?"

"Absolutely."

Roy decided not to enter into cross-examination with Kevin at this time. He had gotten a sudden epiphany. Might be a long shot, but he thought instead he would present Kevin's mother as a witness for the defense to try to counteract the damage. He presented that intent to the Judge and the prosecution. Judge Schram admonished him for not having her on the witness list prior to trial beginning, but allowed it. It was the only small win, and tiny it was, but Roy took it. Best little score since this trial began.

Day two for the prosecution ended with a fizzle and not a bang, but Skip's ship still looked like it was sinking and fast. Roy knew he had a vast ocean to swim ahead of him.

Day three in court was spent largely with the prosecution plowing through some of the more tedious circumstantial and direct evidence from wiretaps, to transcripts, to actual blow by blow descriptions of how accounts were opened, traded or not, and falsified to look like losers. A veritable connect-the-dots session, which delineated the trail and supported the charge of intent to defraud.

Nick took over lead for the prosecution. He reconstructed and reiterated, with the help of charts, graphs and bank statements from across the world, how much money Skip had made stealing from unsuspecting investors. He said, "Mr. Horowitz had some wealthy investors, but many of his investors were regular folks just like you." He looked directly at the jurors. "In another time and place he could have been swindling money from your children's college funds or your retirement plans." He moved over to his props where he provided full color pictures and detailed invoices from Skip's junkets to the Bahamas with his various lady companions, and described the lavish accommodations they stayed at in. "This is Atlantis. It rents for over one thousand dollars per night. Mr. Horowitz spent numerous vacations there." He watched their faces for signs of disgust. "And on this private plane he took weeklong furloughs to Costa Rica, where he went white river rafting, lounged on the Pacific coast beaches, and dined at five star restaurants." He saw the jurors becoming enthralled. He pressed ahead, showing receipts from the Dominican Republic. "These receipts are from the famed Casa De Campo resort and marina. Here Mr. Horowitz entertained a host of local dignitaries and a bevy of young ladies from dusk until dawn."

He concluded the presentation with Las Vegas. "In Las Vegas Mr. Horowitz often rented the entire floor of places like the MGM, Ritz Carlton, Four Seasons, or Grand Barcelona." He stopped, looked at Skip, then at the jury. "And all of this was paid for, was on the tabs, the beguiled heads and shoulders, of his investors who had saved for their children's colleges, their own retirements, or that reserve emergency fund. But they had been convinced that investing in his business prospectus would be the shortcut to their dreams."

He directed everyone's attention again to the display. "There are here, sales slips for hand tailored clothing, totaling well over twenty-two million dollars, thousands of pairs of Italian shoes costing hundreds of thousands of dollars, and keys to vaults filled with expensive one-of-a-kind jewelry, waterfront homes, custom built boats and cruisers. And," he said, waxing loquacious with his best, most oratorical voice and a flamboyant wave at the screen, "luxury automobiles that look more like those of Hollywood celebrities than ordinary people like you and I."

After lunch break, Bob took the reins. Fingers were pointed at Alan Adelman, Ted Romeo, and Jeff Jedlecki for *enhancing or loading accounts* … all done under the watchful direction of Mr. Horowitz and all in the pursuit of profit – for Skip.

Closing out the day were six personal witnesses from various offices who had invested, lost, been told they could recoup those lost funds by investing more, had only lost again, and were now seeking retribution. One of the six was the famed baseball/football player, Leon Sanderson. He played for both the Atlanta Falcons and the Atlanta Braves. He went into detail about how he had walked into the Buckhead office one day and dropped off a few million dollars to open his new account. He said he had made thirteen percent return for a few months, but then had lost those millions and more.

Roy could tell the last half dozen testimonies, especially Mr. Sanderson's, the jury considered credible and extremely convincing, and … a damaging blow to his defense. He tried, without success, to refute those clearly stated facts. His vain attempts bounced off the walls of the courtroom like wild thrown pitches … and likewise, struck out with the jury.

On a break, Jack told Roy that thus far jury commentary had sided mostly with the prosecution. Roy paid him ten thousand for the update and encouraged him to continue to provide insight.

That evening Judge Schram was just finishing a wonderful dinner prepared by his housekeeper, Julia. As he took a last mouthful, she approached him and said, "Judge Schram, Sheriff Jenner is on the phone for you – on your personal line. Do you want to take it or should I take a message?"

He wiped the corners of his mouth with his pressed white linen and refilled his crystal glass with more wine before replying. "No, that's fine. I'll take it in the library."

"As you wish. May I clear the table?"

"Yes, and thank you. That was delicious."

He walked into the library with his Merlot, took a seat in one of his leather club chairs and reached for the phone.

"Hello, this is Judge Schram."

Sheriff Jenner said, "Judge, I sure am sorry to disturb you at home …"

"That's fine, Sheriff … what is it?" He sipped his Merlot.

"We've found what we believe was – is … the gun that killed Frederika Horowitz in a landfill over off I-95 and the Turnpike."

"Have you dusted it for fingerprints?"

"Per chance we have and you will not believe whose prints we found?"

"Nothing surprises me anymore." Judge Schram squelched a burp.

"Yes sir. No sir. It was not Mr. Horowitz if that is what you were thinking."

"Well, who then?" Judge Schram said with an edge of impatience.

"One of Mr. Horowitz' cronies. A Ralph White. Record a mile long."

"Ah, that is interesting indeed." Gets his capo to off the wife. Clever man.

"Looks like maybe he tried to wipe the gun clean before tossing it into the dumpster, but he failed to separate whatever he used to wipe the gun down from the gun itself. My forensics people tell me the oil from his hand, mixed with the powder from the gunshot, gave them a perfect fingerprint."

"Good work, Sheriff," Judge Schram said, and sipped some more.

"Yes, we thought so too. But there is also evidence that she had been aboard Mr. Horowitz's yacht – the Traders Three, that same weekend in question."

"Really?"

"Yes. A neighbor saw her arrive, but never saw her get off the boat." He consulted again his detective's notes, trying his best to decipher the scribbled and clumsy script. "Apparently there were three of them at the beginning of the day … and according to her descriptions I believe they were the man who calls himself Father Zeke, this Ralph White fellow, and Mrs. Horowitz."

"Have you fingerprinted the boat and invited this neighbor to identify these men from a line-up yet?"

"No, but we are working on that as we speak. I just sort of wanted to, ya know – keep you in the loop."

"I appreciate that, Sheriff. Thank you." After another sip of wine he said, "Is there anything else?"

"Not at this time, Your Honor."

CHAPTER FORTY-EIGHT

Sheriff Jenner looked over the report from forensics. Fingerprints and bloodstains recovered from the yacht linked Ralph and Zeke to the disappearance and murder of Frederika Horowitz.

Well I'll be dammed, he thought, still reading, and both of them have been positively identified by a neighbor from a police line-up. He placed a call to have them rounded up and brought in for questioning.

Sheriff Jenner's detectives on the case leaned hard on both Zeke and Ralph. After one hour of badgering and accusing them, they had been unable to get either to cop a plea. Frustrated, the investigators decided to use a 'he ratted on you first' ploy.

Detective Nixon said to Ralph, "Okay, fella ... your buddy – Zeke ..."

"That would be *Father* Zeke," Ralph said with a smirk.

"Whatever ... anyway, that's irrelevant. He's come clean. He's signed a statement that you killed Mrs. Horowitz. Now whaddaya wanna do?"

Ralph cringed at that, in spite of his experience. This was hardly a first time for him, but he'd be damned if he was going to hang alone. Not even for some favorite fucking priest of Skip's. He eased back in his chair and rubbed his chin, eyeing Nixon and sizing up the situation. "Now, that ... isn't quite true."

"Which part isn't quite true?" The detective glared.

"Actually, Skip ..." he fidgeted, "... ah, he asked us to get rid of Fred."

"Get rid of? As in what exactly?"

"Like – you know." He shrugged.

"No, I don't know." Nixon's eyes belied his statement.

"Like kill her."

Detective Nixon couldn't help flashing a smirk. "And Skip was the one who said to do this, eh?" He looped his fingers in his pants and paraded around like a peacock for a few steps. He winked at the one-way mirror, knowing the other detectives were getting and videoing all this. He spun around and returned to his questioning.

"What," he tapped the table with his finger, "exactly," he tapped again, harder, "did this Skip character ... ask you to do." Nixon's eyes penetrated Ralph like a hammer drill. "And give it to me verbatim."

Ralph's hands were not cuffed, but his feet were shackled with plastic strips. He shifted uncomfortably in the metal chair, making an abrasive scraping sound on the concrete floor. The florescent lights added to the already white and sickly pallor of his face. His lips formed a thin straight line as he paused, then said, "He actually asked Zeke ta do it."

Nixon stepped back, opened his mouth and brought his tongue to the roof of it. "Zeke, eh?"

"Yea, Zeke. Zeke asked me to help him out because Skip had suggested that we use the yacht."

"Why the yacht?"

"See, Skip knew that Fred liked to go fishing. So getting her out on the boat was the easy part."

"So you were supposed to take her fishing, right?"

"Yea, that's it. That was the ruse."

"Go on. Then what happened?" Nixon got an update in his earpiece. Father Zeke, in an adjacent interrogation room, was undergoing the same interrogation gambit. He was spilling his guts faster than Ralph. Nixon smiled, eyeing his fallen prey. *Man, are you ever a sorry case. And I am going to so enjoy tossing your pansy ass into the slammer. Loser.*

Ralph continued, sweat forming on his brow. "Okay, look – here's what happened."

"Are ya sure about this? Ya know your friend Zeke is squawking like a seagull."

"I swear to god."

"Well ain't that just the best." *Asshole.*

"I drove the boat and we went out past the color change … ya know, where the water is really, really deep."

"Yea, and?"

"Well we slipped her a mick in her Bloody Mary."

"A mick of what sort?"

"Nothing heavy … just a little sleep aid."

Nixon raised his eyebrows. "Yea?"

"Could I have something to drink? I'm really parched." Ralph cast his eyes to the floor. *God if Skip ever knows I've given him up I am dead!*

Detective Nixon looked into the mirror and said, "Hey could one of you bring him a coke or something?"

A moment later a soda was brought in. Nixon waited while Ralph slugged down half of it and then banged the bottle down on the table with a belch. "Thanks."

"Sure. Go on," Nixon said.

"Anyway, she went to lie down and then we did her in." Ralph threw back his head and belched again.

"We?"

"Yea, like I said – Father Zeke was there, too."

"Who actually pulled the trigger?"

Ralph hung his head and said in a near whisper, "I did. Look – I actually feel bad for doing it, but one never crosses Skip and lives to tell."

"Did you just say that you pulled the trigger?" Detective Nixon knew he had, but wanted it louder for the record.

"Yes," Ralph said, a little louder.

Nixon bent over and put his face in Ralph's. "Louder."

"I pulled the fucking trigger! Okay?"

The detective stood erect and folded his arms. "Uh huh. Then what?"

"We rolled her up in a tarp and dumped her over the side."

"End of story?"

"Yea, we went back to the dock after that."

"So just like that you killed a woman, dumped her out in the ocean, and came back to the dock like it was a round of golf or something."

Ralph said nothing more.

Father Zeke had told the detective who was interrogating him that Skip had offered to pay them a million dollars each. He had transferred half of that ahead of the hit and the remainder was to be paid when he had it confirmed it was done. He admitted to helping dispose of Frederika, but not to the actual killing.

***

Day four in the courtroom. The morning's testimonies for the prosecution came from investigators Doug Walker, Alex Morales, Marek Andropov, Sean McCray, and Shareed Vorhee. Each man added detailed accounts of wiretapped conversations, from their perspectives, which they had compiled over the past seven years of the investigation. All of their testimonies were convincing. Court broke for lunch and resumed at one thirty that afternoon.

***

The media had just caught wind of breaking news about Frederika. Channel seven reported as follows:

We've been watching coverage of the Charles Horowitz investment fraud trial for the past week, but what we didn't know is that his estranged wife, Frederika Horowitz, had been murdered, execution style, aboard his yacht and tossed overboard as fish food. Apparently a fishing boat picked her up off of Savannah, Georgia. Forensic experts were able to get enough DNA to identify her and determine who was responsible for this heinous crime. Details of the investigation are still unfolding, but two of Mr. Horowitz's close friends have been charged with first-degree murder. More details about this murder and other news around this county at four p.m.

***

The afternoon testimony began with Ismail and Amin Singh from American Futures, followed by Vinnie and Stephanie Maracini, Gabe Greenberg, and Natalia Povich. There were also statements from the Keys delegation.

Ismail and Amin both corroborated the testimony from many others with regard to how the accounts were opened, how clients were solicited via the phone and direct mailings, who did the falsifying and how exactly the accounts were doctored, who sent the false statements in to the CFTC, NFA, and SEC., etc. Ismail said there had been times when some monies were traded, but those winnings had been transferred into Skip's offshore numbered accounts and not shared with the people who had been named on the accounts.

Roy tried to place part of the blame for misleading the public squarely on the shoulders of Amin and Ismail – and to some degree it stuck.

Amin said, "I have always tried to run my business on the up and up. When I first met Skip I knew he was not an honest player, but because he had paid us so handsomely I allowed him to use our clearing firm to conduct his deceitful business. I am sorry that I was lured into this deception by his very generous monetary compensation … and I am sorry that I had a hand in his dirty double-dealing. For that lack of conscience I have a black mark that will stick forever on my reputation. Please believe me." He hung his head. "I am so very sorry." Amin looked at the jury. In his eyes they saw sorrow and broken pride.

Vinnie, Gabe, and Stephanie were somewhat less forthright and less contrite about their roles. Stephanie had been fired from the casino's legal team when the story about Skip broke in Nevada and elsewhere. The Nevada bar was considering whether or not to revoke her license to practice in their state. This, more than anything else, caused her to harbor a lot of resentment toward the regulators in general. Her animosity was palpable in her testimony. Roy scored a few points in his cross-examination of those three.

Natalia was the perfect witness for the prosecution, because she had a wealth of experience to draw upon from acting as a double agent for the SAS. She could spin a believable lie and make herself seem the victim.

The jury likes her, Roy thought with a slow shake of the head. Damn. They are buying this shit, believing she's just some innocent pawn in Skip's operations. Any points I may have scored in those last cross-examinations, might as well kiss 'em bye bye.

CHAPTER FORTY-NINE

Nick had done a stellar job for the Federal Government. He had compiled a textbook rendition of information and testimony, carefully constructed by his able associates, led by Bob Hawthorne.

Roy had been busily constructing his rebuttal and defense for Skip. Each day in the courtroom the past week had concerned him that he was perhaps working from the wrong side. But stepping away at this point would have been a failure he was not willing to submit to. Roy had given a short interview to Larry King on CNN at the beginning of the trial and that interview depicted a very different trajectory than his new campaign did. The absolute salvation and total exoneration of Skip might not be possible, but he could make damn sure that the jury saw the witnesses for the prosecution for what they were----opportunists and sleezeballs.

As Skip, Roy, and the rest of his legal team made their way up the wide concrete steps toward the federal building, the questions from the media had changed from his charges to the alleged murder of Frederika and the fate of their daughters who were now left motherless. The morning shows had run various stories about Frederika, depicting who she was and where she had come from. No doubt her family money had catapulted her into her multi-million dollar clothing and jewelry business. There were pictures of family reunions, school recitals, family outings and more. Most reporters drew their own conclusions and they pointed directly at Skip. Phone calls and e-mails depicted the angry uproar that the world felt toward Skip who had shown no signs of remorse – if indeed he had committed this unconscionable act.

Roy and Skip had just entered the courtroom. Roy said, "I can't imagine how those legal representatives from the government manage to get her before us each day."

"Maybe they've got nothing better to do than to try and roast me on a spit?"

"Now's not the time to make jokes, Skip. We've got a hard road to pave today and then some."

"I wasn't joking."

They took their seats. Skip glanced over at the prosecution table. *Asshole regulators.* Then he turned around and blew Veronika a kiss. Veronika had attended every day, seated behind Skip in the first row of spectator seats.

The bailiff walked into the courtroom and said, "All rise for the Honorable Judge Schram."

The gallery of spectators and the tables filled with legal experts rose as Judge Schram ambled in and took his seat. He rapped his gavel and said in clear diction, "The court will come to order."

Jack brought in the jurors. Skip watched each one as they silently filed in and were seated. None of them made eye contact with Skip. Roy had warned him that was a bad omen. Skip fought a shiver and slunk down in his seat. Veronika rubbed his back.

Judge Schram shuffled some papers on his desk, straightened another stack, and then said, "Counselor, are you prepared to continue."

Bob stood and said, "Yes, Your Honor. If things go as we plan them, the government intends to rest today."

"Very well … shall we begin?"

The sketch artist was busy drawing. Cameras flashed.

"Don't you think the jurors look tired," Skip asked Roy, worried.

"Yes, but don't read too much into that … what we need to do is bring them over to our side." *But how?*

"I hope you have a contingency plan." Skip scowled. As much as I'm paying him, he better have more than one contingency plan.

"Don't worry, Skip. I've got everything arranged with Jack. If things look like they will not turn our direction next week, we plan to pay off a few of the ones on the fence," Roy said in a hushed voice. He tried to sound as if he had more confidence than he felt, but the statement was a temporary salve to Skip.

Bob said, "Judge, we've just one more witnesses to hear this morning." He looked down at his notes.

"Get on with it." Judge Schram wagged a hand.

The first witness was Skip and Fredericka's real estate attorney, Clancy Jacobs. Bob led him through a series of questions about their real estate dealings over the years leading up to Skip's most recent purchase, his waterfront estate in Sea Ranch Lakes.

"Mr. Jacobs, what would you estimate Skip's real estate holdings are worth in today's dollars?"

"I would say easily upwards of …" He shifted his glance heavenward and began counting as he spoke, "There were the two homes in Sea Ranch Lakes; a cottage on the northern shore of Maine, the duplex is Scottsdale, the villa in Italy, and the beach house in the Abacos. All of which had appreciated with the swelling economy over the past several years." He stopped and did some mental adding with his forehead wrinkled and rubbing his chin, then said, "I'd have to say in excess of eight hundred million dollars …" he flipped a hand open, "… give or take."

An air sucking sound came from the gallery.

Bob drove this almost inconceivable dollar amount home with the fact that all of this wealth that Skip had been the beneficiary of had been amassed on the broken bank accounts of his investors who had trusted Skip with their life savings only to be told they had been wiped out.

Judge Schram, Roy, Skip, and the entire jury were exhausted when the testimony ended and were grateful for the lunch break.

Roy turned to Skip and said, "It's our turn tomorrow."

"Are we prepared?"

"As prepared as we can be." I hope there are no surprises.

CHAPTER FIFTY

Monday, nine a.m., court reconvened. The usual prosecutorial and defense teams attended, as did an anxious group of media professionals and spectators. The judge and jurors entered and took their seats

Judge Schram looked over his spectacles and said, "Is the defense ready to present its case?"

Roy stood and said, "Yes, Your Honor. Defense calls as its first witness, Tommy Fachuli to the stand."

Tommy walked forward and Judge Schram said, "Please be reminded that you are still under oath. Take a seat."

Tommy did as instructed. Just before coming into the courtroom he had done a big bump and taken a sip of rum for luck and bravado.

Roy pounced like a jackal on a desert rat. He said, "Isn't it true that you are a drug addict and an alcoholic, Mr. Fachuli?"

Nick stood and shouted, "Objection, Judge … irrelevant."

Judge Schram considered this for just a moment and said, "Overruled. I'll allow the question. Continue."

Roy continued, "Well?" Come on, dipshit – say something.

"I'm sorry, I forgot the question." Tommy looked dazed and confused. He glanced furtively between Nick and Roy.

"I was asking you about your drug and alcohol abuse. Will you please tell the jury to what extent you are a … junkie?"

"Ah – well … I do *sometimes* use drugs, but I'm no addict. I occasionally have a drink or maybe two, but just to be sociable." Asshole, who's he think he's talking to?

Roy looked at him. Hard. "Uh huh. And, would you say – an ounce of cocaine is substantial for occasional use or would you say that having that kind of weight in your possession on a regular basis is an indication of an addiction?" Roy smirked.

Tommy looked down. "I never said I keep an ounce on me. As a matter of fact, I never said nothing of the sort." He looked up, a bit defiant. "You're putting words in my mouth."

"Let the records show that Tommy Fachuli has confessed to using cocaine." He spun on his heel and walked back to his table. "That is all at this time, Judge." He looked with renewed confidence at Nick and Bob. "Your witness." Roy felt like at least one wind had changed in his direction. He had placed some serious doubt as to the credibility of Tommy as a witness.

The judge said, "Does the prosecution wish to cross exam?"

"Yes, Your Honor," Nick said as he stood and strode toward the stand. "Mr. Fachuli, your drug and alcohol use – or abuse, as the defense would like to term it, would it be fair to say these harmful habits were in significant measure the result, or by product if you will, caused by the pressure you were experiencing from working in such an unethical job?"

"Yes, oh yes." Tommy nodded several times. "The pressure – it was awful. I felt terrible about what I was being asked to do." The drugs in his system had him frazzled, nerves tingling. He suppressed a whimper. "I just needed some kind of relief. Some kind of escape."

"That's all, judge."

"You may step down," Schram said to Tommy, then addressed Roy. "Call your next witness."

Roy said while rising from his chair, "Defense calls to the stand Mr. Gary Brown.

Gary was reminded he was already sworn in and seated.

Roy referred to his notes on his desk, nodded to himself, then approached the witness stand. "Mr. Brown, isn't it true that Mr. Horowitz took you under his wing when nobody else would. He helped you to establish credit that could in turn help you to buy a new condo and a fine automobile. He handed you a very good opportunity that you blew by not trading as you were told. In fact, you lost for Mr. Horowitz, in one day, over twenty million dollars."

"Yes, I suppose." Brown's tone was as flat as his expression.

"And did Mr. Horowitz ask you to repay the money that you lost?" He squirmed. "No."

"And were you not very highly paid to oversee his Buckhead operation?"

Brown's right eye twitched. "Yes."

Roy scratched his nose and sniffed. "So Mr. Horowitz placed a good deal of trust in you and your brother to do the right thing and he compensated you generously to do so?" He did not wait for Gary to reply. "And wouldn't it also be fair to say that ever since you made that serious error in trading … that twenty four million dollar error, wasn't it? … Mr. Horowitz called you out on it and you've been looking for way to get back at him ever since?"

Gary appeared confused. "I'm not sure where you're going with all this, I …"

Roy leaned forward, "Answer the question. Yes or no, please."

Gary's eyes flashed hostile. "Fine. Look – I lost my license because of that mistake. Because Skip did not stand behind me." He leaned back and folded his arms over his chest.

"So you blame Mr. Horowitz for you inability to make a living?"

"Ah – well …" he wiped his forehead with his hand, "… yeah, sort of."

Roy looked over to the prosecution. "That's all. Your witness."

Nick tried to redirect, but Gary was so confounded that his statements made little sense or impact.

Lunch came and went.

Catherine was the first one to testify after the break. Judge Schram reminded her she was still under oath. She took the seat.

"Ms. O'Reilley," Roy said with an amicable smile, doing a poor job of masking his intentions, "did Mr. Horowitz ever promise you anything that he did not deliver?"

"Mm … well, I guess not, but …"

"Please just answer the question yes or no."

"No," she said, wishing she could elaborate.

"Did Mr. Horowitz ever directly ask you to present his business as something it was not?"

"Not exactly …"

"So you just believed that investigator, Nick Craig, when he told you that Mr. Horowitz had been dirty dealing? You just took his word without even asking for a response to that allegation from Mr. Horowitz, is that right?" Roy's eyes squinted to black flints.

"Yes. But I did ask for proof." Catherine ran a hand through her red locks and looked up with resolution. He's trying to trick me into saying something that I don't want to say. Stay calm.

Roy let that last comment slide by. "And isn't it true that you entertained romantic notions about yourself and Mr. Horowitz … that you may have an axe to grind because he neglected to select you as his next live-in partner?"

Catherine's eyes narrowed. "No, not exactly."

"No further questions, Your Honor." Roy was smiling, pleased at having begun to find his own tempo.

Judge Schram looked at Nick and Bob and asked, "Redirect?"

Bob stood and walked to the witness box. He appeared calm. "Catherine … Ms. O'Reilley, is it not true that you had given up any romantic notions with Mr. Horowitz since meeting Mr. Craig?"

"Yes, that's right." Catherine said. She smiled and appeared to relax some.

"And were they any problems between you and Mr. Horowitz because you had selected to keep company with another man?"

"No, nothing at all."

"No further questions." Bob walked back to the SEC table.

"Any rebuttal?" Judge Schram asked of Roy.

"Not at this time, Your Honor."

The next three witnesses were Lilly the travel agent, Evie, and Mariela. Roy painted a portrait of each woman as a vixen with a penchant for revenge, much the same as he had done with Catherine, but with more damaging results to their credibility. Nick or Bob countered well, but Roy had had a good day overall. Doubt had been placed in the jurors' minds. Better than a draw, he thought, allowing himself a rare smile, and a far sight better than the beating we've taken up until now, but still far from enough to obtain a not guilty verdict.

Roy was feeling good enough about this first day of the defense presentation that he decided to take his entire legal team out to dinner at Dan Marino's restaurant on the New River. They toasted to a successful first round from their corner, and what they hoped was a turning point in the case.

Day two Roy spent trying to refute the evidence used to support the allegations by the prosecution. He marked up their charts and diagrams and in general tried to confuse the elements the prosecution had presented.

After the day's session concluded, Roy met in secret with the Bailiff. Jack told Roy that some of the jurors were not sold on a guilty verdict. He believed they were now ripe for solicitation.

"How many do you think are on the fence?"

"Realistically, I would say four ... maybe five."

"*That* is *good* news. Thank you, Jack." Roy handed Jack a couple of stacks of bills with wrappers stating they were certified for five thousand dollars each. He said, "Spread these out amongst those who are on the fence and tell them there is more where that came from if they can convince the rest to swing our way."

"I'll do what I can," Jack said.

Day three Roy planned to introduce Veronica, and readdress Vinnie, Stephanie, and Gabe. If there was time, he wanted to have Natalia called back, too. His plan was to show the jurors that they were all on the take and therefore could not be trusted as witnesses against Skip.

Veronika was called to the stand first and sworn in. She sat. Roy moved her through a series of light questions that set the tone for her relationship with Skip. He said, "And what type of person would you say Skip is?" He intentionally did not use 'Mr. Horowitz', wanting to seem friendly and amicable. Relax her.

In her Spanish accent she said, "Oh – he's the most wonderful man that ever I have met." Her eyes conveyed her deep and abiding love for Skip. Her youth and innocence played well with the jurors. "He takes such nice care of me." She patted her swollen tummy. "And soon we are three. Please no convict him of any wrong doing. I tell you he is a *very* good man."

Nick and Bob both decided against entering into cross-examination with her. They had nothing to gain by doing so.

Vinnie was next. Again he was reminded he was still under oath. He sat.

"Mr. Maracini, in your association with Mr. Horowitz, have you ever known him to be dirty dealing or dishonest?"

"Well, Vegas ain't known for being sin city for nuthin'." He smiled, looking stupid.

Roy bunched his lips and frowned. "Please just answer the question. Have you ever known Mr. Horowitz to deliberately mislead you?"

"No, not me – but …"

Roy cut him off. "And did he help you to establish a secondary business in Las Vegas, too … the gumball business, isn't it right that was his idea before you decided to do it?"

"Yes, I suppose it was."

"Weren't you very highly paid to run his operation out in Vegas?"

"Yea, I guess so."

"Uh huh. And didn't your wife actually do the misleading?"

Bob bolted upright and roared, "Objection – the counselor is leading the witness."

"Sustained. Please refrain from that line of questioning or rephrase." Schram looked over to the jurors. "The jury will disregard that last statement."

Roy knew he had already scored his point. "Thank you, Your Honor. I have no further questions." He turned, walked back to his table and said to the prosecution without looking their way, "Your witness."

Bob took the turn to redirect with Vinnie. "Mr. Maracini, you were aware that Mr. Horowitz' operation was – how shall we say … borderline legal at best?"

"Yea, yea, sure … I've worked for Skip for a number of years and we've basically run one scam after another, but – we was never caught … 'til now."

Bob's facial gestures toward the jury helped them to tally the last line as first and foremost in importance. "Thank you. That will be all." Bob took his seat and looked over at the jurors whose eyes were glazed over. Damn, he thought, don't they get it? Didn't they hear that?

Stephanie was next. Roy painted her into a corner in the first few minutes. He implied that it was she – not Skip – who provided the impetus for luring high profile CEO's to Skip's business.

"Wasn't it you who brought the purse strings of your clients to Skip's attention and only so you and he could mutually profit from their misadventures? Come now, you are an above average woman intellect wise, you're an attorney for some of the largest casinos in Vegas… and you know a scam when you see it, right? Isn't that exactly what you get paid to do?"

Stephanie said in a flippant tone, "Well, I figured Skip was going to treat them on the up and up, but he let me and them down."

Roy's voice became terse. "The truth of this matter is they would not have been in that predicament if *you* had not led them there, isn't that right?"

Stephanie hesitated. She knew she could not deny she had done her part to walk those people into Skip's unethical net and she knew it was wrong from the onset. She had profited mightily while they lost out. Her forehead furrowed into a frown. "But damn it – I'm not the one being charged with fraud, money laundering, and an assortment of other allegations. He is the one on trial." She pointed to Skip.

Skip sunk even lower in his seat. Fucking Bitch. After all the money I paid her and this is the lousy thanks I get. I hope the cunt gets disbarred.

Judge Schram had waited long enough. His already thin patience had worn completely out. "The witness will please answer the question."

Stephanie snapped out of her selfish musings and said with a flip of her hand, "Fine. Sure – yeah – I had something to do with those big shooters getting' involved with the investments and all. Happy now?"

Roy restrained his urge to do a happy dance. He'd nailed this one good. "No further questions, Your Honor."

Nick tried to soften the damage done by Roy to Stephanie on redirect and did a little, but he also felt that jurors might find her a semi-hostile witness. She had so vociferously defended her own actions in the plot while vilifying Skip to an extreme.

Gabe's testimony revealed nothing new or not previously exposed and therefore did not elicit a redirect.

There was no time to examine Natalia. Day four of the defense would bring her to the stand.

***

Jack had paid off three of the possible five who he felt might be swung over to an innocent verdict with the expressed hope they might be able to convince some of the others.

The jurors took a preliminary vote. Eight sided with a guilty verdict and four felt he was innocent. The three who were on Roy's payola looked at each other. They would have to work twice as hard to illicit an innocent verdict and get paid extra.

CHAPTER FIFTY-ONE

The first three days of defense presentations were over and done. Each evening all the key parties involved in Skip's defense regrouped to decide what to present the following day. The jury majority was still siding with the prosecution, according to Jack's reconnaissance, but Roy had successfully managed to deposit a few lingering seeds of doubt. That added the potential of adding to his arsenal of those who he had already, and those who might be willing to be, paid off. The recipe of money combined with any possibility of innocence created a strong scenario for persuasion.

Natalia was Roy's first witness of the day, also one of his last shots at turning the momentum in his favor. He felt if nothing of great significance was achieved in this round from the three remaining witnesses, he may as well rest his case tomorrow or even at the day's end. He had nothing left.

Natalia was again reminded that she was under oath. She sat primly at the stand. She took a quick glance at Skip and noticed how draining this trial had been on his once handsome and youthful face. Poor racita. Aye, Skip was such a good man and an ardent lover. This is a crying shame. I hope I am able to help him.

"Ms. Povich," Roy said, unbuttoning his suit coat and pulling it open to rest both hands on his hips, "is it true that you came to be in Mr. Horowitz's employ from another man who had been engaged in the same business that you now operate for Skip?"

Natalia shrugged and said in her pronounced Russian accent, "Yes, this is much true."

"Hasn't Mr. Horowitz acted fairly, and even overly graciously, where your needs have been concerned?"

"He has been so much very kind, yes." She smiled, a small one, and cast an endearing look again at Skip.

"I'd say more than kind. Didn't he buy you expensive gifts and take you on lavish vacations?"

"Yes, but I deserved that and more for what I do for him in Costa Rica." She tossed her hair back over her petite shoulder.

Roy was pleased he did not have to trap Natalia into saying something that would discredit her with the jury. She had been credible and trustworthy in her testimony thus far. She was one of the few allies Skip still had in his court. Because he had been so good to her she was not ready to give him up to the prosecution. Roy breathed a rare sigh of relief.

Nick and Bob had no reason to redirect.

Jeff Jedlecki and Alan Adelman were the next two, and final, witnesses for Roy on day four. Jeff was dressed to kill and armed for bull. Before his being seated Judge Schram gave him the customary reminder of his being still under oath. He then instructed Roy to proceed.

"Thank you, Your Honor. Mr. Jedlecki, can you tell us how you came to be in the employ of Mr. Horowitz' firm?"

"My girlfriend actually met Mr. Horowitz first."

"And then how did you two meet?"

"She, my girlfriend … works for the psychic network. And Skip – I mean Mr. Horowitz, regularly called in for advice."

"Advice from a psychic hotline? Isn't that most unusual?"

"Well after a few sessions with Trixi – that's my girlfriend, they had forged a growing relationship. He used to call regularly and ask to speak to her. They built a rapport over a period of time. He confided some things about his business and told her that he was expanding his operations. He even asked *her* to come to work for him, but she gave him my name instead."

"And did you and he finally meet and discuss your working for him?"

"Well, yes he did. We met a few times and discussed an array of things. Over a period of time he and I became friendly, and before long I was his second best broker in the Lauderdale office." Jeff smiled, revealing perfect teeth.

Wipe the fucking grin off your face, Roy wanted to say. Instead, he said, "So your entrance to this work----the brokerage work---was through your girlfriend, right?"

"Right." Again with the smile.

"And do you believe that Mr. Horowitz was being honest and straight with you about his operations?"

"At that time yes, but …"

Roy stopped him short. "And you were handsomely paid for this occupation?"

Jeff's smile morphed into a stern look of indignation. "I earned every penny."

Roy tugged on his chin. "In your experience Mr. Horowitz treated you fairly?"

"Yes, he did." Jeff shifted his weight in his chair.

"Thank you, that will be all. Your witness," Roy said. He believed he was generating momentum for the day. After his good fortune with Natalia and Jeff, he considered Alan a bonus.

On redirect, Bob said to Jeff, "Were you aware that this operation was a scam before you began working there?"

"Yes – you see, Skip knew that my girlfriend's business was also a fraud. They discussed that often. Actually, that's why and how they connected. You know, kindred spirits and all that crap." He had a sheepish laugh at that. Then he cleared his throat, as no one else seemed to find it funny and said, "Anyway – during the course of their lengthy conversations she knew all about his operation. She told everything she knew to me, but despite it being a fraudulent operation I also knew that I could make a lot of money there. So I took the job with my eyes wide open and never looked back."

Shit, Roy was thinking. Should've drilled the punk a lot harder and longer.

Bob continued. "So you opted for the money over doing an honest day's work?"

"Sure. Beats working a regular job for a living." He again had to chortle at his own wit. Nobody else did.

Jeff went on to describe again how they opened accounts, enhanced accounts, occasionally traded those accounts, but never gave much money back to the investors. He closed by saying that Skip treated him quite nicely and that he had worked there happily for six and half years. The impression the jurors got was that he liked Skip and wished him well, but he was looking out for number one above all else.

"How much money would you say you earned on an annual basis with Mr. Horowitz?"

"A couple of million dollars a year plus bonuses and perks." Jeff was smug.

The jury emitted a collective gasp. Some began to murmur amongst themselves, a bit too loud, and Judge Schram had to demand silence in the court.

Bob pressed forward. "If you had to guess how much money the firm made what would you say?"

Roy said in a loud voice while remaining seated, "Objection – that's expert territory and he's no expert. Irrelevant!"

Judge Schram said in a drone with two fingers pressed to his temple, "Over-ruled." He did his 'go ahead" two finger wag motion at Bob and said, "Proceed, the witness will answer the question."

Jeff pursed his lips and twiddled his thumbs as his eyes went up and to the right, thinking. He popped his lips and said, "I believe that it has to total in the hundreds of millions of dollars if not a billion." Another wave of murmurs drifted through the jury and the gallery. "Our offices were expensive. Our splits were high. Skip had numerous properties, airplanes, and boats." Jeff casually looked in Skip's direction. Skip flipped him the bird and mouthed, *fuck you*.

Roy wondered when or if Jeff was going to shut the hell up.

The jurors were wide eyed. The newscasters were scribbling furiously. One sketch artist was drawing Skip's likeness with his finger straight up yours and a sardonic smile on his face.

After Jeff's entertaining and stellar performance, it was Alan Adelman's turn. Alan walked in with his young, pretty wife. He left her seated a couple of rows behind the table for the prosecution before walking to the stand. He too was reminded that he had previously been sworn in and was seated.

Roy pressed Alan through the same basic questions he had asked the rest. He was careful not to ask about money earned or bonuses of any sorts acquired during his employment with Skip. He touched on Skip's fairness and even-handedness with his crew. Alan agreed that Skip was overall a very fair man … to his key employees.

"Your witness," Roy said as he took his seat beside Skip.

Bob again spearheaded the redirect. "Mr. Adelman, you were, I believe, one of the top producer at Mr. Horowitz's firm. Can you please tell us a bit about that?"

Alan cracked his knuckles, looking proud, and said, "I was his *top* producer, numero uno. I earned more than anyone else in his entire organization, almost combined." His two-carat diamond pinky ring shot bolts of rainbow colored lights across the room.

"And just how *much* did you earn?"

"Let's just say in excess of five million dollars per year, and regularly, too."

A loud, collective, air swallowing noise throughout the gallery emptied the entire room of oxygen.

Bob had Alan tell the jury about his big mansion on Jupiter Island and his Carmel colored Rolls Royce Phantom. Having accomplished what he wanted, he said, "Thank you. No further questions."

Alan started to step down, but Roy stood fast with a hand in the air. "Please the court, I'd like to redirect."

Judge Schram shrugged and said, "You may, counselor. Mr. Adelman, please sit back down."

Roy rushed up to the stand and said, "Mr. Adelman are you current with your taxes?"

Bob shot up. "Objection, irrelevant. Mr. Adelman is not the one on trial and therefore what bearing could his taxes have on this case."

Roy said, "Your Honor, if I may be allowed to continue his line of questioning the relevance will become clear."

Judge Schram said with a stern voice, "I am going to allow you a little latitude here, but get to your point and establish relevance in short order, counsel. My patience wears thin."

Roy heeded the warning and quickly got Alan to reveal he cheated on his taxes, but Alan also insisted he had an accountant and was not alone in doing so.

Roy drove that home at full speed. "If you have been dishonest in your taxes are there times in your employ that you have been dishonest with Skip? Times where you served yourself to the detriment of Mr. Horowitz?"

Alan glared and pointed at Roy. "Look. The tax thing was not my doing. And to answer your question, no. I was well compensated by Mr. Horowitz and therefore there was no reason to be dishonest in my dealings with him."

By now Skip suspected that most of his men or women had been skimming on him. He had confided that fact in Roy, and told him to use it to press key points in his defense if he needed to.

Roy zeroed in and bore down, his face intense, leaning foreword with his hands on the witness stand railing. "You do realize that you are under oath and that if we find out otherwise you can be held in contempt and face charges of perjury, Mr. Adelman?"

Alan had just made his best deal ever with the Fed's and he was not about to renege. He said, "I was never in charge of the money. Sammy would've been the one who handled that end of the business."

Roy regarded him, rubbing his chin, and said, "No further questions."

"No redirect at this time, Your Honor," said Bob.

Roy brought his hands together in a soft clap, brought his fingertips to his lips, then stood, leaned over with his palms on the desk and said, "Your Honor, the defense rests."

Lunch was called and the court recessed until one thirty in the afternoon. Closing arguments would conclude the day.

During the break, the news teams updated their audiences about what had occurred thus far. Channel seven's newscaster said, "The second week of this landmark trial is well underway and appears to be wrapping up as early as this afternoon. There has been a host of witnesses for and against Mr. Horowitz. New details have emerged almost daily. More about this important trial coming at six."

Once court reconvened, both the defense and the prosecution were ready to give closing arguments. The courtroom was again filled to capacity.

Nick took the lead for the prosecution. He walked over and spoke directly to the jurors. He leaned on the railing, his navy blue pinstripe suit pressed perfectly, his green eyes sharp and focused, and looked each one in the eye. He smiled. A friendly and disarming demeanor, he knew, would work best – so he used it like a craftsperson's tool. He began, "I want each of you to consider all of the testimony we've heard over the past two weeks. Think about what all of those witnesses said about how Mr. Horowitz conducted his business." He brought back out the props he and Bob had used during their week's work and tied them all back into his remaining words. He wove them all together, striding with confidence as he did so, in one cohesive and easy-to-read story that depicted Skip as an evil, maniacal man who had intentionally sought out unsuspecting and unwitting investors so that he could cheat them out of their money."

Nick stopped in mid-stride to eye the jury, jutted out his chin, raised a forefinger and said, "Place yourself in the same position as these investors who have lost their life savings, college funds, in general their entire financial futures – because of the deviousness of this malevolent man and his devious band of able thieves." He pointed at Skip. "Seek out and search the wisdom of your consciences. And if you really do as I've asked you to today, then there is no way you could come back with any other decision than …" he paused for dramatic swell, leaned in on the rail, and said in an even voice, "… guilty on all counts."

The jurors looked spellbound.

Two thirty p.m., Judge Schram said, "Is the defense prepared for its closing argument?"

Roy rose for his final opportunity to speak to the jury. He wished the closing arguments had been delayed until the following day, when the jury would have been rested and fresh. He hoped they would be open-minded and reflective enough to consider a verdict of not guilty. Roy put on his best form, deciding his demeanor and speech should display an affable and good nature.

"Ladies and Gentlemen of the jury. I would first like to thank you for performing your civic duty in deliberating this difficult case." He broke into his best 'nice guy' smile – all part of the show, his grandstanding and aggrandizing. "You should know some things about my client." He folded his hands and took on an expression of concern and pity. "Mr. Horowitz came from a very poor and sad background. You see, his mother died when he was still a youngster and he never knew his father. He learned to live on the streets – the hard, cold streets were his only home. I am sure many of you can understand the difficulty, perhaps some of you can even relate to such trying and difficult circumstances."

The expression on several jurors' faces indicated they were at least considering Roy's depiction of Skip. Roy stepped up the pace and intensity.

"He taught himself the art of negotiations and read up on the stock markets. He was lucky enough to land his first job on Wall Street when he was only twenty years old. He worked hard and saved his money so he could move to Florida and open up a brokerage firm of his own." Roy paused as he thought of the next best tact to take.

"I am sure some of you are business owners and you know the struggles – or you have a friend or family member who has a business of their own. There comes a lot of responsibility with that onus. You follow me?" He looked each one in the eye, then spun about to continue.

"Before long, Mr. Horowitz found his business was too big … and he needed to expand." He turned back to the jurors and opened his arms wide with both palms up and a congenial smile. "All of us should be so lucky right?" That elicited a few chuckles of agreement from the jury.

"Before long he had managed to open many, very successful businesses." He stopped for emphasis and raised a forefinger. "And he gave a lot back, too. He donated hundreds of thousands of dollars to charity and helped to establish a foundation for at-risk youth." He paraded back and forth in front of the jury box. "The prosecution would have you think that Mr. Horowitz – from day one … set forth to deceive." His timber became louder and stronger as he made the next point. "But nothing could be further from the truth. Mr. Horowitz is a family man who placed his children and wife's lives above all else. The prosecution would have you believe that he was nothing more than a double timing playboy. But there could be nothing further from the truth. He did have *one* transgression and that was that he fell for a young woman from the Dominican Republic and he plans to marry her when his divorce is complete." He waved his hand in the direction of the very pregnant Veronika. Veronika smiled for the jury as Roy carried on.

"But in all the years he had a thriving business it was *never* his intention to deceive his loyal investors. He made them money and paid them higher returns than any of the larger and more prestigious Wall Street firms. He never promised that those returns would continue on forever. Therefore, the charges leveled against Mr. Horowitz were fabricated to make him a scapegoat for a much larger and less conspicuous operation spearheaded by some of his not-so-loyal employees. Mr. Horowitz is only guilty of trusting those people who were closest to him and taking them under his wing. He trusted them, and in return, he was betrayed by them. It is my firm belief that when you have fully considered our evidence, and taken into honest account all the testimonies given, that there will be enough *doubt* as to whether or not he could *possibly* be guilty …" Roy paused, placed his hands on the railing and brought his voice down to an intense, low, laser-like intensity.

"… and ladies and gentlemen of the jury, let me remind you of the importance of two very important words … 'doubt', and 'possibly'. In our great country, an accused person is innocent until proven guilty …"

his voice rose in a crescendo as he stood erect and thrust a finger in the air, "... beyond the *shadow of a doubt!*"

The room became silent enough to hear a tissue fall.

Roy relished the impact for a few seconds and then went for the kill. "The outlandish and preposterous allegations that the prosecution would have you to believe and convict him of are unfounded, and ... definitely *not* proven beyond any shadow of doubt. I beseech you to give this man an opportunity to see his two lovely daughters wed and to see his yet to be born child grow into a teenager and go to college and make a life for himself or herself. Do not take away his freedom based on circumstantial evidence that cannot definitively tie him to fraud or corruption or conspiracy. Vote your consciences! I pray that each of you, in good conscience, being good Americans and abiding by the justice and law of our great nation, will do what you know in your hearts is the right thing to do ... and come back to this court with a verdict ..." he rapped his fist on the railing, "... of *not guilty!*"

Roy thanked them and walked in silence back to his seat. At four o'clock the jurors were instructed by Judge Schram. "You have seen the evidence and heard the arguments for and against the defendant. You must now perform your duty as jurors without bias or prejudice to either party. As I mentioned in the beginning of this trial, the law does not allow you to be governed by sympathy, swayed by public opinion, or bias. Therefore, you must carefully and impartially consider all of the evidence before you. You must follow the letter of the law and reach a unanimous conclusion regardless of consequences. If there is need for clarification, please hand a note to the bailiff who will contact me and I'll provide guidance where guidance is needed." He looked each person in the jury over, turned to the bailiff and said, "You may take the jury to the deliberation room."

The bailiff led them back into the chambers where they would sit, debating the merits and demerits of both sides of the case for whatever length of time necessary.

It was media frenzy time again outside, as each news station struggled for advantageous position and the dissemination of critical information.

One of the CNBC correspondents was before the cameras, saying, "The SEC's case against Mr. Charles Horowitz has just gone to the jury. Deliberations are underway as we speak. As soon as there is a decision we will be the first to update you, so please stay tuned."

Skip, Roy and Veronika went to wait out part of the jury's deliberation period in the conference room adjacent to the courtroom. Skip was pensive and nervous as a woman about to give birth to her first child. Veronika tried to soothe him. Roy had packed a bottle of Old

Granddad into his briefcase that morning. He took a big slug and offered it to Skip and Veronika. Skip took two chugs and Veronika declined because of her unborn child.

Judge Schram went back to his chambers and relaxed. This two-week media circus had been draining. He was as anxious for a decision as the counselors.

At seven o'clock, Bob Hawthorne's eyes widened in surprise when he saw Jack rushing to the judge's chambers. He thought, oh shit, no ... too early, this is not a good sign. As he witnessed Jack enter and close the door he further thought, I'd better go find Nick.

Inside the chambers, Jack said in an out-of-breath voice, "Judge Schram, the foreman of the jury told me, he – they, have a verdict."

Judge Schram said, "Well, Jack, I guess you had better alert the prosecution and defense then."

Jack prepared himself to locate the defense who no doubt would not be pleased to hear that the jury had so rapidly reached a verdict. Jack first checked the conference room where they had previously set up a temporary camp. He found them there. He entered the room filled with trepidation and said, "The jury has arrived at a verdict."

News of the verdict spread faster than an STD in a sex commune. Spectators and newscasters competed for the best seats in the gallery.

The defense came in and were seated, followed by Bob and Nick for the prosecution. The anticipation level was high enough to inflate scores of balloons with all the excited exhalations. Jack had collected the jurors and was now bringing them back into the courtroom.

Judge Schram rapped his gavel twice and said, "This court will come to order, please."

Instantly the room fell silent. All eyes were filled with anxious anticipation, looking back and forth between the counsel and the jury. Skip sat next to Roy, terrified. Roy was only slightly less anxiety-ridden than Skip.

After a few minutes, which felt to Skip like seven years on death row, Judge Schram addressed the jury. "Has the jury arrived at a verdict?"

The foreman stood and said in clear voice, "Yes, Your Honor."

The bailiff walked over to the jury foreman and took the small slip of paper from his hand. He walked it over to Judge Schram. He handed it to him and stood ready. Judge Schram silently unfolded the paper, read its contents, refolded it, and handed back to Jack. Briefly his eye met that of the jury foreman.

None of the jurors had looked at Skip or the table for the defense. They sat mute with their eyes straight ahead.

Jack handed the slip back to the jury foreman, who unfolded it as if performing a dutiful ritual.

Judge Schram said, "Will the defendant please rise and face the jury." Skip stood, feeling and looking shaky, with Roy standing with him. They both turned to face the jury. Judge Schram said, "Will the foreman please read the verdict."

Veronika reached for Skip's hand across the median and took it in hers. Roy stood silently beside Skip, thinking. Damn, that was too fast. A verdict that fast can only mean one thing. Shit.

The jury foreman looked down at the small slip of paper, then up at the defendant, and said, "We find the defendant, Mr. Skip Horowitz ... guilty on all counts."

Skip fell into his seat, covered his face, and sobbed.

Nick and Bob high-fived.

The courtroom rumbled and the doors and windows shook as the newscasters fought to be first out of the courthouse and deliver the verdict on national television.

Judge Schram shouted, "Order!" He banged his gavel three times. "Order! I'll have order in this court!"

CHAPTER FIFTY-TWO

Skip was remanded to home custody once more awaiting his sentencing, scheduled to be three months later. Skip had ample time to consider where he went wrong in his business and how he was able to be caught. He thought he had been clever and covered his tracks. However, he decided, if he had to do it over again, he would do it the same … for the most part. Perhaps he would trust fewer people and be less flamboyant. He would miss the money and the women, but being with Veronika twenty-four-seven was driving him nuts. The idea of prison was almost a relief. And besides, he'd soon be out. Take a break, pay some people off, and start all over.

Veronika gave birth to their son, Trent Charles Horowitz, just before Skip's sentencing and incarceration. Veronika was not looking forward to raising their child alone.

Shamus and Catherine had reconnected toward the end of the Horowitz fiasco and were married soon after Skip went to jail. Their wedding was huge. They had invited practically the entire island of Key West. They spent a blissful weeklong honeymoon at Atlantis because Catherine had heard so much about it during her time working for Skip. When they completed their honeymoon, they bought a five bedroom Victorian house on William Street where they planned to live forever and have lots of sex and babies. Both were elated to be back together and past their whore-mongering days. A few months later Catherine was expecting their first child. Family and friends kept them more than busy and Catherine never once missed the hustle and bustle of Skip's business. The real estate bust finally went boom all across America and everyone was prospering, which was a good thing for them, too. They soon sold their real estate business for a handsome profit. Shamus took over his family's newest bar business and Catherine was happy to be a stay at home mom.

Tommy Fachuli had made it to the Turks and Caicos, but was murdered by the Mafia.

Sammy joined Vinney and Gabe in Vegas where they sold gumball machines for a living.

Ray Georgeakopoulos stuck with Skip's Keys business and went on to make lots of money for him and his investor friends. He did not miss his days of working for the Fed's and sleeping out of suitcases all over the countryside. He and Connie discussed the possibility of taking their relationship to the next step, but both agreed, *if it's not broken why fix it?*

Father Zeke and Ralph White, months after Skip's conviction and imprisonment, were still awaiting their trial in the murder of Frederika, where Skip was also named as co-conspirator. Both felt cheated and played that they had allowed Skip to coerce them into the murdering his wife. To make things worse, they also realized, if they were going to do jail time, the label of 'woman killer' attached to their names was going to sentence them to – 'special treatment' – from the other jailed thugs … at least that's what they'd seen in the movies.

A.J. hooked up with Barbara Allen from Key West. He wanted her to show him her tattoos in person. His curiosity was satisfied.

About the Author

Michelle Malsbury was born and raised in Champaign, Illinois. Currently she resides in Florida. She holds a Bachelors of Science in Business Management and a Masters Degree in Business Management. She has just completed her first year of doctoral studies in the discipline of Conflict Resolution and Peace Studies with high hopes of helping to build nations and sustain peaceful interactions around the globe.

Travels have taken her from Europe through the Caribbean, Central America, Mexico, and across much of the United States.

Michelle is joint founder of the Apalachicola Yacht Club (AYC) and holds the post of secretary/treasurer. For the AYC she drafted the Constitution and Bylaws outlining membership rules, regulations, and guidelines.

She enjoys outdoor activities like sailing, waterskiing, hiking, bike riding, working out, and fishing as well as reading, music, theatre, playing with her two amusing pets (Abu Chez, her 9.5 year old Australian Blue Heeler and Zack, her six year old yellow tabby cat) and writing.

"Three Years With Adonis" was the first to be published of several books that she has written. For more invormation about Michelle Kay Malsbury and her other works, please visit her web site: www.michellemalsbury.com .

ALL THINGS THAT MATTER PRESS ™

FOR MORE INFORMATION ON TITLES AVAILABLE FROM
ALL THINGS THAT MATTER PRESS, GO TO
http://allthingsthatmatterpress.com
or contact us at
allthingsthatmatterpress@gmail.com